THE RASH RESOLVE AND LIFE'S PROGRESS

Chawton House Library Series: Women's Novels

Series Editors: *Stephen Bending*
Stephen Bygrave

Titles in this Series

1 *The Histories of Some of the Penitents in the Magdalen-House*
edited by Jennie Batchelor and Megan Hiatt

2 Stéphanie-Félicité de Genlis, *Adelaide and Theodore, or Letters on Education*
edited by Gillian Dow

3 E. M. Foster, *The Corinna of England*
edited by Sylvia Bordoni

4 Sarah Harriet Burney, *The Romance of Private Life*
edited by Lorna J. Clark

5 Alicia LeFanu, *Strathallan*
edited by Anna M. Fitzer

6 Elizabeth Sophia Tomlins, *The Victim of Fancy*
edited by Daniel Cook

7 Helen Maria Williams, *Julia*
edited by Natasha Duquette

8 Elizabeth Hervey, *The History of Ned Evans*
edited by Helena Kelly

9 Sarah Green, *Romance Readers and Romance Writers*
edited by Christopher Goulding

10 Mrs Costello, *The Soldier's Orphan*
edited by Clare Broome Saunders

11 Sarah Green, *The Private History of the Court of England*
edited by Fiona Price

12 *Translations and Continuations: Riccoboni and Brooke, Graffigny and Roberts*
edited by Marijn S. Kaplan

13 Sydney Owenson, *Florence McCarthy: An Irish Tale*
edited by Jenny McAuley

14 Frances Brooke, *The History of Lady Julia Mandeville*
edited by Enit Karafili Steiner

15 Ann Gomersall, *The Citizen*
edited by Margaret S. Yoon

Forthcoming Titles

Mary Brunton, *Self Control*
edited by Anthony Mandal

Isabelle de Montolieu, *Caroline of Lichtfield*
edited by Laura Kirkley

Mrs S. C. Hall, *Sketches of Irish Character*
edited by Marion Durnin

Eliza Haywood,
The Rash Resolve and Life's Progress

EDITED BY

Carol Stewart

LONDON AND NEW YORK

First published 2013 by Pickering & Chatto (Publishers) Limited

Published 2016 by Routledge
2 Park Square, Milton Park, Abingdon, Oxfordshire OX14 4RN
711 Third Avenue, New York, NY 10017, USA

First issued in paperback 2016

Routledge is an imprint of the Taylor & Francis Group, an informa business

BRITISH LIBRARY CATALOGUING IN PUBLICATION DATA

Haywood, Eliza Fowler, *c.* 1693–1756.
The rash resolve; and, Life's progress. – (Chawton House library series. Women's novels)
I. Title II. Series III. Haywood, Eliza Fowler, *c.* 1693–1756.
Life's progress. IV. Stewart, Carol (Carol Ann)
823.5-dc23

ISBN 13: 978-1-138-23547-2 (pbk)
ISBN 13: 978-1-8489-3336-1 (hbk)

Typeset by Pickering & Chatto (Publishers) Limited

CONTENTS

ACKNOWLEDGEMENTS

My thanks go to the Chawton House Series editors Stephen Bending and Stephen Bygrave for their encouragement and advice as I undertook this project. Gillian Dow speedily organized an Honorary Chawton House Library Visiting Fellowship, which made my research life a great deal easier. Mark Pollard at Pickering & Chatto was positive and supportive. Ian Campbell Ross gave me the benefit of his experience as an editor, and, as ever, was generous with his time. I am particularly grateful to Kathryn R. King, who allowed me to read her fine study, *A Political Biography of Eliza Haywood*, in advance of publication. My debt to her research will be evident in this edition.

INTRODUCTION

The Danger of Giving Way to Passion was the title given to a collection advertised as 'speedily to be publish'd' in the final pages of Eliza Haywood's translation *Letters from a Lady of Quality to a Chevalier* (1720). The anthology was to comprise five 'exemplary novels': *The British Recluse: or, the Secret History of Cleomira, Suppos'd Dead* (1722), *The Injur'd Husband; or, the Mistaken Resentment* (1722), *Lasselia: or, the Self-Abandon'd* (1723), *The Rash Resolve: or, The Untimely Discovery* (1723) and *Idalia: or, the Unfortunate Mistress* (1723).[1] In the end, for reasons that remain unclear, each title appeared individually, and was then republished in Haywood's four-volume *Works* of 1724, along with *Love in Excess* (1719–20), *Letters from a Lady of Quality* and plays and poems. *The Danger of Giving Way to Passion* could, nevertheless, serve as a title for this volume, which brings together two of Haywood's novellas, one early and one late. Neither has appeared before in a critical edition. Both exemplify 'the danger of giving way to passion'. *The Rash Resolve* tells the story of Emanuella, who is seduced by Count Emilius, bears his illegitimate child, and then dies. *Life's Progress through the Passions: or, The Adventures of Natura* (1748) concerns a hero who gives in to sexual and other passions, and finds himself financially entrapped, cuckolded by his own brother, and on the verge of marrying, beneath his class, a yeoman's daughter. By the end of the novel he too is dead. So described, both works could invite the charge levelled at Haywood's novels, in her own time and since, that she wrote rather to indulge her readers' enjoyment of 'warm scenes' than to reform their morals. In the Dedication of *Lasselia* to Edward Howard, eighth Earl of Suffolk, Haywood addresses that criticism:

> My Design in writing this little Novel (as well as those I have formerly publish'd) being only to remind the unthinking Part of the World, how dangerous it is to give way to Passion, will, I hope, excuse the too great Warmth, which may perhaps, appear in some particular Pages; for without the Expression being invigorated in some Measure proportionate to the Subject, 'twou'd be impossible for a Reader to be sensible how far it touches him, or how probable it is that he is falling into those Inadvertencies which the Examples I relate wou'd caution him to avoid.[2]

Neither the avowed cautionary purpose nor the perception of the author's work as mere titillation, however, does justice to these works of fiction.[3]

When *The Rash Resolve* was published in 1723, Eliza Fowler Haywood (*c.* 1693–1756) was enjoying some popular success, and a measure of critical acclaim. Married by 1714, she had returned to England from Dublin, having performed at the Smock Alley Theatre in 1715. In 1717 she was acting at Lincoln's Inn Fields, and by 1719 she was, possibly, a single woman. In a letter dateable to 1728, she speaks of 'the sudden Deaths of both a Father, and a Husband, at an age when I was little prepar'd to stem the tide of Ill fortune'.[4] How old that age was is left unspecified. In another letter, which Kathryn R. King dates to 1729, she refers to two children, 'the eldest not more than 7 years of Age', of which no other record exists.[5] Her first significant literary success was *Love in Excess* (1719–20), originally published in three parts. It went through at least three editions by 1725.[6] Two poems prefaced the second part, one by aspiring poet and playwright Richard Savage (1697/8–1743), and another by an 'Unknown Hand'. Both paid tribute to Haywood's prose, and her power to evoke sympathetic feeling in the reader: 'Soul-thrilling accents all our senses wound', as Savage put it; 'I feel that fire / Your words alone can paint!' writes the anonymous admirer.[7] In the 1722 edition, these poems were joined by another anonymous plaudit, which Haywood later credited to a 'justly celebrated poet'. Eliza, we read, serves the cause of honour, and of love. A correspondent to the *Ladies Journal* in 1727 offered his own response, 'Writ on a blank Leaf of a Lady's *Love in Excess*', and enthuses: 'O could I boast that more than common skill, / Which guides her fancy and directs her quill'.[8] 'MA. A.', female author of *The Prude* (1724), a novel, dedicated it to Haywood as 'a Person whose Merit the World was ... well acquainted with'. She pays particular tribute to the account of Emanuella's love for her child in *The Rash Resolve*:

> Above all, who can read without being inspir'd with uncommon Delight, her maternal Tenderness for little *Victorinus*, when she descends to such mean Offices so unsuitable to her Birth, or the Delicacies of her Frame and Education? Yet in that Distress her Character is most exalted, as if her noble Mind strove by those intolerable Difficulties to make him some Amends for the Severity of Fortune, in the cruel Inhumanity of her Father and her too fond Credulity.[9]

It has to be said that much of the praise comes from those who actually knew Haywood. MA. A. speaks of being favoured with the sight of 'that incomparable Play you were pleased to show me part of in Manuscript' – the play could have been *A Wife to be Lett* (1723). Literary aspirants in the 1720s might have seen an advantage in attaching themselves to a rising author: Richard Savage is another case in point, to whom we will return in a moment.

At the time of publishing *The Rash Resolve*, Haywood was a member of the so-called 'Hillarian' circle that revolved around Aaron Hill (1685–1750), who, in the 1720s, was one of the most significant figures in London literary life.[10] Other significant Hillarians were the poet and later clergyman Edward Young (1683–1765), author of *Night Thoughts* (1742–45), Welsh poet John Dyer (1699–1757), best known for his poem *The Fleece* (1757), Scottish poets David Mallet (*c.* 1705–65) and James Thomson (1700–48), the last of these being the author of *The Seasons* (1726–30), and, most significantly for Haywood, Richard Savage and Martha (*neé* Fowke) Sansom (1689–1736). Savage's earliest forays in writing were pro-Jacobite poems, and he had managed to avoid the charge of treasonable libel in 1717 by virtue of a government amnesty. Moving in theatrical circles, Savage brought to the stage translations of Calderón, and in the dedication of *Love in a Veil* (1718), from *Peor está que estaba* (*From Bad to Worse*), he alluded to his belief that he was the illegitimate son of Richard Savage, fourth Earl Rivers. This was a cause that gained the support of Hill and Haywood, with the latter later underwriting Savage's account of his parentage in *Memoirs of a Certain Island Adjacent to the Kingdom of Utopia* (1724). At the time *The Rash Resolve* appeared in late 1723, literary success was still evading him, as the opening lines of his puff for the novel suggest: 'Doom'd to a Fate, which damps the Poet's Flame, / A Muse, unfriended, greets thy rising Name!' Martha Fowke, by contrast, had enjoyed literary success, with *The Epistles of Clio and Strephon* (1720), written with William Bond (co-author of Aaron Hill's journal, the *Plain Dealer*) in the form of a sequence of Platonic love letters in verse, and poetry appearing in the *New Miscellany* (1720). And Haywood herself was prolific and successful.

The poems that circulated between Haywood, Hill, Savage and Sansom aspired to an idealized Platonic friendship with Hill as muse. Haywood it was who gave Aaron Hill his coterie name of 'Hillarius', and she wrote poems praising him extravagantly, very much in the sublime mode. In 'An Irregular Ode. To Mr. Walter Bowman', she speaks of Hill's 'Cherubial Sweetness' and 'Godlike Majesty'.[11] In 'The Vision', his works are 'matchless'.[12] Hill's poem of the same title ends with the poet waking to behold 'Lovely Eliza, hid with Bay-leaves'.[13] Sansom wrote a poem to Savage exalting Hill. She lies awake at night reading Shakespeare, but: "Tis not for Shakespear that I wake alone; / Another Rival rises to his Fame, / Hillarius!'.[14] Savage, in turn, wrote a poem in praise of friendship entitled 'The Friend. An Epistle to Aaron Hill, Esq.'. However, Sansom's autobiography *Clio: or, A Secret History of the Life and Amours of the Late Celebrated Mrs. S—n—m. Written by Herself, in a Letter to Hillarius*, not published until 1752, shows her nursing an unrequited longing for Hill not of the Platonic kind: 'Oh! If you have a Heart, why did it not beat with *Clio*'s Anguish? Why was it silent when mine was torn to death with Love and Sorrow?'[15] Sansom cast herself as Haywood's teacher, especially in the matter of amorous writing, in 'To Lady E— H—': 'Did I not in Art discover, / How, in Verse, to *hunt* a Lover!'[16] Hill evidently teased Haywood by sending some verses signed 'M.S.' – Martha Sansom – and, recognizing the true author, she wonders what might have happened 'If sacrilegiously with Scorn possess'd, / I'd torn the Paper, which thy Hands have bless'd?'[17] Sansom, in the same poem, is 'vulgar'. This was the least of Haywood's insults. In *The Injur'd Husband*, Sansom appears as the sexually insatiable Baroness de Tortillée, with Savage as her pimp, Du Lache. *Memoirs of a Certain Island* has Sansom as Gloatitia, whose amours it would 'wear out the day, to recount the thousandth part of'.[18] Though Savage, as Riverius, is still pandar for Gloatitia, the author believes that he has been drawn into wickedness and injustice only through Sansom/Gloatitia's influence. She herself 'receiv'd a more than common Injury from him, thro' the Instigations of that female Fury'.[19] Publication of the first part of *Memoirs of a Certain Island* in September 1724 provoked counter-attacks, and ended her association with the Hillarians. Savage, in 'The Authors of the Town' (1725), has Haywood as a 'cast-off Dame' panting for renown, while Clio (Sansom) is crowned with laurels.[20]

These lurid portraits have lent themselves to a narrative of the author's life in which Haywood and Sansom were rivals for Savage's affections. Savage, it was supposed, was the father of one or more of Haywood's illegitimate children, the 'two babes of love' to which Alexander Pope alludes in *The Dunciad*.[21] In this construction of events, Savage left Haywood for Sansom, and Haywood took her (literary) revenge. *The Rash Resolve* has a plot that fits parts of the supposed scandal: the heroine, Emanuella, has an illegitimate child, and the father, Emilius, abandons her. The fault lies not so much with Emilius as with Emanuella's wicked cousin Berillia, who advances the illicit relationship to distract attention from her own amours, and then alienates Emilius by lying about Emanuella's feelings and intentions. So the heroine is left alone to bring up her child by her own labour, of however menial a kind. It is unlikely, though, that Savage would have written a poetic puff for a novel that implicated him in this way; and there is nothing in the poetry, miscellaneous writings or contemporary gossip to indicate that Haywood and Savage, or Sansom and Savage, were lovers. Recent scholarship suggests that it was Hill who was the focus of the women's attention, and that Haywood's venom was directed at Sansom because she saw her as using Savage to alienate Hill, a figure of major importance in her early literary career, but not a lover.[22] *The Rash Resolve* charts a movement from the periphery – the heroine's birthplace in the Spanish West Indies – to a period of adulation at the centre – Madrid – and back to the margins again: possibly an allegory of the author's own experience of the coterie that revolved around Hill.

The Rash Resolve is styled as a cautionary tale, but on closer reading it is difficult to say what, exactly, it cautions the reader against. What is the 'rash resolve' of the title? Emanuella continues to see Emilius when her uncle counsels against it, and it is at this point in the novel that Haywood comments that Emanuella's only fault was self-will. Yet this supposed fault is not really central to the story: it is passed over in a sentence, and it is Berillia rather than Emanuella (or indeed Emilius) who has the agency in developing the relationship between the lovers. Emanuella, like so many of Haywood's heroines, succumbs to the power of her own sexual desires and ultimately suffers as a consequence, but her situation with Emilius is ambiguous. As Haywood puts it: 'the most binding Vows of everlasting Constancy had pass'd between them', and Emilius has asked Emanuella to marry him. Under canon law promises exchanged between a man and a woman could constitute one stage of a marriage process, and were regarded as binding.[23] Emanuella might consider herself as already married under the terms recognized by the Anglican Church at the time, even though common law might not: a situation that could give sexual relations a veneer of respectability. Similar ambiguity attends Natura's relationship with Harriot in *Life's Progress*. Natura asks Harriot to marry him, but she has him sign a contract binding them to each other instead, and: 'NATURA now considering her as his wife, thought himself intitled to take greater liberties than he had ever presumed to do before'. This confusing state of affairs remained in place until the Marriage Act of 1753, which made a public ceremony legally necessary. Emanuella's resistance to a formalization of their marriage actually stems from her desire to remain financially independent – even though Haywood styles it as a generous and disinterested determination to make Emilius, rather than herself, a gainer by their union. When Emilius later discovers Emanuella hiding with their son, she is ready to throw herself out of the window rather than be reunited with him.[24] It is hard to read the story as a programme for conventional morality.

The poems left behind by the Hillarians allow us some insight into Haywood's personal life in the 1720s, but we have far less to go on when trying to piece together Haywood's circumstances in the 1740s. From December 1741 to April 1744 she was 'Mrs. Eliza Haywood, Publisher', running a pamphlet shop at the Sign of Fame on the Great Piazza, next to Russell Street in Covent Garden. (It should be remembered that a 'publisher' in eighteenth-century terms was more like a distributor of printed work, who might or might not have a financial stake in the items sold.) She occupied a four-storey house, and appears to have been able to support a substantial household. When the shop closed in 1744, Haywood sold many items of furniture including what seems to have been a handsome four-poster bed. Haywood's earliest wares as a publisher were anti-Walpole sixpenny pamphlets: other publications were her translations *The Busy-Body* (1741), *The Virtuous Villager* (1742), plays, anti-ministerial satire and pornographic works. In 1742 she translated Claude-Prosper Jolyot de Crébillon's erotic novel *The Sopha* with actor, playwright and pamphleteer William

Hatchett. She produced a conduct-book (*A Present for a Servant-Maid*) and more fiction (*Memoirs of an Unfortunate Young Nobleman*) in 1743, *The Fortunate Foundlings* in 1744, and in April 1744, the first number of the *Female Spectator* (1744–46), her highly successful periodical.

The *Female Spectator* redeemed Haywood in the eyes of at least one near contemporary, Clara Reeve. In *The Progress of Romance* (1785), her history of the evolution of fiction, Reeve reckoned that the mature Haywood 'had the singular good fortune to recover a lost reputation', and that one of the works by which she was most likely to be known to posterity was the *Female Spectator*.[25] Memoirist Laetitia Pilkington noted more acerbically that 'Mrs. *Haywood* seems to have dropped her former luscious Stile ... Her *Female Spectators* are a Collection of trite Stories, delivered to us in stale and worn-out Phrases, bless'd Revolution!'[26] Recent scholarship has judged the *Female Spectator* to be rather more complex than Pilkington allowed. In a collection of essays published in response to the publication of Haywood's periodical as part of the six-volume *Eliza Haywood: Selected Works* (2000–1), critics have noted moral ambivalence, complicity in female revenge, an implied critique of marriage, and a commitment to the Patriot cause in politics.[27]

Haywood's next venture was another periodical, the *Parrot*, which ran for nine numbers from 2 August to 4 October 1746, the eponymous parrot being Haywood's elusive and rather arch persona (or eidolon) in the journal. The *Parrot*, identified as Haywood's by the ascription 'By the authors of *The Female Spectator*', is one of her most overtly political works. It returns repeatedly to the fate of the Jacobite rebels in the aftermath of the '45 Rebellion – a subject on which Numbers 18, 19 and 20 of the *Female Spectator* had been strikingly silent – and recounts the latest developments in the ongoing War of the Austrian Succession. Haywood's Jacobite sympathies are unmistakeable, as is her opposition to the imperial ambitions of Maria Theresa of Austria, who was supported by Britain.[28] The *Parrot* is one of very few openly Jacobite periodicals in the 1740s; opposition to British support for Austria was also very much a minority position. Not for nothing does Haywood's parrot declare: 'I am an Alien ... in these Kingdoms'. The journal relates the story of the devotion of a young lady of good family to the rebel James Dawson, and how she died of grief while he was burned as a traitor. In another issue, the parrot's ironic justification of the behaviour of 'Oram', who pulls off the wings and legs of insects, surely refers to the perceived cruelty of Cumberland at Culloden.

Jacobite sympathies inform *Life's Progress* as well. Natura has to leave England because he is suspected of speaking too favourably of the Chevalier St George (the 'Old Pretender') and incurs 'the odious appellation of a *Jacobite*'. The hero is often in exile, and Natura's travels as part of the Grand Tour give Haywood an opportunity to reflect on the characteristics of different nations and imply her own political position. Opposition to the Williamite succession appears as Natura's disgust with the rough behaviour of the Dutch. Anti-Hanoverian sentiments are expressed in her portrait of Germany as impoverished and wretched. The Viennese people have 'a pride, which comes pretty near ferocity': Haywood's reflection on the character of the Austrian empress. France, in contrast, is the home of gallantry, wit and politeness, always friendly to the interests of women – and the location of amorous adventures much like those we find in Haywood's fiction of the 1720s.

Life's Progress attests to the influence of Henry Fielding, in particular, as he gave fiction a new moral and intellectual credibility in the 1740s. As a fictional biography of a man not of the aristocracy, the novel owes much to *Joseph Andrews* (1742). Fielding begins his novel with introductory words about the value of biography and moral examples: so does Haywood. In the first chapter of book 3 of *Joseph Andrews*, Fielding satirically praises writers who do not follow nature:

> the Authors of those immense Romances, or the modern Novel and *Atalantis* writers; who without any Assistance from nature or History, record Persons who never were, or will be, and Facts which never did nor possibly can happen: Whose Heroes are of their own creation, and their Brains the Chaos whence all their Materials are collected.[29]

Duly chastened – or so the conventional narrative of a reformed Haywood would have us believe – Haywood prefaces her true picture of nature with a surprising disclaimer: 'I am an enemy to all *romances, novels,* and whatever carries the air of them'. Joseph Andrews himself has no heroic attributes, or rather he has only *mock*-heroic attributes; Natura too is styled as ordinary, but still a boy who outdoes the accomplishments of his childhood peers. Fielding's narrative is framed by his own moral commentary: Haywood reflects on the actions of her characters to a much greater extent than she had done before. Indeed, the moral and intellectual framework is the pretext for the novel. Natura is not so much a character as a test case for the proposition that the passions are 'sole authors of all human actions', and that the passions cancel one another out.

If we follow the sequence of events in *Life's Progress* carefully, however, it becomes apparent that this is not a story of passion followed by punishment: it is, rather, a narrative showing that conventional morality, most particularly in the form of marriage, always ends badly. Natura suggests marriage to his first love, Delia, and by the next chapter she has disappeared from the novel. He signs something like a marriage contract with Harriot, and then has to borrow unwisely to supply her with money. He even contemplates stealing from his own father. Natura proposes marriage to a woman of rank simply because he has attained the age when it is expected of him: immediately after she has accepted this proposal he is suspected of Jacobitism, involved in a duel and forced to leave the country. Abroad again, his proposal of marriage to Maria causes her great distress – she is already in love with the socially inferior Humphry – and the episode ends with Humphry's execution for the attempted murder of Natura. Back in England, Natura marries, but his wife dies. To advance his political and social ambitions, he marries the daughter of a minister, but she has many other lovers and the end result is public humiliation. He proposes marriage to a yeoman's daughter in order to produce heirs and prevent his fortune going to his brother, and finds himself pointlessly trapped by the engagement when his brother dies. The only promising relationship is his initially Platonic friendship with Charlotte, but when he marries her, illness and loss of passion soon follow. Natura's fault is not being natural, but not being natural *enough*.

Life's Progress uncannily anticipates the plot of *Tom Jones*, the first three volumes of which appeared in September 1748, six months after Haywood's novel. Natura is motherless from an early age: Tom, as far as the reader knows, is an orphan. Natura is misrepresented by others: 'every little error in him was exaggerated, and he was represented to his father as incorrigible [and] perverse': just as Thwackum and Blifil misrepresent Tom to Allworthy. He has a childhood sweetheart, Delia, just as Tom has one in Sophia. As a naïve but passionate young man, Natura is seduced by Harriot, just as Tom Jones is seduced by Molly Seagrim. When Natura's father finds out about his son's debts he treats him just as Western does Sophia: 'this chamber must be your prison, till I have considered in what fashion I shall dispose of you'. Natura discovers Harriot's true nature when he makes his way to her house and finds her in bed with another man: just like Tom arriving to find Moll entertaining Square. Ashamed of his own folly, he resolves to go to sea: just as Tom makes the same resolution when exiled from Paradise Hall. Halfway through the novel, his transgressions are forgiven by a tolerant father, just as Fielding's hero is forgiven, in the end, by Allworthy. Natura's father thinks to pay Harriot a sum of money to end the relationship: this is Tom's plan with Moll in Fielding's novel, until he discovers that she has had other lovers, namely Square and Will Barnes. Harriot is a good deal more hard-headed than Molly Seagrim, however, and refuses to release Natura from the contract at any price. This unwanted union overshadows the narrative, while Tom and Sophia's wish to be together, in contrast, is what the reader is encouraged to hope for in *Tom Jones*.

Natura is now sent on the Grand Tour. He gets lost in the dark outside Paris and has to sleep in the roughest of inns: Tom, similarly, gets lost at night before taking refuge in the primitive home of The Man of the Hill. Natura is invited to stay at a monastery, where two beautiful nuns fall in love with him, and he is torn between them: just as Tom is attracted to Moll and Mrs. Waters as well as Sophia. As the novel develops in continental Europe, however, the plot takes turns that would be highly unlikely in Fielding's fiction. It would be inconceivable, in terms of Fielding's values, for Sophia to be afforded the same sexual liberty as Tom. Haywood, on the other hand, presents a young married woman of good family overcome by the charms of music at an opera house to such an extent that she throws herself into Natura's arms, and, as Haywood puts it, he 'seized the lucky moment'. Where Fielding, in the end, draws a clear line between virtuous and immodest women, Haywood is at pains to make her heroine's, rather than her hero's, lapse forgivable:

> As this false step was merely accidental, wholly unpremeditated on either side, and by what can be judged by the character of the lady, and her behaviour afterwards, was no more on her part than a surprise on the senses, in which the mind was not consulted, and had not the least share, I know not whether it may not more justly be called a slip of unguarded nature, than a real crime in her; and as for Natura, though certainly the most guilty of the two, whoever considers his youth, his constitution, and above all the greatness of the temptation ... will allow, that he must have been *more*, or *less*, than *man*, to have behaved otherwise than he did.

Where marriage between Tom and his first love is the desired end point in *Tom Jones*, first love is left behind and forgotten in *Life's Progress*, and marriage only ever ends in misery. The outcomes for Natura are so poor that we could read the novel as another of Haywood's revenge narratives.

Twenty-five years ago, it would have been difficult to access any of Haywood's prolific output: now we have more of the fiction and drama, and her important publications, in periodical form. With the publication of *Selected Works of Eliza Haywood* (2000–1), we are moving towards a situation where we can begin to take cognizance of Haywood's range and diversity as well as continuities in her work. Patrick Spedding's *A Bibliography of Eliza Haywood* (2004) works to establish a Haywood canon.[30] *Fair Philosopher*, a collection of essays on the *Female Spectator*, was published in 2006. Kathryn R. King's *A Political Biography of Eliza Haywood* (2012) is a major step in establishing Haywood as a political writer, and raises the standard of Haywood scholarship. It also allows us to see some of the work in its biographical, historical and political context – a project also essayed in this edition. Much work remains to be done, however. There is still sometimes a lack of thorough contextualization when Haywood is discussed, betraying, perhaps, a lingering reluctance to take her entirely seriously. The fiction Haywood published after 1740 is still not available in modern editions, leaving the reader with the Haywood of the 1720s: an absence this edition begins to address. It is to be hoped that the two works made available here further the appreciation of Eliza Haywood as both a significant practitioner of the novel as a genre, and a commentator on, and creator of, her times.

Notes

1. Dates given for the first four of these novels, and for *Letters from a Lady of Quality*, are actual years of publication, rather than the date appearing on the title pages. Books published late in one year commonly appeared with the following year in their imprint.
2. E. Haywood, *Lasselia: Or, The Self-Abandon'd* (1724), bound with *The Injur'd Husband; or, the Mistaken Resentment*, ed. J. C. Beasley (Lexington, KY: University Press of Kentucky, 1999), p. 105.
3. One critic who does take Haywood's moral purpose seriously is K. Lubey, in 'Eliza Haywood's Amatory Aesthetic', *ECS* 39:3 (2006), pp. 309–22.
4. Cited by K. R. King, *A Political Biography of Eliza Haywood* (London: Pickering & Chatto, 2012), p. xii.
5. Ibid.
6. It used to be thought that *Love in Excess* rivalled Daniel Defoe's *Robinson Crusoe* and Jonathan Swift's *Gulliver's Travels* in terms of editions published and copies sold. Patrick Spedding counts six true 'editions' between 1719 and 1741–42, totalling sales of around 6,000 copies. Though successful, *Love in Excess* did not match the sales of Defoe or Swift. See P. Spedding, *A Bibliography of Eliza Haywood* (London: Pickering & Chatto, 2004), pp. 88–9.
7. E. Haywood, *Love in Excess; or, The Fatal Enquiry* (1719–20), ed. D. Oakleaf, 2nd edn (Peterborough, Ontario: Broadview, 2000), pp. 82–3.
8. Ibid., p. 273.
9. MA. A., *The Prude* (London: 1724), p. iv.
10. See C. Gerrard, *Aaron Hill: The Muses' Projector 1685–1750* (Oxford: Oxford University Press, 2003). I am indebted to Gerrard's account of relationships between the Hillarians, especially in ch.4 of her book.
11. E. Haywood, *Poems on Several Occasions*, in vol. 4 of *Works of Mrs. Eliza Haywood* (London: 1724), p. 14.
12. Ibid., p. 12.
13. *Miscellaneous Poems and Translations. By Several Hands. Published by Richard Savage* (London: 1726), p. 76.
14. Ibid., p. 251.
15. *Clio. The Autobiography of Martha Fowke Sansom*, ed. P. J. Guskin (Newark, NJ: University of Delaware Press, 1997), p. vii.
16. Savage, *Miscellaneous Poems*, p. 183.
17. Haywood, *Poems*, p. 14.
18. E. Haywood, *Memoirs of a Certain Island Adjacent to the Kingdom of Utopia* (London: dated 1725), p. 48.
19. Ibid., p. 185.
20. R. Savage, 'The Authors of the Town; A Satire' (London: 1725), p.10.
21. The suggestion was first tentatively put forward by Walter and Clare Jerrold in *Five Queer Women* (New York: 1929), p. 241. It is elaborated by C. Blouch in 'Eliza Haywood', *Selected Works of Eliza Haywood I*, vol. 1, ed. A. Pettit (London: Pickering and Chatto, 2000), p. xxi–lxxxii. The relationship is treated as fact in much work on Haywood.
22. See K. R. King, 'Eliza Haywood, Savage Love, and Biographical Uncertainty', *RES*, New Series, 59:242 (2007), p. 722–39.
23. See R. Probert, *Marriage Law and Practice in the Long Eighteenth Century. A Reassessment* (Cambridge: Cambridge University Press, 2009), p. 35ff.

24. For a different view, see T. Bowers, *The Politics of Motherhood: British Writing and Culture, 1680–1760* (Cambridge: Cambridge University Press, 1996), pp. 124–47.
25. C. Reeve, *The Progress of Romance, through Times, Countries, Manners* ... (London: 1785), p. 121.
26. Cited by King, *A Political Biography,* p. 114.
27. L. M. Wright and D. J. Newman (eds), *Fair Philosopher: Eliza Haywood and* The Female Spectator (Lewisburg, PA: Bucknell University Press, 2006).
28. For readings of Eliza Haywood as a Jacobite, see R. Carnell, 'It's Not Easy Being Green: Gender and Friendship in Eliza Haywood's Political Periodicals', *Eighteenth Century Studies*, 32:2 (Winter, 1998–99), pp. 199–214; R. Carnell, 'The Very Scandal of Her Tea Table: Eliza Haywood's Response to the Whig Public Sphere', in C. Mounsey (ed.), *Presenting Gender: Changing Sex in Early Modern Culture* (Lewisburg: Bucknell University Press, 2001), pp. 255–73; R. Carnell, *Partisan Politics, Narrative Realism, and the Rise of the British Novel,* (New York: Palgrave Macmillan, 2006), ch. 5; N. MacKenzie, 'Eliza Haywood in a "Scrutinising Age"', *Age of Johnson* 16 (2005), pp. 177–97; and C. Stewart, 'Eliza Haywood's *The Fortunate Foundlings*: A Jacobite Novel', *Eighteenth-Century Life* 37:1 (2012), pp. 51–71.
29. H. Fielding, *Joseph Andrews, and his Friend Mr. Abraham Adams* (1742), ed. M. C. Battestin (Oxford: Clarendon Press, 1967), p. 187.
30. Spedding's conclusions have not gone unchallenged. See L. Orr, 'The Basis for Attribution in the Canon of Eliza Haywood', *The Library*, 7th series, 12:4 (2011), pp. 335–75.

SELECT BIBLIOGRAPHY

Primary Sources

A., M.A., *The Prude* (London: 1724).

Addison, J., *Remarks on Several Parts of Italy* (London: 1705).

Clio. The Autobiography of Martha Fowke Sansom, ed. P. J. Guskin (Newark, NJ: University of Delaware Press, 1997).

Fielding, H., *The Adventures of Joseph Andrews, and his Friend Mr. Abraham Adams* (1742), ed. M. C. Battestin (Oxford: Clarendon Press, 1967).

Haywood, E., *Epistles for the Ladies* (1749), in *Selected Works of Eliza Haywood I*, vol. 2, introduced and annotated by C. Blouch, ed. C. Blouch and A. Pettit (London: Pickering & Chatto, 2000).

—, *Lasselia: Or, The Self-Abandon'd* (1724), bound with *The Injur'd Husband; or, the Mistaken Resentment*, ed. J. C. Beasley (Lexington, KY: University Press of Kentucky, 1999).

—. *Love in Excess; or, The Fatal Enquiry* (1719–20), ed. D. Oakleaf, 2nd edn (Peterborough, Ontario: Broadview, 2000).

—, *Poems on Several Occasions*, in vol. 4 of *Works of Mrs. Eliza Haywood* (London: 1724).

—, *Memoirs of a Certain Island Adjacent to the Kingdom of Utopia* (London: dated 1725).

—, *The Female Spectator*, in *Selected Works of Eliza Haywood II*, vol. 2, ed. K. R. King and A. Pettit (London: Pickering & Chatto, 2001).

—, *The Parrot*, in *Selected Works of Eliza Haywood II*, vol. 1, ed. C. Blouch, A. Pettit and R. S. Hanson (London: Pickering & Chatto, 2001).

Locke, J, *Some Thoughts Concerning Education* (1693), ed. J. W. Yolton and J. S. Yolton (Oxford: Clarendon Press, 1989).

Reeve, C., *The Progress of Romance, through Times, Countries, Manners ...* (London: 1785).

Savage, R. 'The Authors of the Town; A Satire' (London: 1725).

Savage, R. *Miscellaneous Poems and Translations. By Several Hands. Published by Richard Savage* (London: 1726).

Secondary Sources

Black, J., *The British Abroad. The Grand Tour in the Eighteenth Century* (Phoenix Mill: Sutton, 1992).

—, *Debating Foreign Policy in Eighteenth-Century Britain* (Farnham, Surrey: Ashgate, 2011).

Blouch, C. in 'Eliza Haywood', *Selected Works of Eliza Haywood I*, vol. 1, ed. A. Pettit (London: Pickering & Chatto, 2000), pp. xxi–lxxxii.

Bocchicchio, R. P. and K. T. Saxton (eds), *The Passionate Fictions of Eliza Haywood. Essays on Her Life and Work* (Lexington, KY: University Press of Kentucky, 2000).

Bowers, T., *The Politics of Motherhood: British Writing and Culture, 1680–1760* (Cambridge: Cambridge University Press, 1996).

—, 'Representing Resistance: British Seduction Stories, 1660–1800', in P. R. Backscheider and C. Ingrassia (eds), *A Companion to the Eighteenth-Century English Novel and Culture* (Chichester: Wiley-Blackwell, 2009), pp. 140–63.

Carnell, R., 'It's Not Easy Being Green: Gender and Friendship in Eliza Haywood's Political Periodicals', *Eighteenth Century Studies*, 32:2 (Winter, 1998–99), pp. 199–214.

—, 'The Very Scandal of Her Tea Table: Eliza Haywood's Response to the Whig Public Sphere', in C. Mounsey (ed.), *Presenting Gender: Changing Sex in Early Modern Culture* (Lewisburg, PA: Bucknell University Press, 2001), pp. 255–73.

—, *Partisan Politics, Narrative Realism, and the Rise of the British Novel* (New York: Palgrave Macmillan, 2006).

Dixon, T., *From Passions to Emotions. The Creation of a Secular Psychological Category* (Cambridge: Cambridge University Press, 2003).

Gerrard, C., *Aaron Hill: The Muse's Projector 1685–1750* (Oxford: Oxford University Press, 2003).

Glover, S. P., *Engendering Legitimacy: Law, Property, and Early Eighteenth Century Fiction* (Lewisburg, PA: Bucknell University Press, 2006).

Hirschman, A., *The Passions and the Interests: Political Arguments for Capitalism before its Triumph* (1977; Princeton, NJ: Princeton University Press, 1997).

Jerrold, W. and C. Jerrold, *Five Queer Women* (New York: 1929).

King, K. R., 'Eliza Haywood, Savage Love, and Biographical Uncertainty', *RES*, New Series, 59:242 (2007), pp. 722–39.

—, 'New Contexts for Early Novels by Women: The Case of Eliza Haywood, Aaron Hill, and the Hillarians, 1719–1725', in P. R. Backscheider (ed.), *A Companion to the Eighteenth-Century English Novel and Culture* (Chichester: Wiley-Blackwell, 2009), pp. 261–75.

—, *A Political Biography of Eliza Haywood* (London: Pickering & Chatto, 2012).

Lubey, K.,'Eliza Haywood's Amatory Aesthetic', *ECS*, 39:3 (2006), pp. 309–22.

Luning, H, 'Disability and the Disenfranchised in Eliza Haywood's *The Rash Resolve*', *Age of Johnson,* 20 (2010), pp. 173–92.

MacKenzie, N., 'Eliza Haywood in a "Scrutinising Age"', *Age of Johnson,* 16 (2005), pp. 177–97.

Orr, L., 'The Basis for Attribution in the Canon of Eliza Haywood', *The Library*, 7th series, 12:4 (2011), pp. 335–75.

Pettit, A., 'Adventures in Pornographic Places: Eliza Haywood's *Tea-Table* and the Decentering of Moral Argument', *Papers on Language and Literature,* 38:3 (2002), pp. 244–70.

Probert, R., *Marriage Law and Practice in the Long Eighteenth Century. A Reassessment* (Cambridge: Cambridge University Press, 2009).

Spedding, P., 'Shameless Scribbler or Votary of Virtue? Eliza Haywood, Writing and Pornography in 1742', in P. Salzman and J. Wallwork (eds), *Women Writing 1550–1750*, (Victoria: Meridian, 2001), pp. 237–51.

—, *A Bibliography of Eliza Haywood* (London: Pickering & Chatto, 2004).

Staves, S., *Married Women's Separate Property in England, 1660–1833* (Cambridge, MA: Harvard University Press, 1990).

Stewart, C., 'Eliza Haywood's *The Fortunate Foundlings*: A Jacobite Novel', *Eighteenth-Century Life*, 37:1 (2012), pp. 51–71.

Wright, L. M. and D. J. Newman (eds), *Fair Philosopher: Eliza Haywood and* The Female Spectator (Lewisburg, PA: Bucknell University Press, 2006).

NOTE ON THE TEXTS

The text of the two novels is based on the respective first editions of *The Rash Resolve* and *Life's Progress* held in the Chawton House Library. Both bear the bookplate of John Charles Hardy, from whose collection the Library is taken. *The Rash Resolve: or, The Untimely Discovery* also bears the armorial bookplate of The Right Honourable the Lord Carmichael, while *Life's Progress through the Passions: or, The Adventures of Natura* has that of Charles Hill. Advertisements appearing in the copy of *Life's Progress* are not included in this edition.

I have intervened as little as possible in the texts. I have silently corrected obvious typographical errors, while as far as possible retaining original punctuation and spelling. The long 's' has been replaced by 's'. In *The Rash Resolve* there are dashes of varying lengths, which I have replaced with a single dash. Paragraphs in italics typically begin with a single roman letter: I have converted these to italic, along with colons or semi-colons in roman type. Running marginal inverted commas have been eliminated from *Life's Progress*. Haywood's spelling is variable, as was common in the eighteenth century, so readers will find *melancholly* and *melancholy*, *secrecy* and *secresy*. Haywood consistently spells *niece* as *neice*.

THE

RASH RESOLVE:

OR, THE

Untimely Discovery.

A

NOVEL.

In Two Parts.

By Mrs. Eliza Haywood.

Woman is soft, and of a tender Heart,
Apt to receive, and to retain Love's Dart:
Man has a Breast robust, and more secure;
It wounds him not so deep, nor hits so sure.
Congreve.[1]

LONDON

Printed for D. Browne *jun*r. at the *Black-Swan*, without *Temple-Bar*; and S. Chapman, at the *Angel* in *Pall-Mall*. 1724.

TO

The Right Honourable

THE

Lady *RUMNEY*.[2]

May it please your LADYSHIP,

THOSE who are acquainted but with part of those shining Qualities which make up the Character of your Ladyship, and consider you only as a Woman of Rank, admirable fine Sense, and the most discerning Judgment in the World; will, perhaps, be astonish'd at my Presumption in throwing at your Feet a Trifle so little capable of meriting your Regard: But those who are happily admitted to a nearer View, and have shar'd the Effects of your condescending Sweetness of Disposition, will easily forgive me when they remember, that the less worthy is the Offering, the greater Goodness is requisite for the Acceptation.

BUT this Reason (tho' certainly a very material one) is not the only one which induc'd me to intreat your Ladyship's Protection. – Flattery is a Vice so much in Fashion, and, I am sorry to say, so much encouraged, that there is nothing more difficult than to find a Patron who not expects, nor would be pleased with it: Where then should a Person, by Nature averse, and by Precept taught to shun it, make an Address of this Nature, but to a Lady whose Perfections strike all Encomiums dumb because they cannot reach her Worth? – a Lady, whose Character is so justly establish'd for all those Graces both of Mind and Body, which can be an Ornament to our Sex, that it would be as needless as vain to attempt a Repetition of them! – You, Madam! are possess'd of Charms which the Soul only can describe! –'tis not in Words to speak them. – We all admire the Diamond's sparkling Lustre; but tho' we gaze never so long on the thousand differing colour'd Rays it casts, no Artist yet had ever skill to paint the Brightness of it.

TO the Motives already mentioned, I cannot forbear adding the Confession of another, that of indulging my Pride in testifying to the World the Honour I receive in your vouchsafing to read the Products of a Genius, which, wanting the Improvements of a learned Education, pretends no farther Merit, than an Aim to please. My Ambition is in this, by your Ladyship's excelling Goodness, sufficiently gratified, and it is this which charms me into a grateful Acknowledgment.

All that I have to offer in Defence of the following little History, is, That there is something so very particular and uncommon in the Misfortunes of her who is the Subject of it, that I think cannot fail of exciting Compassion in a generous Mind: and how blameable soever her Conduct may appear, in one Affair, the Train of Woes it drew on her, prevail to soften the Severity of Censure. – But I will not attempt any thing in her Vindication, let her own unequall'd Sufferings plead for her: I am confident, were the *Fair Unfortunate* still living, She would as readily submit her Fate to the Determination of so *sweet a Judge*, as I do my weak Endeavours to represent it. I am

Madam,

With the most-profound Respect,
Your Ladyship's
Entirely Devoted,
most Faithful and
most Obedient Servant,

Eliza Haywood.

TO

Mrs. *ELIZA HAYWOOD,*

ON HER

NOVEL

CALL'D

The RASH RESOLVE.

DOOM'D to a Fate, which damps the Poet's Flame,
A Muse, unfriended, greets thy rising Name!
Unvers'd in Envy's, or in Flatt'ry's Phrase,
Greatness she flies, yet Merit claims her Praise;
Nor will she, at her with'ring Wreath, repine,
But smile, if Fame, and Fortune cherish thine.

THE *Sister Sciences thy Genius warm,*
And, with their Strength, thy Sex's Softness arm.
In thy full Figures, Painting's Force we find,
As Music charms, thy Language lifts the Mind.
Thy Pow'r gives Form, and touches into Life
The Passions imag'd in their bleeding Strife:
Contrasted Strokes, true Art, and Fancy, show
And Lights, and Shades, in lively mixture flow.
Thus Fear flies Hope, large Reason Love's Controul,
Jealousy wounds and Friendship heals the Soul:
Black Falshood wears bright Gallantry's Disguise,
And the gilt Cloud enchants the Fair One's Eyes.
Thy Dames, in Grief, and Frailties, lovely shine,
And when most mortal, half appear divine.
If, when some Godlike, fav'rite Passion sways,
The willing Heart too fatally obeys,
Great Minds lament, what cruel Censure blames,
And ruin'd Virtue gen'rous Pity claims.

ELIZA, *still impaint Love's pow'rful Queen!*
Let Love, soft Love! adorn each swelling Scene.
Arm'd with keen Wit, in Fame's wide Lists advance!
Spain *yields in Fiction,*[3] *in Politeness,* France.
Such Orient Light, as the first Poets knew,

Flames from thy Thought, and brightens ev'ry View!
A strong, a glorious, a luxuriant Fire,
Which warms cold Wisdom into wild Desire!
Thy Fable glows so rich thro' ev'ry Page,
What Moral's Force can the fierce Heat assuage?

AND *yet, – but say, if ever doom'd to prove*
The sad, the dear Perplexities of Love!
Where seeming Transport softens ev'ry Pain,
Where fancy'd Freedom waits the winning Chain!
Vary'ng from pangs to visionary Joys,
Sweet is the Fate, and charms, as it destroys!
Say then, – if Love to sudden Rage, gives way,
Will the soft Passion not resume its Sway?
Charming, and charm'd, can Love from Love retire?
Can a cold Convent quench th' unwilling Fire?
Precept, if human, may our Thoughts refine,
More, we admire! but cannot prove divine.

RICHARD SAVAGE.[4]

THE

RASH RESOLVE:

OR,

The Untimely Discovery.

Part I

THO' nothing is more laudable than a Firmness of Resolution, yet there is no one thing more apt to bring us into Misfortunes, than too inconsiderately to form them: Whoever fixes a Determination to do, or leave undone any Action of Importance, ought to advise with Time, and deliberately weigh not only all apparent Obstacles, but also all that may possibly arise either to thwart the present Intention, or obligate Repentance if compleated. If the most lively and penetrating Wit that ever was known, a Wisdom wonderful in Youth, a Depth of Learning which scarce any of the Fair Sex could boast, an elevated Genius, and Sublimity of Thought, a Soul composed of Honour, Courage, Gratitude, Generosity, Fortitude, and all those Virtues which wear the Name of *Manly*,[5] joined with Tenderness, Sweetness of Disposition, and every Grace with which the *softer* Specie attracts, and charms, could render the Person possess'd of them happy, the lovely Subject of the following Sheets had been as remarkable for her good Fortune, as the ill Influence of her Stars have made her for the contrary.

Emanuella, so she was call'd, was born in *Porto-Rico*,[6] one of those Islands belonging to the *Spanish West-Indies*,[7] the Government of which had been given to her Father, Don *Alvarez*, by his most Catholick Majesty.[8] She had the misfortune to lose her Mother very young, but notwithstanding that, and the Disadvantage of being educated in a Place which could boast of but little Politeness, the Care and Tenderness of *Alvarez*, whose only Child she was, sufficiently compensated for all other Wants: Perceiving her of an uncommon *Aptitude* for Learning, he sent for the best Masters to instruct her in the *Latin*, *French*, and *Italian* Tongues, in which she became so perfect in a little time, as also in Musick, Dancing, Singing and Painting, that it was hard to say in which she most excell'd: All the *Muses!* all the *Virtues!* all the *Graces!* seem'd assembled in her Soul, and inspir'd her Conversation with such different ways of charming, that what kind soever the Heart was most affected with, one might be sure to find it there: As to the Beauties of her Person, tho' few of the most celebrated ones could boast of more, yet they were so far exceeded by those of the interior Part, that I shall only say the Brightness of her *Mind* shone in her *Eyes*, enliven'd all her Air, and whether she spoke, or look'd, or mov'd, an awe-mix'd Sweetness spread it self around her, at once surprizing, pleasing and commanding.

ADORN'D with all these shining Qualifications, 'tis easy to believe how dear she was to her Father; but alas! it was not many years after she was capable of knowing how happy she was, before she lost it; the good *Alvarez* died when she was about Fifteen, and it was from that fatal Moment she might date the beginning of that Series of continued Woe, which to the end of her Life attended her. Not but she was left in a Circumstance, which, if Wealth could bribe ill Fate, was sufficient to shield her from all the Vexations of Life; but where a Person is destin'd to Misfortunes, that which to *others* would prove a *Blessing*, is to them a *Curse*; the Riches she was possess'd of, serv'd but to attract a Number of *pretended* Friends, but in reality only so to *themselves*, and the open, noble Frankness of her Disposition to lay her liable to their Insinuations. She was so entirely free from all Deceit, and Artifice herself, that till a too dear Experience convinced her, it was very difficult for her to entertain a Belief there was such Baseness in the World.

BUT to go on gradually with the little History I am about to make, the time of Mourning for *Alvarez* was no sooner expired, than she began to have a passionate Desire to leave the Place she was in; the Delicacy of her Taste, joined to the Improvements of her Education, made her uneasy to continue where she could find nothing like herself to converse with. Besides, she had many Relations at *Madrid*, and did not doubt but in so populous a City, she should meet with Entertainments suitable to her Genius.[9] But how great was her Vexation, when having prepared every thing for her Departure, she met with an Obstacle entirely unforeseen? Don *Pedro*, who by her Father's Will, and her own Consent was made her Guardian, having the vast Fortune left her in his Possession, could not think of parting with it so easily; he had a Son, whom ever since the Death of *Alvarez*, he had been casting about how to ingratiate to the Affections of this young Heiress:[10] He had indeed never hinted any such matter to her as yet; nor had the intended Lover made the least Declaration of a Passion, but it was only because the one thought it early enough, and that there being none of a superior Fortune in the Place, there was little danger of the Offer being refused whenever it should be made; and the Silence of the other proceeded from a just Sensibility of his own Demerits, and a true Respect for the engaging *Emanuella*: for he had so little to recommend him in his Person, that had his Soul been possess'd of no greater Beauties, he would have been but little regarded by all that knew him. His Stature was very diminutive, his Limbs unhappily fram'd, his Face cast in a Mould so rough, whoever look'd on it, would have believed that Nature was absent at his Formation, and left the work to Chance; his very Voice was disagreeable, and his hesitating Accents disgrac'd the Meaning he endeavour'd to express. But in this unlovely Out-side, there was a Jewel lock'd, whose Worth made full amends for all his other Wants: He had excellent Sense, Honour, Good-Nature, Generosity, and a thousand other Virtues better described by his own Actions, than by the Pen of any Writer; but had he been possess'd of more good Qualities than ever Man pretended to, it could not be expected that with these interior Charms alone, a Lady so young and beautiful, as *Emanuella*, could be influenced. She was indeed too good a Judge of Wit herself, not to admire it in another; she acknowledged Don *Marco*'s, (for that was his Name) and would often, notwithstanding the Misfortune of his ill manner of Delivery, take Pleasure in hearing his Notions of things. She approv'd of his Conversation, and had a very great Friendship for him, till the Knowledge of his, or rather his Father's Designs, reversed those favourable Thoughts, and turn'd her all into Disdain.

BEING resolv'd to leave the Island with the first Ship, she sent for Don *Pedro*, to advise with him on the ordering her Affairs; she could not think it safe or practicable to take her whole Effects with her, and therefore thought it proper to settle a Correspondence how they might be sent after her, and in what hands trusted. Don *Pedro*, who before had heard of her Design, thought it now high time to discover the Secret he so long had kept; and making her a low Bow, It is easy, Madam, *said he*, for us to contrive means to send your Fortune either to *Madrid*, or any other Place you shall command, but it will not be so easy to bring us to consent to the parting with your self. – You here receiv'd your Being; – here your Education; are a Native – a Property of this Place; and when you attempt to deprive us of that Right we claim of your Presence, the whole Island would rise in Arms; nor ought you to wonder if in so just a Cause I should appear their Head, and force your Stay, if soft Persuasion fails. The old Gentleman was so little accustomed to Gallantry, that *Emanuella* could not help laughing at these Words, which she had not the least Thought were spoke with any other Design; and perceiving he had done, Well well, Don *Pedro! return'd she,* I do not doubt but in such a Cause as this I should be able to make my party good against the Islanders, even tho' you should appear their Head, as you threaten; but to shew you that I am not for War, if Peace may be maintain'd on honourable Terms, pray what have you to offer me here in lieu of those Advantages I may expect else where? That (*reply'd the other hastily*) which if duly weigh'd, is of more Estimation than the whole World beside; a *Love* accompanied by Sincerity, Constancy, and Truth, – a Passion pure as the Zeal which warms the Martyr's Breast, and everlasting as his Reward. All this was so far from giving her any Notion of his Intention, that she had no other Surprize than to find him in a Disposition so different from his former Gravity; and believing he assum'd this Air of Raillery only to divert her, would not baulk his Good-Humour, but return'd an Answer such as she thought suitable to the Occasion: If you were in a Condition (*said she merrily*) I should be half in hope it was of your Heart I had made so great a Conquest; but as you are not yet, nor like to be a Widower, I must entreat you to inform me who it is has felt the Effects of a Power I never had any Reason to have an Opinion of till now. Alas, Madam! (*resumed the Don*) it would ill become the Autumn of my Age to attempt to please the delightful Bloom of yours. – No, no, I would not thus affront your Beauty. – But I have a Son whose Years will not disgrace the Passion he professes. – Nor will his Suit, I hope, be unworthy your Regard. These Words were like a Clap of Thunder to *Emanuella*'s Ears: the manner in which they were spoke joined to a thousand little Passages, which when they happened, were unheeded, but now all at once occur'd to her Remembrance, made her indeed believe he meant what he said: But not yet fully assured, And are you in earnest? *cry'd she*, (with a Voice which testified both her Amazement and Indignation.) But he, whose Pride would not permit him to be easily quell'd, was so far from excusing the Presumption of his Application, that he rather resented the little Deference she paid him. I know not, *resumed he*, for what Reason you should make a doubt of it; there is not so great a Disparity either in Birth or Fortune, to oblige you to think it strange I should offer at an Alliance. – You will leave me to be Judge of that (*answer'd she, growing still more disturb'd*) but I desire not a Repetition of Genealogies, or a Calculation how many Thousands either of us are possess'd of; 'tis sufficient I am not ignorant what is in your hands of mine, which I shall call for in, as soon as I have consider'd of a Person proper to be intrusted in such an Affair. She spoke no more at that time, but continued walking up and down the Room, by her outward Disorders making visible the inward Agitations of her Soul: Don *Pedro*, who had as much Cunning as Pride, observ'd every Motion, and believing he had gone too far, endeavour'd to mitigate the Boldness of his first Expressions, by pleading his Concern for the Welfare of an only Son, who could not live without her. But all he could say to this purpose, was ineffectual to abate the Indignation she had conceiv'd at so disproportionable a Proposal, and the more he endeavour'd at it, the more she grew incensed; till at last weary of his Importunities, she desir'd him to leave her House, and to prepare to make up his Accompts with her by the next day; still assuring him she was determined to take shipping by the first Opportunity. The Chagreen this Accident gave her, was very great; she was disappointed in the Hope of maintaining a friendly Correspondence with a Man who had the Power of being very serviceable to her in those Affairs which she was inexperienced in, and which her Soul, delighting in sublimer Contemplations, was unwilling to be amus'd in. Young as she was, she had a very good guess at the Language of the Eyes, and easily found by his, that she must expect no Obligations from him, unless she could consent to come into his Measures, than which nothing could be more averse to her *Inclinations*, and consequently to her *Designs*; for she was not of a Disposition to resolve on the one, without having first consulted the other: But tho' she foresaw many little Vexations would attend this Quarrel with her *Guardian*, yet she was far from having any Suspicion, he had Baseness enough in his Nature to act in the manner he was already forming, and she soon after experienc'd.

THIS sordid-temper'd Wretch always look'd on every thing as his own that once he had the Possession of; and to think of parting with so much Money as the mistaken good Opinion of *Alvarez* had entrusted him with, was such a Dagger to his Heart, that he had resolv'd rather to have Recourse to any Measures, than to endure it: He therefore contrived a Scheme, which by the Vileness, as well as Cunning of it, one would think could only be suggested by the Devil himself; he pretended that the late Governor, to maintain himself in a Grandeur far beyond what either his Post or Paternal Estate would allow, had at several times borrowed vast Sums of Money of him, some of which had been repaid, and for the Security of the remaining Part, had made over his Jewels, Plate, Houshold-Goods, and all other Moveables to him, and sent Officers to seize immediately on every thing. It was to no purpose that *Emanuella*, surpriz'd as she was, had Presence of Mind to argue on this score more like a Person whom many Years Experience had made perfect in the Law, than a young Virgin, who till this Hour ne'er knew what 'twas to hear a Word which had the sound of Business. – But in vain it was, that she represented the Illegality of the Action, that she might justly sue them for a Robbery, there being nothing really due to Don *Pedro*, or if there had, he could not justify the seizing on her Goods without a long Process, and a Warrant proper for that End; they told her their Business was not to examine into the Merits of the Cause, Don *Pedro* must look to that; they had an Order for what they did, and if she thought herself injur'd, she must make Appeal elsewhere. These sort of Replies were all her fine Reasoning could draw from them, and she would not make use of Reproaches to them, who she knew did but as their Function required, but reserv'd them all for the base *Pedro*. She several times sent to his House, and other Places in search of him; but he was no where to be found, and she was obliged without even the Satisfaction of Complaint, to see her rich Furniture torn down by the Hands of these robust Fellows, her Wardrobe ransacked, her Coffers borne away to the House of *Pedro*, while herself was left without so much as a Bed to lie on, or a second Suit of Clothes to change for those she had on. – She was not without Consideration by what means she should seek Redress for so inhuman, and unexampled a Wrong; but alas! the artful Villain had watch'd his Opportunity, the Persons appointed by her Father's Will *Trustees*, were neither of them at that time on the Island, and the new Governor not being yet arrived, there was no body in whose power it was to examine into this Affair; and against there was, he had provided, if the worst should happen, some to make Oath of Debts contracted by *Alvarez*, and an Inventory of that Part of his personal Estate which he had seiz'd (and might easily do, having them in his Possession) to prove that they were also assigned to him: Nor was this the Extent of his monstrous Stratagem, as she was left in a desolate and naked House, with only three or four of her weeping Servants, not yet determined where or to whom she should fly for Shelter, the same Officers again broke in, and seiz'd her Person, by the same Orders as they had done her Effects: This last Stroke was infinitely more severe to her, than all the rest had been; at Liberty, she was not without hope of some Redress; but to be confin'd, and in the power of so inhuman a Villain, gave her Apprehensions which not all her stock of Courage could enable her to sustain: She fainted several times before they carried her away; the Fellows who at this Sight, hardened as they were, began to feel Compassion, endeavour'd to give her some Consolation, by telling her their Orders were not to carry her to Prison, but to the House of Don *Pedro*, who 'twas possible would come to Terms of Accommodation with her; but this was so far from working the Effect they aim'd at, that it gave an Addition to her Perplexities. O *(said she)* bear me to Prison, to Death, to any thing, rather than place me under the Roof of that consummate Villain! that Fiend more black than Hell it self can furnish! He has no Offers to make me, but such as, wretched as I am, I'd sooner die than accept. – She vented her Passion in many such like Expressions, but neither the steddy Calmness which had appeared in her Countenance, during the whole time of their removing her Goods, nor the Agonies this last Surprize had thrown her in, were of any Force to give a Turn to her Condition; she was in the hands of Persons who are not much accustomed to Remorse, or if by Chance sometimes a little touch'd with it, know how to give a check to Sentiments so contrary to their Profession; she was obliged to go with them to the House of Don *Pedro*, where their Commission being ended, she was left in the Care of some of his Servants; for neither he, nor his Son, were in the way, or at least would not appear till the first Emotions of her Passion were a little abated. But there is a vast difference between those People who are incens'd at every little Accident that happens to thwart their Inclinations, and those whose Passions are not to be raised but on some extraordinary Occasion; – the first as they are immediately angry, so they are as immediately reconciled; but the others, when once provok'd, are for a long time, if ever they are prevail'd on, in the same Humour. Of this last Sort was *Emanuella*; there was scarce a Probability, that had Don *Pedro* recanted, and presently restored her to her Liberty with the Treasures he had so unjustly seiz'd, that she would ever have been brought to forgive the Affront he had put upon her: Nor indeed, can I see why she should, for tho' the World is apt to give to such a Disposition the Epithets of *Malicious* and *Revengeful*, yet as there is certainly a Justice due to our selves as well as to others, in my Opinion to renew a Friendship with a Person whose Unworthiness or Baseness has once forfeited it, is to put it in his power a second time to deceive us, and no other than joining in our own Destruction. Don *Pedro*, however, did not make the tryal, but persisting in the Out-rage he had begun, prepared a Room for her, little different from those in a common Goal;[11] the Windows of it were grated, and the Door always kept close lock'd, except when any Person came in to bring her meat: nor was her Attendance more respectful, he denied her to be waited on by one of her own Sex; fearing, as she was afterwards inform'd, her Tears and Eloquent Manner of expressing her Misfortunes might influence them to pity her Condition, so far as to attempt her Relief. – She had the Privilege of indulging her Melancholy undisturbed for two Days, at the end of which Don *Pedro*, imagining the Violence of her Fury pretty well exhausted, went to make her a Visit. But to what a height does the Sight of the Offender transport the hush'd Disorders? *Emanuella*, whose Philosophy had enabled her to bear the Treatment she had met, with much more Moderation than the generality of the World could have done, and depended entirely on Heaven for the Redress of her Injuries, now lost all Patience; she upbraided him in Terms, which if not severe enough for the Baseness he had been guilty of, yet in such bitter ones, that she herself thought afterwards were unbecoming the Mildness of her Sex; and indeed she had so great an Aversion for Railing, that she has been often heard to say, no Usage could excuse it: – And 'tis certain, the edge of her Invectives had been much less keen, if Don *Pedro*, to his other Crimes, had not in this Visit offer'd an additional Indignity, which to the delicacy of her Soul was less pardonable than his former ones. His earthy and groveling Disposition, rendring him incapable of judging of the Elegance of her's, made him affront her when he meant quite otherwise: Among some other faint Excuses for what he had done, he told her that, he had no other way to force her to marry his Son, – but as soon as ever she consented to that, she should not only be put in possession of all the Care of *Alvarez* had heaped up for her, but also of Treasures which in no other Match she could expect. Not the poor Cottage Maid, who on the mountain Tops, exposed to Winter's Colds, and Summer's Heats, watches her little Flock, nor knows what Grandeur means, had less of Pride than *Emanuella*; yet here, the new, and ne'er till now experienc'd Guest usurp'd the whole Dominion o'er her Soul, and fir'd each Faculty with generous Scorn. – Wretch (*cry'd she*) who ignorant of Merit, and far incapable of judging by what the noble Mind is sway'd, thou thinkest all Dispositions like thy own, and conscious of thy own Depravity of Nature, hast dar'd to hope thou hast the means to force, or bribe me to thy Purpose; – but know, presuming Fool! I view thy executed Spite, and proffer'd Love with equal Eyes, and think them both below my Anger, and fit Subjects only for Disdain. She spoke much more to the same purpose, but Don *Pedro* knowing how entirely he had her in his power, was not at all mov'd at it, and doubted not but in a little time when she found there was no other Possibility of regaining her Liberty, she would recede from her present Haughtiness of Disposition: He did not fail to let her know what his Thoughts were on this Occasion, and expressed them in a fashion so insulting, that it encreased her Rage; 'till finding all she could say ineffectual to bring him to any just Sense of the Villany he was guilty, or to make him see how improbable it was she should ever be brought to yield to what he desir'd by such Methods, she at length desisted, and resolved to speak to him no more. 'Tis probable the old Don was a little nettled at her Behaviour, but he made no shew of it; and only telling her, if she would not be persuaded to become his Daughter, he should take care to be so far a Father to her, as to secure her Person and Fortune from being lavish'd away on a worse Choice, took his Leave. If a Condition such as hers could admit of any Happiness, it was at seeing him depart – the Sight of him was justly detestable to her, and the more so, because being an utter Enemy to Passion, she was almost as ready to condemn her self for the Extravagancies it made her guilty of, as he who had occasioned it: Nothing could be more exemplary than her manner of supporting this Confinement, the Excellence of her Principles made her think it a Crime to *revile* even her greatest Enemies, and the Greatness of her Spirit from any mean Complainings of her ill Fortune: the Servant who was appointed to attend her, protested he never saw her weep, nor utter the least irregular Word. Not that she was insensible of her Misfortunes; not the most repining Mortal, perhaps, ever felt any thing so nearly: being cut off in all probability for ever from all the Pleasures her Youth and Inclinations rendred her suceptible of. – To be robb'd of all that Grandeur she was bred to, – to be denied the Conversation of her Friends, – shut up from all Society, – and in the power of a Man whose Actions testified him to be the greatest of all Villains, one who doubtless would never let her appear in the World again for fear of being call'd to account for what he had done; – one who, 'twas possible, if she yielded not to his Proposal, might, to secure her Fortune, at last contrive her Death: – These were terrible Reflections for so young a Creature, yet I question, by the account I have of her, if the most tenacious of our Philosophers would have bore them with that Resignation she did.

About a Month was past in this Confinement, during which time she had seen no human Face but the Servant, and Don *Pedro* once; for neither his Wife, nor Don *Marco* ever had presumed to come into her Presence, which tho' she was very glad of, she could not help wondering at, not doubting at her first coming there but she should be continually persecuted with the Declarations of him whom her ill Fortune had made her Lover: but she gave herself not much trouble what should be the meaning of it, amusing her self as well as she could with Adventures she had formerly read of; for her cruel Jaylor now denied her the Satisfaction of Books. As she was sitting one Morning pretty early in her usual Meditations, she perceived a Paper lying close to the Door; she started up, and going to take it, perceived by part of it being still under the Door, that it had been thrust in by some body after it was shut: It was impossible but the most incurious in such a Circumstance would have been desirous of seeing what it contain'd, and hastily opening it, she found it was directed to her self, and contained these Lines:

To Donna *EMANUELLA.*

I Heartily lament the unjust Calamity you suffer, but Pity being a poor Consolation, have forbore to give you any Instances of it, till I had the power of testifying it by something more than Words; – if you have Courage enough to trust your self with a Person you know not, you will find more Honour than in those you have confided. – I have provided Means for your Escape, if you think fit to accept it, which let me know by a Line this Night when all the Family are in Bed. – I know you are denied the use of Pen and Ink, but if you can contrive to let a String down from your Window, I will be underneath and fasten one to it, which shall easily go in between the Grate, and by that means I may also receive your Answer, which I will wait the writing of. – Depend that I have no other View in attempting to serve you, than what is consistent with the strictest Honour, whose Votary I profess my self, and the injur'd Emanuella's

Unknown Servant.

P. S. *Three distinct Whistles, about two Minutes each time, shall be the Signal for you to let down the String.*

THE Surprize *Emanuella* was in at reading this, cannot be well express'd; she was sensible there were a great many in the Island, who would make this Offer, if by any means they could have known the need she had of their Service; but then the Improbability there was that Don *Pedro* should let the Truth of this Affair reach the Ear of any one, and much more that they should have an Opportunity of coming into his House, and conveying this Letter under the Door of her Chamber, quite stagger'd her Conjecture: she could not help, however, believing that it was best for her to accept it, since no Condition could be worse than what she was in at present; and if the Person who pretended to so much Honour should have Principles never so different from it, she thought it would be in her power to make a much better Defence at Liberty, and in an open Street, than she could do in this Confinement, in case Don *Marco* (which she was in daily Apprehensions of) should ever make any Attempts on her Honour: Resolv'd therefore, to send an Answer of Consent, she felt a greater Impatience for the approach of Night than yet she had ever known for any Event: At last it came, and between the Hours of Twelve and One she heard the wish'd-for Signal; she had tied her Girdle and Garters together to make a long String ready, which on the third Whistle she immediately let down, and with it drew up a little Standish[12] with a Sheet of Paper roll'd up in it, so careful was the Person that no material should be wanting, she did not delay the use it was convey'd for, but fill'd it in a moment with these Lines:

To the generous Offerer of Life, Liberty, and Deliverance from a thousand Evils.

I Will not give my self leave to suspect you any other than you seem, lest I should by a needless Fear render myself incapable of accepting what you so kindly offer, and justly merit what future Mischiefs may befall me. – I gladly embrace your Proposition, and am ready to do any thing to get free, – I wish you had acquainted me with what Methods I should take, for I can scarce believe there is a Possibility for me to escape: if there be, I beg the Knowledge may not be defer'd. – As you have been too generous to let me know what Reward you expect for so meritorious an Action; I will not pretend to offer any, since it is only in the power of Heaven to make a Retribution suitable to such exalted Virtue; and as that, I am willing to hope, is your only Aim, so that it may be immediately bestow'd in all the choicest Blessings of that eternal Store-House, shall be the incessant Prayers of

The (beyond Expression) obliged
EMANUELLA.

P. S. *The Moon shines to-night with an unusual Splendor, I believe by her favourable Beams you will have Light enough to answer my Impatience with some little Hints by what Means I am to be preserved: If you can without Danger of being observed, I beg you will favour me so far; and that you may do so, I let down your Standish and let the String continue, which I will not draw up till you give a Signal that you have no further Occasion for it.*

NO Whistle being given, she imagin'd he was about to do as she desir'd, and would very fain if possible have seen him, but the Grate was too narrow for her to put her Head through: In a very little time she heard the Whistle, and pulling up the Ribband, found there was a Letter fix'd to it, which contain'd these Lines:

To Donna *EMANUELLA.*

THE *Place I am in not being so private as I could wish, to particularize the Account you desire; I entreat you, will, be satisfied with knowing there is a Way found out to convey the Key of your Prison by the same Means you receive this – ; when it comes to your Hands, it will be also accompanied with a little Ladder made of Silk Cords, and you have no more to do than to unlock your Door and go into a Room adjoining to it, which you will find open, and a Window that looks into a Field whence you may easily descend, and at the bottom find him who will be ready to conduct you where you please, and always glad of an Opportunity to prove how very much he is*

Your most humble Servant.

P.S. *I believe you will have the Ladder and Key to-morrow Night, – therefore do not neglect to watch the Signal.*

If *Emanuella* was before confounded in her Conjectures who it should be that appeared so assiduous to deliver her, she was now much more so; the Key of the Door assur'd her it must be by the Assistance of some Person in the House she was to be befriended: but all the Guesses she could make seeming improbable, she contented her self to wait the Certainty; and the Probability that the worst part of her Misfortune, her Confinement, was near an end, gave her hopes that she should also find Justice to remedy the others also; and she past the remainder of that Night, and the ensuing Day in Contemplations much more tranquil than she had known, since she had been in that House.

The next Night, much about the same Hour, or something later, she heard the Sound she was not a little impatient for; and letting down the String, found it came up with a weight which told her before she saw it, what she expected had not fail'd her: she received both the Ladder and Key, to which was fix'd a little piece of Paper in which was writ these Words:

This Moment is the Crisis of your Fate –; be careful not to lose it – unlock your Door as softly as you can, and go into a Chamber on the left Hand, there is a Balcony to which you may fix your Ladder – ; do not mistake the Room, nor take any Light with you – there are Horses to carry you where you shall command.

It was not without some little Apprehensions this distressed Lady was about to put her self in the power of a Person unknown, at such an Hour, and one who she found had Conveniency to carry her where he pleased, tho' he made her the Compliment of leaving it to her own Choice; but the Exigence of her Affairs, the cruel Restraint she was under, and the Probability of greater Evils, presently banish'd them, and she unlock'd the Door, and in every thing obeyed Directions. The Balcony was so low, that she might almost have jumped from it to the Ground; but the Gentleman who had taken so much pains to serve her, ordered every thing as commodious as possible. She found three Men on Horseback, one of which alighting, lifted her up behind another, and as soon as he was remounted himself, desired her to say where they should conduct her. – The terror she had been in for fear of Discovery while she was in the House, the Confusion to think she was in the Hands of Strangers, and the Uncertainty to which of her Acquaintance the coming in that Hour, and Manner, and the rest of her History, would be the least liable to Censure, made her unable to reply; which one of them perceiving, said to the others, The Lady may by her late Disorders be perhaps, at present, incapable of determining on any thing, 'tis therefore best to ride some distance from hence, no matter which way, to prevent Discovery, till the Power of Consideration is a little return'd to her. *Emanuella*, willing to be farther from Don *Pedro*, assented, and they all went five or six Miles without stopping or speaking to each other; a little House in which there was a Light seem'd to invite them to bait[13] at it, and it being proposed, she having put her self so far into their power, thought it would discover a ridiculous Distrust to scruple bearing them Company into it; and beside, she hoped her Curiosity would be satisfied by discovering to whom it was she was indebted for her Delivery, for they were all so muffled in their Cloaks, that it was impossible for her to know whether she had ever seen them before or not; she had ask'd the Person she rode behind, but he excused himself by telling her that he but obey'd his Principal in what he had done, and without his Leave could not discover any thing. This Secrecy a little alarm'd her, but she was infinitely more so when being come into the House, one of the Persons who she observ'd had never spoke one Word during the whole time of their little Journey, came into the Room, and making a Sign to the others to withdraw, threw off his Cloak, and discovered himself to be Don *Marco.* Astonishment, and Rage, and Fear at once possess'd her – she could not imagine for what Reason he had acted in this manner, unless it was contriv'd so that in flying the Cruelty of the *Father*, she should run into the danger of a more shocking Treatment from the Son. – But she had not time to utter any part of what she thought, before falling on his Knees he accosted her in this Manner: I see Madam, *said he,* with what Regret you find your self under some Obligation to any of the Family of Don *Pedro*; but to convince you that Nearness of Blood does not always occasion a Conformity of Principles, be pleased to accept of this little part of what has been so unjustly taken from you, and believe that *Marco* will never rest till the whole is again at your disposal. In speaking these Words he presented her with a little Amber Box, in which she had been used to keep her Jewels; which opening, she found it still contain'd them, and also Bills to a great Value. 'Tis hard to say whether she was most amazed, or pleased, at so unexpected a piece of Generosity. The Esteem she formerly had for him, which by the late Behaviour of his Father, in which she imagined he had an equal Share, had been converted into as great an Aversion, now return'd with added Vigour, and she rejoiced as much to find she had not been deceived in her first Sentiments of his Virtues, as in the Advantage she receiv'd from them; she expressed herself so obligingly on this Occasion, that Don *Marco* who had the most sincere and disinterested Affection for her that ever was, could not listen to her without feeling a Rapture perhaps superior to that which some who call themselves Lovers are capable of knowing, even in the Gratification of their utmost Wishes. I tremble Madam, *said he*, to appear before you, knowing well that without a Goodness near Divine, the little Service I have now been able to do you, joined with that of my whole future Life is far too small to engage Forgiveness for the Wrongs you have received from my Family; and should not have presumed to discover my self, had not your uncertainty how to bestow your self in safety, obliged me to bring you to this House. You would then, *answer'd she*, have been guilty of a great Injustice to your self, and Unkindness to me; for to be obliged in so profuse a manner, and be ignorant where to pay our Acknowledgments, is, to a grateful Soul, a Pain – : Besides, I feel so great a Satisfaction in the Knowledge, that when I entertain'd a Friendship for Don *Marco* I err'd not in my Choice, that I know not if I could easily have pardon'd the delaying of it. – Be assur'd, I cannot resent the Usage I have met from Don *Pedro* with half that Warmth and Spirit, as I shall endeavour to repay my Obligations to his Son; and that the Virtues of the latter, have entirely disarm'd me from taking that Revenge which the Vices of the other would else have demanded. O I know, resumed Don *Marco*, I know you are too heavenly good, to wish Revenge; but do not, I beseech you, do not let the Memory of what I have done, nor the Belief how much more I would do, were it in my power make you forget what is owing to yourself. – Use all proper means to oblige my cruel Father to restore to you what he has so unjustly taken from you; for much I fear he will not be prevail'd upon by gentle means to deal with Honour by you.

THIS generous Contest lasted for some Time, nor would Don *Marco* give it over, till she had promised to endeavour to do her self Justice; for the Attainment of which, both thought it the most effectual Way for her to pursue her Intention of going to *Madrid*, not only because if she continued where she was, Don *Pedro*'s Artifice might possibly find her out, and contrive some Stratagem again to get her in his power, but also that the King was the only Person who had the Means of redressing her Grievances. He would needs accompany her thither, attended by the two Men whom he had brought to assist her in her Escape; but she opposed it, telling him she had already receiv'd too many Obligations to endure the Thoughts of laying herself under more: However, on his representing the Dangers which of consequence must attend a Person of her Sex, in so long a Voyage, alone; and also the Necessity there was for him to abscond for some time from the Rage of Don *Pedro*, who 'twas probable would be raised to the highest Pitch, on the Discovery how his Designs had been circumvented by the very Person for whose sake they had been form'd: She was at last persuaded, it would not only be extreamly commodious for her, but also far from inconvenient for him; and since his absenting himself from his Father was absolutely necessary, it was as well for him to take a Voyage to *Madrid*, as any other Place. This being concluded on, Don *Marco* advis'd their Immediate Departure, judging it not safe to remain on the Island after Day-Break, if by any means they could leave it sooner; because he knew that in the Morning the Fellow who had the Charge of the Key which he had stole, would discover the Theft, and *Emanuella*'s Escape. One of the Men was therefore immediately dispatch'd to the Sea-side, which they were not above three Miles distant from, to see if there was a Ship ready to go off, and to agree for the Passage. By good Fortune there was one, which on a more than ordinary Gratification, comply'd with their desire of hoisting Sail as soon as they came on board. 'Twould be needless to say with how much Pleasure *Emanuella* heard this News; the ardent Desire she had to leave a place which had so little in it agreeable to her Genius, joined to the late ill Treatment she had met with, and the Apprehensions of being subjected to the same again, is sufficient to make the Reader sensible with what a Welcome she receiv'd the certainty of going.

AN infinity of Contentment sat smiling on her Countenance all the time of their Voyage; a fair Wind, kindly Gales, and an unruffled Sea wafted her smoothly to her desired Port. – No chilling Fears from *within* – No Omens from *without* – No secret Warning from her Guardian Angel gave a Check to the Satisfaction she felt at landing on that fatal Shore where all her Peace of Mind was to be wreck'd! where Mischiefs multiplied, concealed in Clouds – Numberless, nameless Ills – attended her Approach, ready to burst with all their hoarded Venom on her Head.

SHE went immediately to the House of Don *Jabin*,[14] a very near Relation, where having made herself known, and the Particulars of her late Adventure, she was receiv'd with the highest Demonstrations of Kindness – Both he and his Wife assured her they would introduce her to the King, who would doubtless do her Justice as to the Recovery of that part of her Fortune which was still in the possession of Don *Pedro*; and also issue out his Orders for the Punishment so base an Action deserv'd: But this not being done immediately, by reason of his Majesty being at that time at the *Escurial*,[15] from which he did not return so soon as was expected; an Incident entirely unforeseen gave a sudden and vexatious Turn to this Affair, and instead of being *Plaintiff*, reduced her to the State of a *Defendant*.

THE cunning Don *Pedro* had no sooner discover'd her Escape, than he immediately guess'd to what place the was gone; and not doubting but she would take such Measures as could end in no less than his Ruin, had it presently in his head how to preserve himself, and lay the Odium on her: His Son being fled with her, and some few Bills he had taken from him to support himself in his Absence, as well as what of right belong'd to *Emanuella*, furnish'd him with Hints which the prompting Fiend that animated his inventive Brain, took care to improve to form a Story so plausible, that when heard, he should appear the only injured Person, and *Emanuella*, and his Son (whom now he hated) be esteemed no other than Wretches who had contriv'd together to rob him; full of this inhuman Stratagem, and accompanied by some vile Creatures whose Evidence he had purchas'd, as well as Bonds, Notes, and Bills, counterfeiting the dead *Alvarez*'s Hand and Seal, he was at *Madrid* almost as soon as those he follow'd; and being inform'd, his Majesty was at the *Escurial*, he waited not his coming to *Madrid*, but as Vice is always more indefatigable in the pursuit of what it aims at, than a sincere and honest Meaning, he went to wait on him there: And his Age and artful Manner of insinuating what he would have believ'd, wrought so far on the Royal Ear, as to gain him the promise of having it in his power to inflict what Punishment he pleased on the Fugitives, who the cruel Politician had taken care to inform himself where they might be found, before he deliver'd his Petition, tho' he concealed himself from either of them.

NOTHING therefore of his Arrival being suspected, till the News of the King's Return, put Don *Jabin* in mind that his Cousin should make her Appeal, and she was dressing herself to accompany him to Court, when a Messenger from thence came to demand her Appearance. The Surprize of so unlook'd for a Summons, put them all in a Consternation; and Don *Marco*, who tho' he did not lodge there, pass'd most of his Hours with them, and was at that time present, discover'd in his countenance a Horror which extreamly added to it. He was not ignorant of the thousand Artifices his Father was ever Master of, when he was zealous for the Accomplishment of any Design, and fear'd it was by some Emissaries employ'd by him, tho' he was far from imagining he was there himself, that something had been done to pervert that Justice he might very well believe *Emanuella* would claim. He would very fain have persuaded her to suffer him to wait on her, that in case it were as he suspected, he might be a Witness on her Side, against whatever false Suggestions should be offered to her Disadvantage; but that generous Lady would by no means be prevailed on to permit him. She told him she had not the least Fear of making a Defence against all that Malice could form to hurt her; and that she could not consent a Person she call'd Friend, and one who so justly had merited that Title from her, should put so great a Constraint on himself, and endure a Shame so poinant, as must rise from the Accusation of a Parent, tho' never so unworthy a one. She express'd herself in Terms so absolute, that Don *Marco,* tho' with a world of Reluctance, was obliged to obey: and accompanied by Don *Jabin,* his Lady, and the two Servants, who came over with her, and whom it was necessary should appear; she went with a Courage infinitely beyond what could be expected from her Sex and Years; and wholly relying on the Justice of her Cause, and the Care of Heaven, was farther from any dread of the Event, than those to whom it was of less Concern.

NOT but when she was conducted into the Palace, and brought before the King, she was a little alarm'd to see the base Don *Pedro* there: she had however Presence enough of Mind to conceal those little Emotions which she was unable to repel at so unexpected an Interview, and after having paid her Duty to the Royal Presence; If I were not already too well acquainted, *said she,* with your Insolence in maintaining the Injuries you do, I should have hope, Repentance for those you have offered me, had brought you here, so contrary to my Expectation, to make me that Restitution, you might be sure I should endeavour to force you to. There was not a Person in this Assembly, which was very numerous, most of the Nobility being come to congratulate his Majesty on his Return, who the Appearance of *Emanuella*, and the Sweetness which accompanied her Accents, assur'd as they were, did not win to her Interest. – The King himself seem'd to regard her with an uncommon Stedfastness, as surpriz'd at the Graces which attended her; and already suspicious of the Truth of what had been suggested against her: which the watchful *Pedro* observing, throwing himself at his Feet, O my Sovereign! *said he*, if this Woman's Soul had any Affinity with her exterior

Charms, she would at least have had Modesty sufficient to have shun'd the awful Justice of this Place – but I entreat you by that extensive Power which makes Kings Gods on Earth, and by that sacred Regard which to the King of Kings, even from your self, is due! – By Honour, Pity, Justice, by your own Royal Promise, I conjure you not to listen to the false Insinuations of this artful *Siren*, who comes no doubt prepared with well-dress'd Perjuries, and smooth Hypocrisy to evade her Crimes, and turn the Sword of Vengeance against me. 'Twould be very hard to describe any part of what pass'd in the Soul of the injur'd *Emanuella* all the time he was speaking in this manner; scarce could she restrain the struggling Passions, which swell'd almost to bursting in her Breast, and press'd so hard for Vent, 'tis probable no Consideration would have been of force to have withheld them, had not the King with a Countenance somewhat perplex'd commanded him to be silent, telling him Justice should be severely executed on whichever Party should be found the Guilty – Don *Jabin* then, tho' very much confus'd at so strange a Character of his Relation, thought it was his Time to speak, and begg'd to know of what she was accus'd. To which his Majesty assenting, commanded a Person appointed for that purpose to read the Heads of the Charge against her, as they were taken from the Mouth of her Impeacher; which he presently obey'd, and with a loud Voice surpriz'd all who had not heard it before, with the Contents of a Paper which he pulled out of his Pocket, and were as follows:

A brief Abstract of the Crimes alledged against Donna *Emanuella*, Daughter to Don *Alvarez*, late Governor of *Porto-Rico*, an Island in that part of his most Catholick Majesty's Dominions, entitled the *Spanish-West-Indies*: Attested by Don *Pedro*, and a great Number of other Gentlemen upon Oath.

I.

That the said Donna Emanuella, *being privy to the borrowing several large Sums of Money from Don* Pedro, *by her Father; she, after his Death, not only deny'd the Payment of them, but also pretended there was much more owing to her from the said Don* Pedro.

II.

That she seduc'd the Principles of Don Marco, *the only Son of Don* Pedro, *and living with him in a riotous and dissolute manner, soon wasted the little Wealth left her by Don* Alvarez; *on which having recourse to Don* Pedro *for a Supply, and being refus'd by him, she hir'd Assassins to murder him, which he very narrowly escap'd.*

III.

That being, by the Order of the Magistrates of the Place, on Don Pedro*'s Complaint, taken into Custody, and afterwards, by his Compassion and Charity, preserv'd from being carried to Prison, and taken into his own House on her seeming Repentance; she most ungratefully and wickedly contriv'd with his own Son to rob him,* *which they did, and made their Escape together to* Madrid, *with the Value of 5000 Crowns in Jewels, Bills and Money.*

So heavy an Accusation, loaden with so many aggravating Circumstances, was sufficient to have shock'd the most establish'd Fortitude; but *Emanuella* was of that sort of Spirit, which exalts it self the most, when most it is oppress'd: she seem'd rather fuller of Disdain than Anger, while she listned to the invective Scroll; and when she saw Amazement sit on every Face, and those of her own Blood confounded, and unable to offer any thing in her Defence, she thus undertook to plead for herself. Wonder not, Royal Sir! *said she*, that, conscious of my perfect Innocence, and of a Soul too nice to bear such rude Suspicions, as this monstrous Legend may perhaps create, should lodge a Moment in the Breasts of any here; I not await the dull Formalities of Law, nor ask Advice from learned Counsel drawn, but here presume to make my own Defence, unaided but by Truth – Permit me then, great King! to unfold a Story must make my vile Accuser's Heart grow cold within him, tho' warm'd with all the Fires from Hell. She stop'd at these Words, by a beseeching Air expecting his Permission to proceed; which being granted, she related the whole Affair with the greatest Truth and Exactness, neither extenuating her Enemy's Inhumanity, nor diminishing the smallest Tittle of her own Behaviour. Don *Pedro*, and his Accomplices, attempted to interrupt her several times, but they were commanded to be silent, and she was indulg'd in all the freedom she could desire in vindicating herself, and accusing him. When she had finish'd what she had to say, and the Witnesses she brought with her examin'd, there were many, who, confident of her Sincerity, spoke in her Behalf, but it avail'd but little. Don *Pedro*'s continued Asseverations, the number of his Evidences, and the advantage of complaining first, was very near carrying the Cause against her; when Don *Marco*, impatient that they stay'd, and full of fears, which were indeed prophetick, left the House of Don *Jabin,* and came with all speed to the Palace: partly by Persuasions, and partly by Force, he got through the Guards, and entered the Room of Audience just as his Father was entreating Sentence might be past on *Emanuella*. Distracted with what he saw and heard, he ran up to the Chair of State, and begg'd it might be suspended 'till he was heard. The King, whose Sentiments were yet unfix'd, gave him leave to utter what he had to say; and deaf to all other Considerations but those of clearing her, he wildly spoke every thing he knew, and not only confirm'd all *Emanuella* had averr'd, but many more Particulars, of which she was ignorant, concerning his Father's Barbarity; and among the rest, that he really had a design to murder her, the surer to secure her Fortune; which horrid Deed had certainly been perpetrated, had he not timely contrived the means of her Escape. But all that he could urge, was in vain; the King had been so much prepossest by Don *Pedro* of a criminal Correspondence between him and that

Lady, that all he said appeared but as the Effects of Gallantry to save a *Mistress,* who, considering her Attractions, and the Misfortune of his own Form, it was no wonder he should risque every thing for. But, with what Words can so unexampled a Generosity be prais'd! – Perceiving his Zeal to serve, had rather work'd a contrary Effect; the noble-minded *Marco* resolv'd to give a fatal Proof of his Sincerity, once more addressing himself to his Majesty; Since that bad Man, who gave me Being, *said he,* prefers a little shining Dirt to Honour, Truth and Justice, and still persists in his design of ruining an innocent Virgin entrusted to his Care: Thus! *continued he*, (drawing his Sword, and falling on it, before any one cou'd be quick enough to prevent him) Thus! I release myself of the Duty of a Son. – Thus! clear myself of the Crimes he has accus'd me of – and Thus! I hope, convince your sacred Majesty, and the yet unbelieving World, that it contains not a Jewel of more worth than *Emanuella*! – Hear, and believe me, Royal Sir! tho' long, long I have ador'd the charming Maid, conscious of my own Defects, I ne'er presum'd to wound her Ears with the unwelcome Tale; nor would I, 'till my last Moment, have ventur'd on the Declaration, lest she should have *hated*, what I'm too well assur'd she never cou'd have *lov'd.* – If what I now have done, be an Offence to Heaven, I hope you will all supplicate my Pardon: for be assur'd, could I have liv'd with Honour, or with Peace, I had not died so early ; but thus, miserable in all, traduced by him, who ought to have been the Protector of my Fame, justly despis'd by her I wish'd to please, what could I do, but – He could no more; he had given the Wound with such a force, Death found an easy Passage to his Heart, and soon deprived him of the Power of Utterance. The King seemed prodigiously alarmed at so uncommon a Testimony of Affection. The Nobles look'd on one another, struck with a sudden Horror. *Emanuella* forgot her own Misfortunes to lament the untimely Fate of so deserving a Youth. But Don *Pedro*, who, tho' he stood still and motionless for some time, as the Son his Barbarity had deprived him of expired, yet his hurrying Thoughts were busy enough within, and turn'd all his Soul into Confusion. – Long sleeping Conscience rouz'd itself at length, and Self-Conviction, Remorse, and all the Horrors of Desperation at once invaded him. The wild Disorder scorning to prey on any of the meaner Faculties, mounted to the Brain, whirling Reflexion from her Chain of Causes, and quite disjointed Reason. In this sudden Frenzy he uttered enough to make all that heard him sensible of his Guilt; and the King, rightly judging the Cause by the Effect, order'd him to be taken away and secur'd till Time should discover more. The Persons, who had appear'd Confederates in his Design, were sent to the *Inquisition*,[16] there to be instructed in the Pains which perjur'd Wretches like themselves are doom'd to bear in another World; and *Emanuella*, and her Friends, dismiss'd with those Encomiums which her modest, but courageous Behaviour merited, and a Promise given by the King's own mouth, That he would send an immediate Order for the bringing over all that Don *Pedro* had so unjustly seiz'd.

THIS Adventure engross'd the whole Discourse of the Town for a great while; and those who were entirely Strangers to the Person of *Emanuella*, were perfectly well acquainted with her by Report. It is most certain, that her Virtues being rendred by this publick Notice more conspicuous, gain'd her a much greater number of Admirers than otherwise she would have had, if she had been no more seen, nor known than the *Spanish* Ladies ordinarily are; but then the same Reason created also an adequate proportion of Detractors. It is impossible to be remarkably distinguish'd, without being as remarkably envied and hated, especially by those of the same Sex; those who found the greatest improvement in her Conversation, and whom she most instructed in any of those numerous Accomplishments, in which she excell'd, secretly wish'd her less capable of affording it; and those to whom she would not be seen, as finding nothing in them worthy of her Friendship, made it their whole Study by all the little Artifices they were Mistresses of, to lessen the brightness of a Character whose Radiency discover'd the Imperfections of their own: but hers was too well establish'd for any of the Plots laid against her to succeed, and she was so universally applauded by all the knowing part of the World, that it was sufficient to be accounted well thought of by her, to engage the Reputation of being a fine Woman – There were a great many, therefore, who endeavour'd an Intimacy with her in no other View; aiming only at the Character, and neglecting the real Advantages which even those who had been the least indebted either to Nature or Education, might have found in an Acquaintance with her. Nor did her Charity, and Generosity of Disposition, extend only to the embellishing the *Minds* of those to whom she profess'd a Friendship; she could not think a worthy Person under any Distress, without preventing their Requests, by offering every thing in her power to serve them: and tho' the Fortune she was at present possess'd of (till Don *Pedro* had restor'd her the much greater part still in his hands) would not allow very conveniently of such Liberalities; yet she made Presents, which by their Magnificence, had the Receivers been ignorant from whom they came, would rather have been imagin'd to flow from the Purse of a Princess, than that of a private Gentlewoman. Donna *Berillia,* youngest Daughter to her Cousin Don *Jabin*, experienced her Bounty this way; for being condemned much against her Inclinations to a Nunnery (as in *Spain*, where a *Grandee* has a numerous Family, and not an equal Affluence of Wealth, rather than match them below their Birth, 'tis common to bestow one or more of them in that manner, where for eight or nine hundred Crowns they are provided for, for their Lives)[17] the generous *Emanuella* never left solliciting her Father to suspend his Design, till she should receive the remainder of her Fortune as the King had promised she should; assuring him that she would add to what he must be obliged to give to place her in a Cloister, as much as would make her equal to what he design'd for her other Sisters. – Don *Jabin* was very loth to accept of what she offer'd; telling her it was not only a much greater Favour than he was willing to accept, but also a Sum beyond what she could conveniently spare: but she stopp'd his mouth, begging him to believe the Company of *Berillia* was cheaply purchased at that Rate; and that for his other Objection, she would easily make it up, by retrenching Expenses, less pleasing to herself than that would be.

THIS young Lady so highly obliged to *Emanuella* for this Proof of her Friendship, one would think should never have obliterated the Memory of it; but what Engagements are of force to bind a Thankless and Ungrateful Mind! The Aversion she had for a monastick Life, was soon discover'd by the penetrating Eyes of her Cousin, to proceed from her too great Affection for a young Fop, who had nothing to recommend him to the Approbation of of a Woman of Discretion; and talking to her with a little more warmth than was usual on this Occasion, the other resented it as tho' she took that Liberty on the account of what she had promised to her Father, and from that Moment conceiv'd so great a Hatred, that it grew uneasy to herself, because she had no Opportunity to make the other feel the Effects of it – But being naturally as cunning as revengeful, she conceal'd her Sentiments, and under the mask of Friendship, watch'd all her Actions, still hoping some unguarded Minute might arrive, in which she should be able to discover something to expose her for. But not all her Dilligence could furnish what she wanted; *Emanuella*, among the multiplicity of her Adorers, behav'd herself in such a manner, that might defy the strictest Scrutiny – all her Actions – all her Words – all her Looks, were govern'd by Prudence, and her malicious Observer began to think it would be but Labour lost to attempt to blast either her Virtue or Reputation. But alas! what Courage, what Discretion, what cool Reserve, what Sanctity of Wishes can defend the Heart, when once the God of Love has found an Entrance there! that Tyrant Passion lords it o'er the Mind, fills every Faculty, and leaves no room for any other Thought – drives Consideration far away – overturns Reflection – and permits no Image but it self to dwell in Fancy's Region. The soft and tender Soul of *Emanuella,* was a fit Temple for the enslaving Deity to work his utmost wonders in; and that she no sooner felt his Power, was not because she was less susceptible than others of her Acquaintance, but that her Taste was more delicate, and so many different Perfections as were necessary to attract her Admiration, were very difficult to be found in one Man.

BUT Chance, or rather the Character of her Charms, at last, brought a Person to her sight so conformable to the *Idea* she had created in her Mind, of what would please her, that she could not presently distinguish whether it was still the same delightful Vision her extensive Fancy had dress'd up with all the Ornaments of Art and Nature, or a real Substance. This most lovely, this accomplish'd Gentleman, was call'd *Emilius*,[18] a young *Roman* Count, who, having visited almost all the Courts of *Europe,* happen'd at this time to be at *Madrid.* He heard talk of *Emanuella*, as of the greatest wonder there; and having seen all other Curiosities, could not be satisfied to leave the Place, without first being an Eye-witness of those Perfections, which Fame so lavishly reported. The *Carnival* coming on, he had hope the Freedom of the Diversions used in that Season,[19] might afford him an Opportunity he long had vainly languish'd for: Nor was he deceived. *Emanuella*, who had not been accustomed to those severe Restrictions of Behaviour the *Spanish* Jealousy obliges the Females of their Family to observe, was glad to lay hold of all Opportunities to indulge the natural Gaiety of her Humour; and accompanied by Donna *Berillia*, and other Ladies of her Acquaintance, took part in all the innocent Liberties the time allow'd. As they were on their Rambles one day, the watchful *Count*, having Intelligence to whose House they were going, found means to be introduced to the Master of it: There happened to be a great Assembly of Gentlemen and Ladies; but presently informing himself which was *Emanuella*, he singled her out; and in entertaining her, it was difficult to say whether he gave, or receiv'd the greater Pleasure. She thought she had never seen any thing so agreeable and witty, and he found her so far surpassing all the Descriptions had been made him, that tho' he had arm'd himself with all the Resolution he was Master of, to regard her only with *Admiration*, a tenderer Passion, in spite of him, soon took up all his Soul – He could not gaze, without admiring; nor admire, without desiring: But tho' he found that he had very much receded from that Resolution he had form'd before he saw her, yet, till he saw her no more, he knew not how much – The height of Passion is never so truly experienced as in Absence – when from our longing Eyes, the dear lov'd Prospect flies – and our transported Ears no more are blest – what *Sense* cannot bestow *Imagination*'s Force supplies, and brings the Charmer to our ravish'd View – in spite of distance, we see! we hear! we grasp the lovely Phantom, and taste, in *Theory*, ten thousand Joys; till *Reason*, envious of the airy Bliss, chases the bright *Ideas* from our Minds, and shows us what we are.

It was in these waking Dreams the amorous Count beguil'd the Pains of Absence; but he was too much of the Temper of his Sex to content himself without a Happiness more substantial: A perfect Knowledge of his own Attractions, and frequent Experience how little it was in the power of any Woman to withstand the influence of them, made him not despair of finding the same Sensibility in *Emanuella*, as he had done in others; and imagined he wanted nothing but an Opportunity to acquaint her with his Passion, to inspire an equal one in her. The first Step therefore, that he made towards the ingratiating himself, was to write; and, besides the being pretty much accustomed to such kind of *Billets*, the Passion he was at present fir'd with, help'd him to dictate one tender enough to make her believe he lov'd her, and too respectful not to give her an Opinion, his Designs were accompanied with the strictest Honour. The Words were these:

To the Incomparable Donna *EMANUELLA.*

BEFORE *I attempt to make known the impatient Dictates of my Soul, I would call all the Aids of Wit – of pity-moving Eloquence – and soft Persuasion, to inspire my Pen, and teach me Arts to which I am yet a Stranger: But that a secret Impulse from within, bids me beware – tells me* Sincerity *disdains the Ornaments of Words, and looks most lovely in her naked Meaning – Yet dare I not proceed – O that my Guardian Angel – the Witness of my Sighs, my Tears, my long Endurings, my restless Days, and agonizing Nights, would leave his Charge one Moment, and gently whisper in your Ear how much I love – how much I suffer – At length the Secret is reveal'd – O wondrous Force of Passion! that while it drives, restrains, and speaks in Silence – I have confess'd I love – but O what hope that you'll permit me to attest this Truth by all the Services of my future Life? – I have no Parents here, no Friend, no Merits to excuse this bold Presumption, and plead my Cause – but if* Emanuella *has a Penetration such as her Eyes, and Wit, have persuaded me to think,* that *has already told her more in my behalf than any Tongue could utter. The wild Confusion in my Countenance – the Inconnexion of my Words, when all surpriz'd! astonish'd! at the Wonders of your Charms, I by a thousand ways betray'd my Sense of them the few Hours I had the Blessing of entertaining you, at the House of Don* Francisco – *But I am too presuming – I fear the excellent* Emanuella, *so used to conquer, regarded not a Triumph so unworthy of her Observation – If so, I am indeed undone – but as 'tis natural to wish Pity for remedyless Misfortunes, be so divinely good to allow me that; and if you chance to hear of an unhappy Stranger, who falls a Martyr to Love's powerful Flame, know 'tis he who living or dying must be*

Your everlasting Votary,
EMILIUS

P. S. *As I have pass'd many Nights in Contemplation under your Window; permit me to disturb an Hour's Repose of yours with the Musick this Evening about twelve or one a-clock.*

IF what *Emanuella* felt from the first View of *Emilius* was not yet arrived to a Passion, it was enough to afford an infinity of Pleasure in receiving this; which, indeed, she was not without some secret Expectations of, having, as he judiciously enough observ'd, a Discernment which seldom deceiv'd her, and easily inform'd her the Emotions that appear'd in his Face were occasion'd only by her Presence; had she been as quick in discovering the Humours of her own Sex, she had escap'd the greatest part of the Misfortunes which soon after came upon her – But as intimate as she was with Donna *Berillia*, she forbore to acquaint her with this Affair, not out of any suspicion she would betray it, or make any Conjecture to her disadvantage; but that perceiving she still carried on an Amour with that young Spark already mentioned, she thought to acknowledge herself a Lover, would be to lessen the Prerogative she took in advising the other. When Night came, she was very much purplex'd how to get rid of her; and not being willing she should stay till the *Count* came to the Window, made a Pretence of being a little indispos'd, and said she would go to Bed: but the officious Creature would not be so put off; and being of a suspicious Temper, presently imagin'd there was something more than ordinary in the Case, that made her Cousin, contrary to her Custom, so willing she should leave her; and besides, she fancied she had been more thoughtful of late than usual: Therefore putting all this together, she resolv'd, if possible, to find out the meaning of it; and imagining that this Night might produce something which would tend to a Discovery, she stir'd not from the Chamber, under colour of taking care of her, till *Emanuella* had been some time in Bed. Nor after she left her, did she retire to her own Chamber; but putting out the Lights, conceal'd herself in one adjoining to her's, and from which she could easily hear every thing that stir'd in it. She had not long stood Centinel, before she was surpriz'd with the Sound of Musick which the *Count* had brought to serenade his Mistress; she presently drew nearer to a little Window that was in the Room, and the Instruments being tun'd, accompanied a Voice which in very Harmonious Accents sang these Stanzas:

I.

From bright Emanuella's *Charms*,
Ah! – what Relief is found?
She every way the Soul alarms!
And never fails to wound.

II.

Reason and Love, once Foes profess'd,
Their utmost Forces join:
And make the most obdurate Breast,
Confess her all Divine!

III.

Whether she speaks, or looks, or moves,
Strange Passion she inspires!
Scorning the Arts of vulgar Loves,
At once she awes and fires!

Emanuella was so much accustom'd to Gallantries of this kind, that *Berillia* would not have thought any farther of this, than any other *Serenade,* had she not immediately after the Song heard her open her Window: A Condescension she never had made before, to any who aim'd at the Secret to please her, was sufficient to assure the Fair Inquisitive, that whoever the Person below was, he was possess'd of an uncommon Share of *Emanuella*'s Favour, and made her listen to the Conversation they presently after begun, with all the Attention she was able, to discover, if possible, the happy Man so remarkably distinguish'd.

THE moment *Emanuella* appear'd at her Window, *Emilius,* after having made a Sign to those that accompanied him to retire, came as near as he could to it; and in a low Voice, Can you forgive divine *Emanuella! said he*, my keeping you from that Repose which might probably afford you Entertainments more elegant than any you can find abroad. I should be very cruel to my self, *answer'd she,* and unjust to you; should the too nice Reserves of the Country we are in, oblige me to shun a Pleasure such as you have just now afforded me; and as I had my Education in a place of greater Liberties, I shall make no Scruple of continuing to indulge myself in all those innocent ones I have been accustomed to; among which, I account a free Conversation with Persons of your Sex, provided always their Behaviour is what Honour and Decency will allow of. The Man so favour'd (*resum'd the Count*) must be unworthy indeed, who could not form a Humour, if not born with him, suited to those Principles which alone are capable of recommending him to a Woman of less Virtue than the adorable *Emanuella.* O (*continued he, with a beseeching Accent*) that Virtue, Honour, and Sincerity, were the only Requisites to make the Man possess'd of them deserving *Emanuella*'s Favour! The Man who can prove himself (*return'd she*) possess'd of them, needs no other Qualification to a Woman capable of distinguishing what is truly meritorious. A great deal more of this kind of Conversation had doubtless pass'd between them, had they not been interrupted by another Set of Musick, who placed themselves under the Window, for the same purpose the *Count* had done. *Emanuella*, willing to show the Deference she paid him, bad him Good-night, and immediately withdrew: *Berillia*, who had heard every Word that had pass'd, made her own Construction of it, and rejoiced that she had found something wherewith she might let the World know *Emanuella* was not without her Softnesses, as well as those she took the liberty of blaming.

BUT while she pass'd the time in a thousand ill-natur'd Contrivances how to dress up the Affair she had discover'd in the worst Colours, the Lovers were employ'd in Contemplations far different – *Emanuella,* who had been extreamly charm'd with the Person and Behaviour of her new Adorer, from the first time she saw him, was flattering herself with the Idea of a world of Satisfaction in the Proof of his Sincerity; and he, on the other side, was no less transported, that she seem'd willing to be assured he really was what he pretended.

THE next day, at both Morning and Evening Prayers, she did not fail of seeing him; where instead of paying her Devotions to Heaven, she was busied in receiving them herself from the enamour'd *Count.* At Night by Appointment she entertain'd him from her Window, and thus it continued for several Weeks; he still seeming to encrease in the fervency of his Passion, and she in believing it – But while in these Sense-ensnaring Amusements she suffered her Soul to be employ'd, *Berillia* was not idle in reporting all she knew, and a thousand times more, to every one she was acquainted with; and in a little time 'twas grown the common talk that *Emanuella,* the reserv'd discreet *Emanuella,* was fallen in Love with a young Gentleman who was a Stranger in *Madrid*, and from whom she could have no Assurance that he was not already married, or under Engagements, which in Honour she ought not to break through.

EMANUELLA, however, was so much respected by all that knew her, that no one would shock her Ears with any such Discourses; till some of the Old and Grave having got notice of it, and fearing her Behaviour in this Point might serve as a Precedent to their own Daughters and Neices, made no Scruple to speak of this Affair to Don *Jabin* with a good deal of Severity; and he to represent it to her as a very great Solecism in that Decorum she had hitherto so strictly preserved. She could not hear him without a sensible Alarm; but alas! she lov'd and was by this time too far enter'd into the fatal Maze, to be able to extricate herself; there appeared a Prospect of too much Felicity in continuing her Conversation with the charming *Count* for her to resign it for any of those dull Considerations he endeavour'd to inspire her with; and besides all this, tho' she had a Wisdom far above her Years, she in this point and in many others also was apt a little too much to depend on her own Strength of Reason; and the only Fault she was guilty of, was *Self-Will.*

THE Adventure being so publick, she thought she might now communicate it to *Berillia*; little suspecting it was through her means it had first been talked of: and that malicious and designing Creature, glad of this Opportunity to make her Conduct appear yet more blameable, sooth'd the Humour she was in, by all the Arts she was Mistress of – She talk'd continually of the *Count*, she praised his Shape, his Air, his Wit; and whoever has known any thing of Love, will confess, how dangerous it is for a Person, entring into that State, to listen to such Discourses; of an Object which already appears but too Amiable. *Emanuella* suck'd in the delicious Poison, and thought the deceitful Instiller of it her best of Friends: Why, *said she*, should you deprive your self of the Pleasure of conversing with the Man you Love, and who has the tenderest Regard for you, only to satisfy a busy Crowd, who only because they are themselves incapable of tasting those refin'd Delights which Love affords, would deny them to another – These sort of Arguments won the Fair deluded, intirely to resolve on holding a Correspondence with the *Count*: which *Berillia* perceiving, thought she might now act as she pleased; and aiming at her Ruin, took these Means to bring it about.

IT was no difficult matter to inform herself where the *Count* lodg'd; which as soon as she had done, she writ a little Billet to him, the Contents of which were in this manner:

To Count *EMILIUS.*

My Lord,

The Passion which Donna Emanuella *regards you with, is not so much a Secret, but that I know, and pity it: I blame her not for loving a Gentleman of your Accomplishments; but I have too much Friendship for her, not to be angry that she confines herself to a Reserve which makes her so unhappy. I would very fain have you come to a more perfect Understanding of each other's Sentiments; and that you may do so, have contriv'd a way to bring you together, in spite of those dull Formalities which have hitherto kept you at a distance. Be at the Back-Gate, which opens into the little Parade, about the Hour of Twelve this Evening, and you shall be conducted to the Presence of your adored* Emanuella, *by her who would be a Friend to both,*

BERILLIA.

P. S. *I know not to what a height the Affectation of Discretion may transport* Emanuella, *if she should know I sent to you; and besides, it will be better taken, if the Contrivance appears wholly your own – Let this therefore be a Secret; be ready to attest what you shall hear me say – and you may be happy –* Adieu.

Whether *Emilius* was really possess'd of all those Qualities which go to the making up a perfect Lover, the Reader will be able to determine, when his future Behaviour shall be related; but 'tis certain he had all the Assiduity, Impatience, Ardency of Desire of the most Passionate, and could not receive this Intelligence of a Friend so unexpected, and so capable of serving him, without an infinity of Transport – He watched the Hour, and went according to Appointment; where he had not waited a moment, before *Berillia* appeared to introduce him. He made her a thousand Compliments for the Favour she did him; to all which she made but short Answers, having other Matters in her Head – The Family not being all in Bed, she told him he must be content to divert himself in Contemplation, till she could find an Opportunity to get *Emanuella* into the Garden. He bow'd and obey'd, only intreated her to he as expeditious as possible, lest any body coming to walk, as the Sweetness of the Evening might probably invite some one or other, he should be discover'd: Which she assuring him she wou'd, and placing him in an Arbour where he was the least liable to be seen, left him to feast in Imagination on the Pleasures he was shortly to enjoy in Reality.

She kept her Word, and he had waited but a very little Time before he perceiv'd her returning, and *Emanuella* with her: he restrain'd the Transports of his bounding Heart, and continued to conceal himself till he should receive his Cue from *Berillia*; and perceiving they were coming down the Walk which led to the Arbour he was in, stood close behind the shelter of some Jessamin and Fillaree,[20] with which it was covered. As they came pretty near, he heard *Berillia* say to her fair Cousin, Why, my Dear, should you persist in this Severity to yourself and him you love? Had you but heard with how much Tenderness – with how much Zeal – he pleaded for Admittance, and begg'd me to assist his Suit, the Suit of burning, raging, desperate, dying Love, you could not – nay, you ought not to have denied him. But since you have, *answer'd* Emanuella *somewhat peevishly,* why do you now upbraid me with it? Suppose I had not, would you have forgiven me? (*hastily resum'd the other.*) There is no need (*said she*) of asking what I would have done, since you have not put me to the tryal. Well then, (*cry'd* Berillia, *easily perceiving her Inclinations*) suppose I really, in pity of his Sufferings have ventur'd to admit him; suppose he is now in this very Garden full of impatient Wishes, and trembling with Desire to throw himself beneath your Feet; will you consent to pardon what I have done? *Emanuella*, whose Soul was full of disorder'd Emotions, scarcely suffered her to bring out these last Words before, And is he here? *she cry'd.* I will no longer hide it from you (*reply'd* Berillia) and whether you condemn, or thank my Conduct, cannot but take the part of a Passion which to me appears so truly meritorious – But 'tis in his Words, those Words which contrary to the Laws of Friendship, wrought me to introduce him, that I must hope to be clear'd in your Opinion – Appear! my Lord (*continued she, raising her Voice a little*) appear! and charm her to Forgiveness of us both. She had no sooner spoke this, than rushing from behind his leafy Screen, he threw himself at her Feet, embraced her Knees, warm'd her Hands with ten thousand burning Sighs, and missed no Art of soft, seducing Love, to melt her tender Soul, and make it all his own.

As prodigious a share, as all who knew her acknowledged her to have of Wit, she saw not that these were common Arts, which those, least capable of Passion, make use of whenever excited, either by Interest, or Vanity; and that both these Inducements tended powerfully to draw an Attempt of this kind on her, she might have known, had she considered how much the Reputation of having a vast Fortune would gratify the one, and her well-known, and universally admired Perfections the other. But alas! not this Reflection, nor the Remembrance that a thousand times she had heard, from others unmov'd, the selfsame things which now she listen'd to, had any power over her – She lov'd – and lov'd in proportion to the Delicacy of her other Sentiments – Her Notions were more refin'd – her Passion more elegant than those of other Women; and having been bred to believe Sincerity one of the highest Virtues, she could not suspect a want of it in the Man she had so good an Opinion of; nor deviate from the Rules of it so far herself, as to affect an Anger she was far from being possess'd of – Her Words, her Looks, her every Action betray'd the Wishes of her Heart – confess'd her Transport – and told him that he could not sue in vain. *Berillia* was infinitely satisfied in the Observations she made, and that treacherous Creature receiv'd a thousand *publick* Testimonies of Gratitude from the one, and private ones from the other, which she was far from deserving.

THE amorous Pair stay'd not a long time together, lest any Accident should betray their Converse to Don *Jabin* or his Lady, whom *Emanuella* yet was very loth should know the Secret of her Inclinations – but the persuasive *Count* would not depart, without her Permission to return the next Night in the same manner as he had done this – nor would she have been well satisfied, had he appear'd less pressing – And they took leave with less Regret than Lovers usually do, because they both assured themselves of a zealous Promoter of their common Happiness in the Friendship of *Berillia*.

MANY Nights pass'd over as this had done, and at last *Berillia* having brought things pretty near to the pitch she aim'd at, under pretence of waiting in the Garden to receive *Emilius*, would let in her own Lover (who neither being approv'd of by her Father, nor any of her Friends, she could see but by stealth) and when she found *Emanuella* and the *Count* were engag'd in a Conversation which a third Person might be spar'd, she constantly retir'd to another part of the Garden, and receiv'd the double Satisfaction of the Company of the Man she lov'd, and the Probability of undoing the Woman she hated. Not that any thing had yet pass'd between those two amiable Persons, but what was accountable to the strictest Virtue; yet the Passion she found them both possess'd of – the Opportunities she allow'd them – the continual Hints she gave the *Count*, not to let Modesty be his Enemy – and the Artifices she daily, almost hourly, made use of to melt *Emanuella*'s Soul, and turn her all into Desire; gave her liberty (who knew Nature pretty well) to imagine an unguarded Minute might arrive, which might perfectly compleat her base Design, and reduce the envy'd Fair to a Condition both blameable and pitiable.

THEY were now arriv'd to such a height of Love confess'd, that the most binding Vows of everlasting Constancy had pass'd between them[21] – *Emilius* often press'd that the Ceremony of the Church might put it past the power of even Fate it self to deprive him of the Blessing she had made him hope. But *Emanuella* would by no means consent, till the return of the Ships sent for that purpose should make her Mistress of that Wealth which was her Due. As she then was, she might have look'd on a Marriage with the *Count* as extreamly to her Interest; but as she expected to be, the Advantage was wholly on his Side: And among the other Niceties of her Passion, this was one, never to endure to be obliged to the Man she lov'd. Their mutual Vows however, and her firm Resolution to marry him as soon as this Affair was settled, gave, as it were, a Sanction to much greater Freedoms than otherwise he would have dar'd to have taken, or she would have permitted; and at last, O how dangerous is it to transgress, even the least Bounds of that Reserve which is enjoined by Virtue for our Guard! from one Liberty they ventur'd on another, till rapacious, greedy Love, too conscious of his Power, encroached on all, and nothing left for Honour.

DONNA *Berillia* had too much Experience in these Affairs, not to be perfectly sensible of what had happen'd, tho' *Emanuella*'s Modesty, and perhaps already a secret Remorse, would not suffer her to make any one a Confidant in this Part of the Story; and the mischievous Wretch having so much of her Wish compleated, began to study how she should bring about the remainder; that of exposing the Dishonour her Insinuations had in a great measure help'd to occasion, and bring on her unhappy Cousin, the *Shame* and *Misery*, as well as *Guilt*, which waits on a too fond Belief.

FORTUNE seem'd to take pleasure in assisting her Malice; and before she could find an Opportunity to execute any thing she had form'd, gave an unexpected Shock, which without her aid, would have made a Woman of *Emanuella*'s Temper, unfortunate to the last degree; and it was with an infinity of inward Torment she receiv'd the News that all those vast Possessions left her by her Father, and which had been so long detained by the Baseness of Don *Pedro,* having been dispos'd of, and turn'd into ready Cash, and Bills for the Convenience of Exportation, by a sudden Storm were lost, and not above two or three of the Sailors escap'd to bring the fatal Tydings. So dreadful a Misfortune wou'd scarce have been supportable by most young Ladies; but *Emanuella* considered it in a deeper Sense than barely to be reduc'd from one of the *greatest* Fortunes to the *meanest*; she had never set any higher Value on Wealth, than as it might be serviceable to her Friends; and now, having one who was dearer to her than her Soul – one to whom she had made the greatest Condescensions, and one whose Estate she imagined was not very large, and whose Expectations wou'd be strangely disappointed in this Loss, made her regret it with an inconceivable Affliction. She had delay'd marrying him, 'till she was actually in possession of what she knew wou'd make him perfectly easy; and to be certain it never wou'd be in her power to make him any other Present than herself, gave her Agonies which not all her Fortitude could enable her to sustain with Patience, Had she been Empress of the World, *Emilius* should have shar'd that *Grandeur* with her; but she lov'd him with a Passion too refin'd, to be content he should share with her an *abject* State of Life. Her Opinion had set him in so noble a Light, that she doubted not of his Love, Honour, or Generosity, and assur'd herself that it would be wholly her own fault if the Vows he had made her, were not authoriz'd by the Ceremony of the Church.

THE Night after this distracting News was brought, she would not be persuaded to see the *Count*; and when *Berillia* ask'd her what she should say to him, she knew not what to answer. Confus'd, and wild, torn with a thousand different Anxieties, she sometimes bid her reveal the fatal Secret. – Then, with the same Breath, recall'd that Order. – Tell him, I am undone, (*said she.*) Tell him, that cruel Fate, envious of the Blessings of his Love, has ravish'd me for ever from his Sight. – And presently after, No, no, (*resum'd she*) I will not have him know it yet. – I will have the Satisfaction of taking one dear Adieu, yet one more fond Embrace before we part for ever. – 'Tis possible my Grief may rise to that prodigious Height as to destroy me – and at once rid me of the Pain of Thought – of Memory – of curs'd Apprehension. *Berillia* all this while seem'd to endeavour to persuade her to Moderation, and entreated her not to shun his Presence; telling her, she was certain to lose her *Sight* would be an Affliction infinitely more inconsolable to him than that of her Estate: but the Arguments she made use of to convince her, she contriv'd shou'd appear too weak to be of any Efficacy, desiring nothing more than to be entrusted with a Message to him, which she resolv'd to deliver in a manner little conformable to that in which it should be given.

TWICE, or thrice, the perplex'd *Emanuella* sat herself down to write to her belov'd *Emilius*, and as oft lamented her Incapacity; the Emotions of her Soul were too violent to permit any Coherence in her Words. – And after a long debate within herself what would best become her Passion, and her Honour, desir'd *Berillia* to acquaint him with her Misfortune; and gave her leave to let him know she regretted such a Disappointment, only as she thought it rendred her more unworthy of him. *Berillia* rejoic'd beyond measure at this Opportunity of executing what she design'd; assur'd her she would do in every thing as she had commanded. – And by this means, *said the cunning* Ingrate, I shall make a Tryal of his Constancy: for if Men are by Nature so self-interested as they are reported, this Account I have to give him, will prove his noblest Sentiments. The Time for his Approach being arriv'd, broke off any farther Discourse; and she went into the Garden to receive him, leaving the half-distracted *Emanuella* almost drown'd in Tears.

THE impatient *Emilius* was waiting at the Gate, full of a thousand transporting Reflections on the *past*, and pleasing Expectations of *coming* Joys, when *Berillia* open'd it to him, and delaying to say any thing to him of what she had to reveal, 'till she had brought him into the Arbour, the happy Scene which had so lately blest him; she then began to accost him in this manner. My Lord, *said she,* I have a History to relate so little of a piece with those I have already given you of *Emanuella*'s Sensibility of your Merits, that I know not if you will forgive me for relating it. *Emilius*, whose Passion was infinitely greater than what most of his Sex, especially after Enjoyment are possest of, cou'd not hear these Words, and miss *Emanuella* from the place she us'd to be always ready to receive him in, without an inexpressible Disorder; which he could not presently overcome, enough to be able to ask what it was she meant. The artful Traytress, observing his Surprize, encreas'd it, by speaking in this manner. – I see, my Lord, (*resum'd she*) you cannot hear any thing which offers at a discovery of *Emanuella*'s Falshood, without the utmost Concern: Nor do I wonder at it, having been Witness of so many tender Protestations of an ardent Passion on both sides. You may think it strange, perhaps, that I, her Cousin, and her Friend, should tell you this – but what is there in my power to do, which may conceal an Inconstancy, which, tho' I should invent ten thousand Stratagems, in spite of me will show itself? I might indeed have made some Excuse for her not seeing you this Night, which might have seem'd plausible enough; but what cou'd I have said, which cou'd have beguil'd your Impatience in the succeeding ones? – Since then 'tis what you must know, sooner or later, I thought it the more generous part to acquaint you with it early, and arm you for the Misfortune you will doubtless hear of in a little time from other Tongues than mine. The enamour'd *Count* felt his Heart sink in him all the time she had been speaking, and could hardly assume Spirit enough, when she had done, to entreat her to let him know, in few Words, the Accident that had befallen him. I will, my Lord! *said she,* – but first let me deliver the Message I received from *Emanuella*: She bid me tell you, that having this day an Account of that Ship, in which her whole Fortune was trusted, being lost, she cannot think of marrying any Man, but one whose Estate can make up for the Deficiency of hers, and that yours cannot, she has been inform'd: Therefore there being a Necessity of breaking with you, thinks it improper to see you any more – How (*interrupted the* Count) no more but so?[22] *a Necessity of breaking with me – See me no more!*

Good Heaven! is it possible she can so suddenly recede from that height of Passion she last Night profess'd, and all at once degenerate into Coldness and damn'd Indifference! – But you mistake her sure, and what is Over-Tenderness misconstrue Hate – You'll soon be able to judge whether I do not, (*resum'd* Berillia, *affecting an Air of Indignation*) – But I shall give myself no further trouble, but leave you to the Proof. – With these Words she turn'd away, and seem'd as tho' she would have gone out of the Arbour; which *Emilius* perceiving, and repenting of what he had said, catch'd hold of her by her Gown, Stay, Madam, stay, (*cry'd he*:) Pardon the Distraction of a Lover, and ease the Pains you've rais'd by adding more – Confirm the fatal Truth; tell me again my *Emanuella*'s lost – that she is unkind – indifferent – false – and kill me with the Sound. Forbid it Heaven (*resum'd she, softning her Voice and sitting down again*) that Love should have such Power over a Heart like yours – Rouze! rouze, my Lord! your Soul, exert the nobler Faculties, think of her Deceit, Hypocrisy, Perjury, and forget her Charms. Had she refused to marry you, thus fallen as she is from all her Hopes, it had been a generous Proof of Self-denial; but know 'tis all but feign'd, she imagines seeming to *shun,* the more engages your *Pursuit,* and expects to be press'd to what she wishes – and she will yield, depend upon it, if you insist on the Performance of the Contract. Still, still, (*resum'd the impatient Count*) you speak in Riddles – But if ever Pity or Good-Nature sway'd your Soul, let me conjure you, Madam, to explain. I will (*said she*) but you shall swear first by every thing that's Holy, never to utter to *Emanuella* or any other Person what I am about to speak. I do (*cry'd he*) and may just Heaven renounce me when I break it. Know then (*pursued she*) that you have been deceiv'd, betray'd into a fictitious hope of marrying one who has been long since, if Vows have any power, another's Wife: My self was present at the Ceremony; but the unhappy Man was driven from her Arms, e'er Consummation of their Loves. *Emanuella* has a Heart too sensible of the tender Passion, to be long without an Object to inspire it: in the short Interval you happen'd to address her, you know to what a Length her Acceptation of those Addresses has carried her – She vail'd indeed her looser Flame under a Promise of Marriage, which I have already told you was not in her power to make good: However it served for a Pretence, believing (according to the Mutability which is imputed to your Sex) you would be well enough satisfied to decline your Claim before the Return of the Ship – Her Expectations there being crost by your Constancy, and an Account she has lately receiv'd of the sudden Death of her Husband, and the Loss of her Fortune obliges her to act the artful Part, and seem to be averse to what is most her Interest to wish – But now my Lord! (*continued she with a well-counterfeited Concern*) I am arrived to the blackest Point of all her Character, and what indeed induced me to lay open all the rest – She has lately commenc'd a shameful Conversation with a Person whose Name I know not; but whom if you had ever seen, you would with me acknowledge the Depravity of her Taste – But not to grow tedious in a Relation which can afford you but little Satisfaction, she now, tho' not till now, designs to be your Wife, and only waits your protesting not to live without her, to engage her yielding to save you from Despair. Hell first shall seize her (*cry'd the* Count, *transported with the utmost Fury*) let her chuse a Fiend from thence, the fittest *Paramour*, and make the Wretch she has chose her Property. *Berillia* was in so much Rapture at the Success of her Project, that it was very hard for her to counterfeit any longer the Concern she had put on for the Baseness of so near a Relation; and therefore having afresh engag'd his Vows of Secrecy, told him a longer Stay might occasion Suspicion in *Emanuella*; and receiving a thousand Thanks from him for her friendly Caution, took her leave and went to *Emanuella* with the Story she had prepared for her.

She found that unhappy Lady in the Posture she had left her, extended on the Floor, in the most cruel Storm of agonizing Grief, and desperate Love; but it was not in the power of all her Sufferings to turn the Heart of this more than *Barbarian*; and when she saw her rise to meet her, and heard her, with an Accent which might have melted a Heart of Adamant, enquire how 'twas her dear *Emilius* look'd, what 'twas he said, and a thousand such Questions which her Tenderness suggested; she sat for some Moments without making any Reply, and when she did, it was in this manner: I am infinitely troubled, my dear Cousin (*said* Berillia) that you employ'd me in this Errand; I know not what to do, whether to relate the Truth, or amuse you with a Falshood be the most commendable: but summon all your Fortitude, arm your self with Courage to disdain the Baseness, the groveling Disposition of sordid, ungrateful Man. Oh Heaven (*cry'd* Emanuella, *ready to faint with Apprehension*) what means *Berillia,* what has *Emilius* done? All that can compleat a Villain, (*answered she*) a most consummate Villain!

TWICE did the poor *Emanuella* swoon away, before *Berillia* explain'd her cruel Meaning; but being eager to add to her Affliction, as soon as ever she was in a Condition to listen to what she said; Cease, dearest Cousin (*cry'd she*) to mourn; rather let generous Indignation fire your Breast, and arm you to disdain not only the perfidious *Count*, but the whole Race of Man – The cold, insensible, regardless Traytor, heard me with Tears recount your Grief, and speak what you endur'd in the Necessity of parting with him, with so unmov'd an Air, as tho' he were not Man, or were unskill'd in his Sex's Arts of Dissimulation. At last he said he pitied your Misfortune, 'twas very unhappy indeed for a young Lady to be without the means of keeping up the Grandeur she was born to – but that you must study Patience – that doubtless a great many Ladies would be very willing to accept of you as a Companion – and he hoped you would not want – bid me give his Service – and tell you that he wish'd it were in his power to remedy your Misfortunes. – I had not Patience, but revenged the Contempt with all the Revilings that a Woman's Tongue, made keen by the most inveterate Malice, could utter; but he appeared as unconcern'd at this, as at any thing else I had said: and making towards the Door, would fain have left me to rail by myself: but I detain'd him for some time, on purpose to vent the Fury I was possess'd of: but at length he broke from me, and left me almost breathless with the Struggle. Here she stopp'd, expecting what *Emanuella* would reply; but what that Lady felt at so unexpected, so shocking a Relation, was too big for Words! silent, the stormy Passions rolled in her tortur'd Bosom, disdaining the mean Ease of raging or complaining – It was a considerable time before she utter'd the least Syllable; and when she did, she seem'd to start as from some dreadful Dream, and cry'd, It is enough – in knowing one, I know the whole deceiving Sex – Nor will I be a second time betray'd – I'll hide me for ever from their Arts, their soothing Flatteries, their subtle Insinuations – no more I'll hear, or see, or think of Man – The best is base – *Emilius*, *Emilius* whom I lov'd is base – Few Women but in such a Circumstance would have writ, and upbraided the cruel Destroyer of their Peace; but *Emanuella*'s Soul disdain'd those Testimonies of continued Weakness, which however bitter they may appear in the *Expression*, the *Meaning* still is *Love*; for the Indifferent give not themselves the Pains. It was of this Sort she now wish'd to be thought by *Emilius*, and this Disposition help'd *Berillia* to keep any Discovery how much she had injur'd him from her Ears.

BEING determined never to be seen in Publick more, she thought a monastick Life the safest and most convenient Retirement from the World; and communicating her Intentions to Don *Jabin*, and his Wife, (letting them know no other, than that it was the loss of her Fortune which had made her of this Mind) they seem'd to think it the most prudent Method she could use; and the very next Day, without any other Consideration than the flying from a World in which she believ'd it an Impossibility ever to be happy, went into a Nunnery of *Pourclairs*,[23] making choice of that Order as being the severest; resolving to punish her easy Belief, and the Condescension she had made to *Emilius,* in as rigid a manner as was possible. He, who after he had left *Berillia,* and began deliberately to weigh what had been told him, found it very difficult to believe it; and tho' he could not imagine for what Reason that young Lady, who had so much befriended him in the beginning of his Amour, should invent Stories so much to the prejudice of a Relation who lov'd her, only to break off a Correspondence with him; yet he was sometimes about to write to *Emanuella* in such a manner, as without Breach of the Vow he had made to *Berillia,* would have given him some light into the Truth: But the Consideration, that if she was not guilty in the manner she was accused, yet that the Ship in which her Effects were, was lost, was past all doubt; and that to a young Nobleman, full of Ambition, and the Love of Grandeur, was sufficient to abate the Vigour of his other Passion: Beside, he had already enjoy'd her; and where is the Man who dies for a repeated Possession? – He therefore forbore to examine any farther into the Truth of the Affair; and tho' he had some melancholy Reflection for a while, yet the natural Gaiety of his Humour diverted them from doing him any great Prejudice.

THE malicious *Berillia* triumph'd in having remov'd a Person whose superior Graces rendred hers unobservable, and revell'd in the continued Possession of the Man she lov'd without danger of Reproof. *Emanuella* was the only unhappy Person; and it was neither in the power of Time, Absence, Philosophy, or Religion, to obliterate the Memory of *Emilius,* or assuage her Sorrows.

The End of the First Part.

THE

RASH RESOLVE:

OR,

The Untimely Discovery.

Part II.

THE Passion which the *Count* had profess'd for *Emanuella*, was too sincere to be easily thrown off; and tho' in his Circumstances, it was wholly improper he should marry without a Fortune; yet he could not resolve to quit her without the utmost Reluctance – The first Storm of Indignation which the malicious *Berillia* had raised in his Soul, was no sooner over, than a great part of his former Tenderness return'd. He consider'd that what he had heard was so inconsistent with her Character, and with her Behaviour; that had it come from the Mouth of any other Person, it would not have found the least room in his Belief. Nor could he even from her set it down for Truth, in spite of the Improbability there appeared, that she should have any Design in deceiving him into an ill Opinion of a Woman, whom he knew she had Reason to esteem – This Division in his Thoughts, made him for some days sufficiently disquieted. Nor was he a little amaz'd, and alarm'd, when he was told that she was retir'd into a *Monastery* – This Proceeding, he thought vastly incongruous with the Account *Berillia* had given him of her Humour; and he was at the greatest loss in the World what Judgment to form – Fain would he have writ – fain would he have made her a Visit at the Grate of the *Pourclairs*; but the Promise her Cousin had exacted from him, deferr'd him on the one side; and on the other, the Reflection that, in case she should be found Innocent, he should be obliged to renew those Pretensions, which, as she now was, were no way conformable to his Ambition – However, he could not restrain his Inclinations, which were yet very tender to her, and, perhaps, might in time have weighed down *Interest*, if a Chance had not happened in his Affairs, which turn'd the Ballance, and prov'd how little Dependance there is on Man, when *Love* and *Gratitude* are the only Motives to engage his Constancy.

He was one Morning in his Bed full of uneasy and perplex'd Meditations, when his Servant brought him a Letter, in which he found these Lines:

To Count *EMILIUS.*

THAT you have wronged me in the most tender Part, I make no more doubt of, than that you are a Man of Honour enough to endeavour a Defence of what you have done. I desire therefore that you will meet me an Hour hence in the Field of St. Cruzada, *either to repair the Injuries you have done me by your Life, or by depriving me of mine, put an end to the just Resentment of*

OCTAVIO.

THE Surprize with which *Emilius* read this Challenge, was proportionable to the Occasion. He could not imagine for which of his Actions he should be call'd to account by a Gentleman whom he had scarce any knowledge of; whom he had not seen above two or three times, and whom he never had any particular Conversation with: But bethinking himself what a Man of Honour ought to do in such a Case, he ask'd if the Person who brought the Letter waited for an Answer; and being told that he did, he call'd for Pen and Ink, and immediately return'd one in this manner:

To Don *OCTAVIO.*

I Should be very sorry to be guilty of an Injury to any one, and am certain it is as distant from my Power as Inclination, to have done any thing to you which cou'd justly occasion a Summons of the nature I have received: But since I am accus'd of it, am ready to give you such Satisfaction as becomes a Gentleman, and to that end will attend you at the Time and Place appointed; being no less desirous to know the Reason *which has made you my Enemy, than you are to declare yourself one to*

EMILIUS.

HE had no sooner dispatch'd this, than he rose, and making what haste he could to dress, was in the Field little later than his Antagonist; whom, as he came near, he found had his Sword ready drawn, which oblig'd him to put himself also in a Posture of Defence: But being unwilling to fight, without knowing for what Cause – You see, Don *Octavio! said he,* I have obey'd your Summons; but as I am yet unacquainted with the Motive which induc'd you to send it, I desire you will be just enough to inform me, before we engage. You feign an Ignorance (*interrupted the other fiercely*) 'tis impossible you should not know, that Rivalship in Love is what the *Spanish* Honour cannot brook. – Were the adorable *Julia* less worthy of my Passion, the long Addresses I have made to her would scorn to yield to any new Pretender – therefore, defend the Wrong you have had the Boldness to attempt, or tamely fall the unworthy Victim of impatient Jealousy.

THESE Words, and the Name of *Julia* so much surpriz'd the *Count*, that he could neither answer them immediately, nor recollect himself enough to parry the Thrust with which they were accompany'd, and he receiv'd a slight Wound in the Arm, and was very near suffering a second, in a place, perhaps, more dangerous, before he had regain'd Presence enough of Mind to avoid it. But as his Surprize vanish'd, Indignation kindled in his Soul, and he soon let the other know it was not Fear which had rendred him thus long unactive; the Smart of the Wound rais'd him to an equal Fury, and he forbore endeavouring to convince the rash *Octavio* of his Mistake, 'till he had punished his Unadvisedness. Being an excellent Master of his Sword, he not only return'd doubly the Wound he had receiv'd, but by disarming him, rendered him incapable of giving more; but his Rage diminishing with his Adversary's Power, he generously return'd his Weapon, desiring still they might be Friends, and that he would explain what 'twas he meant by Rivalship, and *Julia*; assuring him, that he had no design on any Lady of that Name. *Octavio*, tho' he had too much Honour to renew the Combat with a Person in whose power it so lately had been to have taken his Life, gave him a Look which sufficiently demonstrated the continued Rancour of his Heart, and only telling him, that he knew *Julia* too well to believe she cou'd love a Man without being first belov'd by him, flung sullenly away, leaving *Emilius* in a much greater Consternation, than his Behaviour had put him in before. He cou'd by no means comprehend the meaning of this Adventure, nor from what Source the Jealousy of *Octavio* had sprung. He had heard much Talk of a Lady call'd *Julia*; but he had never seen her, nor was he certain, it was for her sake all this had happened: but from that Moment he conceived a secret Wish, that he were indeed happy enough to be in that Lady's favour, whom he had heard spoke of as one of the greatest Fortunes in *Madrid*, and a celebrated Beauty. The bare Conjecture that there was a possibility, that she might have seen and liked him, went a great way towards the expelling his Passion for a Woman he had already enjoy'd, and who now no longer had it in her power to conduce to the Gratification of his Ambition – He spent that whole Day in Enquiries what sort of a Woman this *Julia* was, how large her Fortune, and who they were that had made Pretensions to her; and from all hands receiv'd such Accounts, as fill'd him with ardent Longings, that *Octavio*'s Jealousy might have something more in it than an imaginary Cause. He was told by some, who seem'd to know a good deal of her Affairs, that, that Gentleman had for a long time profess'd himself her Lover, but had of late been deny'd the privilege of visiting her, tho' for what reason, was yet a Secret; and these Tidings half confirm'd the pleased *Emilius*, that he was more blest than he cou'd have imagin'd.

But, as to inform himself as much as possible of the Truth of this Affair, took up the Day, the Night was employ'd in Contrivances how to make the best Advantage of what had been told. He had found out where she liv'd, and also that being an Orphan, the Riches she was possest of were entirely at her own Dispose; and nothing he thought now remained for him to do, but to form some pretty Stratagem, whereby he might become acquainted with her, without appearing guilty of a Boldness which might forfeit all the Kindness she had for him. Few Men had been more fortunate in Inventions of this nature than himself; and 'tis scarce to be doubted, but that he would soon have found one plausible enough for his purpose, if he had not been spar'd the pains, by receiving in the Morning a Billet of a far different kind than that which had been brought him the Day before. The Contents of it were these.

To Count *EMILIUS.*

SINCE we are taught, that of two Evils 'tis best to chuse the least; to avoid being guilty of Ingratitude, I am oblig'd to break through the Decorum of my Sex, by writing to a Gentleman, to whom, I believe, I am altogether a Stranger.

For the Wound you have received on my account, I can do no less in Honour than apply a Balsam; to which end, I send you the most experienc'd Artist in this Kingdom: And if the Punishment of the Offender may be any Reparation for the Offence, give you my solemn Promise the rash Octavio *shall dearly repent his Insolence, if I have any of that Power over him he pretends.*

And tho' such an Invitation may be thought too great a Freedom, I shall be glad to make you sensible by Word of Mouth, as soon as you are in a Condition to come abroad, how much I regret the Injury has been done you. If a Person, so little qualified to merit your Conversation, has hitherto escap'd your Notice, the Messenger, who brings this, can inform you where you may know more of the Sentiments of

JULIA.

AFTER having mention'd the Inquietudes he was in, to find a proper Method to introduce himself to this Lady, 'twould be needless to express the Pleasure this Letter gave him. He commanded that the Person who brought it shou'd be shew'd up into his Chamber, and finding he appear'd like a Gentleman, used him in the most handsome manner imaginable. The other soon inform'd him, that he was a Surgeon, and that he was order'd by Donna *Julia de Venelli* to attend him with all possible diligence 'till his Wound was cur'd. And tho' the *Count* assur'd him it was but a Scratch, and unworthy his Regard, yet he wou'd needs apply a Plaister to it; and pulling out of his Pocket a Scarf made of Silver Gauze, and curiously embroider'd with Crimson and Green, and a Locket to fasten it together, which had a Cypher in it with the Letters of her Name set round with Diamonds of a very great Value, told him, she had sent him that to bind his Arm. – A Man of less Gallantry, and less Inclination to be well in the Esteem of such a Lady as Donna *Julia*, would scarce have refus'd so obliging a Present; and it is easy to imagine, that he suffer'd it to be put on with a Pleasure suitable to the Favour of the Sender. He intreated him to stay, and order'd a genteel Morning-Repast to be got ready, while he withdrew to his Closet to answer the welcome *Billet*, which he did in these Words.

To the most Excellent Donna
Julia de Venelli.

A HURT so trifling as that which I received from the Hand of Don Octavio *requir'd not a Balsam of that Divine Nature your Goodness has bestow'd. – You rather, Madam! should have reserv'd your Pity for those Wounds the Fame of your Accomplishments has already made but too deep, and which (I had almost said I fear) your Eyes will render incurable, but by Death, or a Condescension, such as 'twou'd be the utmost Vanity to hope – But whatever Destiny you inflict, cannot but be glorious; and certainly, the next Blessing to the Heaven of living in your Favour, would be dying in the Pursuit of it.*

I wear, most angelick of your Sex! the justest Sense of your unmerited Favours at my Heart, and your admirable Scarf on my Arm; which tho' it infuses not Pains of the same nature as those of Hercules*'s Shirt,*[24] *will differ but little in their Consequence, if ever you should discontinue to allow me the Effects of that Infinity of Mercy you seem at present possest of, and refuse me the Privilege of avowing that I am*

The Divine JULIA*'s*
Everlasting Slave,
EMILIUS.

P. S.

If the Sword of Octavio *had emptied my Veins of the best part of their Blood, that Tide of Extasy you have inspired me with, would fill them up again, and give a nobler Life, and added Vigour, to bear me to your Feet with humblest Gratitude and sublimest Joys. – Delay then my impatient Wishes no longer, this day permit me to offer up my Soul, an Oblation worthy of your Acceptation, no otherwise than by its Sincerity.*

THE Surgeon, who easily guess'd at the Lady's meaning who had sent him, went away perfectly pleased that he should be able to give her an Account of *Emilius*'s Behaviour, which he knew would be so much to her Satisfaction. And the *Count* extreamly lifted up at this unexpected Turn of good Fortune, forgot every thing in the Contemplation of the Advantages he should enjoy in marrying a Woman of Donna *Julia*'s Quality and Estate; which that it was in his power to do, he might very well suppose, when she had made him such Advances. It is not to be doubted but that he took all possible Care in the dressing himself that day, to secure the Conquest he had gain'd; and having no Orders to make a Secret of his Visit to her, he went in his Chariot attended by two running Footmen, and four others all in rich Liveries – But alas! there needed not all this Pomp to engage the already enamour'd *Julia*: She had for a long time been the Slave of Love; she ador'd the charming *Count* from the first Moment she beheld him, which happen'd to be at Church soon after his Arrival; and after many fruitless

Endeavours to become acquainted with him, and hearing of his Engagements with *Emanuella*, she fell into a Melancholy, which had like to have cost her her Life – Don *Octavio* had made his Addresses to her for many Months, and at first flatter'd himself with hopes of Success; but perceiving a sudden Alteration in her Humour, immediately imagined it to proceed from the Love of some other Person: and not able to discover any thing of the Truth, he at last found means by bribing a Priest (for what will not Gold influence the Minds of some People to!) to get into the Confessional Chair at the time when she was to come to confess; and by telling her that her Melancholy, if not caused by some spiritual Remorse for any Faults she, might have been guilty of, was sinful; and if she did not disburthen herself to her ghostly Father, and endeavour by Works of Penance to merit Absolution, her Case was more desperate than she was aware of; frighted her so, being naturally pretty much bigotted to[25] the Religion she had been educated in, that she presently confess'd she was in Love. With whom (*cry'd out the pretended Father*) for if it be a Person worthy of you, I will undertake to make you happy with him. To which again she as innocently as before answer'd, *Emilius*, a Roman *Count* lately arriv'd at *Madrid* – She had said more, but the Lover could no longer counterfeit the *Priest*; he threw off his Disguise, and showing himself to be *Octavio,* upbraided her Ingratitude and Falshood, as he term'd it, and vow'd Revenge on his happy Rival. It was in vain she endeavour'd to deter him, by threatning him with those Penalties the Law inflicts on all who dare to prophane the Sacrament of Confession in the manner he had done. His Rage was deaf to all Considerations, either of himself, or the *Priest* who had assisted him in this Stratagem; and he left her in the Church, to ruminate on what had happen'd, while he went and prepared a Challenge for *Emilius*, as has been before related – It is not to be supposed but she had Spies to observe his Motions; but they were either too careless of the Injunction laid on them, or too late to prevent him from fighting with the *Count*: But they brought her Intelligence of all that had happen'd; and since there was no Mischief on either Side, she was not a little contented that she had so good a Pretence to write to *Emilius*. Nor after she had received his Answer, can we imagine she was less diligent in making herself appear as amiable as possible, than he had been. Not only her own Person, but her House and Servants were all set forth to the best Advantage, and every thing seem'd so rich, so fine, so neat, that by the care that was used in making it so, the expected Guest might easily perceive how welcome a one he was.

THE mutual Desire each had to please the other, very much heighten'd the Graces of them both – *Julia* had a Face and Shape to which *Nature* had been so extreamly indulgent, that she stood but little in need of any Aids from Art: but having had Recourse to all that even the most curious had invented, joined to the Pleasure which sparkled in her Eyes, at sight of an Object she had so long and so ardently languish'd to behold; her Beauty appear'd with such an Illustration, as requir'd a Heart better fortified with Constancy than was that of *Emilius* to withstand its Charms. And tho' as handsome as she was, she was by many degrees far less attractive than the abandon'd *Emanuella*; yet he imagined her infinitely more so – O the Enchantments of *Novelty*, the Delights there are in having something to subdue – the pleasing Fears – the sweet Hopes, the tender Anxieties – the thousand nameless, soft Perplexities which fill the roving Soul of Man when in pursuit of a *new* Conquest; but *after Possession* are no more remembred – Then *cold Civility* succeeds *tumultuous Transport* – When *present*, forc'd *Compliments* supply the place of *Ardor*; when *absent*, curs'd *Indifference* that of *impatient Longings* – and dull insipid *Gratitude* is all the *yielding Fair* can hope for, even from the best of Men. *Emilius* now thought he had never seen any thing so lovely as *Julia*, and immediately became possess'd with as much real Passion for her, as a Heart could be, so liable to Mutability as his was. Love and Wit inspir'd him with a thousand engaging Softnesses, which she, eager to credit what she wish'd, believ'd; and tho' she had heard a vast deal of his Pretensions to *Emanuella*, she now imagined him so entirely her own, that it never would be in the power of any other Face to make the least Alteration in his Sentiments to her disadvantage – She lov'd with too sincere and passionate a Flame to be able to disguise it; and what she confess'd not in Words, her Eyes sufficiently inform'd him, and he reaped all the Satisfaction he could hope from this first Visit – He had her Leave to declare himself her Servant – She promised to discharge all others that pretended to that Title – and let him know enough of her Inclinations to sooth Imagination with a belief she would in a short time be brought to yield to all he wish'd – Resolving by his Assiduity to render himself worthy of the Favours he had receiv'd, he waited on her every day, and they were scarce ever asunder but in those Hours which Decency required.

THERE was nothing of this Affair a Secret; the Jealousy of *Octavio,* the publick Visits of *Emilius*, and the undissembled Condescensions of the Lady, engross'd the whole Discourse of the Town. But what became of *Emanuella* when she heard this News, to whom the ill-natur'd *Berillia* immediately convey'd it in the worst and most distracting Description her Malice could invent! She doubted not of his Coldness and Ingratitude before, by the implicit Faith she put in that Wretch who had so cruelly betray'd her; but now to be told, to be assur'd, with a Million of aggravating Circumstances, that he profer'd to another all those Soul-attracting Protestations by which she had been deceiv'd – to know another was in possession of all those Tendernesses – those soft Endearments – those transporting Fondnesses that once she thought were her's for ever, gave her Agonies too terrible to be conceiv'd but by those who have felt the same: Yet, in spite of all she endur'd, she still maintain'd her Resolution, of never seeing or writing to him more, firm and unshaken; and the more she heard of his Perfidiousness, the more she thought it beneath her to take notice of it.

But while she was indulging her Despair for the many Misfortunes which had already befallen her, Don *Jabin*, and his Lady, who were extreamly sincere in their Professions of Friendship to her, were labouring all they could for her Service. They had a very great Interest with the Chief of the Nobility, and were so industrious in exerting it, that the Case of this distress'd Lady being represented to his Majesty's Consideration in terms the most prevailing, engag'd him to command that Don *Pedro*, who was yet at *Madrid*, should out of his own Estate make up some Part of the Losses she had sustained; which tho' happening by the uncertainty of the Sea, were primarily occasioned by him, in refusing to bring over her Effects in a more favourable Season. The avaricious old Monster had no way to avoid this Decree; and the Grief of being obliged to obey it, together with the Stings he felt in his Conscience for the many Crimes he had been guilty of, threw him a second time into a fit of raging Madness, of which in a few Weeks he died unpitied by the whole World. The Provision which by the King's Order he had made for *Emanuella*, gave her kind Relations hope, that they should have her among them again, and they omitted no Persuasions that she would quit that austere Life, and return to the World again; but she had Griefs which were not in the Compass of their power to remedy, she could not endure to think of living where there was the least Probability of seeing the false *Emilius*; and all that was said to move her to the contrary, was no more than throwing Water against the Wind. Don *Jabin* and his Wife were both of them extreamly troubled, that all they had done for her was ineffectual to restore her to her former Chearfulness; but perceiving that their Endeavours to dissuade her from a monastick Life, serv'd only to increase her Obstinacy of persisting in it; they at length gave her over, not without a Belief that the Severities of that Order she had an Intention to embrace, would oblige her to change her Mind long before her Year of Probation was expired; and that she would in a little time be as impatient to quit the Convent, as now she appeared at being persuaded to it.

These good People were not deceived in their Conjectures; they soon saw the Effect: they guess'd, though longer ignorant of the Cause. – In a much less space of time than they imagined, *Emanuella* indeed wish'd herself in any Place, rather than that in which she was; but the Motive which induc'd her to that Desire, nay, inforc'd her to a Necessity of it, was of a nature so shocking, so terrible to be born, that it requires a Pen infinitely more skill'd in Description than mine, to represent a Condition of so consummate a Misery.

It was not many Weeks since she had been among the *Pourclairs*, and in that time had not so much as once thought of the Consequence, which in all probability might attend the guilty Condescensions her Excess of Passion had yielded to *Emilius*: But now the Hour was come which was to make her know, that all she had endur'd from the Cruelty of Don *Pedro* – from the Loss of her Fortune – from the Ingratitude and Falshood of the Man she lov'd, were trifling Woes in competition with those in store for her – She found she was now destined to go through all that can be conceived of Shame – of Misery – of Horror – in fine, she found herself with Child! – with Child without a Husband! – with Child by a Man who she had heard from all hands was going to be married to another! – and what was yet worse, by a Man whom she accounted the vilest, and most perfidious of his Sex! – What Words – nay, what Imagination can paint out her Distress as it deserves! – She was infinitely more wretched than any other Woman would have been in the like Circumstances, by the Addition of a superior Understanding – and the Greatness of her Spirit, and that Fortitude which had so well enabled her to bear all other Misfortunes, serv'd here but to increase the Misery of her Condition, and prevent her from stooping to those Measures by which she alone could hope to secure her Reputation, and screen what had happen'd from the Knowledge of a censorious and unpitying World. Had she now written to the *Count*, there was a Possibility, that in spite of his new Passion for Donna *Julia*, all might have been well; his former Tenderness on the Eclaircissment[26] of her Innocence, and the Treachery of *Berillia*, might, perhaps, have return'd: Or if not so, which indeed after Enjoyment could not be much expected; yet Honour and Gratitude would at least have obliged him to protect and support her in those Miseries, to which her Love for him had reduc'd her: But this was an Expedient she could not bear even to think on; and as often as it came into her mind, she would reject it with all the Contempt imaginable – What (*said she*) shall I descend to ask a Favour from the Man to whom I owe my Ruin? – Shall I, forgetful of my Wrongs, submit to be obliged to that cursed Villain? – that insolent Disdainer of my Truth and Tenderness? No, rather let me suffer all the Plagues that Heaven can inflict, or Flesh endure – Let me be driven to Want, to Beggary – exposed to publick Infamy, the Sport of every Slave – or tarrying here, be buried quick – it will be a less Shock–less Horror than an Obligation to that intolerable Fiend! – the hated, loath'd *Emilius!* Thus did the Haughtiness of her Soul, and fatal Consciousness how little she had deserved the Treatment she had found, suggest. Nor was her *Resentment* less pernicious to her than her *Modesty*; for as the one prevented her from making any Discovery to the *Count*, so did the other also deprive her of the Power of uttering the least Hint of this Affair to Don *Jabin* or his Lady. *Berillia* was the only Person to whom she could persuade her self to reveal it: but Heaven had by this time began to inflict on that false Creature some part of the Punishments her base Actions merited; her criminal Amour had by some means come to her Father's knowledge, and he had sent her under the care of an old Servant into the Country, far from *Madrid*, and the Conversation of her Lover; tho' had she been in the way of being intrusted, 'tis little probable she would have been of any service: But *Emanuella*, who suspected not her Perfidy, received a considerable Addition to her Sorrows, by being told she was gone. Pity is a prodigious Alleviater of Affliction, the most violent Grief finds some Ease in complaining; but when our Woes are of a nature, as will not admit revealing, they prey on our very Vitals, and waste the Spirits with unintermitting Anguish, and seldom fail of bringing on Death or Distraction. Nothing was ever more deserving wonder, than that this wretched Lady did not lay violent hands on her own Life: but tho' the wish'd to die, she forbore being guilty of that Act of Horror: Whenever the Confusion of her Thoughts permitted her the power of Consideration, she would begin to cast about what Course to take; but then the Impossibility there seem'd of her being able to find any, whereby she might conceal her Shame, plunged her afresh into Disorders, which at some times were very little different from Madness. The Cruelties she inflicted on herself in private, such as tearing her Hair, and Flesh, fasting, passing whole Nights together on the Floor; and instead of Rest, giving her self wholly up to the bitter Anguish, would be too tedious, and too melancholy an Account: how terribly she was abandon'd to Despair; and how little she regarded what might befall her, is evident, when the Effects of her now dearly repented Passion, began to grow too great for Concealment. Taking the Opportunity of the *Nunnery* being on some Occasion open, she went out in the Habit she was in, without having taken any thought where to go, or to whom she should apply; it was pretty late in the Evening, and the dusk favour'd her from being taken any notice of; till coming into a great Street where were many Passengers, the sight of them at a distance gave her so much of Thought, as to be apprehensive of being seen, and known; the Cathedral Church therefore of *our Lady* being near, she stepped into the *Porch*, and sitting down in a corner of it, by that means conceal'd herself from the Observation of any body: But what avail'd it, that when the Darkness coming on, the Streets were intirely free; she could direct her Steps to no Place, but where either Shame, or the height of her Spirit would not suffer her to go: yet still keeping up her Resolution, that whatever became of her, and whatever should be the Consequence of her wandering, she never would consent to receive the smallest Shelter or Protection from the ungrateful *Emilius*; she left her Covert, and began her Journey, tho' she was insensible, and wholly incapable of designing any thing: Chance therefore it was which guided her to that part of the Town which led into the great Road to a Village call'd *Aine*: The Knowledge where she now was, for being unaccustomed to walk, made her but little acquainted with the Streets, gave her a kind of a sullen Satisfaction; she car'd not whither she went, so she was out of *Madrid*, and the force of that Desire, strengthen'd her to get a good way from it, before she found herself incapable of going farther: But at last, Weariness and Faintness got the better of Inclination; she could no longer pursue her Pilgrimage, and was constrained to lie down to take such Rest as she could in the Highway – To add to her present Hardship, which considering the Condition she was in, was such as no Woman, but herself, perhaps, ever sustained with Life; it began to rain so excessively, that in a very few Minutes she was wet to the Skin; the Shower was succeeded by a Storm of Wind, and such dreadful Claps of Thunder, as might have struck the most courageous Heart with Dread – But not all the Horrors of this Hurricane, made more terrible by the darkness of the Night, and the forlorn Silence of the Place – Not all she endur'd from its Fury, had the power to make her recede from that Resolution she had form'd, or wish for Shelter from *Emilius.* But in the midst of this dismal Scene, Fortune seem'd to offer her a Gleam of Comfort, as she was lying, her tender Limbs exposed to all the Rage of the unpitying Elements, and pouring forth Tears almost as fast as the Sky did Rain; she perceiv'd, when she least expected it, a Light which seem'd to be in a House not far off. She had so much of Self-Preservation left, as to endeavour to make up to it, which with much ado, numb'd and faint as she was, she did at last; she found it as she wish'd, a little Cottage, for had it been any other, she would rather have continued as she was, than gone to ask Relief where there was a Probability of being known. The poor good Woman of it, who was sitting up tending a sick Child, receiv'd her with as much Hospitality as the Place and her Circumstances would afford: She pluck'd off her wet Clothes, and gave her a Gown of her own to put on, made a Fire and brought her the best Refreshments she had. – But alas! the discontented *Emanuella* was little capable of tasting any; which her kind Hostess perceiving, and guessing by her Garb and Mein that she was a Person little accustomed to such Hardships, intreated to know what had occasioned her travelling alone on foot, and at such a dreadful Hour and Season. This Enquiry threw her unhappy Guest into such Returns of over-pressing Grief, that it was a long time before she could make any Answer; but when she had enough recovered herself to do it, she told her the truth of her having made her Escape from the *Monastery*, only concealing the Reasons why she did so, and her Name: But the Woman having had many Children herself, suspected the former, and pitied her extreamly; she would fain have persuaded her to go to Bed, but the other would not consent; and only throwing herself cross it, she pass'd the remainder of the Night in most bitter Lamentations. When Morning came, she begg'd that she might have those Clothes which had been lent her, believing it might serve as a sufficient Disguise, if by any Accident she should be seen by any that knew her; and told the Woman, she should not only have hers in Exchange, but some Money to boot. – To which the other willingly consented, not only because of her own Profit, but also that believing she was about to prosecute a Journey in which she might be pursued, they might be of service to her. Our unfortunate Traveller felt as much Pleasure at this Opportunity of transmographying herself, as was consistent with her Condition; and designing to go yet farther from *Madrid*, took her Leave. The extream Dirt of the Road made it impossible for her Feet, unused to tread such Ground, to bear her as fast as her Desires would have carried her; but in spite of all she still went on, and without making any stop either to eat or drink, till that Day was almost spent. Evening coming on, she went into an *Inn*, believing now she was far enough from Discovery – Nature beginning to accuse her that she had acted an inhuman Part to the unborn Innocent within her, who bore its share in all the Hardships she endured; she order'd something to be got ready for her to eat, of which having taken as much as her distracted Thoughts would give her leave to do, she went to Bed, and endeavour'd to compose herself. – The extream Weakness she was in, overcoming all those Perturbations which had so long kept her waking, she fell into a sound Sleep, and in the Morning found her Mind as well as Body had been very much refresh'd by it. – She began to consider seriously what it was best for her to do; and that natural Vivacity and Spirit, which had already carried her through so many Difficulties, now by degrees returning, gave her hopes she should also get through this, with less Trouble than her Despair had at first suggested – and resolving to run no farther into Inconveniencies, such as she had pass'd in that little Time since she had left the *Monastery*; she hired a couple of *Mules* and a Guide to conduct her to the next *Town*, which she was inform'd was *Alcala*:[27] From that she designed for *Guadalaxara*,[28] because she thought the other not so far distant from *Madrid*, but that Don *Jabin*, to whom there was a Necessity she must send for Money, might send some Person to know the Reasons of her coming away in so strange a manner. – Reason having now regain'd its force, she no sooner had formed this Design, than she began to put it in execution; and the People of the House furnishing her with *Mules* and a Guide, she got safely to *Alcala*, and from thence to *Guadalaxara*, without any thing happening in her Journey worthy of Remark; unless it were that she, who but a day or two before had so wholly given herself up to Despair, that she seem'd to dare all kind of Miseries, now appeared as careful of her Life, as before she had been the contrary: But this will not be thought strange by any one, who considers how impossible it is for the Excess of any Passion to continue; a weak Constitution, accompanied by a mean Judgment, it immediately destroys, and Death or Madness is the Consequence, as it happened in the Case of Don *Pedro*. But *Emanuella* had a more than ordinary Strength as well of Nature, as of Reason, to struggle with the Torrent of her, for a time, impetuous Grief; which at last enabled her to overcome it, at least so far as 'twas requisite for Self-Preservation, of which for a time she had seem'd wholly regardless.

When she was arrived at *Guadalaxara*, she took Lodgings in a private House; pretending that she had a Husband whom she expected to follow her in a little time: and to prevent all possibility of a Discovery, told the People her Name was *Mercina*. She took the same prudent Care also in the Directions she sent to Don *Jabin*, writing to him in this manner:

To Don *JABIN.*

THE many Proofs I have received of your Friendship, would oblige me to conceal nothing from you, were there no other Person but my self concerned – I entreat, therefore, that you will believe I made a Secret of leaving the Pourclairs *not out of Choice, but Necessity; and as such, vouchsafe to pardon it. – My Affairs requiring an immediate Supply of Money, I beg you will remit in Bills to the value of about two Hundred Crowns, and direct them to be receiv'd by Donna* Mercina, *at* Guadalaxara, *near which place I am; that Lady is my particular Friend, and will not fail to do me Justice in the Trust I repose in her – I desire also that you will write under a Cover to her, an Account of yours and your good Family's Welfare, for which I shall ever most ardently petition Heaven; being (however my present Circumstances may oblige me to appear the contrary) in the sincerest manner,*

Don Jabin's
Most affectionate Kinswoman
and devoted Servant

EMANUELLA.

P. S. *I doubt not but your accustomed Goodness will still extend it self so far in my favour, as to silence whatever Aspersions may happen to be cast on my leaving the* Monastery *so suddenly, by seeming to have been privy to it, and that it was for no other Reason than the too great Severities practised by that Order.*

SHE might have omitted this last Request: She was no sooner miss'd, than the true Reason of her Departure was blazed abroad. One of the *Nuns*, being more quick-sighted than the rest, had discovered her Condition; and after she was gone, related it to the whole Convent. What is in the mouths of such a Number, especially of that Sex which is seldom bless'd with Secrecy, and of that Sort too who have little else to employ their time with, cannot be expected to be with-held from the knowledge of all who have any Conversation with them. *Emilius* among the rest was inform'd of it, which very much help'd to confirm him in the Opinion that all *Berillia* had said concerning her Conduct was true: Judging of her Actions by that of the generality of Women, few of whom would have known themselves to be in the Circumstance she was, without acquainting the Person chiefly obliged to pity, with the Misfortune – He doubted not therefore but that it had happened by him, whom that Monster of Treachery had told him had supplanted him in her Affections, and that that was the Reason she had never written to upbraid the Change of his Humour in his Addresses to *Julia*, as he imagined she would have done, if she had been innocent herself. – And these Conjectures, which tho' in reality the most injurious that could be, appeared so reasonable, that they entirely destroy'd all those small Remains of Tenderness, his new Desire for an Object yet unenjoy'd, had left him: And now entirely devoted to *Julia*, and to the Advantages he proposed by marrying her, left nothing undone which might engage her to consent. – She who was half won before-hand, and had only made some faint Denials for Form's sake, easily suffered herself to seem over-persuaded to follow her Inclinations; and they were married in great Solemnity, in a very little time after *Emanuella* had departed from *Madrid.*

BUT Don *Jabin*, who had but too true a guess at the State of her Affairs, and made no doubt but that *Emilius* was the Man to whom she ow'd her Undoing, forbore to aggravate her Afflictions by sending her any Intelligence either of what was talk'd of concerning herself, or of the Marriage of her Lover: But sending her the Money which she desir'd, and which he easily believ'd she wanted, writ no more to her, than to entreat she would continue to let him hear from her; and that as soon as her Affairs would permit, she would return to *Madrid.*

THIS Supply, and the Belief that every body she had left behind her, were as entirely ignorant of her Circumstances as she could wish, made her as easy in them, as could possibly be expected. Her Courage and usual Fortitude now, with such Success, exerted themselves; that she waited the dreadful Hour, which she knew was shortly to arrive, with all the Resignation and Patience imaginable: and at the appointed time brought a Son into the World, who, from the moment of his Birth, seem'd to promise he would be an Ornament to it.

I am of opinion, that the greatest part of my Female Perusers, will imagine this unfortunate Lady could regard a Child whose begetting had cost her so many Tears but with Indifference, and that she must have look'd on him with more Remorse than Tenderness; but *Emanuella*, as most of her Notions were vastly different from those of the generality of her Sex, so were they also in this. Had the Ceremony of the Church made *Emilius* as much her Husband, as by his Vows he ought to have acknowledg'd himself; and had he never swerv'd in the least tittle from that Constancy he had sworn to maintain inviolable, or that Ardency of Passion which he once profess'd; she could not have loved his Son with greater Fondness – Never did maternal Tenderness reach to a height more elevated than her's – A thousand Lives she would have thought well given to have preserv'd this darling of her Soul – All the Ignominy which this Adventure, if divulg'd, would bring upon her, was now no longer a Concern to her – Even Virtue was become less dear; and she could scarce repent she had been guilty of a Breach of it, so much she priz'd the Effect – and it would only have been with Transports of unconceivable Affection she had beheld the lovely Babe, if the Reflection how little it was in her power to do for him, had not sometimes given a check to the Pleasure she took in calling him her own. – She felt, indeed, all the Mother's *Joy*, but with it infinitely more *Care* than ordinarily attends that Title, and was, as it were, divided in her Thoughts between excess of *Rapture*, and excess of *Pain.* – But however severe the intervals of the *latter* might be, she was sufficiently invigorated by the *former*, to be able to sustain them; and while she had her dear-lov'd Infant in her

Arms, and uninterrupted, gaz'd upon his growing Beauties; nor felt immediate want of any Necessary either for him or herself: she had not the power to think too deeply of what future Miseries might befall her; but her ever-varying Fortune, which would not suffer her to continue long in any settled State of Life, made a sudden Change in her Affairs which obliged her to other Considerations than those which at present took up her Mind.

THE ungrateful *Berillia*, who, as I have before taken notice, had been sent from *Madrid* under the Government of a *Duenna*, some little time before *Emanuella* left the *Pourclairs*: where she was carried, was kept a Secret to every body; for the Cause of her being banished her Father's House, being her Intrigue with a Person he could not approve, he resolv'd to take the most prudent Measures that he could, to prevent the place of her Retirement being discover'd. The Person in whose Charge she was intrusted, had a Sister who lived at a small Village call'd *Tortol*,[29] within a short Mile of *Guadalaxara*, and there she was to be conceal'd for some time. He had as good as made an Agreement for her going into the *Convent* of *Franciscans;* but as he could not be certain, but that she might be in the same Circumstance with her unfortunate Cousin, he was willing to be convinced to the contrary, before her Entrance; and for that purpose plac'd her at this Distance from *Madrid*, where whatever happen'd might be conceal'd. The Place where she was kept being so near *Guadalaxara*, he writ to *Morena*, for that was the Name of her who was appointed Guardian over his Daughter, to make a little Journey thither. He order'd her to enquire for a Woman call'd *Mercina*, and endeavour by her means, if possible, to come to the Speech of *Emanuella*; but if that could not be accomplish'd, to inform herself of the Truth of her Affairs, and give him an account. This Letter happening to be brought when *Morena* was out of the way on some Business, *Berillia* took it in; and knowing it to be her Father's Hand, broke it open. – She had, ever since she had been there, thought of nothing, but how she should get away: and was over-joy'd to find *Emanuella* was so near, resolving to take this Opportunity of making her Escape to her, not doubting but the Power the other's mistaken Friendship had given her over her, would furnish her with Arguments to prevail on her to act according to her Desires. She was kept entirely without Money; and the Belief that she was far from any body who either could or would furnish her with means of making an Escape, in case she should desire it, made her be watch'd with much less Circumspection than otherwise she would have been; and she had an Opportunity to go out of the House the very day she had intercepted the Letter. The Weather favour'd her Design, and it being but a small Walk to *Guadalaxara*, she easily reach'd it before Sun-set.

EMANUELLA had not yet recover'd Strength enough to rise, and was prodigiously surpriz'd when she was told a Lady of a good Appearance enquir'd for Donna *Mercina*, and would not be deny'd the privilege of speaking with her. – She had contracted no Acquaintance in that Place, and could not imagine on what account a Stranger should seem so pressing to see her. – But the People of the House acquainting her that they had already made all the Excuses they could for the Condition she was in, and that every thing was ineffectual to get rid of her, she was at last oblig'd to give leave for her Admittance. The Room was made pretty dark, and the Bed-Curtains clos'd, as is usual in such Cases: So that *Berillia* could not discern who it was she was about to speak to; but desiring that all who were in the Room might leave it, she address'd her in this manner: Donna *Mercina, said she*, there is but one Excuse I can alledge for this Intrusion, but that I hope will be a sufficient one: I doubt not but you are acquainted with the Force of Friendship, and will not think it strange that to prove its Sincerity will carry one to greater lengths than this – I am inform'd it is in your power to let me know where I may find Donna *Emanuella*, a Daughter of the late Governor of *Porto-Rico*. Never was there a more tender Regard between Persons of the same Sex, than that which my Soul paid to this Lady, and which I flatter my self I was favour'd with from her; but some Accidents have for a long time depriv'd me of the Blessing of her Conversation; nor 'till this Day, could I for many Months get the least Intelligence in what Part of the World it was I might hope to find her – I intreat you therefore to direct my Search – I am satisfied she will not take it ill when you shall tell her it is to *Berillia*, her Cousin, her Friend, that you have made this Condescension. – The Astonishment that *Emanuella* was in to find it was she (for she immediately knew her Voice) kept her from interrupting her 'till she came to these Words; but then the Joy she felt at this Recovery of a Friend so long lost, and whom she thought so perfectly in her Interest, broke out in these Expressions – Can it be possible! *cry'd she, throwing open the Curtains*, has Heaven in compassion of my Sufferings sent my dear *Berillia* to me? – Come to my Arms, my best, my only Friend! *Emanuella* will ever bless the Day which brought thee here – 'Tis on thy faithful Breast I may pour out the secret Anguish of my Soul – 'Tis from thee I may assure my self of both Advice and Consolation – Thou who *Lovest* will *Pity* me. – A thousand such like Demonstrations of the sincerest Welcome did she give her, which the other return'd (as soon as the Consternation, at finding her so much sooner than she expected, was a little over) with all the seeming Truth, and tenderest Love imaginable: And what was yet more obliging to her than any thing she could say to herself, she kiss'd and embrac'd the Child with an Ardour so like Sincerity, that one who had less Confidence in her might easily have mistook for it. When the first Raptures of this meeting would permit them to talk of Business, they began to relate to each other all the Particulars of their Adventures since last they parted: But when *Emanuella* heard by what means *Berillia* had been directed to enquire for her, and had read the Letter Don *Jabin* had sent to *Morena*; she found she had but flatter'd herself with an Opinion that the cause of her removal from *Madrid* had been a Secret, and could not forbear expressing how nearly she was touch'd at the loss of that Reputation she had taken so much pains to preserve. And this Regret was of excellent service to further a Contrivance which the wicked *Berillia* had form'd. She presently began to dissuade her from all thoughts of ever returning to *Madrid*: Nor, *said she*, since Don *Jabin* is so diligent in his Inquiries, can you be any longer in private here, tho' I have been so fortunate in intercepting one Letter, he will undoubtedly write again – *Morena* knows you, and in the Person of *Mercina* will *Emanuella* be discover'd, and every Circumstance of this Affair related. I would advise you, since, when one is determined to be conceal'd, all Places are alike, to call in what Money you have in my Father's hands, and quitting *Guadalaxara* with all possible expedition, settle in some other Town. – For my part, if I had less reason to fly from a Father from whom I now no more can hope for Favour, my love for you would oblige me to banish all other Considerations, and continue with you 'till Death enforces a Separation. – The again deceiv'd *Emanuella* highly approv'd of this Advice, and thank'd her for it, and for the Offer she made of living with her, in Terms which the Intentions of the other were far from meriting. Since she had resolv'd to proceed in this manner, the other reminded her, that she must not delay it; because if they tarried till the Account of her making her Escape from *Morena* were sent to her Father, it might possibly make him suspect his Letter had fallen into her hands, and that they were together. – Nothing could be more natural than this Supposition; and for that reason *Emanuella* dispatch'd a Letter to him immediately with a demand of a thousand Crowns, that being the best part of what was her Due; not doubting but by the time it would come to her hands, she should be able to take a Journey. *Berillia* also writ a Letter at the same time to her Lover, but the Contents of it she took care to conceal from her Cousin, only telling her it was to upbraid him for the many Misfortunes her Passion for him had occasioned her. After the Letters were gone, and they had concluded on every thing proper for their Expedition, they began to make what Preparations they could for it, that when the Answers should come, they might have nothing to do, but to depart. – Emannuella had her young Son baptized by the Name of *Victorinus*: A Nurse was provided for him, whose Circumstances would permit her to go with them to any Place they should make choice of; *Mules* and a Man-Servant to attend them were hired, and every thing contriv'd, so as to be ready at a moment's Warning.

How unkindly soever Don *Jabin* might take it, that *Emanuella*, who ow'd the being Mistress of so much Money wholly to his Intercession, seem'd to think him unworthy of her Confidence, which way she design'd to dispose either of that or herself; he did not fail to send it: and tho' her good Sense and the Gratitude of her Nature, gave her some Shocks at treating him in this manner; yet the Artifice of the Treacherous *Berillia*, join'd to the innumerable Perplexities of her Mind, prevented them from taking so great Root in her Reflections, as otherwise they would have done.

ALCALA was the Place they had agreed to go to, not only because they were both of them entirely unknown to any body there, but also, that it being famous for Learning,[30] *Emanuella* thought the young *Victorinus*, when he grew up fit to receive it, might have all the Advantages of it, without her being oblig'd to send him from her sight; a Misfortune, which her Tenderness for him made appear to be the most dreadful that cou'd possibly befall her: And tho' it being much nearer to *Madrid* than the Place they were in, yet both of them resolving to take up other Names, they might live there with as little danger of Discovery as in any other City.

IT being Evening when they set out, they lay that Night at an Inn about the mid-way: *Emanuella*, who was too fond of her little *Victorinus* to suffer him to be one moment from her sight, wou'd needs have his *Nurse* the Partner of her Bed, and *Berillia* had one to herself in another Chamber. Tho' on vastly different Subjects, both these Ladies had sufficient to employ their Minds. – One pass'd away the restless Hours in Contemplation on the many turns of Fortune she had known, and in imploring Heaven, that where she now was going she might find a Settlement for Life – The other was applauding her good Genius, for furnishing her with Artifice to bring about almost whatever she undertook; and flattering herself with a thousand Joys in store, all owing to her own Wit, her own Fertility of Invention, and Perfection in the Art of Dissimulation.

IT was very early in the Morning when *Emanuella* rose, and having order'd the Mules to be got ready, went herself to awake her Cousin; but was not a little surpriz'd, when coming into her Chamber, she was already up, and gone out: however, imagining no more than that, not able to sleep, she had rose, and was gone to take a walk either in the Fields or Garden, bade one of the Servants of the House to call her – O Heaven! *said the Fellow to whom she gave this Command*, do you not know, that the Lady who last Night came with you is gone? – Gone! *cry'd she*, what mean you? she can be gone no farther than to take a little Morning Air, therefore prithee make haste to find her, and let her know we are ready to prosecute our Journey. Alas! *resum'd he*, I fear she has deceiv'd you – I give you my Word, that if she continu'd to ride, as she set out, she is, by this time, some Leagues[31] off. *Emanuella* cou'd by these Words think no other than that he who spoke them was mistaken in the Person she enquir'd for, and therefore took the pains to describe her to him: but he presently told her, that he very well knew who it was she meant; that they had no other Guests in the House but those that came with her, and that a young *Chevalier* well-mounted had come by Day-break, and took her away with him. I leave the Reader to judge what an Astonishment this Intelligence must create in the Mind of her who heard it: She was for some time unable to give any Credit to an Information so highly improbable to be true; but when she return'd to her Chamber, and found that not only every thing that belong'd to her was missing, but also a little Cabinet, which she had entrusted to her Charge, in which was contain'd most of the Money she had receiv'd from Don *Jabin*; 'tis hard to say, whether Amazement for so base and cruel an Action, or Grief for the Misfortunes it must of necessity subject her to, was most predominant in her Soul – to be betray'd, robb'd, and forsaken in so barbarous a manner, by the Person whom of all the World she had placed the greatest Confidence in – to be exposed with her dear Infant, to all the Miseries which attend Poverty – to lose at one Stroke all that she had in the World – No means left her to make the least Provision against Want and Beggary, was something so shocking, so dreadful, as rendred all her Courage useless. – She went into the Room where *Nurse* was dressing her young Master for his Journey, and the Sight of him made the Reflection of the Loss he had sustain'd more terrible to be born: She had not Words presently to relate what had befallen her: and when the good Woman, easily perceiving by her Countenance that something of ill had happen'd, entreated to know the matter; she could get no more from her, for a good while than, O Nurse I am undone! – But that, *cry'd she,* is a trivial Woe, that lovely Babe, that Charmer at your Breast, is ruin'd – we must starve, Nurse! perish for want of Bread – the little All we had, is lost – no means is left us for Support – no Hope but in the Grave. – With these and the like Exclamations did she make the other sensible, something very unfortunate had happen'd; but what it was, she was far from being able to guess; 'till her Mistress having a little more recollected herself, at last acquainted her with the whole Story. Never did any one bear a greater part in the Sufferings of another, than did this faithful Creature in those of *Emanuella*; the Affability and Kindness with which she had been treated by her, had gain'd as great an Interest in her Affections in the short time she had been with her, as tho' she had been bred up with her; and then her Tenderness for the young *Victorinus*, was more than equal to that which Mothers ordinarily feel for their own Children. – She join'd in all her Lamentations, and vented ten thousand Curses on the perfidious and ungrateful Cause of them: But perceiving that this rather encreased the Distraction of *Emanuella*, than any way comforted her, she began to change her Talk, begging her to be as easy as she could, and to proceed in her Journey to *Alcala*; and having enquir'd which way *Berillia* and her Conductor took, and being inform'd, they went towards that Town, she endeavour'd to inspire her with a hope that they might be heard of there. – There was indeed but little Probability in this Conjecture; but as this was not a Place to continue in, the distress'd Lady thought she might as well go there as to any other Place; and complying with the Persuasions of her *Nurse*, they left the Inn, and in a short time arriv'd at *Alcala*.

NURSE's Predictions had so much of Truth in them, that on Enquiry they found that such Persons as those they sought had pass'd through the City, but had stayed no longer than to take a small Refreshment, and were gone on the Road to *Madrid*. – To send any body after them, *Emanuella* knew would be in vain; because it was impossible they would tarry there, on the account of Don

Jabin: therefore she was obliged to sit down with the Misfortune without the least Hope she should ever have any Reparation for it; but with what racking Reflections, those who will but give themselves the trouble of thinking what a Woman in her Circumstances must feel, will be better able to judge, than all the Descriptions I could give, would make them.

WHAT now could this unhappy Lady do? she was in a Place where she was entirely unacquainted, tho' that she was so, was the only Consolation she had; she had no means of providing for herself and little Family, and when the Charges of her Journey were defrayed, had scarce any Money remaining – No Condition sure was ever so calamitous as her's – Her Spirits had doubtless sunk beneath the weight of Sorrow, which oppress'd her, if the Vigour of her Care for her dear Child had not kept them up. – Something must be thought on for the procuring for *him* the Necessaries of Life, whatever should become of herself – and thinking nothing too much to do for him, she threw off the fine Lady, endeavour'd to forget whose Daughter she was, and the Hopes she was bred to, and submitted to the meanest, and most servile Offices for Bread. – She took a little Lodging in the cheapest part of the Town, and leaving her *Nurse* at home to take Care of that which was much dearer to her than all other Considerations, she went every day to a *Convent* in that City; where doing Services for the *Nuns* in the manner of an *Out* or *Lay-Sister*, she made a shift to get as much as maintain'd them, tho' in a manner which none who had known her before these Misfortunes came upon her, could have believ'd she could have liv'd to endure. But what will not Love enable one to go through! what Difficulties are so great but Inclination can Surmount! She condescended to every thing with Chearfulness, for the sake of *Victorinus*; and while she fed her longing Eyes with gazing on his Infant-Charms, and clasped the lovely Innocent in her Arms, she thought herself not wretched; and passing all the Night in that sweet Employment, forgot the Hardships of the Day. In spite of the real Coldness with which she had been treated by *Emilius*, and the monstrous Ingratitude and Baseness she had been made to believe him guilty of, her Soul still confess'd the Graces of his Person; his Image was too deeply impress'd in her Mind, ever to be banished thence, tho' effac'd and blotted by the Memory of his Crimes: The little *Victorinus* had Features so perfectly resembling his, that there wanted but Age to make them appear the same; and this Likeness not a little added to the Fondness she otherwise had for him. All the Passion she once had for the *Father*, was now transmitted to the Son; which join'd to the soft Care which all who are *Mothers* feel, rais'd her's to the most elevated Pitch that Humanity is capable of being inspir'd with.

BUT, to prosecute the melancholy History of her Misfortunes, she had languish'd away (for it could not be call'd living) seven or eight Months at *Alcala* in the manner already represented, without seeing, or being seen by any body she knew; but 'tis probable the one might be owing to the little notice she took of every thing but what concern'd her Business, and the other to the Station she was in, so far different from that in which any one would have imagin'd to have found the accomplish'd, and once so much ador'd *Emanuella*. But one day being at the Cloyster-Gate on her usual Employment, she saw a handsome young *Fryar* waiting to be admitted to speak with the Abbess; happening to stay a little longer than was customary, she had an opportunity of considering his Face, and fancying at first sight she knew him, on looking more heedfully, soon discovered him to be Don *Octavio*, one whom she had formerly many Opportunities of conversing with at the House of Don *Jabin*, and whom she since had heard had fought with *Emilius* on the account of Donna *Julia*. Curiosity made her enquire of some of the *Nuns*, who she perceiv'd knew him, what had been the occasion of his becoming one of the *Religious*; and was told by them, that it was occasion'd by Despair: that Honour preventing him from attempting any thing against a Rival who had given him his Life, he forsook the World as soon as his hopes were at an end, by the Marriage of *Julia* with the *Count*; and that the *Abbess* of that Nunnery being his Aunt, he came there to pay his Duty as he pass'd thro' *Alcala* in his way to some other part of the Country. *Emanuella* had experienc'd too much of Love and Despair, to be surpriz'd at the Effect she found those Passions had caus'd in him, and it was with compassion only she reflected on a Change so little to be expected from that Gaiety, which he was once the the most fam'd for of any *Chevalier* in *Madrid*. She was highly satisfy'd however in her Mind, that her Dress, and the Alteration of her Circumstances had so much disguis'd her, that a Person who had been so perfectly acquainted with her Face, should now not have any notion he had seen it before, and began to live with more security in her thought, that she might continue undiscover'd, tho' she should happen to be seen even by *Emilius* himself, the Person of all the World from whom, as she then was, she most desir'd to be conceal'd. But alas! it was not ordain'd for this unhappy Woman to have any part of her Wishes compleated; she but hoped to live and die in this forlorn Obscurity, and that also was deny'd her: It was but a few days after she had seen *Octavio*, that a Lady, call'd Donna *Jacinta del Florezada*, a young Widow of a vast Estate, who us'd frequently to come and pass some Hours in conversation with the Nuns, desir'd to speak with her; she had often seen her at the *Convent*, and taking more notice of the Delicacy of her Hands and Complexion, the Sweetness of her Voice, and the graceful Manner in which she delivered her Words, than many others who had the same opportunity of observing her, imagin'd she had been educated in a fashion which might deserve a better State of Life than what she at present liv'd in; and having some young Children, believ'd she might be a proper Person for a Governess: She discours'd her on that Head, and putting many questions to make tryal of her Capacity, found it so infinitely beyond what even her good Opinion had suggested, that she immediately made her an offer of coming into her House, and assur'd her of Usage more like a Sister than a Servant.

THIS Proposal, tho' an extraordinary Favour, (for Donna *Jacinta* was not only one of the greatest, but best Women in the Place) was not altogether so agreeable to *Emanuella* as the other expected. – In the first place, she knew not how to part with that dear Babe, whom as yet she had never been absent from one Night, and whom her very Soul was wrapt in. – And in the next, she was unwilling to go into a Family where she knew there was always a great Variety of Company, for fear some one or other might happen to know her. – The first of these Reasons she made no scruple of acquainting Donna *Jacinta* with, and the other she palliated by saying she was of a Disposition too melancholy to endure the sight of many People; and for that cause fear'd she might be unfit for the Employment she would engage her in. – But the obliging Lady would be deny'd by no means; she had taken a fancy to her, and was resolv'd to have her; she told her she commended the Love and Care she seem'd to have of her Child, and that she would be far from endeavouring to alienate an Affection so praiseworthy, or make her unhappy by taking her from that which she so dearly priz'd. You shall have your Child with you, *said she*, both that and a Nurse to look after it shall be as welcome as your self; and as it grows up, I will undertake to give him an Education equal to my own: and as for your other Objections, tho' I think Company the best relief for Melancholy, I will not Press you to come into it – You shall see no body but those whom you think fit. – Nor will I exact any thing from you, but what shall be agreeable to your own Inclinations. There appeared so uncommon a Good-Nature and Frankness in this Lady, as well as Advantage in the Offer she made her, that *Emanuella* must have thought herself both her own and Child's Enemy to have refused it. – She accepted it therefore with all the Acknowledgments of Gratitude with it, and immediately went home to put herself in as good a Capacity as she could, to return to this kind Patroness for good and all. Her poor *Nurse* was over-joy'd when she heard the News, and every thing being ready in a few Hours, all the little Family remov'd, from daily Care, Scarcity, and sometimes Want, to Ease, Plenty, and to Chearfulness: They were receiv'd with a Welcome far beyond their Expectations; had an Apartment assign'd for them, as tho' they had been Guests, not continued Inmates of the House: the Servants were order'd to treat *Emanuella*, who had now given herself the Name of *Placillia*, with all the respect imaginable, and her Nurse with the same Kindness, as if it were their own young Master she attended. Donna *Jacinta*, was so far from promising more than she intended to perform, that on the contrary her *Words* came infinitely short of her *Deeds*. Nor was she of that flashy uncertain Temper which some People are of, tho' accounted Good-humour'd too, of being one day extravagantly fond of those they call Friends, and the next scarce owning they have any such Acquaintance: She was always the same, always in one Temper, unless it were, that her Affections seem'd every day to encrease to her new Companion; but that is little to be wondered at, since this unhappy Fair had a stock of Charms in her Conversation and Behaviour, which were not to be discover'd all at once: The Amendment in her manner of living made also so great a one in her Looks, that she was hardly to be known for the Person who us'd to be employ'd in Messages, or whatever other mean Office the *Nuns* had no more discernment than to put her to. – She now began to resume her former Charms, and appear again herself. *Jacinta* perceiving her Skill in Musick, Painting, Philosophy, and all those Accomplishments which few but those of Quality can afford, or at least take the pains to have their Children instructed in, could not be persuaded but that she was of Noble Descent, and frequently sollicited her to give her the History of her Life; but the other could not be prevail'd upon to relate more than that her Father was a Gentleman in a distant part of *Spain*, and that by marrying against his Consent to a Person who was now dead, she had been reduced to many Misfortunes. This was a Story she had fram'd, for all who enquired into her Affairs; nor could all the kindness of this Lady oblige her to reveal the Truth: Her *Nurse* was also extreamly faithful to the Trust she had reposed in her, nor ever divulged the least Hint of those Affairs she knew, which tho' but a small part, was yet enough to have made all that her Mistress had said appear fabulous.

THUS did she live as happy as a Person can live, who lives dependent on the Favour of another: that good Lady took care to confer her Obligations in such a manner, that they should be as little as possible uneasy to the Receiver; and the other was so sensible of her Favours, that she at length became her's as much thro' Inclination as Duty. – She had continu'd with her about a Year without any thing happening of moment, and she was beginning to think Fortune was grown weary of persecuting her, and would permit her to continue in that Asylum of Tranquillity which she now enjoy'd: She had no reason to imagine she should not live and die with this kind Friend; and the Experience of her Goodness to herself, gave her a certainty that the young *Victorinus* would find the Effects of it in as full a manner as if she were to live. – She would often talk to Donna *Jacinta*, in this manner, who, tho' she never heard her without renewing the Promises she had before made her, yet she endeavour'd to put her off from such kind of Discourses, because she thought them a kind of Food to that Melancholy she seem'd but too much to give way to. They were sitting together one day, when a Gentleman and Lady, attended by a great number of Servants, alighted at the Gate, which oblig'd Donna *Jacinta*, to go to receive them: *Emanuella* continu'd in her Chamber, the other perceiving how much averse she seem'd to be seen by any body but the Family, had for a good while left solliciting her to come into Company; but she had not now remain'd long alone, before she came running into the Room, desiring her she would oblige her so far as to come down – she told her the Persons that came to visit her were her near Relations, and that the Lady, who was most passionately fond of her Husband, and had no Children by him, had happen'd to see the little *Victorinus* at play in the Garden, and imagin'd him so like her Lord, that she express'd a prodigious Impatience to see the Mother. It would be impossible to represent the disturb'd Motions of *Emanuella*'s Soul all the time she heard her speak – she began to think of something, tho' at present she could not well tell of what – a sort of distant Guess – a wild Notion of a Possibility of some wonderful Event – a thousand incoherent unconnected Ideas ran in an instant thro' her Mind, and almost threw her into a Swoon. Donna *Jacinta* was extreamly surpriz'd to find so sudden an Alteration in her Countenance, and ask'd her if she were not well. – No, Madam (*answer'd she, scarce able to speak*) and therefore intreat you would excuse my appearing before this Company. I know not how to do it (*resum'd the other*) since they are so very pressing, but will endeavour it at your Request – tho' I could wish, (*added she*) that I could prevail on you: the Lady, who is my Cousin Germain,[32] is married to a Count of the Empire,[33] and it may be prodigiously in their power to – She had opportunity to say no more, the Person she was speaking to, was now incapable of hearing her, and fallen at her Feet on the Floor, quite senseless. – Amaz'd as she was, she omitted nothing for her Recovery, and throwing Water on her Face, soon brought her to herself; but the Torrent of Tears which gush'd from her Eyes, as soon as she open'd them – the Sighs, which at her return of Breath seeming as tho' they would exhaust it quite, made the good-natur'd Observer half stupefy'd with Grief and Wonder: Nothing was more apparent, than that she had been brought into this Condition only by her being press'd to go into this Company; and not being able to guess the reason of it, and perceiving she did not go about to speak it – For Heaven's sake, *said she*, what have I said to occasion this Confusion of your Soul? or what has Count *Emilius*, or Donna *Julia* done, which should render their Presence so hateful to you? These Words, which so entirely confirm'd her in those Suggestions which already had work'd such sad Effects, were very near throwing her again into those Faintings from which she had so lately been recover'd – but mustering up all the Spirit she had left to stand this Shock, which of all that had befallen her, seem'd the most terrible, she flung herself at the Feet of Donna *Jacinta*, and with trembling Hands catching hold of her Robe, O! pardon me, (*said she, in scarce intelligible Accents*) pardon me, most excellent Lady, that I have abus'd your Goodness with a feign'd Tale – I am not the Person I pretended, but a Wretch unworthy of your Favour – a Wretch, who by one fatal Crime has drawn down all the stor'd Vengeance of high Heaven on her – but, as you have hitherto been so divinely kind – O cast me not off at once – Expose me not to Horrors worse than Death – than Hell – O save me from the Sight of *Emilius*, and you shall hereafter be made sensible of the whole Truth of my unhappy Story. Here she stopp'd, and Donna *Jacinta* was about to make some Reply, when she was prevented, by the sudden coming in of

Emilius and his Lady, with the young *Victorinus* in her hand: The Surprize they were in, that *Jacinta* stay'd so much longer than they expected, their Impatience to see the Mother of a Child whom both of them were so much charm'd with, made them take the Liberty, being told which Room she was in, of coming up. *Emanuella* being opposite to the Door, had the opportunity of seeing them first; and in the instant Distraction that View gave her, incapable of any Thought but how to shun it, a Window by Accident being open, she flew to it, and crying out, *Fate, thou hast done thy worst!* was very near throwing herself out of it, if Donna *Jacinta*, who, tho' equally surpriz'd, had her Thoughts more prepar'd for such an Adventure, had not been very quick in catching hold of her. *Emilius*, who at once saw *Emanuella* and her Despair, stood for some Moments like one depriv'd of Motion – No Words can reach what 'twas he felt at an Object so unexpected! So alarming! – the most strong Surprize, the most violent Grief, the most passionate Tenderness at once possess'd him and he was as unable to express the Force of either, as I am to describe it.

DONNA *Julia*, who had but one Passion to struggle with, soon overcame that enough to ask her Cousin *Jacinta*, what had occasioned the Confusion she beheld, and her own Consternation; but that Lady, who still held the afflicted *Emanuella* in her Arms at the other end of the Room, and was endeavouring to persuade her to Moderation, had not leisure to make any Reply to what she said, or to ease her own Wonder, by enquiring the Source of this Affair; which tho' she guess'd at part of, was far from imagining who *Emanuella* really was, or the Causes she had for Despair. *Emilius* was the only Person who cou'd unfold this Mystery, and believing, that since so much had been discover'd, it were best to reveal the whole, resolv'd to do it, tho' it were so nice a Point, that it requir'd all the Rhetorick he was Master of, to handle without giving Offence to Donna *Julia*: He was also divided in his Sentiments, whether it wou'd not more add to the Disorder of *Emanuella* to relate the Story before her Face or by taking the Company into another Room, leave her in suspence; but after a little debate in his Mind, he at length concluded on the latter as most proper; and drawing nearer to the Place where Donna *Jacinta* and *Emanuella* were, addressing himself to the former, Madam, *said he*, I believe it will be much better for us to retire, and leave this afflicted Lady to that Repose our continuing here may hinder her from enjoying. I will not, Madam! *added he, turning to the other, and bowing very respectfully*, presume to remain in your Sight, nor return to it 'till those Stains the Treachery of the unworthy *Berillia* have cast on my Character are remov'd – then you will find *Emilius* has not been so blameable, as at present he appears; and will, I hope, admit his Presence, without giving him any Tortures by the sight of yours. As much averse as *Emanuella* was to hear him speak, the Name of *Berillia* attracted her Attention, – in the midst of her Agonies, in the midst of that Shock of Nature his sudden coming had given her, she wou'd have been pleas'd at finding him not altogether so guilty as she had believ'd him; and fancying there was a possibility that unfaithful Creature had deceiv'd her, in the Representation she had made of him, as well as in other Affairs, would have been contented to have had him repeat what he knew of her; and finding there was now an absolute Necessity of every thing being discover'd, thought the Recital might as well be made before her Face: she felt something at her Heart, which gave her an Assurance she shou'd not long survive so publick an Eclaircissment of what she had done, and was willing to submit to the shame of it, to gratify her Impatience, to acknowledge herself mistaken in condemning the Man, whom to have found innocent she wou'd, a long time ago, have parted with Life. If, *said she*, my Lord! you have any thing to tell me of the Falshood of that wicked Wretch, more than what I am already appriz'd of, I beg it may be no Secret: Set forth in what terms you please her Faults, and my Misfortunes; I am inur'd to Miseries of all kinds, and can endure even this severest Tryal. – Perhaps, *continu'd she weeping*, with greater Fortitude than the rest, because it is the last – the last of Horrors I can live to know. She made this Request in such a manner, and accompany'd it with so many Sighs, and such Distortion of her Features while she was speaking, that the *Count* made a doubt whether it was best for him to comply with it; and 'tis probable wou'd have evaded it, had she not over, and over again, intreated he wou'd relate all he knew, and put a period to the Amazement which his Wife and Donna *Jacinta* were all this time involv'd in; 'till finding himself press'd past Denyal not only by her, but by those two Ladies, who glad she had propos'd it, seconded her Desire, he was oblig'd to satisfy their Curiosity; which after having a little recollected what he was about to disclose, he did in these, or the like Words.

I believe, *said he*, that for the Satisfaction of all here, I need repeat no more than what *Berillia* herself confess'd, when happening to be taking the Air, about a Mile from *Madrid*, I saw that unhappy Wretch lying on the Grass, weltring in her Blood, wounded in three or four Places, and almost ready to expire: So sad an Object rais'd all that was compassionate in my Soul, but when I went nearer, in hopes to afford her some Relief, Words wou'd but poorly make you sensible what 'twas I felt at knowing her to be *Berillia*, whom I thought one of the sincerest of my Friends. – I began to testify some part of my Concern, by enquiring by what means she had become in that Condition, and offering to bind up her Wounds, but she wou'd not permit me; but discovering all the marks of the most poinant and terrible Despair that ever was, told me, all Care wou'd be in vain, that she was a dead Woman – and that if there was a Possibility for her Wounds to be healed, she wou'd herself make others, which shou'd be beyond the Power of Art. – And then, perceiving my Amazement at hearing her speak in this manner, You (*cry'd she*) *Emilius*, have the least Reason to pity me of all the World – you I have wrong'd in the highest manner. – O! *continued she, in an Agony to which the Rack is mean*, Heaven never can forgive the Injustice I have done you, nor the Ruin I have brought on the innocent *Emanuella* – both – both of you I have betray'd – traduc'd, and tho' she is the greatest Sufferer, 'tis you appear the only Criminal. She then, on my Intreaty, and Assurance of Pardon for whatever she had done, proceeded to inform me, how cruelly she had accus'd me to you, and confess'd, that all the Intelligence she had given me was false concerning your clandestine Marriage with an inferiour Person, who since grown weary of, you had sent to *Andaluzia*,[34] where he died; of a shameful Intrigue you carry'd on with another, even at the time that you permitted my Addresses; and a thousand such like monstrous Inventions, which I do not very well remember; or if I did, shou'd blush to wound your Ears with.

Emanuella cou'd not hear the Recital of such vile Accusations without lifting up her Eyes to Heaven, in token of Astonishment, that there cou'd be such Wickedness permitted; but restrained herself from saying any thing to interrupt him: and he went on in this manner.

It may seem like an idle Excuse, *continu'd the Count*, for me to say in my Defence, that when she endeavour'd to bring me to that Opinion her base Intentions aim'd; she made use of all the Artifice the Devil ever taught, and bound me from revealing, either by Words, or Letters, a tittle of what she had said, by Oaths too terrible to be dispens'd with; so I shall only say, before this Lady who is now my Wife, I at that time thought myself too much the Husband of *Emanuella* to have made my Addresses to any other, had not the Stratagems of the false *Berillia* impos'd so artfully on my Belief, as to make me imagine the Engagements between us had been first dissolv'd by you. – But I will not detain your Attention, by alledging any thing in vindication of a Man, whom, perhaps, you wish not shou'd be clear'd; and who has it not now in his power to repair the Injuries you have suffer'd on his score. – The dying *Berillia*, as I was about to tell you, had Breath enough to confess all this first part of her Barbarity at large, but her Strength decreasing, she run but slightly over that which she afterwards was guilty of to you, in conspiring with a young Man, whom she for a long time had held a criminal Conversation[35] with, to rob you of that Money she had advis'd you to call out of her Father's hands; – and how the Villain, as she was travelling with him to *Toledo*,[36] as he had made her hope, had taken it from her, stabb'd her, and left her in that condition in which I found her. – The Horrors which seiz'd on this poor Wretch, at the approach of Death, wou'd be too dreadful to describe: Never did I sustain a shock like what the sight of them oceasion'd in me; but, base as she had been, I had promis'd her Forgiveness; and indeed, the Penitence she express'd seem'd to deserve it: therefore, after waiting 'till I found she had no longer Sense of Pity or Consolation, I remounted, and rode as fast as I cou'd into the Town, with the melancholy Account of what I had seen and heard to Don *Jabin*, who, not forgetting she was his Child, tho' a disobedient one, sent Servants to fetch her Body, and bury'd it in a Fashion suitable to her Quality.

HERE *Emilius* concluded his Narration, which, as he expected, put an end to the Wonder this little Company had been in, before they had any guess how *Placillia* and he had been acquainted: but not only his Wife, but *Jacinta* had also heard much of *Emanuella*, the Misfortunes which the Avarice of Don *Pedro* had subjected her to, – the Favour she had found from the King, in obliging him to repair part of the Loss she had sustain'd, – the Engagements she had with the *Count*, – their breaking off, – her going afterward among the *Pourclairs*, – her sudden leaving them; – and the Discourse that fill'd the Town for what reason she had been oblig'd to do so. – All this was no Secret to either of them, and from the first Discovery that *Placillia* was *Emanuella*, they ceas'd to be surpriz'd at the effects of such a meeting: but both of them, as well as *Emanuella* herself, expected he would have taken some notice, in his Discourse, of the little *Victorinus*, who, doubtless, had not been left unmention'd by *Berillia*; and whom, since the clearing of his Mother's Innocence, he could make no doubt of being his own Child: – but that was a Subject he fear'd wou'd be too shocking to the well-known Niceness of *Emanuella*'s Modesty. – Besides, he knew not how his Wife might take a Repetition of what, by many Circumstances, she cou'd not but be sensible of without, – But that Lady suspecting the reason of his Silence on that head, and willing to shew how much her Soul disdain'd that mean Passion Wives are too liable to fall into; taking *Emanuella* by the Hand, and pressing it with a most obliging Tenderness; Tho' Madam (*said she*) the Count has Charms, which created in me a Wish to become his Wife, long before I had the least Hope of being so; I beg you will believe me, when I protest by all that's sacred, that had I been appriz'd of the Right you had in him, I would have chose to fall a Martyr to Despair, rather than by gratifying my Desires have been guilty of so much Injustice; nor can I ever yield to be Partaker more of Joys to which you have a superior Claim, unless you vouchsafe to give a Sanction which the Priest had not the power to do: *Emilius* first was yours, – is still yours, by all those Ties which ought to bind an honest Mind; and, if you can forgive the Crime he has been but betray'd to act, I here resign him, and with him, the Title I have innocently so long usurp'd. – *Emanuella*, who had listned with Surprize to this uncommon Generosity, wou'd suffer her to proceed no farther, but interrupting her, – How glad am I (*said she*) to find before I die, one Woman, whose Excellence of Nature will preserve my Sex from those Imputations the monstrous Wickedness of *Berillia* wou'd else draw on it: – But, do not think, most incomparable *Julia*, that I have a Soul so little capable of Gratitude, as to abuse such Goodness; – *Emilius* is only yours; whatever Engagements had pass'd between us, I myself dissolv'd. – When, by the Loss of my Fortune I thought myself unworthy of his Bed, I relinquish'd all the Right his Vows had given me to him; and his enfranchis'd

Heart was free for you, or any Lady whose Deserts might claim the Prize. – I have nothing to accuse him of, and am too much his Friend, not to rejoice that his good Stars directed him, where Beauty join'd with such consummate Virtue cannot fail to give him lasting Happiness. Nothing I cou'd say would be sufficiently Picturess, to paint the various Agitations which perplex'd the Soul of *Emilius* all the time they were speaking; but the Matter was too delicate for him, to offer at an Interposition, and not being able to say any thing but what might possibly cause Distaste either in the one or the other, he chose to remain silent, and leave the noble-minded Ladies to decide the generous Contest, as they pleas'd: When the admirable *Julia* thus prosecuted the Design, which had induc'd her to speak in the manner she had done to *Emanuella*. Since, Madam! (*said she*) either to the Sweetness of your Disposition, which will not suffer you to render a Woman, who, you think, has not sufficient Fortitude to sustain it, miserable by the Loss of all she loves, or to the little Inclination you have to pardon him, who, after the admirable *Emanuella*, cou'd look on any other with a Lover's Eyes: To which soever of these Reasons I am indebted for the continuance of the Name I wear, you must permit me to remind you, there is another Tye, of which you have not the power to disengage *Emilius*: – This lovely Infant (*continu'd she, taking him in her Arms*) whom at first sight attracted my Love, must ever be acknowledg'd as the just Heir of all his Father is possess'd of; – and, give me leave also, to regard him with a Mother's Tenderness; and how many Children soever Heaven shall be pleas'd to bless me with, make him an equal Sharer with them of all the little Fortune I can call my own. – Nay (*added she, after a little pause, and perceiving, by her Looks, the Confusion of* Emanuella*'s Soul at these Words*) as a Testimony that you are not displeas'd at the Interest I pretend to take in this little Charmer, you must consent to live with me as a Sister, – as a Friend. – Here Donna *Jacinta* (pitying from her Soul the Emotions *Emanuella* must feel at such Obligements from her Rival) thought it was her Place to speak; and interrupting her, No, Cousin, (*said she*) I must put a bar to this last Request; – I had a Friendship for *Emanuella*, before I knew who she was, and cannot consent to part with her when I find her so much more worthy my Esteem: – She must continue with me 'till Death inforces a Separation. – She was about to say something more, when *Emanuella*, over-press'd with Shame, with Gratitude, with Tenderness, and perhaps, a mixture of another Passion more difficult to be supported than all the rest; had no longer Strength to struggle with the differing Agitations, and sunk fainting in her Chair: It would he hard to say, whether the Care of bringing her to herself, appear'd most zealous in the Endeavours of Donna *Julia*, Donna *Jacinta*, or *Emilius*; the latter of whom, as soon as she was in a Condition of hearing them, said a thousand tender and obliging things to her; nor did the generous Partner of his Bed conceive the least Displeasure at it, but, on the contrary, thought he never cou'd express a Sense enough of what that unhappy

Lady had suffer'd for him, and wou'd have rejoic'd to have had it in her power to have afforded her any Consolation: but alas! her Misfortunes were now arriv'd at their utmost height, and soon must know a Period with her Life. – Resentment was all which for a long time had kept the Lamp of Life awake, and that being now extinguish'd in a Flood of softer Passions, the other must of necessity expire. – They soon found she was too much disorder'd for Conversation, and therefore, thought it convenient she should be put into a Bed, where perceiving she grew worse, a Physician was sent for to attend; but from the Moment he saw her, he began to doubt any Success of his Prescriptions: In short, she died in three days, of no other Distemper than a broken Heart; equally lamented by Donna *Julia*, as by *Emilius* and *Jacinta*: Nor did they, after her Death, take less Care than they had promis'd of young *Victorinus*; each seem'd to out-vye the other in their Fondness of him: He was bred in all the Accomplishments which can adorn a Youth of Quality; and after the Decease of *Emilius*, and his generous Lady, who never had any Children herself, was left in possession of the Fortunes of them both, with a considerable Addition from the Friendship of *Jacinta*: which he makes use of with a Nobleness of Soul proportionable to the Hopes of those who gave him the Means of expressing it; and is at this day the greatest Ornament of the Kingdom which claims his Birth.

FINIS

THE ADVENTURES OF *NATURA.*

LIFE's

PROGRESS

THROUGH THE *PASSIONS:*

OR, THE

ADVENTURES

OF

NATURA.

By the AUTHOR of

The FORTUNATE FOUNDLINGS.

LONDON:
Printed by T. GARDNER, and Sold at his
Printing-Office, at *Cowley's Head*, opposite *St.
Clement's Church*, in the *Strand*.
M,DCC,XLVIII.

CONTENTS.

LIFE'S
PROGRESS
THROUGH THE
PASSIONS.

INTRODUCTION.

I HAVE often heard it observed by the readers of biography, that the characters are generally too high painted; and that the *good* or *bad* qualities of the person pretended to be faithfully represented, are displayed in stronger colours than are to be found in nature. To this the lovers of hyperbole reply, that *virtue* cannot be drawn too beautiful, nor *vice* too deformed, in order to excite in us an ambition of imitating the *one*, and a horror at the thoughts of becoming any way like the *other*. – The argument at first, indeed, seems to have some weight, as there is nothing, not even precept itself, which so greatly contributes whether to rectify or improve the mind, as the prevalence of example: but then it ought to be considered, that if the pattern laid down before us, is so altogether angelic, as to render it impossible to be copied, emulation will be in danger of being swallowed up in an unprofitable admiration; and, on the other hand, if it appears so monstrously hideous as to take away all apprehensions of ever resembling it, we might be too apt to indulge ourselves in errors which would seem small in comparison with those presented to us.[1] – There never yet was any one man, in whom all the *virtues*, or all the *vices*, were summed up; for, though reason and education may go a great way toward curbing the passions, yet I believe experience will inform, even the *best* of men, that they will sometimes launch out beyond their due bounds, in spite of all the care can be taken to restrain them; nor do I think the very *worst*, and most wicked, does not feel in himself, at some moments, a propensity to good, though it may be possible he never brings it into practice; at least, this was the opinion of the antients, as witness the poet's[2] words:

All men are born with seeds of good *and* ill;
And each shoot forth, in more or less degree:

> One *you may cultivate with care and skill,*
> *But from the* other *ne'er be wholly free.*

THE human mind may, I think, be compared to a chequer-work, where light and shade appear by turns; and in proportion as either of these is most conspicuous, the man is alone worthy of praise or censure; for none there are can boast of being wholly bright.

I BELIEVE by this the reader will be convinced he must not expect to see a faultless figure in the hero of the following pages; but to remove all possibility of a disappointment on that score, I shall farther declare, that I am an enemy to all *romances,*[3] *novels*, and whatever carries the air of them, tho' disguised under different appellations; and as it is a *real*, not *fictitious* character I am about to present, I think myself obliged, for the reasons I have already given, as well as to gratify my own inclinations, to draw him such as he was, not such as some sanguine imaginations might wish him to have been.

I FLATTER myself, however, that *truth* will appear not altogether void of charms, and the adventures I take upon me to relate, not be less pleasing for being within the reach of probability, and such as might have happened to any other as well as the person they did. – Few there are, I am pretty certain, who will not find some resemblance of himself in one part or other of his life, among the many various and surprizing turns of fortune, which the subject of this little history experienced, as also be reminded in what manner the passions operate in every stage of life, and how far the constitution of the *outward frame* is concerned in the emotions of the *internal faculties.*

THESE are things surely very necessary to be considered, and when they are so, will, in a great measure, abate that unbecoming vehemence, with which people are apt to testify their admiration, or abhorrence of actions, which it very often happens would lose much of their *eclat*[4] either way, were the secret springs that give them motion, seen into with the eyes of philosophy and reflection.

BUT this will be more clearly understood by a perusal of the facts herein contained, from which I will no longer detain the attention of my reader.

BOOK the First.

CHAP. I.

Shews, in the example of Natura, *how from our very birth, the passions, to which the human soul is incident, are discoverable in us; and how far the organs of sense, or what is called the constitution, has an effect over us.*

THE origin of *Natura* would perhaps require more time to trace than the benefit of the discovery would attone for: it shall therefore suffice to say, that his ancestors were neither of the highest rank: – that if no extraordinary action had signalized the names of any of them, so none of them had been guilty of crimes to entail infamy on their posterity: and that a moderate estate in the family had descended from father to son for many generations, without being either remarkably improved or embezzled – His immediate parents were in very easy circumstances, and he being their first son, was welcomed into the world with a joy usual on such occasions. – I never heard that any prodigies preceded or accompanied his nativity; or that the planets, or his mother's cravings during her pregnancy, had sealed him with any particular mark or badge of distinction:[5] but have been well assured he was a fine boy, sucked heartily of his mother's milk, and what they call a thriving child. His weaning, I am told, was attended by some little ailments, occasioned by his pining after the food to which he had been accustomed; but proper means being found to make him lose the memory of the breast, he soon recovered his flesh, increased in strength, and could go about the room at a year and some few months old, without the help of a leading-string.

HITHERTO the passions, those powerful abettors, I had almost said sole authors of all human actions,[6] operated but faintly, and could shew themselves only in proportion to the vigour of the animal frame. Yet latent as they are, an observing eye may easily discover them in each of their different propensities, even from the most early infancy. The eyes of *Natura* on any new and pleasing object, would denote by their sparkling a sensation of joy: – *Fear* was visible in him by clinging to his nurse, and endeavouring to bury himself as it were in her bosom, at the sound of menaces he was not capable of understanding: – That *sorrow* has a place among the first emotions of the soul, was demonstrable by the sighs which frequently would heave his little heart, long before it was possible for him either to know or to imagine any motives for them: – That the seeds of *avarice* are born with us, by the eagerness with which he catched at money when presented to him, his clinching it fast in his hand, and the reluctance he expressed on being deprived of it: – That *anger*,[7] and impatience of controul, are inherent to our nature, might be seen in his throwing down with vehemence any favourite toy, rather than yield to resign it; and that spite and revenge are also but too much so, by his putting in practice all such tricks as his young invention could furnish, to vex any of the family who had happened to cross him: – Even those tender inclinations, which afterwards bear the name of *amorous*, begin to peep out long before the difference of sex is thought on; as *Natura* proved by the preference he gave the girls over the boys who came to play with him, and his readiness to part with any thing to them.

In a word, there is not one of all the various emotions which agitate the breast in maturity, that may not be discerned almost from the birth, *hope, jealousy,* and *despair* excepted, which, tho' they bear the name in common with those other more natural dispositions of the mind, I look upon rather as consequentials of the passions, and arising from them, than properly passions themselves: but however that be, it is certain, that they are altogether dependant on a fixation of ideas, reflection, and comparison, and therefore can have no entrance in the soul, or at least cannot be awakened in it, till some degree of knowledge is attained.

Thus do the dispositions of the *infant* indicate the future *man*; and though we see, in the behaviour of persons when grown up, so vast a difference, yet as all children at first act alike, I think it may be reasonably supposed, that were it not for some change in the constitution, an equal similitude of will, desires, and sentiments, would continue among us through maturity and old age; at least I am perfectly perswaded it would do so, among all those who are born in the same climate, and educated in the same principles: for whatever may be said of a great genius, and natural endowments, there is certainly no real distinction between the *soul* of the man of *wit* and the *ideot*; and that disproportion, which we are apt to behold with so much wonder, is only in fact occasioned by some or other of those innumerable and hidden accidents, which from our first coming into the world, in a more or less degree, have an effect upon the organs of sense; and they being the sole canals through which the spirit shews itself, according as they happen to be extended, contracted, or obstructed, the man must infallibly appear.

CHAP. II.

Contains some proofs by what swift degrees the passions gain an ascendant over the mind, and grow up in proportion with our reason.

Natura had no sooner quitted the nursery, than he was put under the direction of the school, to which at first he was every day conducted either by a man or maid-servant; but when thought big enough to be trusted alone, would frequently play the truant, for which he generally received the discipline necessary on such occasions. – He took his learning notwithstanding as well as could be expected; – he had read the testament through at five years old, about seven was put into *Latin*, and began the rudiments of *Greek* before he had attained the age of nine.

As his understanding increased, the passions became stronger in proportion: and here is to be observed the wonderful wisdom of nature, or rather of the

Great Author of nature, in the formation of the human system, that the passions given to us, especially those of the worst sort, are, for the most part, such opposites, that the one is a sufficient check upon the other.[8] – The *pride* of treating those beneath us with contempt, is restrained by the *fear* of meeting the same usage from those above us. – *A sordid covetousness* is controlled by *ostentation.* – *Sloth* is roused by *ambition*, and so of the rest. – I have been told that when *Natura*, by the enticements of his companions, and his own eagerness to pursue the sports suitable to his years, had been drawn in to neglect his studies, he has often ran home on a sudden, and denied himself both food and sleep, till he had not only finished the task assigned him by his school-master, but also exceeded what was expected from him, instigated by the ambition of praise, and hope of being removed to a higher form. – But at other times again his love of play has rendered him totally forgetful of every thing besides, and all emulation in him absorbed in pleasure. – Thus hurried, as the different propensities prevailed, from one extreme to the other; – never in a medium, but always doing either more or less than was required of him.

In like manner was his *avarice* moderated by his *pity:* – an instance of which was this; – One morning having won at chuck-farthing, or some such game, all the money a poor boy was master of, and which he said had been given him to buy his breakfast, *Natura* was so much melted at his tears and complaints, that he generously returned to him the whole of what he had lost. – Greatly is it to be wished, the same sentiments of compassion would influence some of riper years, and make them scorn to take the advantage chance sometimes affords of ruining their fellow-creatures; but the misfortune is, that when we arrive at the state of perfect manhood, the *worst* passions are apt to get the better of the more *noble*, as the prospect they present is more alluring to the eye of sense: all men (as I said before) being torn with the same propensities, it is *virtue* alone, or in other words, a strict *morality*, which prevents them from actuating alike in all. – But to return to the young *Natura.*

He was scarce ten years old when his mother died; but was not sensible of the misfortune he sustained by the loss of her, though, as it afterwards proved, was the greatest could have happened to him: the remembrance of the tenderness with which she had used him, joined to the sight of all the family in tears, made him at first indeed utter some bitter lamentations; but the thoughts of a new suit of mourning, a dress he had never yet been in, soon dissipated his grief, and the sight of himself before the great glass, in a habit so altogether strange, and therefore pleasing to him, took off all anguish for the sad occasion. – So early do we begin to be sensible of a satisfaction in any thing that we imagine is an advantage to our persons, or will make us be taken notice of. – How it grows up with us, and how difficult it is to be eradicated, I appeal even to those of the most sour and cynical disposition.

Mr. *Dryden* admirably describes this propensity in human nature in these lines:

> *Men are but children of a larger growth,*
> *Our appetites as prone to change as theirs,*
> *And full as craving too, and full as vain.*[9]

A Fondness for trifles is certainly no less conspicuous in age than youth; and we daily see it among persons of the best understanding, who wholly neglect every essential to real happiness in the pursuit of those very toys which children cry to be indulged in; even such as a bit of ribband, or the sound of a monosyllable tacked to the name; without considering that those badges of distinction, like bells about an ideot's neck, frequently serve only to render their folly more remarkable, and expose them to the contempt of the lookers on, who perhaps too, as nature is the same in all, want but the same opportunity to catch no less eagerly at the tawdry gewgaw.

Natura felt not the loss of his dear mother, till he beheld another in her place. His father entered into a second marriage before much more than half his year of widowhood was expired, with a lady, who, though pretty near his equal in years, had yet remains enough of beauty to render her extremely vain and affected, and fortune enough to make her no less proud. – These two qualities occasioned *Natura* many rebuffs, to which he had not been accustomed, and he felt them the more severely, as the name of mother had made him expect the same proofs of tenderness from this, who had the title, as he had remembered to have received from her who had been really so.

He endeavoured at first to insinuate himself into her favour by all those little flattering artifices which are so becoming in persons of his tender years, and which never fail to make an impression on a gentle and affable disposition; but finding his services not only rejected, but also rejected with scorn and moroseness, his spirit was too great to continue them for any long time; and all the assiduity he had shewn to gain her goodwill, was on a sudden converted into a behaviour altogether the reverse: he was sure to turn the deaf ear to all the commands she laid upon him, and so far from doing any thing to please her, he seemed to take a delight in vexing her. This occasioning many complaints to his father, drew on him very severe chastisements both at home and abroad; but though while the smart remained, he made many promises of amendment in this point, the hatred he had now conceived against her, would not suffer him to keep them.

His sister, who was five years older than himself, and a girl of great prudence, took a good deal of pains to convince him how much it was both his interest and his duty to pay all manner of respect to a lady whom their father had thought fit to sit over them; but all she could say on that head was thrown away, and he still replied, that since he could not make her love him, he should always hate her.

THIS young lady had perhaps no less reason than her brother to be dissatisfied with the humour of their stepmother; and it was only the tender affection she had for him which made her feign a contentment at the treatment both of them received, in order to keep him within any manner of bounds.

IT may be reckoned among the misfortunes of *Natura*, that he so soon lost the benefit of these kind remonstrances: his fair adviser having a considerable fortune, independent on her father, left her by a grandmother, who had also answered for her at the *font*, was courted by a gentleman, to whom neither herself nor family having any thing to object, she became a bride in a very few months, and went with her husband to a seat he had at a considerable distance in the country.

THIS poor youth was now without any one, either to prevent him from doing a fault, or to conceal it when committed; on the contrary, his mother-in-law, having new-modelled all the family, and retained only such servants as thought it their duty to study nothing but to humour her, every little error in him was exaggerated, and he was represented to his father as incorrigible, perverse, and all that is disagreeable in nature.

I WILL not take upon me to determine whether, or not, the old gentleman had altogether so ill an opinion of his son, as they endeavoured to inspire him with; but it is certain, that whatever his thoughts were on the matter, he found himself obliged for a quiet life to use him with a good deal of severity, which, either because he believed it unjust, or that it was disagreeable to his own disposition, he grew very weary of in a short time, and to put an end to it, resolved to send the child to a boarding-school, tho' he had always declared against that sort of education, and frequently said, that though these great schools might improve the learning, they were apt to corrupt the morals of youth.[10]

FINDING himself, however, under a kind of necessity for so doing, nothing remained but the choice of a convenient place. The wife proposed some part of *Yorkshire*, not only as the cheapest, but also that by reason of the distance, she should not have the trouble of him at home in the holidays; but to this it was not in her power to prevail on his father to consent, and after many disputes between them on it, *Eton* was at length pitched upon.

Natura heard of his intended removal with a perfect indifference: – if the thoughts of parting from his father gave him any pain, it was balanced by those of being eased of the persecuting of his stepmother; but when all things were prepared for his journey, in which he was to be accompanied by an old relation, who was to give the necessary charge with him to those into whose care he should be committed, he was taken suddenly ill on the very day he had been to take leave of his kindred, and other friends in town.

HIS distemper proved to be the small-pox, but being of a very favourable sort, he recovered in a short time, and lost nothing of his handsomeness by that so-much-dreaded enemy to the face: there remained, however, a little redness, which, till intirely worn off, it was judged improper he should be sent where it was likely there might be many young gentlemen, who having never experienced the same, would take umbrage at the sight.

DURING the time of his indisposition he had been attended by an old nurse, who had served in the same quality to his mother, and several others of her family. – The tenderness this good creature shewed to him, and the care she took to humour him in everything, not only while he continued in a condition, in which it might have been dangerous to have put his spirits into the least agitation, but after he was grown well enough to walk abroad, had made him become extremely pettish and self-willed; which shews, that an overindulgence to youth, is no less prejudicial, than too much austerity. – Happy is it for those who are brought up in a due proportion between these two extremes; for as nature will be apt to fall into a dejection, if pressed down with a constant, and uninterrupted severity, so it will infallibly become arrogant and assuming, if suffered always to pursue its own dictates. – Nothing is more evident, than that most of the irregularities we see practised in the world, are owing originally to a want of the medium I have been speaking of, in forming the mind while it is pliable to impression.

THIS was not, however, the case of *Natura*; and though he would doubtless have been what we call a spoiled child, had he been for any length of time permitted to do just what he pleased, yet the nurse being discharged, he fell again under the jurisdiction of his mother-in-law, who had now more excuse than ever for treating him with severity.

HIS father did not want understanding, but was a good deal more indolent than befits a parent. – He had always been accustomed to live at ease, and his natural aversion to all kinds of trouble, made him not inspect into the manners or temperament of his son, with that care he ought to have done. Whenever any complaints were made concerning his behaviour, he would chide, and sometimes beat him, but seldom examined how far he really merited those effects rather of others resentment than his own. Sometimes he would ask him questions on his progress in learning, and praise or dispraise, as he found occasion; but he never discoursed with him on any other topics, nor took any pleasure in instructing him in such things as are not to be taught in schools, but which much more contribute to enlarge the mind; so that had not *Natura*'s own curiosity led him to examine into the sources,[11] first causes, and motives of what he was obliged to read, he would have reaped no other benefit from his *Greek* and *Latin* authors, than meerly the knowledge of their language.

HERE I cannot help taking notice, that whatever inconveniences it may occasion, curiosity is one of the greatest advantages we receive from nature; it is that indeed from which all our knowledge is derived. – Were it not for this propensity in ourselves, the sun, the moon, and all the darling constellations which adorn the hemisphere, would roll above our heads in vain: contented to behold their shine, and feel their warmth, but ignorant of their motion and influence on all beneath, half that admiration due to the Divine Architect, would lye dormant in us. – Did not curiosity excite us to examine into the nature of vegetables, their amazing rise, their progress, their deaths and resurrections in the seasons allotted for these alternatives, we should enjoy the fruits of the earth indeed, but enjoy them only in common with the animals that feed upon it, or perhaps with less relish than they do, as it is agreed their organs of sensation have a greater share of poignancy than ours. – What is it but *curiosity* which renders study either pleasing or profitable to us? – The facts we read of would soon slip through the memory, or if they retained any place in it, could be of little advantage, without being acquainted with the motives which occasioned them. By *curiosity* we *examine,* by *examining* we *compare,* and by *comparing* we are alone enabled to form a right *judgment,* whether of things or persons.

WE are told indeed of many jealousies, discontents, and quarrels, which have been occasioned by this passion, among those who might otherwise have lived in perfect harmony; and a man or woman, who has the character of being too inquisitive, is shunned as dangerous to society. – But what commendable quality is there that may not be perverted, or what *virtue* whose extreme does not border on a *vice*? – Even *devotion* itself should have its bounds, or it will launch into *bigotry* and *enthusiasm*; – *love,* the most *generous* and *gentle* of all the passions, when ill-placed, or unprescribed, degenerates into the very *worst*; – *justice* may be pursued till it becomes *cruelty*; – *emulation* indulged till it grows up to *envy*; – *frugality* to the most sordid *avarice*; and *courage* to a brutal *rashness*; – and so I am ready to allow that *curiosity*, from whence all the *good* in us originally arises, may also be productive of the *greatest mischiefs*, when not, like every other emotion of the soul, kept within its due limits, and suffered to exert itself only on warrantable objects.

IT should therefore be the first care of every one to regulate this propensity in himself, as well as of those under whose tuition he may happen to be, whether parents or governors – Nature, and the writings of learned men, who from time to time have commented on all that has happened in nature, certainly afford sufficient matter to gratify the most enquiring mind, without descending to such mean trifling inquisitions, as can no way improve itself, and may be of prejudice to others.

I HAVE dwelt the longer on this head, because it seems to me, that on the *well*, or *ill direction* of that curiosity, which is inherent to us all, depends, in a great measure, the peace and happiness of society.

Natura, like all children, uncircumscribed by precept, had not only a desire of prying into those things which it was his advantage to know, but also into those which he had much better have been totally ignorant of, and which the discovery of his being too well skilled in, frequently occasioned him much ill will, especially when he was found to have too far dived into those little secrets which will ever be among servants in large families. But reason was not ripe enough in him to enable him to distinguish between what were proper subjects for the exercise of this passion, and what were not so.

THAT impediment, however, which had hitherto retarded his departure being removed, he now set out for *Eton*, under the conduct of the abovementioned kinsman, who placed him in a boarding-house very near the school, and took his leave, after having given him such admonitions as he thought necessary for a person of his years, when more intrusted to himself than he before had been.

BUT *Natura* was not yet arrived at an age wherein it could be expected he should reap much benefit from advice. A settled resolution, and the power of judging what is our real interest to do, are the perfections of maturity, and happy is it for the few who even then attain them. – *Precept* must be constantly and artfully instilled to make any impression on the mind, and is rarely fixed there, till experience confirms it;[12] therefore, as both these were wanting to form his behaviour, what could be hoped from it, but such a one as was conformable to the various passions which agitate human nature, and which every day grow stronger in us, at least till they have attained a certain crisis, after which they decay, in proportion as they increased.

AS *wrath* is one of the most violent emotions of the soul, so I think it is one of the first that breaks out into effects: it owes its birth indeed to *pride*; for we are never angry, unless touched by a real, or imaginary insult; but, by the offspring chiefly is the parent seen. *Pride* seldom, I believe it may be said, *never*, wholly dies in us, tho' it may be concealed; whereas *wrath* diminishes as our *reason* increases, and seems intirely evaporated after the heat of youth is over: when a man therefore has divested himself of the *one*, no tokens are left to distinguish the *other*. – Sometimes, indeed, we shall see an extreme impetuosity, even to old age, but then, it is out of the ordinary course of nature, and besides, the person possessed of it must be endued with a small share of sound understanding, to give any marks of such a propensity remaining in him.

IT is with the utmost justice, that by the system of the *christian* religion, *pride* is intitled the original sin,[13] not only as it was that of the fallen angels, but also as it is certainly the fountain-head from which all our other vices are derived. – It is by the dictates of this pernicious passion we are inflamed with *wrath*, and wild ambition, – instigated to covetousness, – to envy, – to revenge, and in fine, to stop at nothing which tends to self-gratification, be our desires of what kind so-ever.

DURING the school hours, *Natura*, as well as the other young gentlemen, was under too much awe of the master to give any loose to his temper; but when these were over, and they went together into the fields, or any other place to divert themselves, frequent quarrels among them ensued; but above all between those who boarded in the same house; little jealousies concerning some imaginary preference given to the one more than the other, occasioned many bitter taunts and fleers,[14] which sometimes rose to blows and bloody noses; so that the good people with whom they were, had enough to do, to keep them in any tolerable decorum.

THERE is also another branch of *pride* which is visible in all youth, before consideration takes place, and that is, treating with contempt whoever seems our inferior. – A boy who was allowed less money, or wore plainer cloaths, was sure to be the jest of all the rest. *Natura* was equally guilty of this fault with his companions; but when the sarcasms became too severe, and the object of them appeared any way dejected, his generosity often got the better of his arrogance, and he would take part with the weakest side, even till he drew on himself part of those reflections he averted from the other; but this never happened without his resenting it with the utmost violence; for patience and forbearance were virtues not to be expected in this stage of life.

HE was a great lover of gaming, whether of chucking, tossing up for money, or cards, and extremely ill-humoured and quarrelsome whenever luck was not on his side; which shews, that whatever people may pretend, avarice is at the bottom, and occasions all the fondness so many testify for play.

AS for the other ordinary diversions of youth, none could pursue them with more eagerness, nor was less deterred by any ill accident which befel either himself, or any of his companions; one of whom having been near drowning before his face, as they were swimming together, the sight did not hinder him from plunging into the same stream every day; nor could he be prevailed upon from ringing, as often as he had an opportunity, though he had been thrown one day by the breaking of the bell-rope, a great height from the ground, and in the fall dislocated his shoulder, and bruised his body all over. – But it is not to be wondered at, that boys should remember the misfortunes their pleasures have brought on them no longer than the smart continues, when men of the ripest, and sometimes most advanced years, are not to be warned from the gratification of their passions, by the worst, and most frequently repeated ills.

HE, notwithstanding, made a very good progress in those things in which he was instructed, which as yet were only *Latin* and *Greek*; and when the time of breaking up arrived, and he returned to his father's house, none who examined him concerning his learning, could suspect there was either any want of application in himself, or care in his master.

HIS three months of absence having rendered him a kind of stranger at home, his mother-in-law used him with somewhat more civility, and his father seemed highly satisfied with him; all his kindred and friends caressed him, and made him many little presents of such things as befitted his years; but that which crowned his felicity, was the company of a young girl, a near relation of his stepmother's, who was come to pass some time with her, and see *London*, which she had never been in before.

CHAP. III.

The early influence which the difference of sex excites, is here exemplified in the fond but innocent affection of Natura *and* Delia.

NATURA being much of the same age with *Delia* (for so I shall call her) and both equally playful, spirituous, and good-natured, it is hard to say which of them took the greatest delight in the society of the other. *Natura* was never well out of the presence of *Delia*, nor *Delia* contented but when *Natura* was with her.

In walking, dancing, playing at cards, these amiable children were always partners; and it was remarkable, that in the latter of these diversions, *Natura* was never uneasy at losing his money to *Delia*, nor resented any little railleries she treated him with on account of his ill luck, or want of skill in the game, as he had been accustomed to do whenever he received the like from any of his companions. – So forcibly does the difference of sex operate, even before that difference is considered.

Natura was yet too young by much, to know wherefore he found in himself this complaisance, or how it came to pass, that he so much preferred a beautiful and good-humoured girl, to a boy possessed of the same qualifications; but he was not ignorant that he did so, and has often wondered (as he afterwards confessed) what it was that made him feel so much pleasure, whenever, in innocently romping together, he happened to catch hold of her in his arms; and what strange impulse it was, that rendered him so reluctant to part with her out of that posture, that she was obliged to struggle with all her strength to disengage herself.

Hence it is plain, that the passion of love is part of our composition, implanted in the soul for the propagation of the world; and we ought not, in my opinion, to be too severe on the errors which, meerly and abstracted from any other motive than itself, it sometimes influences us to be guilty of. – The laws, indeed, which prohibit any amorous intercourse between the sexes, unless authorized by the solemnities of marriage, are without all question, excellently well calculated for the good of society, because without such a restriction, there would be no such thing as order in the world. I am therefore far from thinking lightly of that truly sacred institution, when I say, that there are some cases, in which the pair so offending, merit rather our pity, than that abhorrence which those of a more rigid virtue, colder constitution, or less under the power of temptation, are apt to testify on such occasions.

Rarely, however, it happens, that love is guilty of any thing capable of being condemned, even by the most austere; most of the faults committed under that function, being in reality instigated by some other passion, such as avarice and ambition in the one sex, and a flame which is too often confounded and mistaken for a pure affection in the other. – Yet such is the ill-judging, or careless determination of the world, that without making any allowances for circumstances, it censures all indiscriminately alike.

THE time prefixed for *Natura*'s remaining with his father being but fourteen days, as they grew near expired, the family began to talk of his going, and orders were given to bespeak a place for him in the stage-coach: he had been extremely pleased with *Eton*, nor had he met with any cause of disgust, either at the school or house where he was boarded, yet did the thoughts of returning thither give him as much disquiet as his young heart was capable of conceiving. – The parting from *Delia* was terrible to him, and the nearer the cruel moment approached, the more his anxiety increased. – She seemed also grieved to lose so agreeable a companion, and would often tell him she wished he was to stay as long as she did.

THOUGH nothing could be more innocent than these declarations on both sides, yet what she said had such an effect on *Natura*, that he resolved to delay his return to *Eton* as long as possible; and that passion which he already felt the symptoms of, though equally ignorant of their nature or end, being always fertile in invention, put a stratagem into his head, which he flattered himself would succeed for a somewhat farther continuance of his present happiness.

THE day before that prefixed for his going, he pretended a violent pain in his head and stomach, and to give the greater credit to his pretended indisposition, would eat nothing; and as it drew toward evening, cried out he was very sick, and must go to bed. – His father, who had the most tender affection for him, could not think of sending him away in that condition. – He went in the morning to his bedside, and finding him, as he imagined, a little feverish, presently ordered a physician, who did not fail to countenance the young gentleman's contrivance, either that he really thought him out of order, or that he had rendered himself so in good earnest, through abstaining from food, a thing very uncommon with him. A prescription was sent to the apothecary for him, and a certain regimen directed.

BUT poor *Natura* soon found this did not answer his purpose: – he was in the same house indeed with his beloved *Delia*, but had not the pleasure of her company, nor even that of barely seeing her, she being forbid going near his chamber, on account of the apprehensions they had that his complaint might terminate in a fever, and endanger her health.

THIS, however, was more than he knew, and resentment for her supposed indifference, joined with the weariness of living in the manner he did, made him resolve to grow well again, and chuse to go to *Eton*, rather than suffer so much for one who seemed so little to regard him.

ACCORDINGLY, when they brought him something had been ordered for him to take, he refused it, saying, he had not occasion for any more physic, and immediately got up, and dressed himself, in spite of all the servant that attended him could do to prevent it. – Word being carried to his father of what he was doing, he imagined him delirious, and immediately got up, and went into his room, nor though he found him intirely cool, could be perswaded from his first opinion. – The doctor was again sent for, who unwilling to lose his perquisite, made a long harangue on the nature of internal fevers, and very learnedly proved, or seemed to prove, that they might operate so far as to affect the brain, without the least outward symptom.

Natura could not forbear laughing within himself, to hear this great man so much mistaken; but when they told him he must take his physic, and go to bed, or at least be confined to his chamber, he absolutely refused both, and said he was as well as ever he was in his life. – All he said, however, availed nothing, and his father was about to make use of his authority to force him to obedience to the doctor's prescription, when finding no other way to avoid it, he fell on his knees, and with tears in his eyes, confessed he had only counterfeited sickness, to delay being sent to *Eton* again; begged his father to forgive him; said he was sorry for having attempted to deceive him, but was ready to go whenever he pleased.

The father was strangely amazed at the trick had been put upon him; and after some severe reprimands on the occasion, asked what he had to complain of at *Eton*, that had rendered him so unwilling to return. *Natura* hesitated at this demand, but could not find in his heart to forge any unjust accusation concerning his usage at that place, and at last said that indeed it was only because he had a mind to stay a little longer at home with him. On which he told him he was an idle boy, but he must not expect that wheedle would serve his turn; for since he was not sick, he must go to school the next day: *Natura* renewed his intreaties for pardon, and assured him he now desired nothing more than to do as he commanded.

This story made a great noise in the family, and the mother-in-law did not fail to represent it in its worst colours to every one that came to the house; but *Natura* having obtained forgiveness from his father, did not give himself much trouble as to the rest. – *Delia* seemed rejoiced to see him come down stairs again, but he looked shy upon her, and told her he could not have thought she would have been so unkind as not to have come to see him; but on her acquainting him with the reason of her absence, and protesting it was not her fault, he grew as fond of her as ever; and among a great many other tender expressions, *I wish,* said he, *I were a man, and you a woman.–Why?* returned she; *because,* cried he, *we would be married. – O fye,* answered the little coquet, *I should hate you, if you thought of any such thing; for I will never be married.* Then turned away with an affected scornfulness, and yet looked kindly enough upon him from the corner of one eye.–*I am sure,* resumed he, *if you loved me as well as I do you, you would like to be married to me, for then we should be always together.* – He was going on with something farther in this innocent courtship, when some one or other of the family, coming into the room, broke it off; and whether it was resumed afterwards, or not, I cannot pretend to determine, nor whether he had opportunity to take any particular leave of her before his departure, which happened, as his father had threatened, the succeeding day.

CHAP. IV.

Shews, that till we arrive at a certain age, the impressions made on us are easily erased; and also that when those which bear the name of love are once rooted in the mind, there are no lengths to which we may not be transported by that passion, if great care is not taken to prevent its getting the ascendant over reason.

THE change of scene did not make any change in the sentiments of our young lover: *Delia* was always in his head, and none of the diversions he took with his companions could banish her from his thoughts; yet did she not so wholly engross his attention, as to render him remiss in his studies; his ambition, as I said before, would not suffer him to neglect the means of acquiring praise, and nothing was so insupportable to him as to find at any time another boy had merited a greater share of it: by which we may perceive that this very passion, unruly as it is, and in spite of the mischiefs it sometimes occasions, is also bestowed upon us for our emolument; and when properly directed, is the greatest excitement to all that is noble and generous. *Natura* seldom had the mortification of seeing any of the same standing with himself placed above him; and whenever such an accident happened, he was sure to retrieve it by an extraordinary assiduity.

BUT to shew that love and business are not wholly incompatible, his attachment to *Delia* did not take him off his learning, nor did his application to learning make him forgetful of *Delia*. He frequently thought of her, wished to see her, and longed for the next breaking-up, that he might re-enjoy that satisfaction, as he knew she intended to stay the whole winter at his father's; but now arrived the time to prove the inconstancy of human nature: he became acquainted with some other little misses, and by degrees found charms in them, which made those he had observed in *Delia* appear less admirable in his eyes: the fondness he had felt for her being in reality instigated chiefly by being the only one of his own age he had conversed with, a more general acquaintance with others not only wore off the impression she had made, but also kept him from receiving too deep a one from the particular perfections of any of those he now was pleased with: – it is likely, however, that the sight of her might have revived in him some part of his former tenderness, had he found her, as he expected he should, on his next coming to *London*: but an elder sister she had in the country, happening to die, she was sent for home, in order to console their mother for that loss; so that he had not any trial on that account; and tho' he thought he should have been glad of her society, during his stay in town, yet her absence gave him small anxiety; and the variety of company which came to the house on account of the baptism of a little son his mother-in-law had lately brought into the world, very well atoned for the want of *Delia*.

NOTHING material happening to him during his stay in town at this time, nor in any other of the many visits he made his father while he continued at *Eton*; I shall pass over those years, and only say, that as he grew nearer to manhood, his passions gathered strength in proportion; and tho' he increased in knowledge, yet it was not that sort of knowledge which enables us to judge of the emotions we feel within ourselves, or to set curbs on those, which to indulge renders us liable to inconveniences.

ALL those propensities, of which he gave such early indications, and which I attempted to describe in the beginning of this book, now displayed themselves with greater vigour, and according as exterior objects presented, or circumstances excited, ruled with alternate sway: sparing sometimes to niggardliness, at others profusely liberal; – now pleased, now angry; – submissive this moment, arrogant and assuming the next; – seldom in a perfect calm, and frequently agitated to excess. – Hence arose contests and quarrels, even with those whose company in some humours he was most delighted with; – insolence to such whose way of thinking did not happen to tally with his own, and as partial an attachment to those who either did, or pretended to enter into his sentiments.

BUT as it was only in trivial matters, and such as were meerly boyish, he yet had opportunity of exercising the passions, his behaviour only served to shew what man would be, when arrived at maturity, if not restrained by precept.

HE had attained to little more than sixteen years of age, when he had gone through all the learning of the school, and was what they call fit for the university, to which his father not intending him for the study of any particular science, did not think it necessary to send him, but rather to bestow on him those other accomplishments, which are immediately expected from a gentleman of an estate; such as fencing, dancing, and music, and accordingly provided masters to instruct him in each, as soon as he came home, which was about the time of life I mentioned.

AS he was now past the age of being treated as a meer child, and also knew better how it would become him to behave to the wife of his father, his mother-in-law seemed to live with him in harmony enough, and the family at least was not divided into parties as it had been, and eighteen or nineteen months past over, without any rub in our young gentleman's tranquility.

SINCE his childish affection for *Delia*, he had not been possessed of what could be called a strong inclination for any particular female; though, as many incidents in his life afterwards proved, he had a no less amorous propensity than any of his sex, and was equally capable of going the greatest lengths for its gratification.

He was but just turned of nineteen, when happening to pass by the play-house one evening, he took it into his head to go in, and see the last act of a very celebrated tragedy acted that night. – But it was not the poet's or the player's art which so much engaged his attention, as the numerous and gay assembly which filled every part of the house. – He was in the back bench of one of the front boxes, from which he had a full prospect of all who sat below: – but in throwing his eyes around on every dazzling belle, he found none so agreeable to him as a young lady who was placed in the next division of the box: – her age did not seem to exceed his own, and tho' less splendid in garb and jewels than several who sat near her, had something in her eyes and air, that, in his opinion, at least, infinitely exceeded them all.

When the curtain dropt, and every one was crowding out as fast they could, he lost not sight of her; and finding when they came out to the door, that she, and a companion she had with her, somewhat older than herself, seemed distressed for chairs, which by reason of the great concourse, seemed difficult to be got, he took the opportunity, in a very polite manner, to offer himself for their protector, as he perceived they had neither friend nor servant with them. They accepted it with a great deal of seeming modesty, and he conducted them through a passage belonging to the house which he knew was less thronged, and thence put them into a hackney coach, having first obtained their permission to attend them to their lodgings, or wherever else they pleased to be set down.

When they arrived at the place to which they gave the coachman a direction, he would have taken leave of them at the door; but they joined in entreating him, that since he had been at the pains of bringing them safe home, he would come in and refresh himself with such as their apartment could supply: there required little invitation to a thing his heart so sincerely wished, tho' his fears of being thought too presuming, would not suffer him to ask it.

He went up stairs, and found rooms decently furnished, and a maid-servant immediately spread the table with a genteel cold collation; but what he looked upon as the most elegant part of the entertainment, was the agreeable chit-chat during the time of supper, and a song the lady who had so much attracted him, gave him, at her friend's request, after the cloth was taken away.

It growing late, his fears of offending where he already had such an inclination to oblige, made him about to take his leave; but could not do it without intreating permission to wait on them the next day, to receive pardon, as he said, for having by his long stay, broke in upon the hours should have been devoted to repose. Tho' this compliment, and indeed all the others he had made, were directed to both, the regard his eyes paid to the youngest, easily shewed the preference he secretly gave to her; and as neither of these women wanted experience in such affairs, knew very well how to make the most of any advantage. *If this lodging were mine,* replied the eldest briskly, *I should have anticipated the request you make; but as I am only a guest, and take part of my friend's bed to-night on account of the hour, will take upon me to say, she ought not to refuse greater favours to so accomplished a gentlemen, and from whom we have received so much civility.*

Natura did not fail to answer this gallantry in a proper manner, and departed highly satisfied with his adventure; tho' probably could find less reasons for being so, than those with whom he thought it the greatest happiness of his life to have become acquainted.

Wonderful are the workings of love on a young heart: pleasure has the same effect as pain, and permits as little rest: it was not in the power of *Natura* to close his eyes for a long time after he went to bed. – He recollected every thing the dear creature had said; – in what manner she looked, when speaking such or such a thing; – how inchanting she sang, and what a genteelness accompanied all she did: – when he fell into a slumber, it was only to bring her more perfectly into his mind; whatever had past in the few hours he had been with her, returned with additional graces on her part, and her idea had in sleep all the effect her real presence could have had in waking.

With what care did he dress himself the next day: – what fears was he not possessed of, lest all about him should not be exact: – never yet had he consulted the great glass with such assiduity; – never till now examined how far he had been indebted to nature for personal endowments.

His impatience would have carried him to pay a morning visit, but he feared that would be too great a freedom, and therefore restrained himself till after dinner, though what he eat could scarce be called so; the food his *mind* languished for, being wanting, the body was too complaisant to indulge itself. – After rising from table, not a minute passed without looking on his watch, and at the same time cursing the tedious seconds, which seemed to him increased from sixty to six hundred. – The hour of five at length put an end to his suspence, and he took his way to the dear, well-remembered mansion of his adorable.

He found her at home, and in a careless, but most becoming dishabillee;[15] the other lady was still with her; and told him she had tarried thus long with miss *Harriot*, for so she called her, meerly to participate of the pleasure of his good company. *Harriot*, in a gay manner, accused her of envy, and both having a good share of wit, the conversation might have been pleasing enough to a man less prepossessed than *Natura.*

The tea equipage was set, and the ceremony of that being over, cards were proposed; as they were three, *Ombre* was the game, at which they played some hours, and *Natura* was asked to sup. – After what I have said, I believe the reader has no occasion to be told that he complied with a pleasure which was but too visible in his eyes. – The time passed insensibly on, or at least seemed to do so to the friend of *Harriot*, till the watchman reminding her it was past eleven, she started up, and pretending a surprize, that the night was so far advanced, told

Natura that she must exact a second proof of that gallantry he had shewn the night before, for she had not courage to go either in a chair or a coach alone at that late hour: – this doubtless was what he would have offered, had she been silent on the occasion; and a coach being ordered to the door, he took leave of miss *Harriot*, though not till he had obtained leave to testify his respects in some future visits.

HAD *Natura* appeared to have more experience of the town, the lady he gallanted home would certainly not have entertained him with the discourse she did; but his extreme youth, and the modest manner of his behaviour on the first sight of him, convinced them he was a person such as they wished to have in their power, and to that end had concerted measures between themselves, to perfect the conquest which, it was easy to perceive, one of them had begun to make over him.

HARRIOT being the person with whom they found he was enamoured, it was the business of the other to do for her what, it may be supposed, she would have done for her on the like occasion. – *Natura* was no sooner in the coach with her, than she began to magnify the charms of her fair friend, but above all extolled her virtue, her prudence, and good humour: – then, as if only to give a proof of her patience and fortitude, that her parents dying when she was an infant, had left her with a vast fortune in the hands of a guardian, who attempting to defraud her of the greatest part, she was now at law with him, *and is obliged to live, till the affair is decided,* said this artful woman, *in the narrow manner you see, – without a coach – without any equipage; and yet she bears it all with chearfulness: – she has a multiplicity of admirers,* added she, *but she assures all of them, that she will never marry, till she knows what present she shall be able to give with herself to the man she shall make choice of.*

TILL now *Natura* had never asked himself the question how far his passion for *Harriot* extended, or with what view he should address her; but when he heard she was a woman of condition, and would have a fortune answerable to her birth; he began to think it would be happy for him if he could obtain her love on the most honourable terms.

IT would be too tedious to relate all the particulars of his courtship; so I shall only say, that humble and timid as the first emotions of a sincere passion are, he was emboldened, by the extraordinary complaisance of *Harriot*, to declare it to her in a few days. – The art with which she managed on this occasion, might have deceived the most knowing in the sex: it is not, therefore, surprizing, that he should be caught in a snare, which, though ruinous as it had like to have been, had in it allurements scarce possible to be withstood at his time of life.

IT was by such degrees as the most modest virgin need not blush to own, that she confessed herself sensible of an equal tenderness for him; and nothing is more strange, than that in the transport he was in, at the condescensions she made him, that he did not immediately press for the consummation of his happiness by marriage; but tho' he wished for nothing so much, yet he was with-held by the fears of his father, who he thought would not approve of such a step, as the fortune he imagined she had a right to, was yet undetermined, and himself, tho' an elder son, and the undoubted heir of a very good estate, at present wholly dependant on him. – He communicated his sentiments to *Harriot* on this head with the utmost sincerity, protesting at the same time that he should never enjoy a moment's tranquility till he could call her his own.

SHE seemed to approve of the caution he testified, – said it was such as she had always resolved religiously to observe herself; *tho' I know not,* cried she, looking on him with the most passionate air, *how far I might have been tempted to break thro' all for your sake; but it is well one of us is wise enough to foresee and tremble at the consequences of a marriage between two persons whose fortunes are unestablished*. – Then, finding he made her no other answer than some kisses, accompanied with a strenuous embrace, she went on; *there is a way,* resumed she, *to secure us to each other, without danger of disobliging any body; and that is by a contract: I never can be easy, while I think there is a possibility of your transferring your affection to some other, and if you love me with half that degree of tenderness you pretend, you cannot but feel the same anxiety.*

NATURA was charmed with this proposition, and it was agreed between them, that her lawyer should draw up double contracts in form, which should be signed and delivered interchangeably by both parties. Accordingly, the very next day, the fatal papers were prepared, and he subscribed his name to that which was to remain in her custody, as she did her's to that given to him. Each being witnessed by the woman with whom he first became acquainted with her, and another person called into the room for that purpose.

NATURA now considering her as his wife, thought himself intitled to take greater liberties than he had ever presumed to do before,[16] and she had also a kind of a pretence for permitting them, till at last there remained nothing more for him to ask, or her to grant.

ENJOYMENT made no abatement in his passion; his fondness was rather increased by it, and he never thought himself happy, but when with her; he went to her almost every night, and sometimes passed all night with her, having made an interest with one of the servants, who let him in at whatever hour he came: – so totally did she engross his mind, that he seemed to have not the least attention for any thing beside: nor was the time he wasted with her all the prejudice she did him: – all the allowance made him by his father for cloaths and other expences, he dissipated in treats and presents to her, running in debt for every thing he had occasion for.

BUT this was insufficient for her expectations; she wanted a sum of money, and pretending that her law-suit required a hundred guineas immediately, and that some remittances she was to have from the country would come too late, told him he must raise it for her some way or other.

THIS demand was a kind of thunder-stroke to *Natura*; not but he doated on her enough to have sacrificed infinitely more to her desires, if in his power; but what she asked seemed so wholly out of reach, that he knew not any way by which there was the least probability of attaining it. The embarrassment that appeared in his countenance made her see it was not so easy for him to grant, as it was for her to ask. *I should have wanted courage,* said she, *to have made you this request, had I not considered that what is mine must one day be yours, and it will be your own unhappiness as well as mine, should my cause miscarry for want of means to carry it on. – Severe necessity!* added she, letting fall some tears, *that reduces me to intreat favours where I could wish only to bestow them.*

THESE words destroyed all the remains of prudence his love had left in him; he embraced her, kissed away her tears, and assured her that though, as he was under age, and had but a small allowance from his father, it was not at this time very easy for him to comply with her demand, yet she might depend upon him for the money the next day, let it cost what it would, or whatever should be the consequence.

HE left her that night much sooner than was his custom, in order to consult within himself on the means of fulfilling his promise to her, which, to have failed in, would have been more terrible to him than death.

CHAP. V.

That to indulge any one fault, brings with it the temptation of committing others, is demonstrated by the behaviour of Natura, *and the misfortunes and disgrace which an ill-judged shame had like to have involved him in.*

NEVER had *Natura* experienced so cruel a night; a thousand stratagems came into his head, but for some reason or other all seemed alike impracticable, and the morning found him in no more easy a situation. – He put on his cloaths hastily, and resolved to go to all the acquaintance he had in the world, and try the friendship of each, by borrowing what sums he thought they might be able to spare: but first, going into his father's closet, as was his custom every morning to pay his duty to him, he found a person with him who was paying him a large sum of money: the sight of what he so much wanted filled him with inexpressible agitations: – he would have given almost a limb to have had in his possession so much of that shining ore as *Harriot* expected from him; and wished that some sudden accident, even to the falling of the house, would happen, that in the confusion he might seize on some part of the treasure he saw before him.

THE person, after the affair which brought him there was over, took leave of the father of *Natura*, who having thrown the money into his bureau, to a large heap was there before, waited on him down stairs, without staying to lock the drawer.

OFTEN had *Natura* been present when his father received larger sums than this, and doubtless had the same opportunity as now to make himself master of some part, or all of it; but never till this unhappy exigence had the least temptation to do so. – It came into his head that the accident was perfectly providential, and that he ought not to neglect the only means by which he could perform his promise; – that his father could very well spare the sum he wanted, and that it was only taking before the time what by inheritance must be his own hereafter. – In this imagination he opened the drawer, and was about to pursue his intention, when he recollected that the money would certainly be missed, and either the fault be laid upon some innocent person, who might suffer for his crime; or he himself would be suspected of a thing, which, in this second thought, he found so mean and wicked, that he was shocked almost to death, for having been capable of even a wish to be guilty of it. – He shut the drawer again, – turned himself away, and was in the utmost confusion of mind, when his father returned into the room; which shews that there is a native honesty in the human nature, which nothing but a long practice of base actions can wholly eradicate: and I dare believe that even those we see most hardened in vice, have felt severe struggles within themselves at first, and have often looked back upon the paths of virtue, wishing, tho' fruitlesly, to return.

NATURA, however, did not give over his pursuit of the means of performing his promise: on the contrary, he thought himself obliged by all the ties of love, honour, and even self-interest, to do it; but difficult as he believed the task would be, he found it much more so than he could even have imagined: his intimacy being only with such, as being much of his own age, and like him were at an allowance from their parents or guardians, it was not in the power of any of them to contribute a large sum toward making up that he wanted; the most he got from any one being no more than five guineas, and all he raised among the whole amounted to no more than twenty, and some odd pounds.

DISTRACTED with his ill fortune, he ventured to go to an uncle he had by the mother's side, and after many complaints of his father's parsimony, told him, that having been drawn into some expences, which, though not extravagant, were more than his little purse could supply, he had broke into some money given him to pay his taylor, whom he feared would demand it of his father, and he knew not how far the ill-will of his mother-in-law might exaggerate the matter; concluding with an humble petition for twenty guineas, which he told him he would faithfully return by degrees.

AS *Natura* had the character of a sober youth, the good old gentleman was moved by the distress he saw him in, and readily granted his request, tho' not without some admonitions to confine for the future his expences to his allowance, be it ever so small.

THUS *Natura* having with all his diligence not been able to raise quite half of the sum in question, was quite distracted what to do, and as he afterwards owned, more than once repented him of those scruples which had prevented him from serving himself at once out of his father's purse; tho' had the same opportunity again presented itself, it is scarce possible to believe by the rest of his behaviour, that he would have made use of it, or if he had, that he could have survived the shame and remorse it would have caused in him.

IN his desperation he ran at last to the house of a noted money-scrivener,[17] a great acquaintance of the family, and in his whose hands his father frequently reposed his ready cash: to this man he communicates his distress, and easily prevails with him to let him have fifty pounds, on giving him a note to pay him an hundred for it when he should come of age, his father having said he would then make a settlement on him.

THIS, however, was still somewhat short of what *Harriot* had demanded; but he left his watch at a pawn-broker's for the rest; and having compleated the sum, went transported with joy, and threw it into the lap of that idol of his soul; after which, he was for some days perfectly at ease, indulging himself with all he at present wished for, and losing no time in thought of what might happen to interrupt his happiness.

BUT while he battened in the sun-shine of his pleasures, storms of vexation were gathering over his head, which, when he least expected such a shock, poured all their force upon him.

THE first time his uncle happened to see his father, he fell on the topic of the necessity there was for young gentlemen born to estates, and educated in a liberal manner, to be enabled to keep his equals company; adding, that if the parsimony of a parent, denied them an allowance, agreeable to their rank, it might either drive them to ill courses, or force them to associate themselves only with mean, low-bred people, among whom they might lose all the politeness had been inculcated into them. The father of *Natura*, well knowing he had nothing to answer for on this account, never suspected this discourse was directed to him in particular, and joined in his brother-in-law's opinion, heartily blaming those parents, who, by being too sparing to their children, destroyed all natural affection in them, and gave them some sort of an excuse for wishing for their death: – he thanked God he was not of that disposition, and then told him what he allowed *per* quarter to *Natura*, *with which,* added he, *I believe he is intirely satisfied.* The other replying, that indeed he thought it more than sufficient, the conversation dropped; but what sentiments he now began to conceive of his nephew it is easy to conceive; the father however thought no farther of this, till soon after the scrivener came to wait on him: – he was a perfect honest man, and had lent

Natura the money meerly to prevent his applying to some other person, who possibly might have taken advantage of his thoughtlessness, so far as even to have brought on his utter ruin, too many such examples daily happening in the world: to deter him also from going on in this course, he demanded that exorbitant interest for his money abovementioned, which, notwithstanding, as he assured his father, in relating to him the whole transaction, he was far from any intention to make him pay.

NEVER was astonishment greater than that in which the father of *Natura* was now involved: – the discourse of his brother-in-law now came fresh into his mind, and he recollected some words which, tho' he did not observe at the time they were spoken, now convinced him had a meaning which he could not have imagined there was any room for. – He had no sooner parted from the scrivener, than he flew to that gentleman, and having related to him what had passed between him and the scrivener, conjured him, if he could give him any farther lights into the affair, not to keep him in ignorance: on which the other thought it his duty to conceal nothing, either of the complaints or request had been made him by his nephew: – after some exclamations on the extravagance and thoughtlessness of youth, the afflicted father went in search of more discoveries, which he found it but too easy to make among the tradesmen, all of whom he found had been unpaid for some time.

IT would be needless to go about to make any description of the confusion of mind he was in: – he shut himself in his closet, uncertain for some time how he should proceed; at last, as he considered there was not a possibility of reclaiming his son from whatever vice had led him thus all at once into such extravagancies, without first knowing what kind of vice it was; he resolved to talk to him, and penetrate, if possible, into the source of this evil.

ACCORDINGLY the next morning he went into the chamber where *Natura* was yet in bed; and began to entertain him in the manner he had proposed to himself: – first, he let him know, that he was not unacquainted with every step he had taken for raising a sum, which he could not conceive he had any occasion for, as well as his having with-held the money he had given him to discharge his tradesmen's bills: – then proceeded to set before his eyes the folly and danger of having hid, at his years, any secrets from a parent, concluding with telling him, he had yet a heart capable of forgiving what was past, provided he would behave in a different manner for the future.

WHAT *Natura* felt at finding so much of what he had done revealed to his father, was greatly alleviated, by perceiving that the main thing, his engagement with *Harriot*, was a secret to him: – he did not fail to make large promises of being a better œconomist, nor to express the most dutiful gratitude for the pardon the good old gentleman so readily offered; but this he told him was not sufficient to deserve a re-establishment in his favour, he must also give him a faithful account by what company, and for what purposes he had been induced to such ill husbandry; *for,* added he, *without a sincere confession of the motives of our past transactions, there can be little assurances of future amendment.*

NATURA to this only answered, that it was impossible to recount the particulars of his expences, and made so many evasions, on his father's still continuing to press his being more explicit, that he easily perceived there would be no coming at the truth by gentle means; and therefore, throwing off at once a tenderness so ineffectual, he assumed all the authority of an offended parent, and told the trembling *Natura,* that since he knew not how to behave as a *son,* he should cease to be a *father,* in every thing but in his authority: – *be assured,* said he, *I shall take sure measures to prevent you from bringing either ruin or disgrace upon a family of which you are the first profligate: – this chamber must be your prison, till I have considered in what fashion I shall dispose of you.*

WITH these words he flung out of the room, locking the door after him; so that when *Natura* rose, as he immediately did, he found himself indeed under confinement, which seemed so shameful a thing to him, that he was ready to tear himself in pieces: – it was not the grief of having offended so good a father, but the disgrace of the punishment inflicted on him, which gave him the most poignant anguish,[18] and far from feeling any true contrition, he was all rage and madness, which having no means to vent in words, discovered itself in sullenness: – when the servant to whom he intrusted the key came in to bring him food, he refused to eat, and could scarce restrain himself from throwing in the man's face what he had brought.

IT is certain, that while under this circumstance, he was agitated at once by every different unruly passion: – pride, anger, spleen, thinking himself a man, at finding the treatment of a *boy,* made him almost hate the person from whom he received it. – The apprehensions what farther meaning might be couched in the menace with which his father left him, threw him sometimes into a terror little different from convulsive; – but above all, his impatience for seeing his dear *Harriot,* and the surprize, the grief, and perhaps the resentment, he imagined she must feel on his absenting himself, drove him into a kind of despair.

IN fine, unable to sustain the violence of his agitations, on the third night, regardless of what consequences might ensue from giving this additional cause of displeasure to his father, he found means to push back the lock of his chamber, and flew down stairs, and out at the street-door with so much speed, that it would have been impossible to have stopped him, had any one heard him, which none happened to do, it being midnight, and all the family in a sound sleep.

THAT he went directly to the lodgings of *Harriot,* I believe my reader will make no doubt; but perhaps her character does not yet enough appear, to give any suspicion of the reception he found there.

In effect, she was no other than one of those common creatures, who procure a miserable subsistance by the prostitution of their charms; and as nature had not been sparing to her on that score, and she was yet young, though less so than she appeared thro' art, she wanted not a number of gallants, who all contributed, more or less, to her living in the manner she did: several of these had happened to come when *Natura* was with her; but she having had the precaution to acquaint them with her design of drawing in this young spark for a husband, they took the cue she gave them, each passing before him either for a cousin, or one of the lawyers employed in her pretended suit.

It was with one of these equally happy, tho' less deluded rivals of *Natura*, that finding he did not come, she had agreed to pass this night; and her maid, as the servants of such women, for the most part, imitate their mistresses, happened to be at the door, either about to introduce, or let out a lover of her own; – the sight of a man at that time of night, with one who belonged to his beloved, immediately fired *Natura* with jealousy: – he seized the fellow by the collar, and in a voice hoarse with rage, asked him what business he had there? To which the other replied only with a blow on the face, the wench shrieked out, but *Natura* was either stronger or more nimble than his competitor; he presently tripped up his heels, and ran up stairs. – *Harriot* and her lover hearing somewhat of a scuffle, the latter started out of bed, and opened the chamber-door, in order to listen what had occasioned it, just as *Natura* had reached the stair-case. – If his soul was inflamed before, what must it now have been, to see a man in his shirt, and just risen from the arms of *Harriot*, who still lay trembling in bed: – he flew upon him like an incensed lion; but the other being more robust, soon disengaged himself and snatching his sword, which lay on a table near the door, was going to put an end to the life of his disturber; when *Harriot* cried out, *Hold! hold! – for heaven's sake! – It is my husband!* –*Natura* having no weapon wherewith he might defend himself, or hurt his adversary, revenge gave way to self-preservation; and only saying, *husband, no; – I will die rather than be the husband of so vile a woman*, run down with the same precipitation he had come up.

Impossible it is to describe the condition of his mind when got into the street: – his once violent affection was now converted into the extremest hatred and contempt; – he detested not only *Harriot*, and the whole sex, but even himself, for having been made the dupe of so unworthy a creature, and could have tore out his own heart, for having joined with her in deceiving him. – Having wandered about some time, giving a loose to his fury, the considerations of what he should do, at last took their turn: – home he could not go, the servant who used to admit him knew nothing of his being out, and he durst not alarm the family by knocking at the door, having passed by several times, and found all fast.

In this perplexity, as he went through a street he had not been used to frequent, he saw a door open, and a great light in a kind of hall, with servants attending: – he asked one of them to whom it belonged, and was told it was a gaming-house, on which he went in, not with any desire of playing, but to pass away some time; finding a great deal of company there, he notwithstanding engaged himself at one of the tables, and tho' he was not in a humour which would permit him to exert much skill, he won considerably.

THE company did not break up till five in the morning, and he then growing drowsy, and yet unable to find any excuse to make to his father, he could not think of seeing his face, so went to a bagnio[19] to take that repose he had sufficient need of, the fatigues of his mind having never suffered him to enjoy any sound sleep, since his father's discovery of the extravagance he had been guilty of.

ON his awaking, the transaction of the preceding night returned to his remembrance with all its galling circumstances, and the more he reflected on his disobedience to his father, the less he could endure the thoughts of coming into his presence: – in fine, that shame which so often prevents people from doing amiss, was now the motive which restrained him from doing what he ought to have done. – Had he immediately gone home, thrown himself at his father's feet, and confessed the truth, his youthful errors had doubtless merited forgiveness; but this, though he knew twas both his duty, and his interest, he could not prevail on himself to do; and to avoid the rebukes he was sensible were due to his transgressions, he resolved to hide himself as long as he could from the faces of all those who had a right to make them.

IN fine, he led the life of a perfect vagabond, sculking from one place to another, and keeping company with none but gamesters, rakes, and sharpers, falling into all manner of dissolution; and whenever his reason remonstrated any thing to him on these vicious courses, he would then, to banish remorse for one fault, fly to others, yet worse, and more destructive.

IT is true, he often looked back upon his *former* behaviour, and was struck with horror at comparing it with the *present*; – the reflection too how much his mother-in-law might take advantage of the just displeasure of his father against him, to prejudice him in his future fortune, even to cause him to be disinherited, sometimes most cruelly alarmed him; yet, not all this, nor the wants he was plunged in on an ill run at play, (which was the sole means by which he subsisted) were sufficient to bring him to do that which he now even wished to do, tired with the conversation of those profligates, and secretly shocked at the scenes of libertinism he was a daily witness of.

HIS thoughts thus divided and perplexed, he at length fell into a kind of despair; and not caring what became of himself, he resolved to enter on board some ship, and never see *England* again, unless fortune should do more than he had reason to hope for in his favour.

CHAP. VI.

Shews the great force of natural affection, and the good effects it has over a grateful mind.

IF children could be sensible of parental tenderness, or knew what racking cares attend every misdoing of an offending offspring, the heart of *Natura* would have been so much touched with what his father endured on his account, as to have enabled him to have got the better of that guilty shame, which alone hindered him from submitting to him; but conscious of deserving only the severest reproofs, he could not flatter himself there was a hope of ever being reinstated in that affection he had once possessed, and was too proud to content himself with less.

THAT afflicted parent being informed of his son's plight, spared no cost or pains to find out the place of his retreat; but all his enquiries were in vain, and he was wholly in the dark, till it came into his head to search a little escritoire which stood in his chamber, and of which he had taken away the key: on breaking it open, he found the counterpart of his contract with *Harriot*, and by that discovery was no longer at a loss for the motives which had obliged his son to raise money, not doubting but the woman was either extremely indigent, or a jilt: but to think the heir of his estate had been so weak as to enter into so solemn and irretrievable an engagement, with a person of either of these characters, gave him an inexpressible disquiet. All his endeavours were now bent on finding her out, not in the least questioning but his son was with her: the task was pretty difficult, the contract discovering no more of her than her name, and the parish in which she lived; yet did the emissaries he employed at last surmount it: they brought him word not only of the exact place where she lodged, but also of her character, as they learned it from the neighbours; they heard also that a young gentleman, whose description answered that of *Natura*, had been often seen with her, and that she had given out she was married to him.

THE father having received this information, consulted with his brother-in-law what course was to be taken, and both being of opinion, that should any enquiry be made concerning *Natura*, it would only oblige them to quit their lodgings, and fly to some place where, perhaps, it would be more difficult to trace them; it was agreed to get a lord chief justice's warrant, and search her lodgings, without giving any previous alarm.

THIS was no sooner resolved than put in execution: the father and uncle, attended by proper officers, burst into the house, and examined carefully every part of it; but not finding him, they sought, and perfectly perswaded *Harriot* could give intelligence of him, they threatened her severely, and here she displayed herself in her proper colours; – nothing ever behaved with greater impudence: – she told them, that she knew nothing of the fool they wanted; but if she could find him, would make him know what the obligations between them exacted from him: in fine, it was easy for them to perceive, there was nothing satisfactory to be obtained from her, and they departed with akeing hearts, but left not the street without securing to their interest a person in the neighbourhood, who promised to keep a continual eye upon her door, and if they ever saw the young gentleman go in, to send them immediate notice.

It is needless to acquaint the reader how fruitless this precaution was: *Natura* was far from any inclination ever more to enter that detested house, and in that desponding humour, already mentioned, had certainly left the kingdom, and compleated his utter undoing, if Providence had not averted his design, by the most unexpected means.

He was at *Wapping*, in the company of some persons who used the sea, in order to get into some ship, he cared not in what station, when a young man, clerk to an eminent merchant of his father's acquaintance, happened to come in, to enquire after the master of a vessel, by whom some goods belonging to his master were to be shipped: he had often seen *Natura*, and though much altered by his late way of living, knew him to be the person whom he had heard so great a search had been made after: he took no notice of him however, as he found the other bent earnestly in discourse did not observe him, but privately informed himself of all he could relating to his business there, and as soon as he came home acquainted his master with the discovery he had made, who did not fail to let his father know it directly.

It is hard to say, whether joy at hearing of his son, or grief at hearing he was in so miserable a condition, was most predominant in him; but the first emotions of both being a little moderated, the consideration of what was to be done, took place: – the clerk having found out that he was lodged in an obscure house at that place, in order to get on board the first ship that sailed, the father would needs go himself, and the merchant offering to accompany him in their little journey, a plan of proceeding was formed between them, which was executed in the following manner.

They went together into a tavern, and sent to the house the clerk had directed, under pretence, that hearing a young man was there who had an inclination for the sea, a master of a ship would be glad to treat with him on that affair. – *Natura*, happily for him, not having yet an opportunity of engaging himself, obeyed the summons, and followed the messenger: – his father withdrew into another room, but so near as to hear what passed, and there was only the merchant to receive him; but the sight of one he so little expected in that place, and whom he knew was so intimate in their family, threw him into a most terrible consternation. He started back, and had certainly quitted the house, if the merchant, aware of his intention, had not catched hold of him, and getting between him and the door, compelled him to sit down while he talked to him.

HE began with asking what had induced him to think of leaving *England* in the manner he was going to do; – reminded him of the estate to which he was born, the family from which he was descended, and the education which he had received; and then set before his eyes the tenderness with which his father had used him, the grief to which he had exposed him, and above all the madness of his present intentions: – *Natura* knew all this as well as he that remonstrated to him; but as he had not been capable of listening to his own reflections on that head, all that was said had not the least effect upon him, and the merchant could get no other answer from him, than that as things had happened, he had no other course to take.

THE truth was, that as he could not imagine by what means the merchant was apprized of his design, he thought his father was also not ignorant of it; and as he did not vouchsafe either to come in person, or send any message to him from himself, and perhaps was even ignorant that the merchant had any intention of reclaiming him, he looked upon it as a confirmation of his having intirely thrown off all care of him, and in this supposition he became more resolute than ever in his mind, to go where he never might be heard of more.

WHAT though, said the merchant, *you have been guilty of some youthful extravagancies, I am perfectly assured there requires no more than your submitting to intreat forgiveness, to receive: come,* continued he, *I will undertake to be your mediator, and dare answer I shall prevail. – No, sir,* replied Natura, *I am conscious of having offended beyond all possibility of a pardon; – nor can I ever bear to see my father again.*

THE merchant laboured all he could to overcome this mingled pride and shame, which he perceived was the only obstacle to his return to duty; but to no purpose, *Natura* continued obstinate and inflexible, till his father, having no longer patience to keep himself concealed, rushed into the room, and looking on his son with a countenance which, in spite of all the severity he had endeavoured to assume, betrayed only tenderness and grief. – *So, young man,* said he, *you think it then my place to seek a reconciliation, and are perhaps too stubborn to accept forgiveness, even though I should condescend to offer it.*

NATURA was so thunderstruck at the appearance of his father, and the manner in which he accosted him, that he was far from being able to speak one word, but threw himself at his feet, with a look which testified nothing but confusion: that action, however, denoting that he had not altogether forgot himself, melted the father's heart; he raised him, and forcing him to sit down in a chair close by him; *Well,* Natura, said he, *you have been disobedient to an excess; I wish it were possible for your distresses to have given you a remorse in proportion; – I am still a* father, *if you can be a* son. – He would have proceeded, but was not able: – the meagre aspect, dejected air, and wretched appearance of a son so dear to him, threw him into a condition which destroyed all the power of maintaining that reserve which he thought necessary to his character.

NATURA, on the other hand, was so overcome with the unhoped-for gentleness of his behaviour,[20] that he burst into a flood of tears. – Filial gratitude and love, joined with the thoughts of what he had done to deserve a far different treatment, so overwhelmed his heart, that he could express himself no other way than by falling on his knees a second time, and embracing the legs of his father, with a transport, I know not whether to say of grief or joy; continued in that posture for a considerable time, overwhelmed at once with shame, with gratitude, and love: – at length, gaining the power of utterance, – *O sir*, cried he, *how unworthy am I of your goodness!* – but then recollecting as it were somewhat more; *yet sure,* pursued he, *it is not possible you can forgive me all. – I have been guilty of worse than, perhaps, you yet have been informed of: – I am a wretch who have devoted myself to infamy and destruction, and you cannot, nay ought not to forgive me.*

THE father was indeed very much alarmed at this expression, as fearing it imported his distresses had drove him to be guilty of some crime of which the law takes cognizance. – *I hope,* said he, *your having signed a contract with an abandoned prostitute, is the worst action of your life?*

IT is impossible to describe the pleasure with which *Natura* found his father was apprized of this affair, without being obliged to relate it himself, as he was now determined to have done: – all his obduracy being now intirely vanquished, and converted into the most tender, affectionate, and dutiful submission.

CAN there be a worse? replied he, renewing his embraces, *and can you know it, and yet vouchsafe to look on me as your son!* – *If your penitence be sincere*, said the good old gentleman, *I neither can, nor ought refuse to pardon all: – but rise*, continued he, *and freely give this worthy friend and myself, the satisfaction we require; – a full confession of all your misbehaviour, is the only attonement you can make, and that I can expect from you:*[21] *– remember I have signed your pardon for all that is past, but shall not include in it any future acts of disobedience, among which, dissimulation, evasion, or concealment, in what I demand to be laid open, I shall look upon as of the worst and most incorrigible kind.*

HE needed not have laid so strong an injunction on the now truly contrite *Natura*; – he disguised nothing of what he had done, even to the mean arts of gaming, to which he had been obliged to have recourse after his voluntary banishment from all his friends; and then painted the horrors he conceived at the things he daily saw, and the despair which had induced him to leave *England*, in such lively colours, that not only his father, but the merchant, were affected by it, even to the letting fall some tears.

BUT not to be too tedious in this part of my narration, never was there a more perfect reconciliation: – the father till now knew not how much he loved his son, nor the son before felt half that dutiful affection and esteem for his father.

IT now remained to conclude how the forgiven youth was to be disposed: – there were two reasons which rendered it imprudent for him to go home; first, on the score of his mother-in-law, who being better informed than her husband could have wished, of the errors of his son, he feared would have behaved to him in a fashion which, he easily foresaw, would be attended with many inconveniences; even perhaps to the driving him back into his late vicious courses; and secondly, on that of the contract, which it would be more difficult to get *Harriot* to relinquish, if *Natura* were known to be re-established in his father's favour, than if concealed and supposed still in disgrace with him. – The generous merchant made an offer of an apartment in his house; but *Natura*, who had not seen his sister of a long time, proposed a visit to her; as thinking the society of that dear and prudent relation, would not only console, but establish him in virtue.

THE father listened to both, and after some little deliberation, told his son, that he approved of his going to his sister for a month or two, or three, at his own option; *but*, said he, *it is not fit a young man like you should bury yourself for any long time in the country*; – *you are now of a right age to travel, and I would have you enlarge your understanding by the sight of foreign manners and customs: – I would, therefore, have you make a short visit to my daughter, after which, accept of my friend's invitation, and in the mean time I shall prepare things proper for your making the tour of* Europe, *under a governor who may keep you in due limits.*

HAD *Natura* never offended his father, the utmost he could have wished from his indulgence, was a proposal of this kind; – he was in a perfect extasy, and knew not how sufficiently to express his gratitude and satisfaction; on talking, however, more particularly on the affair, it was agreed he should go first to the merchant's, in order to be new cloathed, and recover some part of those good looks his late dissolute way of life had so much impaired.

EVERY thing being settled so much to the advantage of *Natura*, even a few hours made some alteration in his countenance; so greatly does the ease of the mind contribute to the welfare of the body! – he parted not till night from this indulgent parent, when he went home with the merchant, and had the next day tradesmen of all kinds sent for, who had orders to provide, in their several ways, every thing necessary for a young gentleman born to the estate he was. – As youth is little regardless of futurity, he forgot, for a time, what consequences might possibly attend his contract with *Harriot*, and was as perfectly at ease, as if no such thing had ever happened. When fully equipped, he went down into that country where his sister lived, and if the least thought of his former transactions remained in him, they were now intirely dissipated, by the kind reception he there met with, and the entertainments made for him by the neighbouring gentry.

BUT his heart being bent on his travels, and receiving a letter from his father, wherein he acquainted him that all things were ready for his departure, he took leave of the country, after a stay of about nine weeks, and returned to the merchant's, where his father soon came to see him, and told him, he had provided a governor[22] for him, who had served several of the sons of the nobility in that capacity, and was perfectly acquainted with the languages and manners of the countries through which they were to pass.

THIS tender parent moreover acquainted him, that having consulted the lawyers, on the score of that unhappy obligation he had laid himself under to *Harriot*, and finding they had given it as their assured opinion, that it was drawn up in the most binding and authentic manner, he had offered that creature a hundred guineas to give up her claim; but she had obstinately rejected his proposal, and seemed determined to compel him to the performance of his contract; or in case he married any other woman, to prosecute him for the moiety of whatever portion he should receive with her.

THE mention of this woman, who had given *Natura* so much disquiet, and who indeed had been the primary cause of all his follies and misfortunes, together with the thoughts of what future inconveniencies she might involve him in, both on the account of his fortune and reputation, made him relapse into his former agitations, and afterwards rendered him extremely pensive, and he could not forbear crying out, that he would chuse rather to abandon *England* for ever, and pass the whole remainder of his days in foreign climates, than yield to become the prey any way of so wicked, so infamous a wretch, *whom*, said he, *I shall never think on, without hating myself for having ever loved.*

THE good-natured merchant, as well as his father, perceiving these reflections began to take too much root in him, joined in endeavouring to alleviate the asperity of them, by telling him, that it was their opinion, as indeed it seemed highly probable, that when he was once gone, she would be more easily prevailed upon; especially as the reconciliation between him and his father was to be kept an inviolable secret. The old gentleman also added, in order to make him easy, that how exorbitant soever she might be in her demands, and whatever it should cost, though it were the half of his estate, he would rid him of the contract; which second proof of paternal affection, renewed in *Natura*, as well it might, fresh sentiments of love, joy, and duty; and the same promise being again and again reiterated, he soon resumed his former chearfulness, and thought of nothing but the new scenes he was going to pass through.

IN fine, not many days elapsed before he departed, with his governor and one footman, who had been an antient servant in the family. – As their first route was to *France*, they went in the *Dover* stage, and thence embarked for *Calais*, without any thing material happening, except it were, that on sight of the ocean, *Natura* was fired with a devout rhapsody at the thoughts of finding himself upon it, in a manner so vastly different from that, in which, but a few months since, his despair had led him to project; and the resolution he made within himself never to be guilty of any thing hereafter, which should occasion a blush on his own face, or incur the displeasure of a father, to whom he looked upon himself as much more indebted, for the forgiveness he had received, than for being the author of his existence.

So great an effect has mercy and benevolence over a heart not hardened by a long practice of vice! How far *Natura* persevered in these good intentions, we shall hereafter see; but the very ability of forming them, shews that there is a native gratitude and generosity in the human mind, which, in spite of the prevalence of unruly passions, will, at sometimes, shine forth, even in the most thoughtless and inconsiderate.

BOOK the Second.

CHAP. I.

The inconsideration and instability of youth, when unrestrained by authority, is here exemplified, in an odd adventure Natura *embarked in with two nuns, after the death of his governor.*

NOVELTY has charms for persons of all ages, but more especially in youth, when manhood is unripened by maturity, when all the passions are afloat, and reason not sufficiently established in her throne by experience and reflection, the mind is fluctuating, easily carried down the stream of every different inclination that invites, and seldom or never has a constant bent.

FROM seventeen or eighteen to one or two and twenty, I look upon to be that season of life in which all the errors we commit, will admit of most excuse, because we are then at an age to think ourselves men, without the power of acting as becomes reasonable men. It was in the midst of this dangerous time, that *Natura* set out in order to make the tour of *Europe*, and his governor dying soon after their arrival in *Paris*, our young traveller was left to himself, and at liberty to pursue whatever he had a fancy for.

THE death of this gentleman was in effect a very great misfortune to *Natura*; but as at his time of life we are all too apt to be impatient under any restraint, tho' never so mild and reasonable, he did not consider it in that light; and therefore less lamented his loss, than his good nature would have made him do, had he been the companion of his travels in any other station than that of governor, the very name of which implied a right of direction over his behaviour, and a power delegated by his father of circumscribing every thing he did. I believe, whoever looks back upon himself at that age, will be convinced by the retrospect, that there was nothing wonderful in *Natura*'s imagining he had now discretion enough to regulate his conduct, without being under the controul of any person whatever; and could not, for that reason, be much afflicted at being eased of a subordination not at all agreeable to his humour, and which he thought he had not the least occasion for.

The baron d'*Eyrac* had often invited him to pass some days with him, at a fine villa he had about some ten leagues[23] from *Paris*; but his governor not having approved that visit, he had hitherto declined it. – He now, however, took it into his head to go, and as the distance was so short, went on horseback, attended by his footman, with a portmanteau containing some linnen and cloaths, his intention being to remain there while the baron stayed, which, as he was informed, would be three weeks, or a month; – it being then the season for hunting, and that part of the country well suited for the diversion.

He had been on a party of pleasure a considerable way on this road before, so thought he had no occasion for a guide, and that he should easily be directed to the house; but it so happened that being got about twenty miles from *Paris*, he missed his route, and took one the direct contrary, and which at last brought him to the entrance of a very thick wood: – there was not the least appearance of any human creature, nor the habitation of one, and he was beginning to consult with his servant whether to go back, or proceed till they should arrive at some town or village for refreshment, when all at once there fell the most terrible shower of hail and rain, accompanied with thunder, that ever was heard; – this determined them to go into the wood for shelter: – the storm continued till night, and it was then so dark, that they could distinguish nothing: – they wandered, however, leading their horses in their hands, for it was impossible to ride, hoping to find some path, by which they might extricate themselves out of that horrid labyrinth.

Some hours were passed in this perplexed situation, and *Natura* expected no better than to remain there till morning, when he heard a voice at a little distance, cry, *Who goes there?* Never had any music been half so pleasing to the ears of *Natura*. *Friends,* replied he, *and travellers, that have lost their way*. On this the person who had spoke, drew nearer, and asked whither they were bent. *Natura* told him to the villa of the baron d'*Eyrac*. The baron d'*Eyrac*, said the other, *he lives twelve miles on the other side the wood, and that is five miles over*. – He then asked if there were no town near, to which he could direct them. – *No,* replied the other, *but there is a little village where is one inn, and that is above half a league off: – you will never find your way to it; but if you will pay me, I will guide you. Natura* wished no more, and having agreed with him for his hire, followed where he led.

Nothing that was ever called an inn, had so much the shew of wretchedness; nor could it be expected otherwise, for being far from any great road, it was frequented only by shepherds, and others the meanest sort of peasants, who worked in the adjacent grounds, or tended the cattle.

In this miserable place was *Natura* obliged to take up his lodging: – he lay down, indeed, on the ragged dirty mattress, but durst not take off his cloaths, so noisome was every thing about him: – fatigued as he was, he could not close his eyes till towards day, but had not slept above two hours before the peasant who had served him as a guide, and had also stayed at the inn, came into his room, and waked him abruptly, telling him the lady abbess desired to speak with him. – *Natura* was much vexed at this disturbance, and not sufficiently awaked to recollect himself, only cried peevishly, *What have I to do with abbesses,* and then turned to sleep again.

On his second waking, his footman acquainted him, that a priest waited to see him: – *Natura* then remembered what the peasant had said, but could not conceive what business these holy people had with him; he went down however immediately, and was saluted by a reverend gentleman, who told him, that the lady abbess of a neighbouring monastery (whose almoner[24] he was) hearing from one of her shepherds the distress he had been in, had sent to intreat he would come, and refresh himself with what her convent afforded.

Natura was now ashamed of having been so rough with the peasant, but well atoned for it by the handsome apology he now made; after which he told the almoner, that he would receive the abbess's commands as soon as he was in a condition to be seen by her. – This was what good manners exacted from him, tho' in truth he had no inclination for a visit, in which he proposed so little satisfaction.

He then made his servant open the portmanteau, and give him such things as were proper to equip him for this visit; and while he was dressing, was informed by his host, that this abbess was a woman of quality, very rich, and owned the village they were in, and several others, which brought her in more rent.

If the vanity so natural to a young heart, made *Natura*, on this information, pleased and proud of the consideration such a lady had for him while unknown, how much more cause had he to be so, when being shewn by the same peasant into the monastery, he was brought into a parlour, magnificently furnished, and no sooner had sat down, than a very beautiful woman, whom he soon found was the lady abbess, appeared behind the grate, and welcomed him with the most elegant compliments.

He had never been in a monastery before, and had a notion that all the nuns, especially the abbesses, were ill-natured old women: he was therefore so much surprized at the sight of this lady, that he had scarce power to return the politeness she treated him with. – Her age exceeded not twenty-four; she was fair to an excess, had fine-turned features, and an air which her ecclesiastic habit could not deprive of its freedom; but the enchanting manner of her conversation, her wit, and the gaiety that accompanied all she said, so much astonished and transported him, that he cried out, without knowing that he did so, *Good God! – is it possible a monastery can contain such charms!* – She affected to treat the admiration he expressed, as no other than meer *bagatelle*; but how serious a satisfaction she took in it, a very little time discovered.

A monastery, said she, *is not so frightful a solitude as you, being a stranger to the manners of this country, have perhaps painted to yourself: – I have companions in whom I believe you will find some agreements.* – She then rung a bell, and ordered an attending nun, or what they call a lay-sister, to call some of the sisterhood, whose names she mentioned; and presently came two nuns, with a third lady in a different habit; the least handsome of these might have passed for a beauty, but she that was the most so I shall call *Elgidia*; she was sister to the abbess, but wanted a good many of her years, and being intended for a monastic life by their parents, had been sent there as a pensioner,[25] till she should be prevailed upon to take the veil.

THE abbess, having learned from *Natura* that he was from *England*, told them, in a few words, what she knew of him, and the motive of the invitation she had made him; then desired they would entertain him till her return, having some affair, which called her thence for a small time.

As *Elgidia* appeared by her dress to be more a woman of this world than her companions, he directed his discourse chiefly to her; but whether it were that she had less gaiety in her temper, or that she was that moment taken up with some very serious thought, *Natura* could not be certain, but he found her much less communicative, than either of those, whose profession seemed to exact greater reserve.

As *Natura* spoke *French* perfectly well, and delivered all he said with a great deal of ease, they were very much pleased with his conversation; and yet more so, when, at the return of the abbess, that wit and spirit they before found in him, seemed to have gained an additional vigour.

THE truth is, the first sight of this beautiful abbess had very much struck him; and a certain prepossession in her favour, had rendered him not so quick-sighted as he might otherwise have been to the charms of her sister: – not that he was absolutely in love with her, nor entertained the least wish in prejudice to the sanctity of her order; it was rather an *admiration* he was possessed with on her account, which the surprize, at finding her person and manner so widely different from what he had expected, contributed very much to excite in him.

THE breakfast, which consisted of chocolate, tea, coffee, rich cakes, and sweetmeats, was served upon the *Turnabout*;[26] but the abbess told him, that their monastery had greater privileges than any other in *France*; for they were not restrained from entertaining their kindred and friends, tho' of a different sex, within the grate; *as you shall experience*, said she, with the most obliging air, *if you will favour us with your company at dinner.*

NOTHING could be more pleasing to *Natura* than this invitation, and it cannot, therefore, be supposed he hesitated much to comply with it; however, as the hour of their devotion drew nigh, and forms must be observed, he was desired to take a tour round about the village till twelve, at which time they told him dinner would be on the table.

HE was still in so much amazement at what he had seen and heard, that he was not sorry at having an opportunity of being alone, to reflect on all had passed; but the deeper he entered into thought, the more strange it still seemed to him; till happening accidentally to fall into some discourse with a gentleman in the village, he was told by him, that the nunnery they were in sight of, was called, *Le Convent de Riche Dames*; that none but women of condition entered themselves into it, and that they enjoyed liberties little different from those that live in the world: – *It is true,* said this person, *the gay manner in which they behave, has drawn many reflections on their order, yet I know not but they may be equally innocent with those of the most rigid.*

THIS was enough to shew *Natura*, that the civilities he received, were only such as any stranger, who appeared of some rank, might be treated with, as well as himself; and served to abate that little vanity which, without this information, might have gained ground in his heart; at least it did so for the present: what reasons he founds afterwards for the indulging it, the reader will anon be enabled to judge.

HE was not, however, without a good deal of impatience for the hour appointed for his return, which being arrived, the portress admitted him into a fine room behind the grate, where he found the abbess, *Elgidia*, the two nuns he had seen in the morning, and another, which, it seems, were all the abbess thought proper should be present.

THE table was elegantly served, and the richness of the wines, helped very much to exhilerate the spirits of the company. – *Elgidia* alone spoke little, tho' what she said was greatly to the purpose, and discovered that it was not for want either of sentiment or words she retained so great a taciturnity. – *Natura* saying somewhat, that shewed he took notice how singular she was in this point, the abbess replied, that her sister did not like a convent, that the comedy, the opera, and ball, had more charms for her than devotion. On which *Natura* made some feint attempts to justify a *goûte* for those public diversions, but was silenced by the abbess, who maintained the only true felicities of life were religion and friendship. *What then do you make of love, madam?* cried he briskly: *love, the first command of Heaven, and the support of this great universe: – love, which gives a relish to every other joy, and* – he was going on, but the abbess interrupted him, *Hold! – Hold!* said she, *this is not a discourse fit for theses sacred precincts.* – But these words were uttered in a sound, and accompanied with a look, which wholly took away their austerity, and it was easy for *Natura* to perceive by the manner in which they were spoke, as well as by a sigh, which escaped *Elgidia* at the same time, that neither of these ladies were in reality enemies to the passion he was defending.

SOME little time after dinner was over, *Natura* was about to take his leave; but the abbess told him, that she had formed a design to punish him for pretending to espouse the cause of love; *and that is,* said she, *by detaining you in a place, where you must never speak, nor bear a word, in favour of it: – we have,* continued she, *a little apartment adjoining to the monastery, tho' not in it, which serves to accommodate such friends as visit us, and are too far from home to return the same day: – you must not refuse to pass at least one night in it; and I dare promise you, that you will not find yourself worse lodged, than the preceding one: – your servant may also lie in the same house, and I will send your horses to a neighbouring farmer, who will take care of them.*

THE manner in which this request was urged, had somewhat in it too obliging, for *Natura* to have denied, in good manners, even if his inclinations had been opposite; but indeed he was too much charmed with the conversation of the lovely abbess, and her fair associates, to be desirous of quitting it. – He not only stayed that night, but also, on their continuing to ask it, many succeeding ones. – He lay in the apartment above-mentioned, breakfasted, dined, and supped in the convent, as if a pensioner in the place, always in the same company, and ambitious of no other.

THE gallantries with which he treated the abbess, were as tender as innocence would permit; nor did he presume to harbour any views of being happier with her than he was at present.

BUT see! the strange caprice of love! It was not through a coldness of constitution, nor any considerations of her quality and function, which rendered him so content with enjoying no more of her than her conversation; nor that hindered him from taking advantage of many advances she made him, whenever they were alone, of becoming more particular; but it was the progress *Elgidia* every day made in his esteem: – the more he saw that beautiful young lady, the more he thought her charming; and every time she spoke discovered to him a new fund of wit, and sweetness of disposition: – it was not in her power to erase the first impression her sister had made on him, but it was to stop the admiration he had for her from growing up into a passion: – whenever he saw either of them alone, he thought her most amiable he was with; and when they were together, he was divided between both.

FOR upwards of a month did he continue in the same place, and in the same situation of mind; but then either the abbess's own good sense, or the advice of some friend, remonstrating to her, that so long a stay of a young gentleman, who was known to be not of her kindred, might occasion discourses to her disreputation, and that of the monastery in general; she took the opportunity one day, when he was making an offer of going, as he frequently did, to speak to him in this manner:

I know not how, said she, *to part with you, and I flatter myself you think of going, rather because you imagine your tarrying here for any length of time, might be inconvenient for us, than because you are tired of the reception you have found here.*

Ah madam! cried he, *be assured I could live for ever here*; – *and that I only grieve that such a hope is impossible.* – *If what you now say is sincere,* answered she, *you may at least prolong the happiness we at present enjoy:* – *but I shall put you to the proof* continued she, looking on him with eyes in which the most eager passion was visibly painted, – *to hush the tongue of censure, you shall remove to a town about seven miles distant, where there are many good houses, in one of which you may lodge, under pretence of liking the air of this country, and visit us, as other of our friends do, as frequently as you please, without endangering any remarks, even though you should stay with us three or four nights at a time.*

Natura was so ravished at this proposal, and the kind, almost fond manner, in which it was made, that he catched hold of her hand, and kissed it, with a vehemence not conformable to a *Platonic* affection: – she seemed, however, far from being offended at his boldness, which had perhaps proceeded to greater lengths, had not *Elgidia* at that instant come into the room – The abbess was a little disconcerted, but to conceal it as well as she could, *sister,* said she, *I have made our guest the proposal I mentioned to you this morning, and leave you to second it:* with these words she withdrew.

Elgidia appeared in little less confusion than her sister had done; but *Natura* was in infinitely more than either of them. – The sudden sight of her who possessed at least half of his affections, just in the moment he was in a kind of rapture with another, struck him like the ghost of a departed mistress; and tho' he had never made any declaration of love either to the one or the other, yet his heart reproached him with a secret perfidy, and he durst scarce lift his eyes to her face, when with a timid voice he at last said, *Madam, may I hope you take any interest in what your sister has been speaking of?* – *You may be sure I do,* replied he, *in all that concerns the abbess; as to my farther sentiments on your staying or going, they can be of no consequence to you.* – *How, madam!* resumed he, by this time a little re-assured, *of no consequence! You know nothing of my heart, if you know it not incapable of forming the least wish but to please you.*

He said many other tender and gallant things to her, in order to engage her to add her commands to those of the abbess; but, either the belief that he was wholly devoted to that lady, or the natural reserve of her temper, would suffer her to let him draw no more from her, than that she should share in the happiness her sister proposed to herself, in his continuing so near them.

But tho' *Elgidia* could command her words, she could not have so much power over her eyes as to keep them from betraying a tenderness not inferior to that of her sister; and *Natura* had the satisfaction of finding he was beloved by both these amiable women, without thinking himself so far attached to either, as not to be able to break off whenever he pleased.

BUT to what end tended all this gallantry! to what purpose was all this waste of time, in an amour, which either had no aim in view, or if it had, must be such a one, as must turn to the confusion of the persons concerned in it! – These indeed are questions any one might naturally ask, but could not have been resolved by *Natura*, who took a pleasure in prosecuting the adventure, and neither examined what he proposed by it himself, or considered what consequences might ensue; and herein he but acted as most others do of his age, who rarely give themselves the pains of consulting what *may*, or *will be*, when pleased with what *is*.

HE went to the place the abbess had directed, but imagined he should be very much at a loss for amusement, being wholly a stranger to every body. He would doubtless have been so, had his retreat been in any other country than *France*;[27] but as it is the peculiar characteristic of that nation to entertain at first sight with the same freedom and communicativeness of a long acquaintance, he soon found himself neither without company nor diversion: – whether he had an inclination to hunt, or dance, or play, he always met with persons ready to join in the party, so that the intervals he passed there, between his visits to the monastery, seemed not at all tedious to him.

THE ladies, however, were far from being forgotten by him; ten days had not elapsed, before he returned to renew, or rather to improve, the impression he had both given and received. – The abbess appeared all life and spirit at his return, but *Elgidia* was more melancholly than when he left her; but it was a melancholly which had in it somewhat of a soft languor, which was very engaging to *Natura*, especially as he had reason to believe, by several looks and expressions, which in some unguarded moments fell from her, that he had the greatest interest in it.

THE oftener he saw her, the more he was confirmed in this conjecture; but as he could not be assured of it, never treated her in a manner which should give her room to guess what his thoughts were, for fear of meeting with a rebuff, which would have been too mortifying to his vanity: – but as the belief of being beloved by her, rendered her insensibly more dear to him; the regards he paid her, and the sighs which frequently issued from his breast when he approached her, did not escape the notice of the quick-sighted abbess; and disdaining a competitorship in a heart she thought she had wholly engrossed, resolved to be more plain than hitherto she had been, in order to bring him to declare himself.

WITH this view she led him one day into the garden, and being seated in a close arbour, where there was no danger of being overheard, – *Natura*, said she, *I doubt not but you may perceive, by the civilities I have treated you with, that you are not indifferent to me; but as you cannot be sensible to how great a degree my regard for you extends, it remains that I confess to you there is but one thing wanting to compleat the intire conquest of my heart; and that is,* continued she, fixing her eyes intently on his face, *that you will cease for the future to pay those extraordinary assiduities to* Elgidia *you have lately done.*

How much soever *Natura* was transported at the beginning of this discourse, the closure of it gave him an inexpressible shock, insomuch that he was wholly unable to make any reply, to testify the sense he had of the obligation she conferred on him. *I see,* said she, *the too great influence my sister has over you leaves me no room to hope any thing from you: – I did not think the sacrifice I exacted from you so great, that the purchase of my heart would not have atoned for it; but since I find it is otherwise, I repent I put you to the trial.*

IN speaking these words she rose up, and flew out of the arbour: the confusion *Natura* was in, prevented him from endeavouring to detain her; and before he could resolve with himself how to behave in so critical a conjuncture, she was out of sight. – Whatever tenderness he had for the other, he could not bear the thoughts of having offended this lady: the confession she had just made him, seemed to deserve all his gratitude; and tho' the price she demanded for her heart was too excessive for him to comply with, yet he resolved to make his peace with her the first time he found her alone, on the best terms he could.

THIS was an opportunity, however, not so easily attained as he had imagined: – the abbess conceived so much spite at the little inclination he had testified to comply with her demand, that she kept one or other of the nuns with her the whole remainder of that day, and he could only tell her by his eyes how desirous he was of coming to an eclaircisement.[28]

BUT as if this was a day destined to produce nothing but extraordinary events, perceiving the abbess industriously avoided speaking to him, he had retired into the parlour to ruminate on the affair, when *Elgidia* came in to him, and with somewhat more gaiety than she was accustomed to, cried, *What, alone,* Natura! *but I suppose you attend my sister, and I will not be any interruption*; and then turned to go out of the room. All the discontent he was in for the displeasure he found he had given the abbess, could not keep him from getting between her and the door: – *I have no other way to convince you of the injustice of your suspicion*, said he, *than to detain you here; tho' perhaps,* added he, looking on her with an unfeigned tenderness, *while I am clearing myself in one article, it may not be in my power to prevent betraying my guilt in another, which it may be you will find yet less worthy of forgiveness.*

I know not, replied she, with a smile too enchanting to be resisted, *that I ever gave you any tokens of a rigid disposition; and besides, I am inclined to have so good an opinion of you, that I look to your giving me any cause of offence, as one of the things out of your power.*

EMBOLDENED by these words, *Suppose, madam,* resumed he, *I should confess to you that I was indulging the most passionate tenderness for the beautiful* Elgidia!

– that her sweet idea is always present with me, and that I sometimes am presuming enough to cherish the hopes of not being hated by her: – tell me, continued he, *what punishment does this criminal deserve?*

To be treated in the same manner, answered she blushing, *if he is sincere; and to be made know that he cannot have formed any designs upon the heart of* Elgidia, *which* Elgidia *has not equally harboured upon that of* Natura. – A declaration so unexpected might very well transport a young man, even beyond himself, and all considerations whatever: – forgetful of the respect due to her quality and virtue, and regardless of the place they were in, he seized her in his arms, and almost smothered her with kisses, before she could disengage herself; at length, breaking from him, *It is not by such testimonies as these,* said she, *that I expected you should repay the acknowledgment I have made; but by a full laying open your bosom, as to what passes in it, in regard to my sister: – I know very well she loves you, and am apt to believe she has not been more discreet than myself in concealing it from you; but am altogether at a loss as to the returns you may have made her passion.*

Natura now really loving her, hesitated not to do as she desired; neither making any secret of the admiration which the abbess had raised in him at first sight, nor the discourse she had lately entertained him with, and the injunction she had laid upon him. *Elgidia* took this as so great a proof of his affection, that she made no scruple to ratify the confession she had made him by all the endearments that innocence would permit: – after which, they consulted together how he should behave to the abbess, whose temper being violent, it was not proper to drive to extremes; and it was therefore agreed between them, that he should continue to treat her with a shew of tenderness: *Elgidia* even proposed, that he should renounce her, in case the other continued to insist upon it; but *Natura* could not consent his insincerity should go so far.

They parted, mutually content with each other; and *Natura* himself believed his inclinations were now fixed, by the assurance *Elgidia* had given him of the most true and perfect passion that ever was: but how little do we know of our own hearts at his years! the next time he saw the abbess alone, he relapsed into the same fluctuating state as before, and found too much charms in the kindness she expressed for him, to be able to withdraw himself intirely from her.

That lady, who loved to an excess, could not be any long time without affording him the means of reconciliation; and the next morning, as soon as breakfast was over, descended alone into the garden, giving him a look at the same time, which commanded him to follow: – he did so, and perceiving she took her way to the same arbour they had been in before, he went in soon after her, affecting, rather than feeling, a timidity in approaching her. *Well,* Natura, said she, *have you yet examined your heart sufficiently, to know whether the full possession of mine, can atone for your breaking with my sister;* – to which he replied, that as he had no engagements with *Elgidia*, nor had ever any other thoughts of her, than such as were excited by that respect due to her sex and rank, he was wholly ignorant in what manner it was exacted from him to behave: – *but,* added he, *if vowing that from the first moment I beheld your charms, I became absolutely devoted to you, may deserve any part of that affection you are pleased to flatter me with, I am ready to give you all the assurances in the power of words.*

THIS asseveration could not be called altogether false, because he had really a latent inclination in him towards her, which all the tenderness he had for *Elgidia* could not eradicate; and this it was that gave all he said such an air of sincerity as won upon the abbess, to believe her jealousy had misinterpreted the looks she had sometimes seen him give her sister, and at length made her desist from reproaching him on that score.

THE tranquility of her mind being restored, she gave a loose to the violence of her passion, in such caresses as might well make the person who received them forgetful of all other obligations: – in these transporting moments the lovely abbess had his whole soul: – he now, unasked, abjured not only *Elgidia*, but all the sex beside, and even wondered at himself for having ever entertained a wish beyond the happiness he enjoyed at present.

THE abbess was too well versed in the affairs of love, not to be highly satisfied with the proofs he gave of his, than which, it is certain, nothing for the time could be more sincere or ardent; death was it to them both to put an end to this inchanting scene, but as they were seen to go into the garden soon after one another, and too long a stay together might occasion a suspicion of the cause, they were obliged to separate, though not without a promise of meeting in the same place at night, after the nuns were all retired to their respective chambers.

THE abbess passed through a back-way into the chapel, it being near the time of prayers, and *Natura* returned by the great walk into the outward cloister, where *Elgidia* seeing him at a distance, and alone, waited his coming, to know of him how he had proceeded with her sister. – *Natura,* yet full of the abbess and the favours he had received from her, would have gladly dispenced with this interview; but she was too near, before he perceived her, for him to draw back with decency.

FAR from suspecting any change in him, and judging of his integrity by her own, *I was impatient,* said she, *to hear the event of your conversation with the abbess; tell me therefore in a few words, for the bell rings to chapel, whether you have succeeded so far as to stifle all jealousies of me? Yes, madam*, replied he, recovering himself as well as he could from his confusion, *we may be easy for the future, as to that particular. – I long for the particulars of your discourse,* resumed she, *but cannot now stay to be informed; meet me in the garden after the sisterhood are in bed; this,* continued she, putting a key into his hand, *will admit you by the gate that leads to the road: – do not fail to be there at nine.* – The haste she was in to be gone, would not have permitted him time to make any answer, if he had been provided with one, and he could only just kiss her hand as she turned from him.

BUT what was the dilemma he was now involved in! the hour, and place she appointed, were the very same in which he was to meet the abbess! impossible was it for him to gratify both, and not very easy to deceive either: – he went back into the garden, ruminating what course he should take in so intricate an affair; at first he thought of writing a little billet, and slipping it into *Elgidia*'s hand, acquainting her that the abbess had commanded him to attend her in the garden at the time she mentioned, and telling her that he thought it necessary to obey, to prevent all future suspicion: – but he rejected this design, not only as that young lady might possibly have the curiosity to conceal herself behind the arbour, and would then be a witness of things it was no way proper she should be informed of, but also because his heart reproached him for having already done more than he could answer, and forbad him to deceive her any farther; in fine, that he might be guilty of perfidy to neither, he resolved to quit both, at least for that night, but knew not yet on what he should determine for the future.

DIVINE service being over, he repaired to the parlour, where, after they were sat down to dinner, he said, addressing himself to the abbess, that having sent his servant that morning to his lodgings, he had received letters of the utmost importance, which required immediate answers; and that he must be obliged for that reason to take his leave; *though with what regret*, added he, *it is easy to perceive, by the long stay I always make here.*

THE abbess insisted upon it, that he should not go; – told him he might write what he pleased there without interruption; and that his man might carry his dispatches to the post: but all she urged could not prevail, and both that lady and her sister had the mortification to hear him give orders that his own horse should be got ready with all expedition; as for his servant he was left behind for a few hours, on the account of packing up some things he had brought him in the design of staying a longer time.

IN fine, he went away, with a promise of returning in a short time. The abbess was inwardly fretted at the disappointment, but imagined it was only occasioned by the motive he pretended, till a young nun who was her confidante in all things, and had happened to cross the cloyster when *Natura* and *Elgidia* were talking together before prayers, and had seen him kiss her hand, informed her of this passage, and added, of her own conjecture, that the abrupt departure of *Natura* was owing to somewhat that lady had said to him: – there needed no more to inflame the passionate and jealous abbess; she doubted not of being betrayed, and flew directly to her sister's chamber, accused her of being guilty of the most criminal intercourse with a stranger, and threatened if she did not confess the whole truth to her, and swear never to see him more, she would send an account of her behaviour to their parents, who would not fail to thrust her into a less commodious convent, and compel her to take the veil directly.

THE mild and timid disposition of *Elgidia,* could not sustain this shock; she immediately fainted away, and help being called to bring her to herself, in opening her bosom a paper fell out of it, which the abbess snatching up, ran to her chamber to examine, and found it contained these words:

'To prevent my dear angel from being surprized at my sudden departure, know that it is to avoid the abbess, who obliged me to give her a promise of meeting her this night in the garden: – at my next visit you shall be informed at full of all that passed between us in the morning. Adieu.

NATURA.'

As *Natura* had no opportunity to make an excuse to *Elgidia*, he had slipt this billet into her hand on taking leave; and though no more was meant by it than to make her easy till his return, there was sufficient in the expression not only to convince the abbess that her sister was indeed her rival, but also to make her think herself had been the dupe to their amour. – Impossible would it be to describe the force of those passions, which, in this dreadful instant, overwhelmed her soul; so I shall only say, it was as great as woman could sustain, and which the impatience of venting on their proper object, put it into her head to go to him in a disguise, and upbraid his perfidy. As she seldom listened to any dictates, but those of her passion, this design was no sooner formed than preparations were made for the execution, nor could all her confidante urged, on the danger and scandal of the attempt, deter her from it.

THERE was a fellow who was frequently employed about the monastery, in whom she could confide: – him she sent to a farmer, with orders to hire three horses, one for herself, another for her confidante, who, in spite of all her apprehensions on that account, she would needs make accompany her, and the third for the man, who was to attend them as a valet, the little road they had to travel. This fellow was directed to bring the horses about ten o'clock at night, at which time it would be dark, to the corner of a wall at the farther end of the garden, when she and her companion were to mount, and away on this wild expedition.

BUT while the abbess was busy on her project, *Elgidia* had also another, though of somewhat a less desperate kind; her sister's temper gave her but too much reason to believe she would revenge herself on her by all the ways in her power; and trembling at the thoughts of being exposed to her parents, and the censure of the world, as the other had threatened, which she knew no way to avoid, but by *Natura* making up this quarrel; and tho' she knew it could only be done by his renouncing all pretensions to herself, yet she rather chose to lose the man she loved, than her reputation. As she knew not whether the abbess would delay the gratification of her malice any longer than the next morning, she resolved to send for *Natura* that same night, in order to engage him to a second reconciliation with her sister, let the terms be never so cruel to herself.

SHE had no sooner laid this plot, than she ran to see if the servant he had left behind was yet gone, and finding he was not, bad him wait a little, that she might send a letter by him to his master. The contents of her epistle were as follow:

'SOMETHING has happened, which lays me under a necessity of speaking to you this night: – the only consolation I have under the severest of all afflictions, is, that I did not take back the key I gave you in the morning: I beg you will make use of it, and let me find you in the close arbour as soon as the darkness will permit your entrance unobserved: – fail not, if you have any regard for the honour, the peace, and even the life of the unfortunate

ELGIDIA.'

NATURA had no sooner received this billet from the hands of his servant, than all his tenderness for the fair authoress of it revived in him, which, joined to his impatient curiosity for the knowledge of the accident she mentioned, easily determined him to do as she desired.

HE set out at the close of day; but the moon rising immediately after, shone so extremely bright as proved her, no less than the sun, an enemy to the design he was at present engaged in; he was therefore obliged to wait till that planet had withdrawn her light, before he durst approach the convent.

THE abbess and her companion having dressed themselves in riding habits, went at the abovementioned hour to the gate where they expected the man and horses were attending their coming; but there was not the least appearance of any. – the abbess, emboldened by her impatience and despair, would needs venture out some paces beyond the gate, to listen if she could hear any sound of what she wanted, but had not long continued in that posture, before she discovered by the twinkling light of the stars, two men on horseback, galloping directly to the place where she stood: – impossible was it for her to discern what sort of persons they were, but easy to know, as there were two men, and no more than two horses, that they were not those she looked for; on which she ran with all the haste she could back into the garden, and clapping the gate after her, in her fright stopped not till she was almost at the entrance of the cloyster: – both she and her companion were out of breath; but when they had a little recovered it, the latter took the liberty of railying her on the terror she had been in, at the sight of two persons, who were, doubtless, only pursuing their own affairs, without any thought or notice of them: –the abbess acknowledged the pleasantry was just, and returned again to the gate, which having opened, they found two horses tied to a tree, at a little distance from it, without any person to look after them. She imagined they belonged to the farmer, but could not guess wherefore there was not a third, or how it happened that the man was not with them. – The two lady-adventurers waited in hopes of seeing their attendant with another horse, till the abbess, fearing the night would be too far spent for the execution of her design, and grown quite wild with rage and vexation, resolved to go without a guide; and accordingly she and the young nun that was with her, mounted the horses they found there, and rode away.

LITTLE did this distracted woman imagine to whom she was indebted for the means of conveying herself where she wished to be; for in effect these horses were *Natura*'s, and it was no other than himself, attended by his man, who had put her into that fright, which occasioned her running so far back into the garden, as gave him time to enter, without being either seen or heard by her: – he was no sooner within the gate, than his servant tied the horses to a tree, as has been related, and retired to a more convenient place, either to lye down to sleep, or on some other occasion. – Thus did an accident which had like to have broken all *Elgidia*'s measures, turn wholly to the advantage of them, and she found as much satisfaction, as a person in her situation could possibly take, in finding *Natura* so punctual to the summons she had sent.

IT was with a flood of tears she related to him all that had passed between the furious abbess and herself after his departure, and concluded her discourse with beseeching him to see her in the morning, and omit nothing that might pacify her, *even*, said she, *to forswear ever speaking to me more.*

NATURA was touched to the very soul at the grief he saw her in, and equally with the tender consideration she had for him; and now more devoted to her than ever, would have done any thing to prove the sincerity of his passion, but that which she demanded of him: – it was in vain she urged the impossibility of keeping a correspondence together under the same roof with a rival who had all the power in her own hands; or that she represented how much better it would be for both to break off so dangerous an intercourse of themselves, before the rage of the abbess should put her upon doing it, in a manner which might involve them all in destruction: – all the arguments she made use of, only served to render him more amorous, and consequently less able to part with her. – The difference he found between these two sisters; the outrageous temper of the one, compared with the prudence, sweetness, and gentleness of the other, rendered the comparison almost odious to him; and as he could not but acknowledge the impractibility of maintaining a conversation with the latter, without the participation of the former; nor though he should even consent to divide himself between them, would either of them be content, he told *Elgidia*, that the only way to solve these difficulties, was, for her to fly from the monastery, and be the partner of his fortune, as she was the mistress of his heart.

SUCH a proposition made her start! – to abandon all her friends, and put herself wholly in the power of a stranger, of whose fortune, family, or fidelity, she could not be assured, gave her very just alarms; but whatever was her reluctance at the first mention of such an enterprize, the extreme passion she had for him, rendered all her apprehensions, by degrees, less formidable: – he told her he had no other wishes, than such as were dictated by honour; – that he would marry her as soon as they should arrive at a place where the ceremony could be performed with safety – that he was heir to a considerable estate after his father's death, that on his return to *England* he should have a handsome settlement out of it, and that his present allowance was sufficient to keep them above want. – People easily believe what they wish, especially from the mouth of a beloved person. – *Natura* indeed had uttered no untruths as to his circumstances, but as to the main point, his marrying her, it is impossible to judge whether in that he was sincere, because he knew not himself whether he was so, tho' in the vehemence of his present inclinations he might imagine he did so, and at that time really meant as he said.

Be that as it may, *Elgidia* suffered herself to be won by his perswasions; and being so, the present opportunity was not to be lost. – He had horses at the gate, could conduct her, he said, where she might be concealed till they got quite out of the reach of her kindred, and failed not to remonstrate, that if she delayed, but even till the next morning, not only the jealousy of the abbess, but a thousand other accidents, might separate them for ever.

As the lovers past their time in this manner, the distracted abbess was prosecuting her journey, in quest of him she had left behind: as the way she had to go was so short, there was no great danger of any mischief attending it, neither did any happen; but how great was her confusion! when arriving at the house where *Natura* lodged, she was told he went out in the evening, on the receipt of a billet brought him by his servant. – This disappointment destroyed all the remains of temperance had been left in her; she presently guessed the billet came from no other than *Elgidia*, doubted not but they were together, and figured in her mind a scene of tenderness between them so cruel to her imagination, that frenzy itself scarce exceeded what she endured: – she rode back with even more precipitation than she had set out, and being alighted at the gate thro' the great walk, supposing *Elgidia* had brought him into her chamber, where, if she found them, thought of nothing, but sacrificing one or both of them to her resentment.

In this situation of mind, it cannot be imagined she had any thought about the horses; but her companion having more the power of reflection, and judging them to be the farmer's, thought it best to tye them to a tree within the garden, that so they might be secured, and sent to him in the morning; which having done, and shut the gate, she was going to follow the abbess, when she met her coming back: – *I have considered,* said she, *that my perfidious sister would rather chuse the close arbour for her rendezvous, than her own chamber, where there would be more danger of being overheard by the nuns who lie near her; – go you therefore,* continued she, *and wait me in my apartment, while I search the garden.*

THE nun obeyed, glad to be eased of this nocturnal attendance, and the abbess drew near, as softly as she could, to the arbour; and standing behind the covert of the greens of which it was composed, heard the consent *Elgidia* gave to accompany *Natura*, and saw her quit him, with a promise of returning, as soon as she had put on a habit somewhat more proper for travelling.

HAD she followed the first dictates of her passion in this stabbing circumstance, she had either pursued her sister, and inflicted on her all that vindictive malice could suggest, or run into the arbour, and discharged some part of her fury on *Natura*: – each alike shared her resentment, but divided between both, lost its effects on either: – a revenge more pleasing, and less unbecoming of a female mind, at length got the better of those furious resolves; – she thought, that as every thing favoured such a design, and she was equipped for the purpose, to take the place of her sister, would afford her an exquisite triumph over the disappointment she should occasion them: accordingly, after staying long enough to encourage the deception, she came round the arbour, and entered at the passage by which *Elgidia* had gone out: – *Natura*, not doubting but it was his beloved, took her in his arms, saying, *How transporting is the expedition you have made in your return; and indeed we had need of it, for the night is far exhausted, and it is necessary you should be out of this part of the country before day-break.*

THE abbess answered not to what he said, but gave him her hand; on which he led her towards the gate, entertaining her with the most endearing expressions as they walked, to all which she was still dumb. *Natura* was not surprized at it, as imagining she was too much engrossed by the thoughts of what she was about to do, to be able to speak: – but how great was his mortification, when having opened the gate, he found his servant, who having missed the horses, was just come back from a fruitless search of them. – He drew his sword, and had not the fellow stept nimbly aside, had certainly killed him: – while he was venting his passion in the severest terms, the abbess shut the gate upon him, and locked it with her own key, which, leaving in the lock, the one he had made use of, could now be of no service. – A caprice he had so little reason to expect in *Elgidia*, might very well surprise him, especially at a time when both had so much cause to be more grave! –he called to her, he complained, he even reproached the unkindness, and ill-manners of this treatment, while the abbess indulged on the other side the most spiteful pleasure in his vexation.

SHE left him railing at fate and womankind, without convincing him of his error, when as she was going to the monastery, she met *Elgidia* just coming out, and directing steps towards the arbour: – they were in the same path, and facing each other: – *Elgidia*, full of the fears which usually attend actions of the nature she was about to do, no sooner perceived the form of a woman, and habited in the same manner as herself, than she took it for a spirit; and terrified almost to death, cried out, *a ghost! a ghost!* and ran, shrieking, with all her force to the cloyster, resolved, as much as it then was in her power to resolve on any thing, to desist from her enterprize. – She made no stop, till she got into her chamber, where she threw herself on the bed, in a condition not to be described.

THE abbess was so well satisfied with the success of this last stratagem, that it greatly abated the thoughts of taking any further revenge: – she went laughing to her confidante, and told her the whole story, who congratulated her upon it, and said, that in her opinion, she might take it as a peculiar providence of Heaven, that had disappointed her first design, which could only have increased her confusion, and probably brought a lasting scandal on the order. The abbess wanted not reason, when her passion would permit her to exert it, and could not help confessing the truth of what the other remonstrated; – she now easily saw they were *Natura*'s horses they had made use of, but how it came to pass that those she had bespoke, or the man she had ordered to bring them, happened to fail, remained a point yet to be discussed: – the morning, however, cleared it up; – the fellow acquainted her, that the farmer had no horses at home, and that as he was coming to let her know it, he saw two men at the gate, one of whom entered, so that he imagined she had provided herself elsewhere: – she then bad him turn out *Natura*'s horses, which the nun having said how she had disposed of them, not thinking herself obliged to take any care of what belonged to a man, who had treated her with so much ingratitude.

NATURA was all this time in the utmost perplexity, not only at the usage he imagined had been given him by *Elgidia*, but also for the loss of his horses; and at being told when he came home, that two women, in riding habits, well mounted, but without any attendants, had been to enquire for him: – all these things, the meaning of any one of which he was not able to fathom, so filled his head, that he could not take any repose: – pretty early in the morning, a letter was brought him from *Elgidia*, which he hastily opened, but found nothing in it, but what served to heighten his amazement and discontent.

SHE told him that she could not dispense with letting him know the occasion of her breach of promise; that intending nothing more than to perform it, she was hastening to the arbour, when, in the middle of the garden, she was met by an apparition, which, as near as she could discern, had the resemblance of herself; – that the terror she was in had obliged her to retire; and that as she could look on what she had seen, as no other than a warning from Heaven, she had determined to use her utmost endeavours for extinguishing a passion obnoxious to its will; to which end she desired he would make no farther attempts to engage her to an act so contrary to her duty, or even ever to see her more.

NATURA had so little notion of spirits and ghosts, that at first he took this story only as a pretence, to cover a levity he had not suspected her to be guilty of; but when he reflected on the silence of the person he had taken for her, and the description of those who had been to enquire for him, he began to imagine, as he had not the least thought of the abbess, that something supernatural had indeed walked the garden that night, and had also been at his own lodgings in order to perplex him more: – a thousand little tales he had been told in his infancy, concerning the tricks played on mortals by those shadowy beings, now came fresh into his mind; and as the belief of what *Elgidia* had wrote gained ground in him, was not far from being of her opinion, that it was a warning from Providence, and to repent of having attempted to snatch from the altar a woman devoted to it.

It is doubtless accidents such as this, that have given rise to so many stories of apparitions, as have been propagated in the world; and had not *Natura* been afterwards informed of the whole truth, it is likely he would have been as great a defender of those ideas, as any who are accounted superstitious: – but however that might have been, it wrought so strongly on his mind at present, that joined with the considerations of those perpetual perplexities which must infallibly attend an ecclesiastical intrigue; besides, those which the abbess would involve him in, made him resolve to obey *Elgidia*'s commands, and pursue the matter no farther, but go directly to the baron d'*Eyrac*'s, who he heard was still at his country-house.

The loss of his horses, however, very much vexed him; he bought them, because he preferred that way of travelling to a post-chaise: they had cost him forty *louis d'ores* in *Paris*, and knew not whether the country he was in would afford him any so fit for his purpose: – he was just sending his man to enquire where others were to be had, when his own were at the door, without the least damage done either to themselves or saddles: – the farmer who had the care of them while he was at the monastery, found them wandering in the field, and easily knowing to whom they belonged, brought them home.

This was some consolation to him for the loss of his mistresses; and he began to resolve seriously on his departure; but thinking it would be the highest ungenerosity to quit the convent, without acknowledging the favours he had received there, he wrote a letter to the abbess, full of gratitude and civility, telling her, that tho' the necessity of his affairs required he should take an eternal leave of that place, he should always preserve the memory of those honours he had received in it. – To *Elgidia* he wrote in much the same strain she had done to him, and concluded with desiring her to believe it was to Heaven alone he could resign her. These letters he sent by his man, and ordered him to leave them with the portress, to avoid any answers which might have drawn him into a longer correspondence than he desired, or perhaps even have occasioned a revival of those inclinations in him, which he was now convinced of the folly and danger of.

THIS was the first proof he gave of a firmness of resolution, and was indeed as great a one as could have been expected from a man of the age he was: – it must be owned, that at that time love is the strongest passion of the soul, and as neither *Elgidia* nor the abbess wanted charms to inspire it, and he had been but too sensible of the force of both, to be able, I say, to tear himself away in the manner he now did, was a piece of heroism, which I wish every one in the like circumstance may have power to imitate.

HE hired another horse and guide, that he might not lose his way a second time, and departed the same day for the baron's, where he was received by that young nobleman with the utmost kindness as well as politeness, and found so much in his conversation, and those who came to visit him, and the continual amusements of that place, as made him soon forget all he had partook in the monastery: – he remained there while the baron stayed, and then came with him to *Paris*.

ON his return he frequented the same company, and pursued the same pleasures he had done before; but as nothing extraordinary befel him, I shall not enter into particulars, my design being only to relate such adventures as gave an opportunity for the passions to exert themselves in influencing the conduct of his life.

CHAP. II.

The pleasures of travelling described, and the improvement a sensible mind may receive from it: with some hints to the censorious, not to be too severe on errors, the circumstances of which they are ignorant of, occasioned by a remarkable instance of an involuntary slip of nature.

OF all the countries *Natura* intended to see, *Italy* was that of which he had entertained the most favourable idea: – his curiosity led him to convince himself whether it really deserved to be intitled *the garden of the world*;[29] and therefore it was thither he resolved to make his next progress. – Being told that in so long a journey he would find an excessive expence, as well as incommodity, in travelling on horseback, by reason he must be obliged to hire a guide from one place to another, he sold his horses, and after having hired a post-chaise, took leave of his acquaintance, and of a place where he had enjoyed all the pleasures agreeable to a youthful taste.

HE went by the way of *Burgundy*, and passing through *Dijon* proceeded to *Lyons*,[30] where the sight of the ruins of some *Roman* palaces yet remaining there, the fine churches, and beautiful prospect that city affords, being situated at the confluence of the rivers *Rhone* and *Soane*, tempted him to stay some days. – He was one evening sitting with his landlord in the inn-yard, when a post-chaise came in, out of which alighted a gentleman and a lady, just by the place where they were. – The man got up with all the obsequiousness of persons of his calling, to bid them welcome, and shew them into a room: – the lady, in passing, looked earnestly at *Natura*, and his eyes were no less attached on her: he thought he saw in her face features he was perfectly acquainted with, but could not, at that instant, recollect where he had been so. Not so with her, she easily remembered him, and in less than half an hour he received an invitation by his name from these new guests to sup with them, which he accepted of with great politeness, but said at the same time, he could not imagine to whom he was obliged for that honour. – On his coming into the room, *Difference of habit*, said the lady, smiling, *joined with the little probability there was of meeting me in this place, may well disguise me from your knowledge; but these impediments to remembrance, are not on your account*; *monsieur* Natura *is the same in person at* Lyons, *as at the convent of* Riche Dames, *though perhaps*, added she, *somewhat changed in mind*. There needed no more to make him know she was one of the two nuns who always dined, when he was there, with the abbess, and was her particular confidante. – *By what miracle, madam, are you here?* cried he: *by such another*, answered she, *as might have brought* Elgidia *here, had not an unlucky spirit put other thoughts into her head*.

SHE then proceeded to inform him, that loving, and being equally beloved by the gentleman who was with her, she had made her escape with him from the monastery, and was going with him into one of the *Protestant* cantons of *Switzerland*,[31] of which he was a native, and where they were certain of being safe from any prosecutions, either from her kindred, or the church.

NATURA, after having made his compliments to the gentleman on the occasion, enquired of her concerning the abbess and *Elgidia*; on which she informed him of all the particulars related in the preceding chapter; adding, that after the receipt of the two letters he had sent, the sisters came to a mutual understanding, each confessed her foible to the other, and the cause of their quarrel being for ever removed, a sincere reconciliation between them ensued.

AS gratitude is natural to the soul, and never is erased but by the worst passions that can obtrude upon the human mind, *Natura* had enough for these ladies to make him extremely glad no worse consequences had attended their acquaintance with him, but was extremely merry, as they were all indeed, at the story of the supposed spirit: – they passed the best part of the night together in very entertaining discourses, and the next day the two lovers proceeded on their journey to *Switzerland*, as *Natura* the following one did his to *Avignon*.[32]

HERE again he halted for some time, to feast his eyes, and give subject for future contemplation, on the magnificent buildings, fine gardens, churches, and other curiosities, which he was told of, gave him a sample, tho' infinitely short, of what he would find in *Rome*: – the grandeur in which the nobility lived, the elegance and politeness in the houses of even the lowest rank of gentry, and the masquerades, balls, and other public diversions, which every night afforded, made him already see that neither the pleasures, nor the delicacies of life were confined to *Paris*.

THE desire of novelty is inherent to a youthful heart, and nothing so much gratifies that passion as travelling: – variety succeeds variety: – whether you climb the craggy mountains, or traverse the flowery vale; – whether thick woods set limits to the sight, or the wide common yields unbounded prospect; – whether the ocean rolls in solemn state before you, or gentle streams run purling by your side, nature in all her different shapes delights; each progressive day brings with it fresh matter to admire, and every stage you come to presents at night customs and manners new and unknown before.

THE stupendous mountains of the *Alps*, after the plains and soft embowered recesses of *Avignon*, gave perhaps a no less grateful sensation to the mind of *Natura*: he wanted indeed such a companion as death had deprived him of in his good governor, to instruct him how to improve contemplation, and to moralize on the amazing and different objects he beheld;[33] yet as his thoughts were now wholly at liberty, and his reason unclouded by any passions of what kind soever, he did not fail to make reflections suitable to the different occasions.

WHOEVER has seen *Rome* will acknowledge he must find sufficient there to exercise all his faculties; but though the architecture, and the paintings which ornament that august city might have engrossed his whole attention, the many venerable reliques which were shewn him of old *Rome*, appeared yet more lovely in his eyes; which shews the charms antiquity has for persons even of the most gay dispositions: but this, according to my opinion, is greatly owing to the prejudice of education, which forces us as it were to an admiration of the antients, meerly because they are so, and not that they are in any essential respect always deserving that vast preference given them over the moderns:[34] –this may be easily proved by the exorbitant prices some of our virtuoso's give for pieces of old copper, which are reckoned the most valuable, as the inscriptions or figures on them are least legible.

NATURA, however, was not so absorbed in his admiration of the ruined corner of a bath, or the half-demolished portico of an amphitheatre, as to neglect those entertainments which more affect the senses, and consequently give the most natural delight; – the exquisite music performed at the churches,[35] carried him there much oftener than devotion would have done, and rarely did he fail the opera at night.

As the *Romans* are allowed to be the best bred people upon earth,[36] especially to strangers, be they of what country or perswasion soever, neither the being an *Englishman* or a *Protestant* hindered him from making very good acquaintance, and receiving the greatest civilities from them; but the person to whom he was most obliged, and who indeed had taken a particular fancy to him, was the younger son of the family of *Caranna*: this nobleman, knowing his taste for music, would frequently take him with him to his box at the opera-house, most persons of condition having little closets or boxes to themselves, of which every one keeps his own key, and none can be admitted but by it: – nothing can be more indulging, as there are curtains to draw before them, and the seats are made in such a manner, that the person may lie down at his ease.

THE signior of *Caranna* being otherwise engaged one night, when a celebrated piece was to be performed, he lent his key to *Natura*, unknowing that his wife, who had also one, had made a compliment of her's to a young lady of her acquaintance.

NATURA by some accident being delayed from going till after the opera began, on entering was surprized to find a very beautiful young person there, stretched on the sopha: – as he had been told the box would be intirely empty, he knew not whether he ought to retire or go forward and seat himself by her: – this consideration kept him some minutes in the posture he was in, and perceiving she was too much taken up with the music, either to have heard him open the door, or see him after he came in, he had the opportunity of feasting his eyes, with gazing on the thousand charms she was mistress of; all which were displayed to a great advantage by the shadowy light which gleamed from the stage thro' a thin crimson taffety curtain, which she had drawn before her, to the end she might neither be seen by others, nor see any thing herself which might take off her attention from the music.

IN fine, he drew near, and had placed himself close by her before she observed him; but no sooner did so, than she started, and appeared in some confusion: he made a handsome apology for the intrusion, which he assured her, with a great deal of truth, was wholly owing to chance, and said he would withdraw, if his presence would be any interruption to the pleasure she proposed: – she seemed obliged to him for the offer, but told him she would not abuse the proof he gave of his complaisance by accepting it; on which he bowed, and continued in his place.

BOTH the music, and the words, seemed intended to lull the soul into a forgetfulness of all beside, and fill it only with soft ideas: – it had at least this effect upon the lady, who had closed her eyes, and was in reality lost to every other sense than that of hearing. –*Natura*, either was, or pretended to be, equally transported, and sunk insensibly upon her bosom, without any opposition on her part: – she had possibly even forgot she was not alone, and when an air full of the most inchanting tenderness was singing, was so much dissolved in extasy, that crying out, *O God, 'tis insupportable!* she threw her arms over *Natura*'s neck, who was still in the same posture I just mentioned; – he spoke not a word, but was not so absorbed in the gratification of one faculty, as to let slip the gratification of the others: – he seized the lucky moment; – he pressed her close, and in this trance of thought, this total absence of mind, stole himself, as it were, into the possession of a bliss, which the assiduity of whole years would perhaps never have been able to obtain.

REASON and thought at last returned; she opened her eyes, she knew to what the rapture she had been in had exposed her, and was struck with the most poignant shame and horror: – she broke with all her force from that strict embrace in which he had continued to hold her; and being withdrawn to the farther corner of the closet – *What have I done*, cried she, *What have I done!* – these words she repeated several times, and accompanied them with tears, wringing her hands, and every testimony of remorse. – It was in vain for him to attempt to pacify her, much less to prevail on her to suffer any second proofs of his tenderness; – she would not even give him leave to touch her hand, and on his offering it, pushed him back, saying, *No, stranger! you have taken the advantage of my* insensibility, *but shall never triumph over my* reason, *which enables me to hate you, – to fly from you for ever, as from a serpent.*

NATURA said every thing that love and wit could inspire, to reconcile her to what had past; but she remained inflexible, and only condescended to request him to leave the place before the opera was ended, that they might not be seen coming out together, and that he would tell signior *Carrana*, that having unexpectedly found a lady in the box, he had withdrawn without entering. – He then begged she would entertain a more favourable opinion of an action, which her beauty, the bewitching softness of the entertainment, and the place they were in, had all concurred to make him guilty of; but she would listen to nothing on that head, insisted on his never taking the least notice of her, wherever they might chance to meet; and only told him, that tho' she was unalterably fixed in this resolution, yet he might depend upon it she hated him less than she did herself.

FINDING she was not to be moved, he obeyed her commands, and straight went out of the box, more amazed at the oddness of the adventure, than can be well expressed; and yet more so, when he afterwards heard she was the wife of a person of great condition, was in the first month of her marriage with him, and had the reputation of a woman of strict virtue.

AS this false step was meerly accidental, wholly unpremeditated on either side, and by what can be judged by the character of the lady, and her behaviour afterwards, was no more on her part than a surprize on the senses, in which the mind was not consulted, and had not the least share, I know not whether it may not more justly be called a slip of unguarded nature, than a real crime in her; and as for *Natura*, though certainly the most guilty of the two, whoever considers his youth, his constitution, and above all the greatness of the temptation, which presented itself before him, will allow, that he must either have been *more*, or *less*, than *man*, to have behaved otherwise than he did.

LET the most severely virtuous, who happily have never fallen into the same error, but figure to themselves the circumstances of this transgressing pair, and well consider in what manner nature must operate, when thus powerfully excited, and if they are not rendered totally incapable of any soft sensations, by an uncommon frigidity of constitution, they will cease either to wonder at, or too cruelly condemn, the effects of so irresistible an impulse.

WERE it not for the precepts of religion and morality, the fears of scandal, and shame of offending against law and custom, man would undoubtedly think himself intitled to the same privileges which the brute creation in this point enjoy above him; and it is not therefore strange, that whenever reason nods, as it sometimes will do, even in those who are most careful to preserve themselves under its subjection, that the senses ever craving, ever impatient for gratification, should readily snatch the opportunity of indulging themselves, and which it is observable they ordinarily do to the greater excess, by so much the longer, and the more strictly they have been kept under restraint.

CHAP. III.

The uncertainty of human events displayed in many surprizing turns of fortune, which befel Natura, *on his endeavouring to settle himself in the world: with some proofs of the necessity of fortitude, as it may happen that actions, excited by the greatest virtue, may prove the source of evil, both to ourselves and others.*

NATURA stayed but six months in *Rome*, and then passed on to *Florence*, where having seen all the curiosities that place afforded, he only waited to receive some remittances from his father, after which he intended to cross the *Appenines* to *Bolognio*, then proceed to *Venice*, and so through the *Tirolose*[37] to *Vienna*, and flattered himself with having time enough to visit all the different courts which compose the mighty empire of *Germany*.[38]

THESE remittances were delayed much longer than he had expected, and when they arrived, were accompanied by a positive command from his father to put an end to his travels, and return to *England* with all the expedition he could. – His surprize at so unlooked for an order, would have been equal to the mortification it gave him, if he had not received a letter from his sister at the same time, which informed him, that his being so suddenly recalled was wholly owing to the misfortunes in which their family was at present involved: – that soon after his departure, their father had discovered an intercourse between his wife and a person who pretended to be a relation, no way to the honour of either of them; – that frequent quarrels had at length separated them; – that he was engaged in a law-suit with her, and also in several others, with people to whom she, in revenge, as it was supposed, had given bonds, dated before marriage, for very great sums of money, pretended to have been borrowed of them by her; – that tho' the imposition was too gross not to be easily seen through, yet the forms of the courts of judicature could not be dispensed with, and the continual demands made upon him had laid him under such inconveniencies as obliged him even to lessen the number of his servants, and retrench his table: – she added, that he spoke of his dear *Natura* with the utmost tenderness, and was under a very great concern that the necessity of his affairs would not permit to send him any more such supplies as were requisite for the prosecution of his travels.

Natura at first felt a very great shock at this account; but it is the peculiar blessing of youth, not to be for any length of time affected with misfortunes; his melancholly soon dissipated, and he thought of nothing more than compliance with the command he had received, and also to perform it in the cheapest manner he could. – On speaking of his intentions of returning home, he was advised to go to *Leghorn*,[39] which being a very great port, it would be no difficulty to find a ship bound for *Holland* or *England*, in which he might take his passage at an easy rate. He had certainly taken this method, but meeting with an *English* gentleman, who was on his travels, and had not yet been at *Rome*, was perswaded by him to go back, on his offering to bear the whole expences of that route, for the pleasure of his company. – After a stay of two or three months there, they pursued their journey to *Paris*, where *Natura* renewed all the former acquaintance he had there: – the baron d'*Eyrac*, with whom he had contracted an intimate friendship, and from whom he concealed nothing of his affairs, was extremely concerned to hear the occasion of his being recalled so much sooner than he had expected, and made him an offer which suited very well with *Natura*'s inclination to accept: it was this.

That an old officer in the army having obtained leave to dispose of his commission, *Natura* should become the purchaser; and to enable him to do so, the baron would advance a sum of money, to be returned at several easy payments, as he received the profits arising from his troop.

Love and gallantry had already had their turns with *Natura*; ambition, and the pride of being in an independent state, began now to work in him: – as *France* was in alliance with *England*, there was neither shame nor danger in entering into her service:[40] – besides, he considered, that as his father was no longer in a condition to supply him with money abroad, he could not expect any settlement to be made on him at home that would be answerable to his former expectations; – and that by a captain's pay, joined to some assistance he might hope to receive sometimes from *England*, he should be enabled to make a very good figure in the world, till the misfortunes of his family should be retrieved, and if they never were so, he should at least have a provision for life, in a country he was not weary of.

He therefore made no hesitation of accepting this proof of the baron's friendship, who immediately went about making good his promise; and what with his money, and the great interest he had, both with the court and army, *Natura* was dispensed with, for not having been in the service before; and in a very few days saw himself at the head of a troop of horse.

His father, to whom he wrote an account of the step he had taken, with his motives for it, was far from being offended at it; tho' he told him it added to his trouble, to think his eldest son should be compelled, by his having entered into a second marriage, to have recourse to any avocation whatever for bread; but concluded with telling him, that in the severe necessity of their present circumstances, he could not have pitched on any thing more agreeable to his inclinations, or more honourable in itself.

This letter served to compose all the disquiets *Natura* had of disobliging a parent, for whom he retained the most tender, as well as dutiful regard, ever since the kind forgiveness he received from him at *Wapping*, which shews the great effect of lenity over a mind, where gratitude and generosity are not wholly extinguished; which, as I before observed, they never are, but by a long habitude of vice.

He was now as happy as he had any need to wish to be, enjoying all the pleasures of life in a reasonable way, and rarely transgressing the bounds of moderation; and when at any time, through the prevalence of example, or the force of his own passions, he was hurried to some little excesses, they were never such as could incur the censure of dishonourable or mean. He was punctual to his payments with the baron, and had the satisfaction of seeing himself intirely out of debt at three years end; which manner of behaviour so endeared him to that gentleman, that few friendships are to be found more sincere, than that which subsisted between them.

But as good sometimes arises out of evil, so what is in itself a real happiness, is not always without consequences altogether the reverse; as it proved to *Natura*, who from the most contented situation, all owing to the baron's friendship, was, on a sudden, by that very friendship, thrown into one of the greatest trouble and danger.

One morning, as he was dressing, the baron entered his chamber, with a countenance which before he spoke, denoted he had somewhat of importance to communicate: – *Natura* easily perceived it, and to put him out of pain, ordered his valet to leave the room; on which the other immediately told him, he was come to desire a proof of that sincere good-will he had professed for him. – *I should*, replied he, *be the most unworthy of mankind, if I had not in reality much more than is in the power of words to express, and not look on an opportunity given by you of testifying it, equal to any favour you have bestowed on me.*

The baron was at present in too much agitation of spirit to answer this compliment as he would have done at another time; and made haste to inform him, that the countess d'*Ermand*, who on some misunderstanding with her husband, had been confined in a monastery for several months, without any hopes of obtaining her release, had found means to convey a letter to him, earnestly requesting he would assist her in her escape: –*she has acquainted me*, continued he, *with the plot she has laid; – there is nothing impracticable in it; but I cannot do what she desires without the help of some trusty friend, and it is you alone I dare rely upon, in a business, which, if not carefully concealed, as well as resolutely acted, may be of very ill consequence.*

Natura did not greatly relish this piece of knight-errantry; but as he thought he ought to refuse nothing to the baron, hesitated not to assure him of the most ready compliance; on which the other told him, he must get two or three of his soldiers, who, disguised like peasants, but well mounted, and their swords concealed under their cloaths, must attend the expedition, and be at hand in case they should meet with any resistance, which, however, he said he did not apprehend, it being but ten small miles to the monastery, the road but little frequented, and the time agreed upon for the execution of the project twelve at night; so there was no great danger of any interruption, unless some unfortunate accident should happen. – *The lady*, continued he, *informs me she has observed the place where the portress constantly hangs up the key of the outer gate every night, and when the nuns are gone into the chapel to their midnight devotions, can easily slip out: – we have only therefore to be there exactly at the time, and be ready to receive her; and as for the rest, I have already provided a place where she may remain undiscovered, till something can be done for her.*

The baron added many things concerning the ill treatment she had received; but *Natura* did not give himself any trouble to examine into the merits of the cause, it was sufficient for him to do what he requested of him; and that night being the same had been appointed by the lady for the business to be done, he went immediately about preparing for it.

Accordingly, he selected from out of his troop three who seemed most proper to be employed in such an enterprize, and after having sworn them to secrecy in whatever they saw, or should happen, though without acquainting them with the main of the affair, or mentioning the baron d'*Eyrac*, told them in what manner they were to disguise themselves, and ordered they should attend him at the *Fauxbourg*,[41] a little after ten o'clock the same night.

Rejoiced at an opportunity of obliging their officer, especially as they doubted not of being well gratified, each gave a thousand oaths instead of the one required of him, to be both punctual and faithful in the discharge of the trust reposed in him.

In fine, all was conducted with a care and caution becoming of the gratitude and esteem *Natura* had for the baron, and as if he had himself approved of this undertaking, which, as I before observed, he could not do in his heart.

The two gentlemen, muffled up in their cloaks and vizarded, repaired to the *Fauxbourg*, at the appointed time, where they found the soldiers on the post allotted for them by their officer; on which they all rode off together, and arrived before the walls of the monastery some few minutes before twelve, at which hour precisely the gate was opened, and a woman appeared at it. – To prevent the loss of time, it had been concluded, that the baron should not dismount, but *Natura* perform the office of an equerry, in placing her behind him: just as he had alighted, and taken her in his arms, in order to perform that office, a great noise was heard; and in an instant, our adventurers found themselves surrounded by more than a dozen armed men, who rushed upon them from the covert of a wood: – the lady shrieked, and ran back into the convent, on *Natura*'s letting her go, in order to draw his sword against these antagonists who seemed resolute, either to kill or take him and his associates prisoners: – the fight was obstinate on both sides, tho' the baron finding his design defeated, had not entered into it at first, but trusted to the goodness of his horse for his escape, if his consideration for *Natura*, who being on foot, must have been immediately seized, had not prevented him. – At length, however, having received two or three wounds, and convinced of the impossibility of maintaining their ground against such an inequality of numbers, self-preservation prevailed; he broke thro' those that encompassed him, and setting spurs to his horse, had the good fortune to avoid the mischief which he knew must inevitably befal those he left behind.

THE three troopers gallantly defended their captain for some time, nor was he idle in making those who approached him too near, feel the sharpness of his sword; but not being able to get on horseback, all his courage, or that of his men, could not prevent him, and them, from being made prisoners. Several of the conquering party being officers of justice, they conducted them to *Paris*, where the soldiers were disposed of in the common goal,[42] but *Natura* who was known, was committed to the care of an exempt,[43] who treated him with the good manners his station demanded; he had received a pretty deep wound in the shoulder, and a surgeon was presently sent for; but no artery nor sinew being touched, no ill consequence was like to attend it.

IT may be imagined he passed the remainder of this night in a good deal of disquiet, as having lived long enough in *France* to know that an attempt of the nature he had been engaged in would find little mercy from the law. – A good part of the next day was passed, before they carried him to the magistrate, whose office it was to examine into such causes, his adversaries not having prepared their accusation; the heads of which were, that he had attempted a rape upon a married woman of quality; that he had contrived, with other persons, to take her out of the monastery, and had come with an armed force for that purpose. These articles having been deposed upon oath, the magistrate told him his crime was of a double nature, that he had violated both the civil and ecclesiastic laws; but as his office extended no farther than the former, he had only to demand of him what defence he had to make for himself in that part.

Natura had no other remedy than to deny all that was laid to his charge: – he protested, as he might truly do, that he was so far from entertaining any criminal designs on any lady in that monastery, that he did not so much as know the face of any one of them; and pretended, that being only riding out for the benefit of the air, he found himself attacked by persons unknown, with whom he confessed he had fought in his own defence.

But this availed not at all to his justification: – his own soldiers, who had been examined before himself, had confessed, that they were commanded by their officer to attend him on a certain enterprize, in which they were to behave with secresy and resolution; but said, they did not know of what sort it was, till they saw a woman come to the gate of the monastery, whom their captain presently took in his arms, but with what intent they could not pretend to say.

A letter also was produced, which madame d'*Ermand* had dropt, and which had occasioned this discovery of the intrigue, as it contained the whole method by which she was to be taken away; and tho' there was no name subscribed, appearances were strong against *Natura* as the author, and tho' he offered to bring many witnesses to prove it was a hand very different from what he wrote, yet it served at least to prove that it was sent by some one person in the company, and that if he were not the principal in this conspiracy, yet being the agent and abettor, as it was plain he was, by his bringing his own soldiers, he could not be judged less guilty.

After a long examination he was remanded to the exempt's house, till the sitting of the judges, which they told him would be in eight days; in which interval he was allowed to prepare what defence he had to make, and for that purpose advocates were allowed to come to him, but no other person whatever, not even his own servant, and he received attendance from those belonging to the exempt, who also fetched from his lodgings change of apparel, and all such necessaries as he had occasion for; care being taken to search every thing before it came to his hands, in order to prevent any letters being conveyed to him that way.

In this melancholly situation did he pass his time; but that was little in regard to his apprehensions of the future: – as his case stood there was little expectation of any thing less than a shameful death, perhaps ushered in by tortures worse than even that: – his advocates, however, and it is likely his accusers too, were of opinion that he had been in reality no more than an agent in this business, and therefore gave him to understand, that if he laid open the whole truth, and declared the name of the person chiefly concerned, it would greatly mitigate the severity of the laws in such cases; but this he would by no means be prevailed upon to do, resolving rather to suffer every thing they could inflict upon him, than be guilty of so mean and dishonourable an action as breach of trust, even to a person indifferent, but to a friend villainous in the most superlative degree: alike unmoved by arguments, as inflexible to menaces or perswasions, he persisted in answering, that he was ignorant of what they aimed at: – that he knew nothing of madame d'*Ermand* himself, was an intire stranger to her, and equally so to the ill designs on her they mentioned, either on his own account, or that of any other person.

He was neither so weak nor vain as to flatter himself his positiveness in denying what could be proved by so many witnesses, would be of any service at his trial; but as it was expected he should say something in his defence, and could say nothing else, without giving up his friend, he was determined not to depart from what he had alledged at first.

The count d'*Ermand*, who possibly had a suspicion of the truth, as it seems he long had entertained some jealous thoughts of the baron d'*Eyrac*, who had taken all opportunities of testifying an uncommon gallantry to his wife, would have given almost a limb to satiate his revenge against that gentleman: – the soldiers had been re-examined several times concerning that other person who was with them at the monastery, and had made his escape; but as they had neither seen his face, nor heard his name, it was impossible for them to make any discoveries: – these poor wretches were afterwards put to the torture, but that had, nor indeed could have, any other effect, than to make them curse their officer, who had been the cause of their sufferings.

In fine, monsieur d'*Ermand*, and the kindred of his wife, joined with the instigations of the clergy, who thought they had an equal right for revenge in this point, prevailed so far upon the civil magistrates, as to procure an order that *Natura* should himself undergo the same tortures his soldiers had done, thereby to extort that confession from him they could no otherwise procure: – this, notwithstanding, they had the lenity to inform him of, the day before that which was prefixed for the execution, thinking perhaps, that the menace of what he was condemned to endure, would be sufficient: but tho' human nature could not but shrink under such apprehensions, yet did his fortitude remain unshaken, and he thought of nothing but how to arm himself, so as to bear all should be inflicted on him with courage.

But there were no more than a few hours in which he had to meditate on what he had to do, when his affairs took a very different turn, and by the most unthought-of means imaginable: It was towards the close of day, when the wife of the exempt came into his chamber, and having locked the door, *I am come, captain,* said she, *to offer you life, liberty, and what is yet more, to put it in your power to avoid those dreadful tortures, which are preparing for you! – what would you do to gratify your preserver?* – The surprise *Natura* was in, did not hinder him from replying, that there was nothing with which he would not purchase such a deliverance, provided the terms were not inconsistent with his honour: – *No,* resumed she, *I know by your behaviour since in custody, and the resolution with which you have withstood all the temptations laid before you, for the unravelling an affair, you have, it is the opinion of every one, been led into only by your friendship to some person, that you regard nothing so much as honour; what I have to propose will be no breach of it; – but,* continued she, *time is precious, and opportunities of speaking to you are scarce; therefore know, in a few words, that I am weary of my husband's ill usage, desire nothing so much as to go where I may never see him more; and if you will make me the companion of your flight, and swear to take care of me till I shall otherwise dispose of myself; I have disguises for both of us prepared, and this night you shall be free.*

Natura had little need to hesitate if he should accept this proposal: – he saw there was at least a chance for escaping the dangers to which he was exposed; and should the woman's plot miscarry, and he detected of being an accomplice in it, his condition could not, even then, be worse than it was at present; he therefore embraced her with a fervor which she seemed very well pleased with, and assured her in the most solemn manner he would return all the obligations she conferred on him, by such ways as should be most agreeable to her. She then told him she had not slept for some time in the same bed with her husband, and therefore might easily come to him again as soon as the family were gone to their respective apartments; and having said this, went out of the room hastily, tho' not without returning his salute, and telling him he was worthy of greater risques than those she was about to run.

He was no sooner left alone, than he began to reflect on the capriciousness of his destiny, which to preserve him from suffering for a crime he was innocent of, was about to make him in reality guilty of one of the very same nature: it is likely, however, he was not troubled with many scruples on this head; or if any arose in his mind, they were soon dissipated in the consideration of what he owed to his own safety, which he yet could not greatly flatter himself with the hope of, as he was not ignorant how difficult it was for a delinquent to elude the diligence of those sent in search of him. The chance of such a thing notwithstanding was not to be neglected; and he waited with an impatience adequate to the occasion, for the hour in which he expected his deliverance.

It was little more than eleven o'clock, when she came into the chamber in the habit of a country fellow, which so intirely disguised her, that till she spoke, he took her for one of those who attend the prisoners in the circumstances he then was, and imagined some accident had prevented the execution of her plot; but he was soon convinced of his error, by her speaking, and at the same time presenting him with a coat, wig, and every thing proper to make him pass for such as she appeared herself: – the reader may suppose he wasted not much time in equipping himself, or in making any idle compliments; it was scarce midnight, when they both got safely out of the house, the door of which she shut softly after her.

She then proposed to him to go to the *Fauxbourg*, whence they might, without any suspicion, as passing for poor countrymen, get into the open road before day-break; but he would needs stop at the baron d'*Eyrac*'s, judging with good reason that they might be more securely concealed in his house, till the search should be over, than to pretend to travel in any shape whatever. She, who knew not what obligations the baron had to be faithful to him in this point, at first opposed it; but he at length prevailed, and they went boldly to the door; the family not being all in bed, it was immediately opened, but in the dress they were, found some difficulty to be admitted to the baron, who, the servant told them, was asleep; but *Natura*, with an admirable presence of mind, replied, that he had brought a letter from a friend in the country of the utmost importance, and must be delivered into the baron's own hands directly; on which he was at last won to let them come into the hall, while he sent to let his lord know.

WHETHER the baron had any suspicion of the truth, or not, is uncertain, but he ordered the men should be brought up; *Natura*, however, thought it most proper to speak to him alone, therefore left his companion below: – never was surprize greater than that of this nobleman, when the other discovered himself to him, and the means by which he had been set free. After the first demonstrations of joy and gratitude for the integrity he had shewn in resolving to endure every thing, rather than betray the trust reposed in him, it was judged necessary to send for his deliverer, to whom on her coming up, the baron made many compliments.

ON discoursing on what method was best for them to take, in order to prevent discovery the baron would by no means suffer them to pursue that of endeavouring to quit *France* till the search would be made should be entirely over; he told them, he had a place where he could answer with his life for their concealment, which indeed was that he had provided for the countess d'*Ermand*, in case they had not been disappointed in their designs. – *There*, said he, *you may remain, and be furnished with all things necessary*; – *I can come frequently to you, and inform you what passes, and when you may depart with safety, after we have contrived the means.*

THE exempt's wife, as well as *Natura*, highly approved of this offer; and the baron knowing any stay in his house might be dangerous both to himself and them, presently dressed himself, and went with them to the house he mentioned, where having seen them safe lodged, took his leave for that night, but seldom let a day pass without seeing them.

THIS was doubtless the only asylum which could have protected them from the strict search was made the next day; the house of every person, with whom either *Natura* or the woman had the least acquaintance, was carefully examined; but this scrutiny was soon over in that part, they supposed them to have left the city, and officers were sent in pursuit of them every road they could be imagined to take; so that had they fled, they must unavoidably have been taken. But not to be too tedious, it was five weeks before the baron could think it safe for them to leave *Paris*; and then hearing their enemies had lost all hope of finding them, and that the general opinion was, that they were quite got off, he told *Natura* that he believed they now might venture to go, taking proper precautions. On taking leave, he compelled *Natura* to accept of bills to the value of his commission, which, as he said, being lost meerly on his account, it was his duty to re-imburse: –nothing could be more tender than the parting of these two faithful friends; – necessity, however, must be obeyed; – they separated, after having settled every thing between them, and mutually promised to keep a correspondence by letters.

IT was judged best, and safest for them, to keep still in the same disguise till they should be entirely out of the *French* dominions, which happily at length they were, without the least ill accident befalling them, none suspecting them for other than they appeared, though the search after them was very strict, and a great reward offered for apprehending them. – As soon as they arrived at *Dover*, both threw off their borrowed shapes; *Natura* was again the fine gentleman, and his companion a very agreeable woman, who was so well satisfied with what she had done, and the behaviour of *Natura* towards her, that she had lost nothing of her good looks by the fatigue of her journey.

HERE they waited some time for the arrival of his servant, who knew nothing what was become of his master, since he had made his escape from the exempt, till he was entirely out of the kingdom, but had, all this while, been kept in good heart by the baron, who still had told him he was safe and well, and that he should soon hear news of him to his satisfaction; this faithful domestic, whom they had no pretensions to detain, now came with all his baggage, and *Natura* returned to *London*, in an equipage, not at all inferior to that in which he had left it.

THE first thing he did was to place the exempt's wife in a handsome lodging, and then went to wait upon his father, who had been much alarmed, at not having received any letter from him for a much longer time than he had been accustomed to be silent. The old gentleman was rejoiced to see him, after an absence of near six years, but sorry for the occasion, as his affairs were greatly perplexed, on account of the law-suits before mentioned, which being most of them in chancery,[44] were like to be spun out to a tedious length; but *Natura* soon informed him that he was in a condition, which at present did not stand in need of any assistance from him, and that he was determined to enter into some business for his future support.

BUT in the midst of these determinations, the remembrance of his unhappy contract with *Harriot* came into his mind; he thought he had reason to fear some interruption in his designs from the malice and wickedness of that woman: but being loth to renew the memory of his former follies, he forbore making any mention of it to his father, till that tender parent, not doubting but it would be a great satisfaction to him, to know himself entirely freed from all claims of the nature she had pretended to have on him, acquainted him, that after he was sent away, the first step he had taken, was to get the contract out of her hands.

THE transported *Natura* no sooner heard he had done so, than he cried out, *By what means, dear sir, was she prevailed upon to relinquish a title, by which she certainly hoped to make one day a very great advantage?*

Indeed, said the father, *I know not whether all the efforts I made for that purpose, would have been effectual, if fortune had not seconded my design: – she withstood all the temptations I laid in her way, rejected the sum I offered, and only laughed at the menaces I made, when I found she was not to be won by gentle means; and I began to despair of success, so much as to give over all attempts that way, when I was told she was in custody of an officer of the* compter,[45] *on account of some debts she had contracted: – on this your uncle put it into my head to charge her with several actions in fictitious names; so that being incapable of procuring bail, and going to be carried to prison, when I sent a person to her with an offer to discharge her from all her present incumbrances, on condition she gave up the contract, which I assured her, at the same time, she would not be the better for, it being my intention you should settle abroad for life.*

This, continued he, *in the exigence she then was, she thought it best to accept of, and I got clear of the matter, with much less expence than I had expected; her real debts not amounting to above half what I had once proposed to give her.*

NATURA was charmed to find himself delivered from all the scandal, and other vexations, with which he might otherwise have been persecuted his whole life long, both by herself and the emissaries she had always at hand, and might have employed against him: nor was he much less delighted to hear that she had also received some part of the punishment her crimes deserved, in the disappointment of all her impudent and high-raised expectations.

HAVING nothing now to disturb him in the prosecution of his purpose, he set about it with the utmost diligence; and as he had a considerable quantity of ready money by him to offer either by way of præmium, or purchase, there was not, indeed, any great danger of his continuing long without employment, nor that, so qualified, he might not also be able to chuse out of many, one which should be most agreeable to his inclinations.

ACCORDINGLY he in a little time hearing of a genteel post under the government that was to be disposed on, he laid out part of his money in the purchase of it, and with the remainder set up the exempt's wife in a milliner's shop, in which, being a woman of a gay polite behaviour, she soon acquired great business, especially as she pretended to have left *France* on the score of religion, and went constantly every day to prayers, after having formally renounced the errors of the church of *Rome: Natura* visited her very often out of gratitude, and perhaps some sparks of a more warm passion; and they had many happy hours together, which the talk of their past adventures contributed to heighten, as afflictions once overcome, serve to enhance present happiness.

SEVERAL matches were now proposed to *Natura*, but he rejected them all; whether it were that he had not seen the face capable of fixing his heart, or whether he was willing to wait the determination of his father's affairs, in order to marry to greater advantage, it is hard to say; tho' probably the latter was the true reason; for ambition now began to display itself in his bosom, and by much got the better of those fond emotions which a few years past had engrossed him: he now began to think that grandeur had charms beyond beauty, though far from being insensible of that too, he was not without other amours than that he still continued with the *French* woman: the raising his fortune was, however, his principal view, and for that purpose he neglected nothing tending to promote it; he made his court to those of the great men, who he knew could be serviceable to him with so much success, that he had many promises of their interest for a better post, as soon as opportunity presented.

FORTUNE for a while seemed inclined to favour him in a lavish manner; his mother-in-law died, and with her many of the vexatious suits dropped, and others were compromised at an easy rate, so that his father was soon in a condition to make a settlement upon him sufficient to qualify him for a seat in parliament, which, on the first vacancy, thro' favour, he got into, though at that time the house was not crowded with placemen, as it since has been: in fine, he was beloved and caressed by persons of the highest rank, and every one looked upon him as a man who, in time, would make a very considerable figure in the world.

HIS friends remonstrating that as he was twenty-nine, it was time for him to think of marriage, and a proposal being made on that account with a young lady, of an ancient and honourable family, who, besides a large fortune in her own hands, had the reputation of every other requisite to render that state agreeable, he hesitated not to embrace it: – he made his addresses to her, she accepted of them, and in as short a time as could be expected, contented to give him her hand; – the kindred on both sides were very well pleased, and tho' her family had some advantages in point of birth over his, yet as he seemed in a fair way of doing honour to it, there was not the least objection made; but articles were drawn, and a day appointed for the wedding.

BUT how little dependance is to be placed on fortune! how precarious are the smiles of that uncertain goddess, when most secure of her promised favours, and just upon the point, as we imagine, of receiving all we have to wish from her, she often snatches away the expected good, and showers upon us the worst of mischiefs treasured in her store-house! – Some few days before that which was to crown his hopes, he happened in company to be discoursing of his travels, and mentioning some things he had seen in *France*, a gentleman who imagined he spoke too favourably of the chevalier *St. George*,[46] and pretended he had also been there, took upon him to contradict almost all he said concerning that place and person: *Natura* knowing himself in the right, and being a little heated with wine, maintained the truth of what he alledged, with more impetuosity than policy perhaps would have suffered him to have done at another time; and the other no less warmly opposing, passion grew high on both sides; – the lie was given and returned; – each was no less quick with his sword than his repartee, several passes were made, but the company parted them: and though they stayed together, neither of them was reconciled, nor in good humour for what was past.

In going home *Natura* and one gentleman kept together, as their way happened to be the same, when, see the wild effects of party-rage! all on a sudden, the person who had been his antagonist, and, it seems, had followed, came up to them, with his sword drawn, and told *Natura* he was a scoundrel, and a fool, for what he had said; his words, and the sight of his weapon, made him put himself immediately in a posture of defence, which indeed he had need of; for had he been less nimble, he had received the sword of the other in his body, before the gentleman who was with him could do any thing to separate them; nor were his efforts for that purpose sufficient to prevent them from engaging with a vehemence, which permitted neither of making use of much skill: it was however the chance of *Natura* to give his adversary a wound, which made him fall, as he imagined, dead; on which the disinterested person made the best of his way, as being afraid of being taken up by the watch, who were then just coming by: – *Natura* did the same, and thinking it improper to go home, went to the house of a friend, in whom he could confide, and who, on enquiry the next day, brought him an account, that the person with whom he had fought was dead, but had lived long enough to acquaint those who took him up, by whom he had received his hurt; and that warrants were already out for apprehending the murderer, as he was now called.

What now was to be done! *Natura* found himself under the necessity of going directly out of the way, and by that means endanger the loss of his employment, and also of his intended bride; or by staying expose himself to a shameful trial at the *Old Bailey*, which, he had reason to fear, would not end in his favour, the deceased having many friends and relations at the bar; and the very person who had been witness of their combat, somewhat a-kin to him: – it was therefore his own inclination, as well as the advice of his friends, that prevailed on him to make his escape into some foreign part, while they were looking for him at home; which he accordingly did that same hour, taking post for *Harwich*, where, through the goodness of his horse, he arrived that night, and immediately embarked in a fishing-smack, which carried him into *Holland*.

He had leisure now to reflect on his late adventure, which afforded the most melancholly retrospect; the happy situation he had been in, and the almost assured hopes of being continued in for life, made his present one appear yet worse, than in reality it was: he now looked on himself as doomed to be a vagrant all his days, driven from his native country for ever, and the society of all his friends, and torn beyond even a possibility of recovering, from a lady, to whom he was so near being united for ever, whom he loved, and whose fortune and kindred had given him just expectation of advancement in the world.

THESE gloomy thoughts took him wholly up for some days, but he was not yet arrived at those years, in which misfortunes sink too deeply on the soul; these vexatious accidents by degrees lost much of their ferocity, and he began to consider how much beneath a man of courage it was to give way to despair at any event whatever, and that he ought to look forward, and endeavour to *retrieve*, not *lament*, the mischief that was past. He wrote to his father an exact account of every thing, and intreated his advice: he sent also a letter to the young lady, full of the most tender expressions, and pressures for the continuance of her affection; though this latter was more for the sake of form than any hope he had of being granted what he asked, or as he was circumstanced, any benefit he could have received from it, if obtained.

THE answer his father sent, gave him both pain and pleasure; it informed him, that the wounds he had given the person with whom he fought, were not mortal; that it was only the vast effusion of blood which had thrown him into a fainting, which occasioned the report of his death, and that he was now in a fair way of recovery; so that he, *Natura*, might return as soon as he pleased, there being no danger on account of the rencounter; but that the occasion of that quarrel being a party-affair, and represented in its worst colours by some private enemies, it had reached the ears of the ministry, who, looking on him as a dissaffected person, had already disposed of his employment; he also informed him, that he must not flatter himself with being able ever hereafter to be thought qualified to hold any place or office under the government: – he also added, that the friends of his intended bride were so incensed against him, that they protested, they would sooner see her in her coffin, than in the arms of a man who had incurred the odious appellation of a *Jacobite*; and that she herself expressed her detestation of the principles he was now accused of, with no less virulence and contempt; – had torn the letter he had sent to her in a thousand pieces; and to shew how much she was in earnest, had accepted the addresses of a gentleman, who had been long his rival, and to whom it was expected she would soon be married.

IF *Natura* rejoiced to find himself cleared of having been the death of a fellow-creature, he was equally mortified at having rendered himself obnoxious to those who alone were capable of gratifying his ambition: as for the change in the lady's sentiments concerning him, he was under much less concern; he thought the affection she professed for him must have been very small, when a difference of opinion in state-affairs, and that too but supposed, could all at once erace it, and rather despised, than lamented, the bigotry of party-zeal, which had occasioned it: – his good sense made him know, that to deny all the good qualities of a person, meerly because those good qualities were not ornamented with the favours of fortune, was both unjust and mean; and the proof she gave of her weakness and ungenerosity in this point, intirely destroyed all the passion he once had for her, and consequently all regret for the loss of her.

He could not, however, think of returning to *England* yet a while; his father's letter had given some hints, as if there was a design on foot, and he was confirmed soon after of the truth of it, for expelling him the house; and he thought it was best to spare his enemies that labour, and quit it of his own accord: and in this he found himself intirely right, when on writing to some persons of condition, with whom he had been most intimate, he found by their answers, that it was now known he had been in the *French* service, which both himself and his father had kept a secret, even from their nearest kindred; not there was any thing in it which could be confirmed into a crime, as the nations were then in alliance, but because as he could not possibly enjoy a commission there, without conforming to the ceremonies of the *Romish* church,[47] it must infallibly be a hindrance to his advancement in a *Protestant* country. It is certain, *Natura* was of a temper to make good the proverb, *That when one is at* Rome, *one must do as they do at* Rome: – and though he had gone to hear *mass,* because it was his interest, and the necessity of his affairs obliging him in a manner to seek his bread at that time, yet was he far from approving the superstitions of that church: all that he could write, however, or his friends urge for him on this head, was ineffectual; he passed for a *papist* and a *jacobite* with every body: pursuant therefore to his resolution of continuing abroad, till these discourses should be a little worn out, he wrote again to his father, and settled his affairs so as to receive remittances of money, at the several places to which he intended to go.

CHAP. IV.

The power of fear over a mind, weak either by nature, or infirmities of body: The danger of its leading to despair, is shewn by the condition Natura *was reduced to by the importunities of priests of different perswasions. This chapter also demonstrates, the little power people have of judging what is really best for them, and that what has the appearance of the severest disappointment, is frequently the greatest good.*

As to lose the memory of his disgrace, or at least all those gloomy reflections it had occasioned, was the chief motive which had made *Natura* resolve to travel a second time, it was a matter of indifference to him which way he went. He first took care to make himself master of all that was worth observation in *Holland,* where he found little to admire, except the *Stadthouse,*[48] and the magnificence with which king *William,* after his accession to the crown of these kingdoms, had ornamented his palace at *Loo;*[49] but the rough, unpolite behaviour of the people, disgusted him so much, that he stayed no longer among them than was necessary to see what the place afforded, and then passed on to *Brussels, Antwerp,* and, in fine, left no great city, either in *Dutch* or *French Flanders* unvisited; thence went into *Germany*, where his first route was to *Hanover*, having, it seems, a curiosity of seeing a prince, whose brows were one day to be incircled with the crown of *England*;[50] but this country was, at that time, in so low and wretched a condition, that whether he looked on the buildings, the lands, or the appearance of the inhabitants, all equally presented a scene of poverty to his eyes; he therefore made what haste he could out of it, having found nothing, except the Elector himself, that gave him the least satisfaction. He was also at several other petty courts, all which served to inspire in him not the most favourable idea of *Germany*.

AT length he arrived at *Vienna*, a city pompous enough to those who had never seen *Rome* and *Paris*; but however it may yield to them in elegance of buildings, gardening, and other delicacies of life, it was yet more inferior in the manners of the people; – he perceived among the persons of quality, an affectation of grandeur, a state without greatness, and in the lower rank of gentry, a certain stiffness, even to the meanest, and an insufferable pride, which came pretty near ferocity:[51] – the costly, but ill-contrived parades frequently made, discovered less their riches than their bad taste, and appeared the more ridiculous to *Natura*, as they were extolled for their magnificence and elegance; but, even here, as indeed all over *Germany*, the courts of *Berlin* and *Dresden* excepted, you see rather an *aim* of attracting admiration and respect, than the *power* of it. These, however, were the sentiments of *Natura*, others perhaps may judge differently.

BUT whatever may be the deficiencies of *Germany* in matters of genius, wit, judgment, and manners, there is none in good eating, and good wine; and though their fashion of cookery is not altogether so polite, nor so agreeable to the palates of others as their own, yet it must be confessed, that in their way, they are very great epicures; but though they generally eat voraciously, they drink yet more; and so nimbly do they send the glass about, that a stranger finds it no small difficulty to maintain his sobriety among them.[52]

NATURA'S too great compliance with their intreaties in this point, had like to have proved fatal to him: – the strength of the wines, and drinking them in a much larger quantity than he had been accustomed to, so inflamed his blood, that he soon fell into a violent fever, which for some days gave those that attended him, little hopes of his recovery; but by the skill of his physician, joined to his youth, and the goodness of his constitution, the force of the distemper at last abated, yet could not be so intirely eradicated, as not to leave a certain pressure and debility upon the nerves, by some called a fever on the spirits, which seemed to threaten either an atrophy or consumption; his complexion grew pale and livid, and his strength and flesh visibly wasted; and what was yet worse, the vigour of his mind decayed, in proportion with that of his external frame, insomuch that, falling into a deep melancholy, he considered himself as on the brink of the grave, and expected nothing but dissolution every hour.

WHILE he continued in this languishing condition, he was frequently visited by the priests, who in some parts of *Germany*, particularly at *Vienna*, are infinitely more inveterate against *Protestantism* than at *Paris*, or even at *Rome*, though the *papal* seat; as indeed anyone may judge, who has heard of the many and cruel persecutions practised upon the poor *Protestants* by the emperors, in spite of the repeated obligations they have had to those powers who profess the doctrines of *Calvin* and *Luther*;[53] but gratitude is no part of the characteristic of a *German*.

THESE venerable distracters of the human mind, were perpetually ringing hell and damnation in his ears, in case he abjured not, before his death, the errors in which he had been educated, and continued in so many years, and by acts of penance and devotion, reconcile himself to the mother church; they pleaded the antiquity of their faith, brought all the fathers they could muster up, to prove that alone was truly orthodox, and that all dissenting from it was a sin not to be forgiven.

ON the other hand, the *English* ambassador's chaplain, who knew well enough what they were about, omitted nothing that might confirm him in the principles of the reformation, and convince him that the church of *England*, as by law established, had departed only from the errors which had crept into the primitive church, not from the church itself, and that all the superstitious doctrines now preached up by the *Romish* priests, were only so many impositions of their own, calculated to inrich themselves, and keep weak minds in awe.

NATURA, who had till now contented himself with understanding moral duties, and had never examined into matters of controversy between the two religions, now found both had so much to say in defence of their different modes of worship, that he became very much divided in his sentiments; and each remonstrating to him by turns, the danger of dying in a wrong belief, wrought so far upon the present weakness of his intellects, as to bring him into a fluctuation of ideas, which might, in time, either have driven him into despair, or made him question the very fundamentals of a religion, the merits of which its professors seemed to place so much in things of meer form and ceremony.[54]

BY this may be seen how greatly *christianity* suffers by the unhappy divisions among the professors of it: – much it is to be wished, though little to be hoped, that both sides would be prevailed upon to recede a little from their present stiffness in opinion, or be at least less virulent in maintaining it; since each, by endeavouring to expose and confute what they look upon as an absurdity in the other, join in contributing to render the truth of the whole suspected, and not only give a handle to the avowed enemies, of depreciating and ridiculing all the sacred mysteries of religion, but also stagger the faith of a great many well-meaning people, and afford but a too plausible pretence for that sceptism[55] which goes by the name of *free-thinking*, and is of late so much the fashion.

In another situation, perhaps, *Natura* would have been little affected with any thing could have been said on this score; but health and sickness make a wide difference in our way of thinking:[56] – when surrounded by the gay pleasures of life, and in the full vigour and capacity of enjoying them, we either do not reflect at all, or but cursorily on the evil day; but when cold imbecility steals upon us, either through age or accidents, and death and eternity stare us in the face, we have quite other sentiments, other wishes: – whoever firmly believes, that in leaving this life, we but step into another, either of happiness or misery, and that which ever it proves, will be without end, or possibility of change, and that the whole of future welfare depends on the road we take in going out of this world, will be very fearful lest he should chuse the wrong; and it is not therefore strange, that while, with equal force, the *papist* pulled one way, and the *protestant* another, the poor penitent should be involved in the most terrible uncertainty.

Happy, therefore, was it, both for the recovery of his mind and body, that his physicians finding all their recipes had little effect, advised him to seek relief from the waters of the *Spa*,[57] and as it was their opinion, they would be of more efficacy, when drank upon the spot, he accordingly took his journey thither, but by reason of his weakness, was obliged to be carried the whole way in a litter.

It is very probable, that being eased of the perplexities the incessant admonitions of the priests of different opinions had given him, contributed as much as the waters to his amendment; but to which ever of these causes it may be imputed, it is certain that he every day became better, and as his strength of body returned, so did that of his mind, in proportion; with his apprehensions of death, his disquiets about matters of religion subsided also, and whenever any thing of that kind came cross his thoughts, it was but by starts, and was soon dissipated with other ideas, which many objects at this place presented him with.

But that to which he was chiefly indebted for the recovery of his former gaiety of temper, was meeting with an *English* family, with whom he had been extremely intimate; the lady had come thither for the same purpose he had done, her husband being very tender of her, would needs accompany her, and they brought with them their only daughter, a young lady of great beauty, and not above eighteen, in hopes, as they said, of alleviating a certain melancholly, to which she was addicted, without any cause, at least any that was visible, for it.

Natura had often seen the amiable *Maria* (for so she was called) but had never felt for her any of those pleasing, and equally painful, emotions, which a nearer conversation with her now inspired him with: – he had always thought her very handsome, but she now appeared perfectly adorable in his eyes: – the manner of her behaviour, that modest sweetness which appeared through her whole deportment, and seemed, as it were, a part of her soul, had for him irresistible charms; and as he very well knew the circumstances of her family such, as his friends could make no reasonable objections against, nor his own such as could be thought contemptible by those of her kindred, he attempted not to repel the satisfaction which he felt, in the hopes of being one day able to make an equal impression on her heart.

THE very first use he made of his intire recovery from his late indisposition, was an endeavour to convince her how much her presence had contributed to it, and that the supremest wish his soul could form, was to enjoy it with her in the nearest, and most tender union, as long as life continued. – She received the declarations he made her of his passion with great reserve, and yet more coldness; and affected to take them only for the effects of a gallantry, which she told him was far from being agreeable to a person of her humour: but he imputing her behaviour only to an excess of that extreme modesty which accompanied all her words and actions, was so far from being rebuffed at it, that he acquainted her parents with his inclinations, and, at the same time, intreated their permission for prosecuting his addresses to her.

BOTH of them heard his proposals with a joy which it was impossible for either, especially the mother of that lady, to conceal: – each cried out, almost at the same time, that the sentiments he expressed for their daughter, was an honour they hoped she had too much good sense not to accept with the utmost satisfaction, and added, that they would immediately lay their commands upon her, to receive him in the manner she ought to do.

AS their families and fortunes were pretty equivalent, and *Maria*, besides her being an heiress, had beauty enough to expect to marry, even above her rank, *Natura* could not keep himself from being a little astonished at the extravagance of pleasure they testified at the offer he had made: parents generally take some time to consider, before they give their assent to a proposal of this sort; and as he knew they were very well acquainted with the occasion of his leaving *England* this second time, and were of a party the most opposite that could be to that he was suspected to have favoured, their extreme readiness to dispose of their only daughter, and with her their whole estate, to him seemed the more strange, as he had been, ever since he conceived a passion for *Maria*, in the most terrible apprehension of meeting with a different reception from them, meerly on the account of his supposed principles.

THE transport, however, that so unexpected a condescension gave him, prevented him from examining too deeply what might be the motives that induced them to it, and he gave himself wholly up to love, gratitude, and the delightful thoughts of being in a short time possessed of all he at present wished, or imagined he ever should ask of Heaven.

BUT how were all these rapturous expectations dashed, when soon after going to visit *Maria*, he found her lovely eyes half drowned in tears, and her whole frame in the utmost disorder: – *What, madam*, cried he, with a voice which denoted both grief and surprize, *can have happened, to give you any cause of the disquiet I see in you! – You,* replied she, snatching away her hand, which he had taken, *you alone are the cause; – what encouragement did I ever give you,* continued she, *that should make you imagine the offers you have made my parents would be agreeable to me? – Did I ever authorize you to ask a consent from them, which I was determined never to grant myself, and which, I will suffer a thousand deaths rather than ratify.*

THE confusion *Natura* was in at these words was so great, that it prevented him from making any answer; but he looked on her in such a manner as made her ashamed of what she had said, and perhaps too of the passion that had so far transported her; and perceiving he still continued silent, *I own myself obliged for the affection you express for me,* resumed she, with more mildness, *though it is at present the greatest misfortune could have happened to me. Could I have thought you would have declared yourself in the manner you have done to my father and mother, I would have convinced you how impossible it would be for you to reap any advantage from it, and that by so doing you would only make me the most wretched creature in the world; but all is now too late, and I foresee the cruel consequence.* – Here her tears interrupted the passage of her words, and *Natura* having recollected himself, began to complain of the severity of his destiny, which compelled him to *love* with the most violent passion a person who could only return it with an equal degree of hate. – *Love,* replied she, with a deep sigh, *is not in our power; – let me therefore conjure you, by all that which you pretend to have for me, to proceed no farther in this business, nor endeavour to prevail on my parents to force an inclination, which no obligations to them, services from you, or length of time can ever influence in your favour; for be assured, that if you do, you will only see the hand should be given you at the altar, employed in cutting my own throat or plunging a dagger in my breast.*

WITH these words, and an air that had somewhat of wildness in it, she flung out of the room, leaving him in a consternation impossible to describe, almost to conceive; her mother came in immediately after, and judging by his countenance how her daughter had behaved, told him he must not regard the coyness of a young girl; that she doubted not but *Maria* would soon be convinced what was her true happiness; and that a little perseverance and assiduity on his side, and authority on theirs, would remove all the scruples, bashfulness alone had created in her: *No, madam,* answered he, with some impatience, *there is somewhat more than all this you have mentioned, against me; – there is a rooted detestation to me in the very soul of* Maria, *which as I cannot but despair of being ever able to remove, common reason bids me attempt no farther.*

THE mother of *Maria* appeared very much perplexed, and said a great deal to perswade him that his apprehensions were without foundation; but the young lady had expressed herself in terms too strong for him not to be perfectly assured she was in earnest; and being willing to ruminate a little on the affair, he took leave, though not without the other extorting a promise from him, of coming again the next day.

Natura had not given himself much time to reflect, before he conceived great part of the truth: – he could not think either his person or qualifications so contemptible, as to inspire a heart unprepossessed by some other object, with an aversion such as *Maria* had expressed: he therefore concluded, she had disposed of her affections before she knew of his: it also seemed plain to him that her parents were not ignorant of her attachment, and being such as they could not approve of, it was that which had rendered them both so ready to snatch at his proposal, without any mention of those considerations they would otherwise naturally have had of jointure, settlements, and all those things, previous to marriage, between persons of condition.

He was the more confirmed in this belief, when the father came to his lodgings the next morning; and without seeming to know anything of what had passed between him, either with his wife, or *Maria*, asked, in a gay manner, how the latter had received his addresses? To which *Natura* answered in the same manner as he had done to her mother; adding only, that he could not avoid believing her heart was already engaged to some more worthy man, and was sorry his own unhappy passion had occasioned any interruption. The father left nothing unsaid that might dissipate such a conjecture, and affected to railly him on a jealousy which, he said, was common to lovers; and then told him a long story how himself had formerly suffered much by the same vain imagination. But all this was so far from making *Natura* doubt the truth of his conjectures, that, seeing through the artifice, he was the more convinced they were intirely right.

He went, notwithstanding, in the afternoon, either because he had promised to do so, or because he could not all at once resolve to banish himself from a person he took so much pleasure in beholding, though now without hopes of ever being able to obtain: – being left alone with *Maria*, both of them remained in a kind of sullen silence for some minutes, till at last the force of his passion in spite of himself made him utter some complaints on the cruelty of fortune, and his own insensibility, which had denied him the opportunity of discovering the thousand charms he now found in her, till too late to have his adoration of them acceptable to her. *I have not less reason,* said she, *to accuse the chance which at this time brought us together, than you can possibly have; since the love you profess for me, and which I once more assure you I can never return, has laid me under the severest displeasure of my parents; – but I had hopes,* continued she, *after the declaration I made you yesterday, that you would have renounced all pretensions to me, and had generosity enough in your nature, not to have taken the advantage of my father and mother's power over me, to force me into a compliance, which must be fatal to one or both of us.*

No, madam, answered he, much surprized, *I am far from even a wish of becoming guilty of what you accuse me with; – dear as I prize your person, I would not attempt to purchase it at the expence of your peace of mind; nor could I be truly blessed in the enjoyment of the* one, *without the* other; *– it is only to* Maria *herself I would have been obliged, not to the authority of her parents.*

Will you then quit me, cried she hastily, *and let the act appear wholly your own? – I will,* replied he, after a pause, *difficult as it is to do so, and irresolute and inconstant as it will make me seem. That,* said she, *will be an action truly deserving my esteem; and in return, know I am much more your friend in refusing your addresses, than either my parents in encouraging, or your own mistaken wishes in offering them: – but,* pursued she, *I beg you will enquire no farther, but leave me, and break off with my parents in the best manner you can.*

FAIN would he have obtained a farther explanation of words, which seemed to him to contain some mystery, as indeed they did; but she was no less inflexible to his intreaties on that score, than she had been to those of his love; and perceiving his presence gave her only pain, he went out of the house with an aking and agitated heart, but resolved to do as she desired and he had promised, whatever pangs it cost him.

HE had not gone above an hundred paces on his way home, before he was accosted by a man who seemed like an upper-servant in a gentleman's family, and who, with a low bow, delivered him a letter, which, on seeing directed to himself, he hastily opened, and found contained these lines:

'SIR,

IF you have any thing in you of the gallantry, generosity, or gratitude, for which your country is famed, come where the bearer will conduct you, to a woman, who has suffered much on your account, and can be extricated from an unhappy affair only by your advice.'

NATURA was little in a humour to pursue an adventure of the kind this seemed to be; but curiosity got the better of his spleen, and he bad the fellow lead the way, and he would follow; which he accordingly did, till they were out of the town, and from the sight of all the houses.

BEING come into a field which was a kind of an inclosure, and a theatre proper enough for the tragedy intended to be acted on it, the fellow turned back, and drew a pistol, which he instantly discharged at the head of *Natura*, crying at the same time, Maria *sends you this.* – Heaven so directed the bullets, that the one passed by his ear, and the other only grazed upon his shoulder, without doing any farther damage, than taking away a small piece of his sleeve. It is easy to judge of his surprize, yet was it not so great as to disable him from drawing his sword in order to revenge himself on the assassin; but the wretch, in case his fire-arms should miscarry, had provided a falchion[58] concealed under his coat, with which, the same instant, he ran furiously on *Natura*, and had certainly cleft him down, tho' perhaps in doing so, he might have received his own death's wound at the same time from the sword of his antagonist; but both these events were happily prevented by the peculiar interposition of Divine Providence: some reapers, who had lain asleep under an adjacent hedge, being roused with the noise of the pistol, ran to the combatants, and with their hooks beat down both their weapons; while at the same fortunate crisis, two gentlemen attended by three servants, who happening to cross a road which had a full prospect over the field, had seen, at a distance, all that had passed, and came galloping up to the assistance of *Natura*, who was then beginning to interrogate the villain on the occasion of this attempt; but he refused to give any satisfactory answer to what he said, so was dragged by the countrymen, and others, who by this time were gathered together, back into the town, and carried immediately before a magistrate, who, on his obstinately refusing to make any confession, committed him to prison.

Natura, who imagined nothing more certain, than that *Maria* had set this fellow on to murder him, as the surest way to get rid of his addresses, went directly to the house where she lodged, full of a resentment equal to the detestable crime of which he thought her guilty; – he found her in the room with her father and mother, of whom he took little notice, but stepped forwards to the place where she was sitting; and seeing her a little surprized, which indeed was occasioned only by his sudden return, and the abrupt manner in which he entered: – *You find, madam*, said he, with a voice broke with rage, *your plot has miscarried*; – Natura *still lives, though it must be owned your emissary did all could be expected, to obey your commands, for my destruction.*

It is hard to say, whether *Maria*, or her parents, were in the greatest consternation at these words; but he soon unravelled the mystery, by relating the whole story, not omitting what the assassin said in presenting the pistol, and then as a confirmation throwed the letter he had received into *Maria's* lap, and at the same time shewed the passage one of the bullets had made through the sleeve of his coat: – the young lady no sooner cast her eyes upon the letter, than she gave a great shriek, and crying out, *O* Humphry, Humphry! *every way my ruin!* immediately fell fainting on the floor; her father, without regarding the condition she was in, snatched up the paper, the hand-writing of which he presently recollected, as having, it seems, intercepted several wrote by the same person; –*Abandoned, infamous creature*, cried he; – *shame of thy sex and family*, added the mother, striking her breast in the utmost agony: – in fine, never was such a scene of distraction and despair! – *Natura*, injured as he had been, could not behold it without compassion; – he ran by turns to *Maria*, endeavouring to raise her, – then to her parents, beseeching them to moderate their passion, – then to her again: – *You are too generous*, said the father, *let her die, happy had it been if she had perished in the cra-*

dle: – Just as he spoke these words she revived, and lifting up her eyes, *O, I am no murd'ress*, cried she, *guilty as I am, in this Heaven knows my innocence. – It is false, it is false*, said the father; *but were it true, canst thou deny, thou most abandoned wretch, that thou wert also ignorant that the villain who wrote this letter had followed us to* Spaw,[59] *and bring a second shame upon us?* – She answered to this only with her tears, which assuring him she had no defence to make on this article, his rage grew more inflamed; he loaded her with curses, and could not keep himself from spurning her with his feet, as she still lay groveling on the ground, and might perhaps have proceeded to greater violences, had not *Natura*, by main force, withheld him, while her mother, tho' little less incensed against her, dragged her in a manner out of the room, more dead than alive.

THE unhappy object removed from his sight, the provoked father grew somewhat more calm, and turning to *Natura, You see now, sir*, said he, *how unworthy this wretched girl is of that affection with which you once honoured her*; *but how shall I obtain your pardon for what the too great tenderness for an only child has made me guilty of to you; – all I can say is, that I hoped she had been reclaimed, and so far from even a wish to repeat her crimes, that she had only an utter detestation for the villain that had seduced her.*

NATURA knew very well how he ought to judge of this affair; but as he had an aversion to dissimulation, and was unwilling to add any thing to the affliction he was witness to, he said little in answer to the other's apology, but that he was extremely sorry for *Maria*, and the misfortunes she had brought on the family; and then took his leave as soon as decency would permit; but with a firm resolution to hold no farther conversation, wherever they should hereafter happen to meet, with persons who had all of them, in their several capacities, used him so ill.

THE assassin was soon after brought to a public tryal, where tortures making him confess the truth, he acknowledged, that having been a servant in the family, the beauty of *Maria* had inspired him with desires, unbefitting the disparity between them; – that emboldened by an extraordinary goodness she shewed to him, he had declared his passion, and met with all the returns he wished; – that she became pregnant by him, and had made a vow to keep herself single, till the death of her father should leave her at liberty to marry him; but that an unlucky accident having discovered their amour, he was turned out of the house, and the grief *Maria* conceived at it occasioned an abortion; but that after her recovery she contrived means to meet him privately, and to support him with money, that he might not be obliged to go to service any more; that she had acquainted him with their coming to the *Spa*, and not only knew of his following them in disguise to that place, but contrived a rendezvous where they saw each other often, and he learned from her the addresses of *Natura*, and the positive commands laid on her by her parents of marrying him, in order to retrieve her honour and reputation; that as besides the extreme love he had for her, his own interest obliged him to hinder the match, if by any means he could; and finding no other than the death of his rival, he had attempted it by the way already mentioned: but cleared *Maria*, however, of all guilt on this score, who, he assured the court, knew nothing of his intentions of murder.

THE sentence passed on him was, to be hanged in chains, which was accordingly executed in a few days; though *Natura*, pitying his case, in consideration of the greatness of the temptation, laboured for a mitigation of his doom. – He never saw the unfortunate *Maria* afterwards, but heard she was in a condition little different from madness, which making her parents think it improper she should return to *England*, they conveyed her to *Liege*, where they placed her as a pensioner in the convent of *English* nuns, there to remain till time and reflection should make a change in her, fit to appear again in the world; which proceeding in them shewed, that whatever aversion some people have to *this*, or *that* form of religion, they can countenance, nay, pretend to approve it, when it happens to prove for their convenience to do so.

NATURA was now intirely cured of his passion, but could not avoid feeling a very tender commiseration for her, who had been the unhappy object of it; he found also, on meditating on every passage of this adventure, that she was infinitely less to blame, in regard to him, than her parents had been; and that what he had accused, as cruel in her, was much more kind than the favour they had pretended for him. – When he reflected on the gulph of misery he had so narrowly escaped, he was filled with the most grateful sentiments to that Providence which had protected him; and also made sensible, that what we often pray for, as the greatest of blessings, would, if obtained, prove the severest curse: – a reflection highly necessary for all who desire any thing with too much ardency.

CHAP. V.

Shews that there is no one human advantage to which all others should be sacrificed: – the force of ambition, and the folly of suffering it to gain too great an ascendant over us: – public grandeur little capable of atoning for private discontent; among which jealousy, whether of love or honour, is the most tormenting.

THE desire of being well settled in the world is both natural and laudable; but then great care ought to be taken to moderate this passion, in order to prevent it from engrossing the mind too much; for it is the nature of ambition, not only to stop at nothing that tends to its gratification, but also to be ever craving new acquisitions, ever unsatisfied with the former. – One favourite point is no sooner gained, than another appears in view, and is pursued with the same eagerness: – what we once thought the *summum bonum* of our happiness, seems nothing when we have attained to the possession of it, while that which is unaccomplished, fires us with impatience, and robs us of every enjoyment we might take in life.

NATURA having now been absent two years, thought the idle rumours concerning him, as to his principles in party-matters, would be pretty much silenced, so began to think of returning to *England*; he was the more encouraged to do so, as he found by his letters, that those in the ministry, who had appeared with most virulence against him, had been removed themselves, and that a considerable change in public affairs had happened. Accordingly, he set forward with all the expedition he could, feeling not the least regret for leaving a country he had never liked, nor where he had ever enjoyed any real satisfaction, and had been so near being plunged into the worst of misfortunes, that of an unhappy marriage: – no ill accident intervening, he arrived in *England* and proceeded directly to *London*, where he was received with an infinity of joy by his father and sister, who happened at that time to come to town with her spouse, in order to place a young son they had at *Westminster* school.[60]

THE better genius of *Natura* now took its turn, and prevailed over his ill one: the person whose turbulent zeal had occasioned his late misfortune, had since, being detected in some malpractice in other affairs, been cashiered from an office he held under the government, and was in the utmost disgrace himself: every body was now assured, that *Natura* had done no more than what became any man of spirit and honour; and those who before had condemned, now applauded his behaviour: in fine, every thing happened according to his wishes, and, to crown his happiness, he married about ten months after his arrival, a young beautiful lady, of his father's recommendation, and who had indeed all the qualifications that can render the conjugal state desirable.

THE promotion of a member of parliament to the house of peers for that county, in which their estate lay, happening soon after, he stood for the vacant seat, and easily obtained it; – nothing now seemed wanting to compleat his perfect happiness, yet so restless is the heart of man, that gaining much, it yet craves for more; *Natura* had always a great passion for the court, meerly because it was a court, and gave an air of dignity to all belonging to it; he longed to make one among the shining throng; he was continually sollicitingit, with an anxiety which deprived him of any true enjoyment of the blessings of his life; nor could all the arguments his father used to convince him of the vanity of his desires, nor the soft society of a most endearing and accomplished wife, render him easy under the many disappointments he received in the prosecution of this favourite aim.

THE death of his father soon after, however, filled his bosom with emotions which he had never felt before in any painful degree; he was for some time scarce able to support the thoughts of having lost so tender and affectionate a parent: but as nothing is so soon forgot as death, especially when alleviated by the enjoyment of a greater affluence of fortune, his grief wore off by pretty swift degrees, and he was beginning to renew his pursuits after preferment, with the same assiduity and ardency as ever, when his wife died in bringing into the world a son.

This second subject of sorrow struck indeed much more to his heart than the former had done, as he now wanted that comforter he had found in her. – All the consolation he had was in that little pledge of their mutual affection she had left behind; and it was for the sake of that dear boy, at least he imagined it so, that his ambition of making a great figure in the world again, revived in him, if possible, with greater energy than ever.

As he was now in possession of a very fine estate, had an agreeable person, rendered yet more so by all the advantages of education and travel, and not quite six-and-thirty, when he became a widower, his year of mourning was scarce expired, before all his friends and acquaintance began to talk to him of another wife, and few days past without proposals of that nature being made; but either the memory of the former amiable partner of his bed, or the experience he had in his own family of the ill effects that second marriages sometimes produce, made him deaf, for a long time, to any discourses on that head, though urged by those who, in other matters, had the greatest ascendant over him.

Though he was far from being arrived at those years which render a man insensible of beauty, yet he was past those which had made him look on the enjoyment of it as the supremest bliss: – the fond desires that once engrossed him, had for some time given way to the more potent ardors of ambition; – he now made not love his *business* but *amusement*; the amours he had were only transient, and meerly to fill the vacancy of an idle hour: his thoughts were so wholly taken up with advancing himself, and becoming a man of consequence in the world, that it may be reasonably supposed, by his behaviour, and the manner in which he rejected all the offers made to him, that had he met with a woman, in whom all the perfections of the sex were centered, she would not have been able either to engage him to a serious attachment, or to have quitted those more darling pursuits, which the desire of greatness fired him with.

Thus fortified by his present inclinations against all the charms of youth, of wit, of beauty, there was but one temptation he had not the power of withstanding, and that one his ill fate at length presented to him. A certain great person, who at that time was at the head of public affairs, had a neice, who for many private reasons, he found it necessary to dispose of in marriage: *Natura* was the man he happened to pitch upon, as one who seemed to him a very proper person, and accordingly made him the offer, accompanied with a promise of getting him into a great post, which he knew he had been for a long time, and was still, solliciting, though without any prospect of success, without his assistance.

The young lady was not ugly, yet far from being mistress of charms capable of captivating a heart which had been filled with so many images of different beauties; but, as I have already said, love was not now the reigning passion of *Natura*'s soul, and had she been much less amiable, the dowery she was to bring, sufficiently compensated for all other deficiencies, according to his present way of judging.

He hesitated not a moment to accept the minister's proposal; and a long courtship, as things were ordered between them, being needless, he became again a husband, in a very few days after the first mention had been made of it, and at the same time was put in possession of what was much more welcome to him than his bride, even tho' she had been endowed with every virtue, every grace.

All for a time went smoothly on: – he saw himself in a rank and precedence, his birth could never have expected: – his wife's uncle loaded him with favours; he procured a commission of lieutenant in the guards for his younger brother by his mother-in-law, whom, in spite of the ill usage, with which both himself and his father had been treated by her, he had a very great affection for; – he also got employments for several others of his kindred; – his house was the rendezvous of the gay and titled world; – his friendship was courted by all his acquaintance, and his interest at court created him so many dependants, that his levee[61] was little inferior to that of the minister himself.

This full attainment of all he wished, and even more than he had ever dared to indulge the hope of, might well render him extremely contented; – he was indeed pleased to excess, but the gladness of his heart was so far a virtue in him, as it prevented him at first from shewing any tokens of that pride, which a sudden variation of fortune frequently excites.

It is certain, his behaviour was such as gained him an equal share of love and respect; and he had this addition to his other blessings, of not having his advancement envied; a thing pretty rare about a court, where there are so many gaping after every office that falls.

They say ambition is a lust that is never quenched; and that the enjoyment of much brings with it only an impatience for more; that fresh objects, and new acquisitions, still presenting themselves, the mind is ever restless, ever anxious in the endless pursuit. – It is very likely this maxim might indeed have been verified in the mind of *Natura*, after the hurry of transport for what he had already obtained had been a little worn off, and made way for other aims; but he had scarce given over congratulating himself on his success, before a strange alteration, and such as he had least dreaded of, happened in his humour, and rendered him wholly incapable of retaining the least relish for all the blessings he possessed, and in which he so lately placed the ultimate of his wishes.

The compliments paid to him on his promotion and marriage, the giving and receiving visits from all his kindred and friends, together with the duties of his post, so much engrossed him for the first two or three months, that he had not time to give any attention to his domestic affairs, and happy would it have been for his peace if he had always continued in a total negligence in this point, as the fatal inspection plunged him into such distractions as required many long years to compose.

IN fine, he now discovered such dispositions to gallantry in his wife, as inflamed him with jealousy, to such a degree as it would be impossible to describe; – not that he had ever been possessed of any extraordinary love or fondness on her account; but the injury which he imagined was offered to his honour, by the freedoms with which she entertained several of those young courtiers which frequented his house, made him in a short time become the most discontented man alive.

UTTERLY impossible was it for him to conceal his disquiets; though the fears he had of displeasing the minister made him attempt it, as much as possible, and conscious of his ill dissimulation that way, the little notice she took of a chagrin he knew she could not but observe, very much added to it, as it seemed a certain proof of her indifference for him; a behaviour so widely different from the amiable tenderness of his former wife, dissipated all the little affection he had for her, and it was not long before she became even hateful to him; his jealousy however abated not with his love, her dishonour was his own, her person was his property by marriage,[62] and the thoughts of any encroachment on his right were insupportable to him.

WHETHER she was in fact as yet guilty of those violations of her duty, which his imagination incessantly suggested to him she was, neither himself, nor the world, were ever able to prove; but it is certain her conduct was such, in every shape towards him, as gave but too much room for suspicion in the least censorious, and which growing every day more disagreeable to him, he at length had not the power of feigning an inattention to it. – He remonstrated to her the value every woman, especially those in high life, ought to set on her reputation; – told her plainly, that the severest censures had been past upon her, and without seeming to believe them just himself, intreated her to act with more reserve for the future.

ALL this, though delivered in the most gentle terms he could invent, had no other effect than to set her into an immoderate laughter: nothing could be more provoking, than the contempt with which she treated his advice; and on his insisting at last, in terms which she might think were somewhat too strong, on her being less frequently seen with some persons he mentioned to her, she answered in the most disdainful tone, that when she came to his years, she might, perhaps, look on the pleasures of life with the same eyes he did; but while youth and good humour lasted, she should deny herself no innocent indulgencies, and was resolved, let him and the world say what they would, not to anticipate old age and wrinkles.

As *Natura* was not yet forty, in perfect health, and consequently not past the prime of manhood, this reflection cast upon his years, could not but add to his disgust of her that made it, and he replied with a spite which was very visible in his countenance, that whatever disparity there was between their ages, it would soon diminish by the course of life she followed, and which, if she persisted in, would, in a very little time, make her become an object below the voice of censure.

THEY must know little of the sex, that do not know no affront can be so stinging as one offered to their beauty, even tho' conscious of having no great share of it; but the wife of *Natura* had heard too many flatteries, not to inspire her with the highest idea of her charms, which the little respect he now testified to have for them, did not at all abate, and only served to make her despise his stupidity, as she termed it.

NO measures after this were kept between them; she seemed to take a pleasure in every thing that gave him pain; she coquetted before his face with every handsome man that came in her way, and in fine gave herself such airs as the most patient husband could not have permitted her long to persist in. Making use of the authority the laws had given him,[63] he, in a manner, forced her into the country, upwards of an hundred miles from *London*, though it was then in the depth of winter, and placed persons about her, with orders to prevent her from all means of returning, till he should judge it proper for her so to do.

ON this she wrote to her uncle, complaining of the hard treatment she received, and beseeching him to take some measures to oblige her husband to restore her liberty. The minister, who had at that time much greater concerns upon his hands on his own account, did not care to give himself any trouble about private family affairs; he only just mentioned to *Natura* the letter she had sent to him, and the purport of it; and on his relating to him the reasons that had compelled him to put this restraint on her behaviour, told him, he should not interfere between them; so that *Natura* found he had nothing to apprehend for what he had done.

FINDING this step had produced nothing for her purpose, she at last condescended to submit to her justly offended husband; and on her solemn and repeated promises of regulating her conduct for the future in such a manner as he should approve, he was prevailed upon by her seeming contrition, to consent to make trial how far her heart corresponded with her professions: – it was agreed, to prevent the town from inspecting too deeply on what had passed, that she should pretend her absence from town had been the effect of her own choice, and for giving the better colour, he went down himself, and brought her up. – They lived together, after this, much better than they had done for some months before their quarrel, and were now, in appearance, perfectly reconciled; I say, in appearance, for all was outward shew, neither of them had in their hearts the least true affection, nor could forgive the other for what had passed between them.

THE excessive constraint which both put upon themselves, in order to conceal the real sentiments of their hearts from each other, as well as from the world, could not but be extremely painful: – *Natura* suffered her as little as possible out of his sight, though he could have wished a possibility of avoiding her for ever, and was obliged to do all he could, to make that pass for a fondness of her presence, which was indeed only the effect of his jealousy of her behaviour in absence: – she affected to think herself happy in his company, for no other reason, than to win him to an assurance of her reformation, as might render him less observant than he had been of what she did, even at the time (as was afterwards discovered) when she seemed most sorry and angry with herself for having given him any cause of suspicion since their marriage.

BOTH, in fine, endured all that could make marriage dreadful, especially *Natura*, who having with his former wife experienced all the felicity of that state, was the more wretched by the sad alternative; and as he could not sometimes forbear comparing the present with the past, fell frequently into perfect convulsions of grief and remorse, for having plunged himself into it.

A PERPETUAL dissimulation is what human nature finds among the things which are impossible to perform; – and I am pretty certain, that the most artful person that ever breathed, could not, at all times, and in all circumstances, restrain so far his real inclinations, as to give no indications of them to an observing eye; and it is scarce probable, but that the very attempt in *Natura* and his wife, gave rise to as many reflections on their conduct in this point, as there was too much room to make on others.

IT was indeed a kind of farce acted by this unhappy pair, in which both played their parts so aukwardly, that the real character would frequently peep out, and though each dissembled, yet neither was deceived; but as I said before, this could not last for ever; and the ice being once broke in some unguarded humour either on the one or the other side, I cannot pretend to affirm on which, the torrent of their mutual disgust burst out with the greater force, for having been so long pent up: it is hard to tell which testified the most virulence, or expressed themselves in the most bitter terms: – all that can be determined is, that those of *Natura* shewed most of *rage*, and those his wife made use of, most of *hatred.*

AFTER having fully vented all that was in their souls against each other, both became more calm; and agreed in this, as, the only resource for ease in their present unhappy situation, to banish for the future all deceit between them, and never more pretend the least kindness or good-will to each other when in private, to lie in separate beds, and to be as seldom as possible alone together; but for the sake of both their reputations to continue in the same house, and before company to behave with reciprocal politeness.

THESE terms rid *Natura* of a great part of that insupportable constraint he had been under, but gave not the least satisfaction, as to his jealousy of honour; he doubted not but she would be guilty of many things, injurious in the highest degree to their public character, and which yet it would not so well become him to exert his authority in opposing, and these reflections gave him the most terrible inquietude; which shews, that though *jealousy* is called the child of *love*, it is very possible to feel all the tortures of the *one*, without being sensible of any of the douceurs of the *other* passion.

HOW dearly now did *Natura* pay for the gratification of his ambition! – What availed his grandeur, the respect paid him by his equals, and the homage of the inferior world! –What the pride of having it in his power to confer favours, when he had himself a heart torn with the most fierce convulsions, and less capable of enjoying the goods of fortune, than the most abject of those indigent creatures, who petitioned for relief from him! – By day, by night, alone, or in company, he was haunted with ideas the most distracting to his peace. – A smile on the face of his wife, seemed to him to proceed from the joy of having made some new conquest; a grave or melancholly look, from a disappointment on the account of a favourite gallant: yet as her person was the least thing he was tenacious of, the behaviour of others gave him greater pain than any thing she could do herself; –whoever spoke handsomely of her, he imagined insulted him; and those who mentioned her not at all, he thought were sensible of her levity, and his misfortune: – every thing he saw or heard, seemed to him a sad memento of his dishonour; and though he could not assure himself she had in fact been guilty of a breach of her virtue, he was very certain she had been so of that reserve and modesty which is the most distinguishable characteristic of it, and took from him the power of vindicating her innocence, or his own honour, even though he had believed them safe, as becomes a husband, whose wife is more cautious of her conduct in this point.

TOO delicate of the censure of the world, it gave him the utmost anxiety how to carry himself, so as not to afford any room to have it said he was either a jealous, or a too credulous husband; yet in spite of all his care, he incurred both these characters: – those who had heard of his sending her into the country, without being acquainted with the motives for his so doing, looked on him as the former; and those who saw her manner of behaviour, and the seeming politeness of his treatment of her, imagined him the latter: –so difficult is it for any one, who only sees the outside of things, to judge what they are in reality; yet the vanity of having it believed they are let into secrets, makes a great many people invent circumstances, and then relate for matters of fact, what are indeed no more than the suggestions of imagination, or, what is yet worse, the coinage of their own brain, without believing themselves what they take upon them to report to others.

THIS undoubtedly happened on the score of *Natura* and his wife, and occasioned not only many idle stories at tea-table conversation, but also many oblique hints to be sometimes given to himself, which, perhaps, there was not the least grounds for, but which greatly added to his disquiets; as when we think we have reason to believe part, we are ready to give credit to all we hear, especially in cases of this nature; it being the peculiar property of jealousy, to force the mind to grasp with eagerness, at every thing that tends to render it more afflicted and perplexed.

BOOK the Third.

CHAP. I.

Shews in what manner anger and revenge operate on the mind, and how ambition is capable of stifling both, in a remarkable instance, that private injuries, *how great soever, may seem of no weight, when* public grandeur *requires they should be looked over.*

NOTHING is so violent as anger in its first emotions, it takes the faculties by surprize, and rushes upon the soul like an impetuous torrent, bearing down all before it: its strength, however, is owing to its suddenness; for being raised by some new and unexpected accident or provocation, reason has no warning of its approach, and consequently is off her guard, and without any immediate power of acting: the sweetest, and most gentle disposition, is not always a sufficient defence for the mind, against the attacks of this furious passion, and may be hurried by it to deeds the most opposite to its own nature; but then as it is fierce, it is transient also; should its force continue, it would lose its name, and be no longer anger, but revenge; which, though the worst and most fiend-like propensity of a vicious inclination, is sometimes excited by circumstances, that seem in a great measure to alleviate the blackness of it: – repeated and unprovoked insults, friendship and love abused, injuries in our person, our fortune, or reputation, will sour the softest temper, and are apt to make us imagine it is an injustice to our selves, not to retaliate in kind, the ill treatment we receive. Religion, indeed, forbids us to take our own parts thus far, and philosophy teaches, that it is nobler to forgive, than punish wrongs; but every one is not so happy as to have either of these helps; and I do not find but those who boast both of them in the most superlative degree, stand in need of something more, to enable them to restrain this prevailing impulse; and that it is not so much to the precepts they receive from others, as to some dictates from within, that many people are indebted for the reputation of patience and forbearance.

IT is the peculiar providence of Heaven, as I took notice in the beginning of this work, that the more ignoble passions of human nature, are, generally speaking, opposites, and by that means serve as a curb to bridle the inordinancy of each other; so that, though *one alone* would be pernicious to society, and render the person possessed of it obnoxious to the world, *many* will prevent the hurt, and make the man himself tolerable.

THE adventure I am now going to relate, will prove that *Natura* had the greatest excitements, and the greatest justification both for wrath and revenge that could possibly be offered to any one man: yet did another passion, not more excusable than either of these, suppress all the turbulent emotions of both, and quench the boiling flames within his soul, insomuch as to make him appear all calmness and contentedness.

BUT though I made use of the word passion to express the now prevailing propensity of *Natura*'s soul, I do not think that ambition, strictly speaking, can come under that denomination: – to me it rather seems the effect of an assemblage of other passions, than a passion simple of itself, and natural to the mind of man; and I believe, whoever examines it to the fountain head, will find it takes its origin from pride and envy, and is nourished by self-love, nor ever appears in any great degree, where these do not abound. – Were it born with us, there would doubtless be some indications of it in childhood, but it is observable, that not till man arrives at maturity, and, even not then, unless the sight of objects above himself excites it, he discovers the least sensation of any such emotion. – In fine, it is an inclination rarely known in youth, ordinarily declines in age, and never exerts itself with vigour, as in the middle stage of life, which I reckon to be from about five-and-twenty to fifty, or somewhat more, according to the strength of the natural stamina, or constitution. – But to go on with my history.

SINCE *Natura* had been in what they call a settled state in the world, it had always been his custom to distinguish the anniversary of that day which gave him birth, by providing a polite entertainment for his friends and kindred: he had now attained to his fortieth year, and though it had been that in which he had known more poignant disquiets, than in any one of his whole life before; yet thinking that to neglect the observation of it now, would give occasion for remarks on his reasons for so doing, he resolved to treat it with the usual ceremony.

IT was in that delightful season of the year, when nature, adorned with all her charms invites the senses to taste that regale[64] in the open air which the most elegant and best concerted entertainments within doors cannot atone for the want of. After dinner was over, the whole company, which was pretty numerous, adjourned from the table to the garden, a small, but well ordered spot of ground, at the lower end of which was a green-house, furnished with many curious exotic plants. While *Natura* was shewing this collection to those of his guests, who had a taste that way, others were diverting themselves with walking in the alleys, or sat down in arbors according as their different fancies inclined, as it is common for people to divide themselves into little parties, when there are too many for all to share in a general convention.

As they were thus employed, the minister, who though he had not thought it beneath the dignity of his character to do honour to the birth-day of the husband of his neice, yet had his mind taken up with other things than the amusements of the place, took *Natura* aside on a sudden, and asked him if he had not a paper in his custody, which he had some time before put into his hands; to which the other answering in the affirmative, *There are some things in it I do not well remember*, said the great man; *and a thought just now occurs to me, in which they may be of use: – Natura* then offered to fetch it; *No*, replied the other, *I will go with you, and we will examine it together.*

THERE was no need of making any apology to the company, they being, as I have already said, dispersed in several parts of the garden; but had they not been so, the statesman was absolute master wherever he came, and no one would have taken umbrage at *Natura*'s following him.

THEY went hastily up stairs together, and the door of a room, thro' which they were to pass to *Natura*'s study, being shut, he gave a push against it with his foot, and it being but slightly fastened, immediately flew open, and discovered a sight no less unexpected than shocking to both; – the wife, and own brother of *Natura*, on a couch, and in a posture which could leave no room to doubt of the motive which had induced them to take the opportunity of the company separating themselves, to retire, without being missed, which, but for this accident, they probably would not have been.

IT is easy to conceive what a husband must feel in so alarming a circumstance, nor will any one wonder that *Natura* behaved in the manner he did, in the first emotions of a rage, which might very well be justified by the cause that excited it. – Not having a sword on, he flew to the chimney, on each side of which hung a pistol; he snatched one off the hook, and was going to revenge the injury he had received on one or both the guilty persons, when the minister, stepping between, beat down that arm which held the instrument of death, crying at the same time, *What, are you a madman! – would you to punish them expose yourself! –* The passion with which *Natura* was overwhelmed was too mighty for his breast; it stopped the passage of his words, and all he could bring out was *villain! – whore!* – while those he called so, made their escape from his fury, by running out of the room. In attempting to follow them he was still with-held; and the minister having with much ado got the pistol from him, began to expostulate with him, in order to disarm his mind from pursuing any future revenge, as he had done his hand from executing the present.

Consider, said the statesman, *that these are but slips of nature, that there are in this town a thousand husbands in the same situation: – indeed the affair happening with your own brother, very much enhances the crime and the provocation; but as the thing is done, and there is no remedy, it will but add to your disgrace to make it public.*

LITTLE would it have been in the power of all the arguments in the world, if made use of by any other person, to have given a check to that just indignation *Natura* was inflamed with: but as patience and moderation were prescribed him by one to whom he was indebted for all the grandeur he enjoyed, and by whose favour alone he could hope for the continuance of it, he submitted to the task, difficult as it was, and consented to make no noise of the affair. The minister assured him he would oblige his brother to exchange the commission he was at present possessed of, for one in a regiment that was going to *Gibraltar,*[65] *which,* said he, *will be a sufficient punishment for his crime, and at the same time rid you of the sight of a person who cannot but be now detestable to you; –as to your wife, I expect you will permit her to continue in your house, in consideration of her relation to me, but shall not interfere with the manner of your living together; – that shall be at your own discretion.*

As neither of them imagined the lady, after what had happened, would have courage enough to go down to the company, it was agreed between them to make her excuse, by saying, a sudden disorder in her head had obliged her to absent herself.

Natura cleared up his brow as much as it was possible for him to do in such a circumstance, and returned with the minister to his guests, among whom, as he supposed, he found neither his wife nor brother; as for the latter, much notice was not taken of his absence, but the ladies, by this time, were full of enquiries after her; on which he immediately made the pretence above-mentioned; but unluckily, one of the company having been bred to physic, urged permission to see her, in order to prescribe some recipe for her ailment. – *Natura* was now extremely at a loss what to do, till the minister, who never wanted an expedient, relieved him, by telling the doctor, that his neice had been accustomed to these kind of fits from her infancy, that it was only silence and repose which recovered her, which being now gone to take, any interruption would be of more prejudice than benefit.

This passed very well, and no farther mention was made of her; but the accident occasioned the company to take leave much sooner than otherwise they would have done, very much to the ease of *Natura,* who had been in the most intolerable constraint, to behave so as to conceal the truth, and longed to be alone, to give a loose to the distracting passions of his soul.

The more he ruminated on the wrongs he had sustained, the more difficult he found it to preserve that moderation the minister had enjoined, and he had promised: he had long but too much reason to believe his wife was false; but the thought that she had entered into a criminal conversation[66] with his own brother, rendered the guilt doubly odious in them both. – Had not his own eyes convinced him of the horrid truth, he could have given credit to no other testimony, that a brother, whom he had always treated with the utmost affection, and whose fortune it had been his care to promote, should have dared to harbour even the most distant wish of dishonouring his wife. He seemed, in his eyes, the most culpable of the two, and thought the banishment intended for him much too small a punishment for so atrocious a crime. It is certain that this young gentleman had not only broke through the bands of duty, honour, gratitude, and every social obligation, but had also sinned against nature itself, by adding incest to adultery. – *Natura* could not indeed consider him as any thing but a monster, and that as such he ought to be cut off from the face of the earth; and neither reason nor humanity could alledge any thing against the dictates of a revenge, which by the most unconcerned and disinterested person could not be called unjust. – Strongly did its emotions work within his soul, and he was more than once on the point of going in search of him, in order to satiate its most impatient thirst, but was as often restrained, by reflecting on the consequences, – *Suppose,* said he to himself, *I should escape that death the law inflicts for murder, in consideration of the provocation, I cannot hope to preserve my employments. – I must retire from the world, live an obscure life the whole remainder of my days, and the whole shameful adventure being divulged, will render me the common topic of table conversation, and entail dishonour and contempt upon my son.*

THUS did ambition get the better of resentment; – thus did the love of grandeur extirpate all regard of true honour, and the shame of private contempt from the world lie stifled in the pride of public homage.

THE minister in the mean time kept his word; he let the offending brother know it was his pleasure he should dispose of his commission in the guards, and purchase one in a regiment he named to him, which was very speedily to embark for *Gibraltar*: the young gentleman obeyed the injunction, and doubtless was not sorry to quit a place, where some accident or other, in spite of all the care he had resolved to take, might possibly bring him to the sight of a brother he had so greatly injured, the thoughts of whose just reproaches were more terrible to him, than any thing else that could befal him.

THE wife of *Natura* being also privately admonished by her uncle how to behave, kept her chamber for some days, not only to give the better colour to the pretence had been made of her indisposition, but also to avoid the presence of her husband, till the first emotions of his fury should be a little abated; – he, on the other hand, profited by this absence, to bring himself to a resolution how to behave, when the shock of seeing her should arrive: – as her crime was past recall, reproaches and remonstrances would be in vain to retrieve her honour, or his peace; and if they even should work her into penitence, what would it avail? unless to soften him into a pity, which would only serve to render him more uneasy, as there was now no possibility of living with her as a wife. – Having, therefore, well weighed and considered all these things, it seemed best to him to say nothing to her of what had happened, and indeed to avoid speaking to her at all, except in public.

WHAT she thought of a behaviour she had so little reason to expect, and what effect it produced on her future conduct, shall hereafter be related; I shall only say at present, that *Natura* gave himself no pain to consider what might be her sentiments on the occasion, as long as he found her uncle was perfectly satisfied with his manner of acting in this point, which he had no reason to doubt of, not only by the assurances he gave him in words of his being so, but by a more convincing and substantial proof, which was this; an envoy extraordinary being about to be sent to a foreign court, on a very important negociation, he had the honour of being recommended, as a gentleman every way qualified for the duties of that post. – The minister's choice of him was approved by the king and council, and he set out on his embassy, with an equipage and state, which, joined to the attention he gave to what he was employed in, greatly dissipated the chagrin of his private affairs, and he seemed to have forgot, for a time, not only the injuries he had received, but also even the persons from whom he had received them.

CHAP. II.

Shews at what age men are most liable to the passion of grief: the impatience of human nature under affliction, and the necessity there is of exerting reason, to restrain the excesses it would otherwise occasion.

THERE are certain periods of time, in which the passions take the deepest root within us; what at one age makes but a slight impression, and is easily dissipated by different ideas, at another engrosses all the faculties, and becomes so much a part of the soul, as to require the utmost exertion of reason, and all the aids of philosophy and religion to eradicate. – Grief, for example, is one of those passions which, in extreme youth, we know little of, and even when we grow nearer to maturity, has rarely any great dominion, let the cause which excites it be never so interesting, or justifiable: it may indeed be poignant for a time, and drive us to all the excesses imputed to that passion; but then it is of short continuance, it dwells not on the mind, and the least appearance of a new object of satisfaction, banishes it entirely; we dry our tears, and remember no more what so lately we lamented, perhaps with the most noisy exclamations: – but it is not so when riper years give a solidity and firmness to the judgment; – then as we are less apt to grieve without a cause, so we are less able to refrain from grieving, when we have a real cause. – Grief may therefore be called a reasonable passion, tho' it becomes not a reasonable man to give way to it; – this, at first sight, may seem a paradox to many people, but may easily be solved, in my opinion, on a very little consideration; – as thus, – because to be sensible of our loss in the value of the thing for which we mourn, is a proof of our judgment, as to refrain that mourning for what is past retrieving, within the bounds of moderation, is the greatest proof we can give of our reason: – a dull insensibility is not a testimony, either of wisdom or virtue; we are not to bear afflictions like *statues*, but like men; that is, we are allowed to *feel*, but not to *repine*, or be *impatient* under them: – few there are, however, who have the power of preserving this happy medium, as I before observed, tho' they are such as have the assistance both of precept and experience.

In a word, all that can be expected from the best of men, when pressed with any heavy calamity, is to struggle with all his might to bear up beneath the weight with decency and resignation; and as grief never seizes strongly on the mind, till a sufficient number of years gives reason strength to combat with it, that consideration furnishes matter for praise and adoration of the all-wise and all-beneficent Author of our being, who has bestowed on us a certain comfort for all ills, if we neglect not to make use of it; so that no man can be unhappy, unless he will be so.

Motives for grief which happen on a sudden merit excuse for the extravagancies they sometimes occasion, because they surprize us unawares, reason is off her guard, and it cannot be expected we should be armed against what we had no apprehensions of; – presence of mind is an excellent, but rare quality, and we shall see very few, even among the wisest men, who are such examples of it, as to behave in the first shock of some unforeseen misfortune, with the same moderation and calmness of temper, as they would have done, had they had previous warning of what was to befal them.

Much, however, are the effects of this, as of all other passions, owing to constitution: – the robust and sanguine nature soon kindles, and is soon extinguished; whereas the phlegmatic is slow to be moved, and when so not easily settled into a calm: and tho' the difference of age makes a wide difference in our way of thinking, yet as there are old men at twenty, and boys at three-score, that rule is not without some exceptions. But to take nature in the general, and allowing for the different habits of body and complexion, we may be truly said to be most prone to particular passions at particular ages: – as in youth, love, hope, and joy; – in maturity, ambition, pride, and its attendant ostentation; – when more advanced in years, grief, fear, and despair; – and in old age, avarice, and a kind of very churlish dislike of every thing presented to us.

But to return to *Natura*, from whose adventures I have digressed; but I hope forgiveness for it, as it was not only the history of the man I took upon me to relate, but also to point out, in his example, the various progress of the passions in a human mind.

He acquitted himself of the important trust had been reposed in him, with all the diligence and discretion could be expected from him; and returned honoured with many rich presents from the prince to whom he had been sent, as a testimony of the sense he had of his abilities.

But scarce had he time to receive the felicitations of his friends on this score, before an accident happened to him, which demanded a much more than equal share of condolance from them. – His son, his only son, the darling of his heart, was seized with a distemper in his head, which in a very few days baffled the art of medicine, and snatched him from the world. – What now availed his honours, his wealth, his every requisite for grandeur, or for pleasure? – He, for whose sake chiefly he had laboured to acquire them, was no more! – no second self remained to enjoy what he must one day leave behind him. – All of him was now collected in his own being, and with *that* being must end. –Melancholly reflection! – yet not the worst that this unhappy incident inflicted: – his estate, all at least that had descended to him by inheritance, with the vast improvements he had made on it, must now devolve on a brother he had so much cause to hate, and whose very name but mentioned struck horror to his heart.

THE motives for his grief were great, it must be allowed, and such as demanded the utmost fortitude to sustain; – he certainly exerted all he was master of on this occasion; but, in spite of his efforts, nature got the upper hand, and rendered him inconsolable: – he burst not into any violent exclamations, but the silent sorrow preyed on his vitals, and reduced him, in a short time, almost to the shadow of what he had been.

ONE of the most dangerous effects of melancholy is, the gloomy pleasure it gives to every thing that serves to indulge it: – darkness and solitude are its delight and nourishment, and the person possessed of it, naturally shuns and hates whatever might alleviate it; – the sight of his best friends now became irksome to him; – he not only loathed, but grew incapable of all business; – he shut himself in his closet, shunned conversation, was scarce prevailed on to take the necessary supports of nature, and seemed as if his soul was buried in the tomb of his son, and only a kind of vegetative life remained within him.

HIS sister, who loved him very affectionately, and for whom he had always preserved the tenderest amity, being informed of his disconsolate condition, came to town, flattering herself with being able to dissipate, at least some part of his chagrin. To this end she brought with her all her children, some of whom he had never seen, and had frequently expressed by letter, the desire he had of embracing them, and the regret he had that the great affairs he was always constantly engaged in, would not permit him time to take a journey into the country where she lived.

BUT how greatly did she deceive herself; – he was too far sunk in the lethargy of grief, to be roused out of it by all her kind endeavours; – on the contrary, the sight of those near and dear relatives she presented to him only added to his affliction, by reminding him in a more lively manner of his own loss; and the sad effect she found their presence had on him, obliged her to remove them immediately from his eyes.

SHE could not, however, think of quitting him in a state so truly deplorable, and so unbecoming of his circumstances and character: – she remained in his house, would pursue him wherever he retired, and as she was a woman of excellent sense, as well as good-nature, invented a thousand little stratagems to divert his thoughts from the melancholly theme which had too much engrossed them, but had not the satisfaction to perceive that any thing she could say or do, occasioned the least movement of that fixed sullenness, which, by a long habit, appeared like a second nature in him.

THIS poor lady found also other matters of surprize and discontent, on her staying in town, besides the sad situation of her brother's health: – as she had never been informed of the disunion between him and his wife, much less of the occasion of it, the behaviour of that lady filled her with the utmost astonishment: – to perceive she took no pains to alleviate his sorrows, never came into the room where he was, or even sent her woman with those common compliments, which he received from all who had the least acquaintance with him, would have afforded sufficient occasion for the speculation of a sister; yet was this manifest disregard, this failure in all the duties of a wife, a friend, a neighbour, little worthy of consideration, when put in comparison with her conduct in other points.

AFTER the adventure of her detection, finding the minister was resolved to support her, and that her husband durst not come to any open breach with her, she immediately began to throw aside all regard for decorum; – she seemed utterly to despise all sense of shame, and even to glory in a life of continual dissolution; – the company she kept of both sexes, were, for the most part, persons of abandoned characters: whether she indulged herself in a plurality of amours, is uncertain, though it was said she did so; but there was one man to whom she was most particularly attached; – this was a person who had formerly enjoyed a post under the government, but was turned out on the score of misbehaviour, and had now no other support than what he received from her: – with him she frequently passed whole nights, and took so little care in concealing the place of their meeting, that the sister of *Natura* easily found it out.

ON relating the discovery she had made to some of their relations, they advised her to tell her brother, imagining this glaring insult on his honour would effectually rouse him out of the stupidity he languished under: – he was of the same opinion, and took the first opportunity of letting *Natura* into the whole infamous affair, not without some apprehensions, that an excess of rage on hearing it, might hurry him into a contrary extreme; but her terrors on this head were presently dissipated, when having repeated many circumstances to corroborate the truth of what she said, there appeared not the least emotion in his countenance; and on her urging him to take some measures to do himself justice, or at least to put a stop to this licentiousness of a person whose dishonour was his own; all she could get from him was, that he had neither regard enough for her to take any pains for the reclaiming her, nor for the censure of the world on himself, and desired she would not trouble him any farther on this point.

THIS strange insensibility afforded cause to fear his faculties were all too deeply absorbed in melancholy, for him ever to become a man of the world again, and as she truly loved him, gave both her, and all his other friends, an infinite concern.

CHAP. III.

The struggles which different passions occasion in the human breast, are here exemplified; and that there is no one among them so strong, but may be extirpated by another, excepting revenge, *which knows no period, but by gratification.*

THOUGH it must be acknowledged, that the passions, generally speaking, operate according to the constitution, and seem, in a manner, wholly directed by it, yet there is one, above all, which actuates alike in all, and when once entertained, is scarce ever extinguished: – it may indeed lie dormant, for a time, but then it easily revives on the least occasion, and blazes out with greater violence than ever. I believe every one will understand I mean *revenge*, since there is no other emotion of the soul, but has its antedote; *grief* and *joy* alternately succeed each other; – *hope* has its period in possession; – *fear* ceases, either by the cause being removed, or by a fatal certainty of some dreaded evil; – *ambition* dies within us, on a just sense of the folly of pursuing it; – *hate* is often vanquished by good offices; – even greedy *avarice* may be glutted; and *love* is, for the most part, fluctuating, and may be terminated by a thousand accidents. – *Revenge* alone is implacable and eternal, not to be banished by any other passion whatsoever; – the effects of it are the same, invariable in every constitution; and whether the man be phlegmatic or sanguine, there will be no difference in his way of thinking in this point. The principles of religion and morality indeed may, and frequently do, hinder a man from putting into action what this cruel passion suggests, but neither of them can restrain him who has revenge in his heart, from wishing it were lawful for him to indulge it.

THIS being so fixed a passion, it hardly ever gains entrance on the mind, till a sufficient number of years have given a solidity to the thoughts, and made us know for what we wish, and why we wish. – Every one, however, does not experience its force, and happy may those be accounted who are free from it, since it is not only the most unjustifiable and dangerous, but also the most restless and self-tormenting emotion of the soul.

THERE are, notwithstanding, some kind of provocations, which it is scarce possible, nor indeed consistent with the justice we owe to ourselves, to bury wholly in oblivion; and likewise there are some kinds of revenge, which may deserve to be excused; of these, that which *Natura* put in practice, as shall presently be shewn, may be reckoned of the number.

I DOUBT not, but my readers, as well as all those who were acquainted with him at that time, will believe, that in the situation I have described, he was for ever lost to the sense of any other passion, than that which so powerfully engrossed him, and from which all the endeavours hitherto made use of, had been ineffectual to rouse him. But it often happens, that what we least expect, comes most suddenly upon us, and proves that all human efforts are in vain, without the interposition of some supernatural power.

I HAVE already said, that the bad conduct of his wife had been repeated over and over to him without his discovering the least emotion at it; yet would not his sister cease urging him to resent it as became a man sensible of his dishonour, that is, to rid himself, by such ways as the law puts it in the power of a husband so injured, to get rid of her; and imagining that an ocular demonstration of her crime, would make a greater impression on him, than any report could do, she set about contriving some way to bring him where his own eyes might convince him of the truth of what he had been so often told: – but how to prevail on him to go out of his house, which he had not now seen the outside of for some months, was a difficulty not easily surmounted: – the obstinacy of grief disappointed all the little plots they laid for their purpose, and they were beginning to give over all thoughts of any future attempts, when chance accomplished the so-much desired work.

HE had ordered a monument to be erected over the grave of his beloved son; which, being finished, and he told that it was so, *I will see*, said he, *if it be done according to my directions.* Two or three of his kindred were present when he took this resolution, and one of them immediately recollecting, how they might make it of advantage to their design, said many things in praise of the structure; but added, that the scaffolding and rubbish the workmen had left, not being yet removed, he would have him defer seeing it, till it was cleaned. To this he having readily agreed, spies were placed, to observe the time and place, where the lady and her favourite lover had the next rendezvous. As neither of them had any great caution in their amour, a full account was soon brought to the sister of *Natura*, who, with several of their relations, came into his chamber and told him that the tomb was now fit to be seen in all its beauty.

ON this he presently suffered himself to be dressed, and went with them; but they managed so well that, under pretence of calling on another friend, who, they said, had desired to be of their company in this melancholly entertainment, they led him to the house where his wife and enamorato were yet in bed. The sister of *Natura* having, by a large bribe, secured the woman of the house to her interest, they were all conducted to the very scene of guilt, and this much injured husband had a second testimony of the perfidy of his wife; but alas! the first had made too deep an impression on him to leave room for any great surprize; he only cooly turned away, and said to those who had brought him there, that they needed not have taken all this pains to make him a witness of what he was convinced of long before.

HIS wife, however, was frighted, if not ashamed, and hid herself under the bedcloaths, while her gallant jumped, naked as he was, out of the window; but though *Natura* discovered very little emotion at all this, yet whether it was owing to the arguments of his friends, or that the air, after having been so long shut up from it, had an effect on him, they could not determine, but had the satisfaction to find that he consented an action in his name should be awarded against the lover, and proper means used for obtaining a bill of divorce from his wife.

THE real motive of this change in him none of them, however, could penetrate: – grief had for a while obliterated the thoughts of the injustice and ingratitude of his brother, but what he had now beheld reminding him of that shocking scene related in the first chapter of this book, all his long stifled wishes for revenge returned with greater force than ever; and thinking he could no way so fully gratify them, as by disappointing him of the estate he must enjoy at his decease, in case he died without issue, a divorce therefore would give him liberty to marry again; and as he was no more than three-and-forty years of age, had no reason to despair of having an heir, to cut entirely off the claim of so wicked a brother. Having once began to stir in the affair, it was soon brought to a conclusion. – The fact was incontestable, and proved by witnesses, whose credit left no room for cavil; a bill of divorce was granted on very easy terms,[67] and the gallant fined in so large a penalty, that he was obliged to quit the kingdom, to avoid imprisonment for life.

THUS did revenge produce an effect, which neither the precepts of religion, philosophy, or morality, joined with the most tender and pressing remonstrances of his nearest and dearest friends, could ever have brought about; – and this instance, in my judgment, proves to a demonstration, that it is so ordered by the all-wise Creator, that all the pernicious passions are at continual enmity, and, like counter-poisons, destroy the force of each other: and tho' it is certain, a man may be possessed of many passions at once, and those also may be of different natures, and tend to different aims, yet will there be a struggle, as it were, between them in the breast, and which ever happens to get predominance, will drive out the others in time, and reign alone sole master of the mind.

CHAP. IV.

Contains a further definition of revenge, *its force, effects, and the chasm it leaves on the mind when once it ceases. The tranquility of being entirely devoid of all passions; and the impossibility for the soul to remain in that state of inactivity is also shewn; with some remarks on human nature in general, when left to itself.*

I HAVE already shewn, in the example of *Natura*, how not only resentment for injuries, but even the extremest and most justifiable *rage*, may be subjected to *ambition*, and afterwards how that *ambition* may be quelled and totally extinguished by *grief*; and also that *grief* itself, how violent soever it appears, may subside at the emotions of *revenge*. – This last and worst passion alone finds nothing capable of overcoming it, while the object remains in being. It is true, that we frequently in the hurry of resentment, threaten, and sometimes act every thing in our power, against the person who has offended us, yet on his submission and appearing sorry for what he has done, we not only forgive, but also forget all that has past, and no longer bear him the least ill will; but then, this passion, by which we have been actuated, is not properly *revenge*, but *anger*, of which I have already sufficiently spoke, and, I flatter myself, proved how wide the difference is between these two emotions.

NATURA had no sooner taken it into his head to revenge himself in the manner above related, on his transgressing brother, than he resumed great part of his former chearfulness, conversed again in the world as he had been accustomed; nor, though he perceived his interest with the minister fall off ever since he had been divorced from his neice, and easily foresaw, that he would, from his friend, become in time his greatest enemy, yet it gave him little or no concern, so wholly were his thoughts and desires taken up with accomplishing what he had resolved.

HE was, however, for some time deliberating within himself to whom he should direct his addresses on this score; the general acquaintance he had in the world, brought many ladies into his mind, who seemed suitable matches for him; but then, as they were of equal birth and fortunes with himself, he reflected, that a long formal courtship would be expected, and he was now grown too indolent to take that trouble, as he was not excited by inclination to any of them, and had determined to enter a third time into the bonds of matrimony, meerly through the hope of depriving his brother of the estate.

BESIDES, the accidents which had lately happened to him, had very much altered his way of thinking, and though he had shaken off great part of the chagrin they had occasioned, yet there still remained a certain languor and inactivity of mind, which destroyed all the relish he formerly had of the noisy pleasures of life: – he began now to despise that farce of grandeur he once testified so high a value for, and to look on things as they really deserved; – he found his interest with those at the helm of public affairs, was very much sunk, and he was so far from taking any steps to retrieve it, that he seldom went even to pay that court to them, which his station demanded from him; – he grew so weary of the post which he had, with the utmost eagerness, sought after, and thought himself happy in enjoying, that he never rested till he had disposed of it, which he did for a much less consideration than it was really worth, meerly because he would be in a state of perfect independency, and at full liberty to speak and act, according to the dictates of his conscience, or his inclination.

HE was no sooner eased of his attendance at court by this means, than he retired to his country seat, in which he now thought he found more satisfaction, than the town, with all its hurrying pleasures could afford; there he intended to pass the greatest part of the remainder of his days, with some woman of prudence and good nature, which were the two chief requisites he now wished to find in a wife. – There were several well-jointured widows in the county where he resided, and also young ladies of family and fortune, but he never made the least overtures to any of them, and behaved with that indifference to the sex, that it was the opinion of all who conversed with him, that he never designed to marry again, when at the same time, he thought of nothing more than to find a partner in that state, such as promised to prove what he desired.

To this end he watched attentively the behaviour of all those he came in company with, and as he was master of a good deal of penetration, and also no small experience in the sex, and besides was not suspected to have any views that way, it is certain he had a good chance not to be deceived.

It was not among the fine ladies, the celebrated beauties, nor the great fortunes, he sought himself a wife; but among those of a middling rank; he only wished to have one who might bring him children, and be addicted to no vice, or caprice, that should either scandalize him abroad, or render him uneasy at home, and in all his inspection, he found none who seemed so likely to answer his desires in every respect as a young maid called *Lætitia*; she was the daughter of a neighbouring yeoman, not disagreeable in her person, or behaviour, yet possessed of no accomplishments, but those which nature had bestowed: her father was an honest plain man, he had four sons and two daughters, who had been married some time, and had several children; *Lætitia* was his youngest, and promised to be no less fruitful than her sisters; and this last was the chief inducement which made *Natura* fix his choice upon her.

Having resolved to seek no farther, he frequently went to the old man's house, pretending he took delight in country affairs, would walk with him about his grounds, and into his barns, and see the men who were at work in them. One day he took an opportunity of going when he knew he was abroad, designing to break his mind to the young *Lætitia*, who, being her father's housekeeper, he did not doubt finding at home: accordingly she was so; and, after some previous discourse, a little boy of one of her sisters, being playing about the room, *This is a fine child*, said he; *when do you design to marry, pretty Mrs.* Lætitia? – *Should you not like to be a mother of such diverting little pratlers? – It is time enough, sir*, replied she modestly, *for me to think of any such thing, – If you get a good husband*, resumed he, *it cannot be too soon: – Nor, if a bad one, too late*, cried she, *as there are great odds on that side. – That is true*, said he, *but I believe there are many ill husbands, who owe their being such, to the ill conduct of their wives: – now I fancy*, continued he, *whoever is so happy as to have you, will have no such excuse; for I firmly believe you have in you all the requisites to make the marriage state agreeable*. To this she only made a curtesy, and thanked him for his good opinion: *I do assure you*, resumed he, *it is so sincere, that I should be glad to prove it, by making you my wife. What say you*, pursued he, *could you be willing to accept of my addresses on that score?* With these words he took hold of her hand, and pressing it with a great deal of warmth, occasioned her to blush excessively. – The inability she was in of speaking, through the shame this question had excited in her, gave him an opportunity of prosecuting what he had begun, and saying many tender things, to convince her he was in earnest; but when at last she gave him an answer, it was only such as made him see she gave little credit to his professions. – Some people coming in on business to her father, and saying they would wait till he came home, obliged *Natura* to take his leave for that time, well satisfied in his mind, that he had declared himself, and not much doubting, but that in spite of this first shyness, she would easily be prevailed upon to correspond with his desires, when his perseverance in them, should have assured her of their sincerity.

HE was, notwithstanding, a good deal surprized, when, going several times after to the house, he could scarce see her, and never be able to exchange a word with her in private, so industriously did she avoid coming into his presence. – Such a behaviour, he thought, could proceed only from one of these two motives, either thro' an extraordinary dislike to his person, or through the fears of giving any indulgence to an inclination, which the disparity between them might make her mistake for a dishonourable one. Sometimes he was tempted to think the one, sometimes the other; but not being of a humour to endure suspence, he resolved to take effectual measures for coming at the certainty.

HE went one day about noon, and told the yeoman he was come to take a dinner with him, on which the other replied, that he did him a great deal of honour; but should have been glad to have been previously acquainted with it, in order to have been prepared to receive a gentleman of his condition. – *No,* said *Natura, I chose to come upon you unawares, not only to prevent you from giving yourself any superfluous trouble on my account, but also because I would use a freedom, which should authorize you to treat me with the same; – we are neighbours,* continued he, *and neighbours should be friends, and love one another.*

SOME other little chat on trivial affairs passed away the short time between the coming of *Natura*, and dinner being brought in; on which, the yeoman intreated him to sit down, and partake of such homely food as he found there. – *That I shall gladly do*, answered *Natura, but I waited for your fair daughter; I hope we shall have her company. I do not know*, said the yeoman, *I think they told me she was not very well, had got the head-ach, or some such ailment: – go, however,* pursued he, to a servant, *and see if* Lætitia *can come down. – But, sir*, cried he, perceiving his guest discovered no inclination to place himself at the table, *do not let us wait for her.*

NATURA on this sat down, and they both began to eat, when the person who had been sent to call *Lætitia* returned, and said, she begged to be excused, being very much indisposed, and unfit to be seen. – The old man seemed to take no notice, but pressed *Natura* to eat, and somewhat embarrassed him with the many apologies he made for the coarseness of his entertainment; to all which he gave but short answers, till the cloth was taken away, and they were alone. – Then, *I could not wish to dine more to my satisfaction*, said he, *if the sweetness of your meat had not been imbittered by your daughter's absence; – to be plain*, continued he, *I fear I am the disease which occasions her retirement. – You, sir!* cried the father, affecting a surprize, which he was not so well skilled in the art of dissimulation, to make appear so natural, but that *Natura* easily saw into the feint, and told him with a smile, that he found the *country* had its arts as well as the *court: – but let us deal sincerely with each other*, pursued he, *I am very certain, it is from no other motive, than my being here, that your daughter refused to come to table; and I also faithfully believe you are no stranger to that motive: – be therefore free with me; and to encourage you to be so, I shall acquaint you, that I have made some overtures to Mrs.* Lætitia, *– that I like her, and that my frequent visits to you have been entirely on her account: – now, be as sincere with me, and let me know, whether the offers I made her will be approved.*

THE yeoman was a little dashed on *Natura* speaking in this manner, and was some moments before he could recollect himself sufficiently to make any reply; and, when at last he had, all he could bring out was, *Sir, my girl is honest, and I hope will always continue so.*

I am far from doubting her virtue in the least, answered *Natura* hastily, *but I think I cannot give a greater testimony of the good opinion I have of her, than by offering to make her my wife. – Ah, sir*, cried the yeoman, interrupting him, *you must excuse me, if I cannot flatter myself you have any thoughts of doing us that honour. – I am a mean man, of no parentage, and it is well known have brought up a large family by the sweat of my brow. –* Lætitia *is a poor country maid: – it is true, the girl is well enough, but has nothing, – nothing at all, alas! in her to balance for that vast disparity of birth and fortune between you.*

Talk no more of that, said *Natura*, taking him by the hand, *such as she is, I like her; and I once more assure you, that I never had any dishonourable intentions on her, but am ready to prove the contrary, by marrying her, as soon as she approves of me, and you agree to it.*

THE old man looked very earnestly on him all the while he was speaking, and knew not well whether he ought to give credit to what he said, or not. – Natura, perceiving his diffidence, continued, by sparing neither arguments, nor the most solemn imprecations, to remove it, till he was at last assured of a good fortune, which, as he said, he had thought too extraordinary to happen in his family. He then told *Natura* he would acquaint his daughter with the happiness he intended for her, and dispose her to receive it with that respect and gratitude that became her. On which *Natura* took his leave till the next day, when he found *Lætitia* did not make any excuse to avoid his presence, as she had lately done. – He addressed himself to her not in the same manner he would have done to a woman of condition, but yet in very tender and affectionate terms: –

her behaviour to him was humble, modest, and obliging; and though she was not mistress of the politest expressions, yet what she said discovered she wanted not a fund of good sense and understanding, which, if cultivated by education, would have appeared very bright. He easily perceived, she took a great deal of pains to disguise the joy she conceived at this prospect of raising her fortune, but was too little accustomed to dissimulation, to do it effectually, and both the one and the other gave him much satisfaction.

CIRCUMSTANCES being in the manner I related, it is not natural to suppose any long sollicitation was required. – *Lœtitia* affected not an indifference she was free from, and *Natura* pressing for the speedy consummation of his wishes, a day was appointed for the celebration of the nuptials, and both the intended bride and bridegroom set themselves about making the necessary preparations usual in such cases.

BUT see, how capable are our firmest resolutions of being shaken by accidents! – the most assured of men may be compared to the leaf of a tree, which veers with every blast of wind, and is never long in one position. – Had any one told *Natura* he had taken all this pains for nothing, and that he would be more anxious to get off his promise of marrying *Lœtitia*, than ever he had been to engage one from her for that purpose, he would have thought himself highly injured, and that the person who said this of him was utterly a stranger to his sentiments or character; yet so it happened, and the poor *Lœtitia* found all her hopes of grandeur vanish into air, when they they seemed just on the point of being accomplished. – The occasion of this strange and sudden transition was as follows:

TWO days before that prefixed for his marriage, *Natura* received a packet from *Gibraltar*, which brought him an account of the death of his brother. – That unfortunate young gentleman, being convinced by his sufferings, and perhaps too by his own remorse, and stings of conscience of the foulness of the crime he had been guilty of, fell into a languishing disorder, soon after his arrival in that country, which left those about him no expectations of his ever getting the better of. – Finding his dissolution near, he wrote a letter to *Natura*, full of contrition, and intreaties for forgiveness. This epistle accompanied that which related his death, and both together plunged *Natura* into very melancholly thoughts. – The offence his brother had been guilty of, was indeed great; but, when he remembered that he had repented, and was now no more, all resentment, all revenge, against him ceased with his existence, and a tender pity supplied their place: – what, while *living*, he never would have forgave, when *dead* lost great part of its atrocity, and he bewailed the fate of the transgressor, with unfeigned tears and lamentations.

THIS event putting an end to the motive which had induced *Natura* to think of marriage, put an end also to his desires that way; – he was sorry he had gone so far with *Lœtitia*, was loth to appear a deceiver, in her eyes, or in those of her father; but thought it would be the extremest madness in him to prosecute his intent, as his beloved sister had a son, who would now be his heir, and only had desired to be the father of one himself to hinder *him* from being so, whose crimes had rendered him unworthy of it.

THE emotions of this revenge having entirely subsided, he now had leisure to consider how oddly the world would think and talk of him, if he perpetrated a marriage with a girl such as *Lœtitia;* – he almost wondered at himself, that the just displeasure he had conceived against his brother, should have transported him so far as to make him forgetful of what was owing to his own character; and when he reflected on the miseries, vexations, and infamy, his last marriage had involved him in, he trembled to think how near he had been to entering into a state, which tho' he had a very good opinion of *Lœtitia's* virtue, might yet possibly, some way or other, have given him many uneasinesses.

HE was, however, very much embarrassed how to break with her handsomely; and it must be confessed, that after what had passed, this was no very easy matter to accomplish. – Make what pretence he would, he could not expect to escape the censure of an unstable fluctuating man. – This is indeed a character, which all men are willing, nay industrious, to avoid, yet what there are few men, but some time or other in their lives, give just reason to incur. – *Natura* very well knew, that to court a woman for marriage, and afterwards break his engagements with her, was a thing pretty common in the world; but then, it was a thing he had always condemned in his own mind, and looked upon as most ungenerous and base: – besides, though he had made his addresses to *Lœtitia*, meerly because he imagined she would prove a virtuous, obedient, and fruitful wife, and was not inflamed with any of those sentiments for her which are called love; yet, designing to marry her, he had set himself as much as possible to love her, and had really excited in his heart a kind of a tenderness, which made him unable to resolve on giving her the mortification of being forsaken, without feeling great part of the pain he was about to inflict on her.

ALL he now wished was, that she might be possessed of as little warmth of inclination for him as he had known for her, and that the disparity of years between them, might have made her consent to the proposed marriage, intirely on the motive of interest, without any mixture of love, in order that the disappointment she was going to receive, might seem the less severe: as the regard he had for her made him earnestly wish this might be the case, he carefully recollected all the passages of her behaviour, her looks, her words, nay, the very accents of her voice, were re-examined, in hope to find some tokens of that happy indifference, which alone could make him easy in this affair; but all this retrospect afforded him no more than uncertain conjectures, and imaginations which frequently contradicted each other, and indeed served only to increase his doubts, and add to his disquiets.

THE mourning for his brother was, however, a very plausible pretence for delaying the marriage; and as he was willing the disappointment should come on by degrees, thinking by that means to soften the asperity of it, he contrived to let both father and daughter have room to guess the event before hand. – He seldom went to their house, and when he did, made very short visits, talked as if the necessity of his affairs would oblige him to leave the country, and settle again entirely in town: – rather avoided, than sought any opportunity of speaking to *Lætitia* in private, and in all his words and actions, discovered a coldness which could not but be very surprizing to them both, though they took not the least notice that they were so before him, but behaved towards him in the same manner, as when he appeared the most full of affection.

THIS was a piece of prudence *Natura* had not expected from persons of their low education and way of life: – he had imagined, that either the one or the other of them would have upbraided this change in him, and by avowing a suspicion, that he had repented him of his promises, given him an opportunity either of seeming to resent it, or by some other method, of breaking off: but this way of proceeding frustrated his measures in that point, and he found himself under a necessity of speaking first, on a subject no less disagreeable to himself, than he knew it would be to those to whom his discourse should be directed.

HOWEVER, as there was no remedy, and he considered, that the longer to keep them in suspence, would only be adding to the cruelty of the disappointment; he sent one morning for the yeoman to come to his house, and after ushering in what he was about to say, with some reflections on the instability of human affairs, told him that some accidents had happened, which rendered it highly inconvenient for him to think of marrying; – that he had the utmost respect and good will for *Lætitia*, and that if there were not indissoluble impediments to hinder him from taking a wife, she should be still his choice, above any woman he knew in the world; – that he wished her happy with any other man, and to contribute to making her so, as also by way of atonement for his enforced leaving her, he would give her five hundred pounds, as an addition to her fortune.

THIS was the substance of what he said; but though he delivered it in the softest terms he could possibly make use of, he could find it was not well received by the old man; his countenance, however, a little cleared up at the closure of it: – the five hundred pounds was somewhat of a sweetener to the bitter pill; and after expatiating, according to his way, on the ungenerosity of engaging a young maid's affection, and afterwards forsaking her, he threw in some shrewd hints, that as accidents had happened to change his mind as to marriage, others might also happen, which would have the same effect, in relation to the present he now seemed to intend for her.

To prevent that, cried *Natura* hastily, *you shall take it home with you*; and with these words turned to a cabinet, and took out the sum he had mentioned; after counting it over, he put it into a bag, and delivered it to the yeoman, saying at the same time, that though it might not be so proper to come to his house, yet if he would send to him in any exigence, he should find him ready to assist him; *for you may depend*, added he, *that though I cannot be your son, I shall always be your friend.*

THESE words, and the money together, rendered the yeoman more content than *Natura* had expected he would be; and by that he hoped he knew his daughter had not imbibed any passion for him, which she would find much difficulty in getting rid of, and that this augmentation to her portion, would very well compensate for the loss of a husband, of more than twice her years.

A SMALL time evinced, that *Natura* had not been altogether mistaken in his conjectures. – *Lætitia* became the bride of a young wealthy grazier in a neighbouring town, with whom she removed soon after her marriage; and this event, so much desired by *Natura*, destroyed all the remains of disquiet, his nicety of honour, and love of justice, had occasioned in him.

BEING now wholly extricated from an adventure, which had given him much pain, and no less free from the emotions of any turbulent passion, he passed his days and nights in a most perfect and undisturbed tranquility; a situation of mind to which, for a long series of years, he had been an utter stranger.

TO desire, or pursue any thing with too much eagerness, is undoubtedly the greatest cruelty we can practise on ourselves; yet how impossible is it to avoid doing so, while the passions have any kind of dominion over us: – to *acquire*, and to *preserve*, make the sole business of our lives, and leave no leisure to *enjoy* the goods of fortune: – still tost on the billows of passion, hurried from care to care the whole time of our existence here, is one continued scene of restlessness and variated[68] disquiet. – Strange propensity in man! – even nature in us seems contradictory to herself! – we wish *long life*, yet shorten it by our own anxieties; – nothing is so dreadful as *death*, yet we hasten his approach by our intemperance and irregularity, and, what is more, we know all this, yet still run on in the same heady course.

NATURA had now, however, an interval, a happy chasm, between the extremes of pleasure and of pain; – contented with his lot, and neither aiming at more than he possessed, nor fearful of being deprived of what he had. He, for a time, seemed in a condition such as all wise men would wish to attain, tho' so few take proper methods for that purpose, that those who we see in it, may be said to owe their felicity rather to chance, than to any right endeavours of their own.

CHAP. V.

Contains a remarkable proof, that tho' the passions may operate with greater velocity and vehemence in youth, yet they are infinitely more strong and permanent, when the person is arrived at maturity, and are then scarce ever eradicated. Love and friendship are then, and not till then, truly worthy of the names they bear; and that the one *between those of different sexes, is always the consequence of the* other.

THE inclination we have, and the pleasure it gives us to think well of our abilities, leads us frequently into the most gross mistakes, concerning the springs of action in our breasts. We are apt to ascribe to the strength of our reason, what is in reality the effect of one or other of the passions, sometimes even those of the worst kind, and which a sound judgment would most condemn, and endeavour to extirpate. – Man is a stranger to nothing, more than to himself; – the recesses of his own heart, are no less impenetrable to him, than the worlds beyond the moon; – he is blinded by vanity, and agitated by desires he knows not he is possessed of.

IT was not *reason* but *revenge*, which dissipated the immoderate grief of *Natura* on the death of his son; – it was not *reason* but *pride*, which made him see the inconveniencies of marrying with *Lœtitia*, – and yet doubtless he gave the praise of these events to the strength of his prudence: to that too he also ascribed the resolution he now took of living single during the remainder of his life; whereas it was in truth only owing to his being at present acquainted with no object capable of inspiring him with the tender passion.

AS he was now entirely free from all business, or avocation of any kind whatsoever, it came into his head to go and pass some part of the summer season with his sister: – he accordingly crossed the country to her seat, and was received with all imaginable demonstrations of joy, both by herself and husband.

HE found their family increased by the addition of a lady, who preferring a country to a town life, had desired to board with them, which was readily granted by the sister of *Natura*, not only as she was a relation of her husband, but also for the sake of having a companion so perfectly agreeable as this lady was in every respect.

CHARLOTTE, for so she was called, had been left a widow within three months after her marriage, and had never entertained any thoughts of entering into a second engagement, though her person, jointure, and accomplishments, had attracted many sollicitations on that score. She was about thirty years of age when *Natura* found her at his sister's; and through the chearfulness of her temper, and the goodness of her constitution, had preserved in her countenance all the bloom of fifteen. – The charms of her person, however, made no impression on *Natura* at his first acquaintance with her; he thought her a fine woman, as every one did who saw her, but her charms reached not his heart, nor gave him any emotions, either of pain or pleasure.

BUT it was not for any long time he remained in this state of insensibility. – *Charlotte* had graces which could not fail of conquest, sooner or later: – where those of her eyes wanted the power to move, her tongue came in to their assistance, and was sure of gaining the day: – there was something so resistless in her wit, and manner of conversation, that none but those who by nature, or want of proper education, were too dull and stupid to understand, but must have felt an infinity of satisfaction in it.

BESIDES all this, there was a sympathy of humour between this lady and *Natura*, which greatly contributed to make them pleased with each other: – both were virtuous by nature, by disposition gay and chearful: – both were equally lovers of reading, had a smattering of philosophy, were perfectly acquainted with the world, and knew what in it was truly worthy of being praised or contemned; and what rendered them still more conformable, was the aversion which each testified to marriage. – *Natura*'s treatment from his wife, had made him speak with some bitterness against a state, which had involved him in so many perplexities; and *Charlotte*, though so short a time a wife, having been married against her inclination, and to a man who, it seems, knew not her real value, had found in it the beginning of disquiets, which prognosticated worse mischiefs, had not his death relieved her from them, and made her too thankful for the deliverance, to endure the thoughts of venturing a second time to give up her freedom.

THIS parity of sentiments, inclinations, and dispositions, it was which, by degrees, endeared them to each other, without knowing they were so.

NATURA became at last impatient out of the company of *Charlotte*, and *Charlotte* found a restlessness in herself whenever *Natura* was absent; but this indeed happened but seldom: – the mutual desire they had of being together, made each of them industriously avoid all those parties of pleasure, in which both could not have a share: – *Natura* excused himself from accompanying his brother-in-law in any of those diversions where women were not admitted; and *Charlotte* always had some pretence for staying at home when the sister of *Natura* made her visits to the ladies of the country; – yet was this managed on both sides with such great decency and precaution, that neither the one nor the other perceived the motive which occasioned their being so rarely separated; much less had the family any notion of it.

IT is certain, that never any two persons were possessed of a more true and delicate passion for each other: – the flame which warmed their breasts, was meerly spiritual, and platonic; – the difference of sex was never considered: – *Natura* adored *Charlotte*, not because she was a lovely woman, but because he imagined somewhat angelic in her mind; and *Charlotte* loved *Natura*, not because he had an agreeable person, but because she thought she discovered more charms in his soul, than in that of any other man or woman.

THE acquaintance between them soon grew into an intimacy, and that intimacy, by degrees, ripened into a friendship, which is the height and very essence of love, though neither of them would allow themselves to think it so: they made no scruple, however, of assuring each other, of their mutual esteem, and promised all the good offices in the power of either, with a freedom which they would not have done (especially *Charlotte*, who was naturally very reserved) had they been sensible to what lengths their present attachment might in time proceed.

WINTER now drew on, but *Natura* was too much rivetted to think of departing, and would doubtless have made some pretext for living altogether with his sister, had not an accident happened, which made his going a greater proof of the regard he had for *Charlotte*, than his staying could have done, and perhaps made him know the real sentiments he was possessed of on her account, much sooner than he should without it.

THAT lady had some law-affairs, which required either herself, or some very faithful and diligent friend to attend. Term was approaching,[69] and the brother-in-law of *Natura* had promised to take a journey to *London* for that purpose; but he unfortunately had been thrown from his horse in a hunting match, and broke his leg, and *Charlotte* seemed in a good deal of anxiety, who she should write to, in order to entrust with the care of her business, which she justly feared would suffer much, if left wholly to the lawyer's own management.

NATURA on this offered his service, and told her, if she would favour him with her confidence in this point, he would go directly to *London*, where she might depend on his diligence and fidelity in the forwarding her business: – as she had not the least doubt of either, she accepted this testimony of his friendship, with no other reluctance, than what the being long deprived of his conversation occasioned. – Her good sense, notwithstanding, got the better of that consideration, which she looked upon only as an indulgence to herself, and committed to his care all the papers necessary to be produced, in case he succeeded so well for her, as to bring the suit to a trial.

THE manner of their taking leave was only such as might be expected between two persons, who professed a friendly regard for each other; but *Natura* had no sooner set out on his journey, than he felt a heaviness at his heart, for having left the adorable *Charlotte*, which nothing but the consideration that he was employed on her business, and going to serve her could have asswaged.

THIS was, indeed, a sweet consolation to him, and on his arrival in town, set himself to enquire into the causes of that delay she had complained of, with so much assiduity, that he easily found out she had not been well treated by her lawyers, and that one of them had even gone so far as to take fees from her adversary; – he therefore put the affair into other hands, and ordered matters so, that the trial could not, by any means, be put off till another time.

YET, in spite of all this diligence, it was the opinion of the council, that there was an absolute necessity for the lady to appear herself: – it is hard to say, whether *Natura* was more vexed or pleased at this intelligence; he was sorry that she could not, of himself, accomplish what he came about, and spare her the trouble of a journey he had found was very disagreeable to her, not only on account of her aversion to the town, and the ill season of the year for travelling, but also because the person she contended with was a near relation, and she was very sensible would engage many of their kindred to disswade her from doing herself that justice she was resolute to persist in her attempts for procuring. – The thoughts of the perplexity this would give her, it was that filled him with a good deal of trouble; but then the reflection, that he should have the happiness of seeing her again, on this account, much sooner than he could otherwise have done, gave him at least an equal share of satisfaction.

THE gentlemen of the long robe employed in her cause, and whose veracity and judgment he was well assured of, insisting she must come, put an end to his suspence, and he wrote to her for that purpose: the next post brought him an answer which, to his great surprize, expressed not the least uneasiness on the score of this journey, only acquainted him, that she had taken a place in the stage, should set out next morning, and in three days be in *London*; against which time, she begged he would be so good to provide her a commodious lodging, she being determined to go to none of her kindred, for the reason abovementioned.

BEING animated with exactly the same sentiments *Natura* was, that inclination which led him to wish her coming, influenced her also to be pleased with it, and rendered the fatigue of the journey, and those others she expected to find on her arrival, of no consequence, when balanced against the happiness she proposed, in re-enjoying the conversation of her amiable and worthy friend.

BUT all this *Natura* was ignorant of; nor did his vanity suggest to him the least part of what passed in his favour in the bosom of his lovely *Charlotte*; but he needed no more than the knowledge she was coming to a place where he should have her company, with less interruption than he had hitherto the opportunity of, to make him the most transported man alive. As he had no house of his own in town to accommodate her with, he provided lodgings, and every thing necessary for her reception, with an alacrity worthy of his love, and the confidence she reposed in him; and went in his own coach to take her from the stage some miles on the road. She testified her gratitude for the care he took of her affairs, in the most obliging and polite acknowledgments; and he returned the thanks she gave him, with the sincerest assurances, that the thoughts of having it in his power to do her any little service, afforded him the most elevated pleasure he had ever known in his whole life.

WHAT they said to each other, however, on this score, was taken by each, more as the effects of gallantry and good breeding, than the real motives from which the expressions they both made use of, had their source: – equal was their tenderness, equal also was their diffidence, it being the peculiar property of a true and perfect love, always to fear, and never to hope too much.

NATURA had taken care to chuse her an apartment very near the place where he lodged himself, which luckily happened to be in an extreme airy and genteel part of the town; so that he had the pleasure of seeing her, not only every day, but almost every hour in the day, on one pretext or other, which his industrious passion dictated; and this almost continual being together, and, for the most part, without any other company, very much increased the freedom between them, though that freedom never went farther, even in a wish, on either side, for a long time at least, than that of a brother and sister.

THOUGH all imaginable diligence was used to bring the law-suit to an issue, those with whom *Charlotte* contested, found means to put it off for yet one more term, she was obliged to stay that time; but neither felt in herself, nor pretended to do so, any repugnance at it: – *Natura* had enough to do to conceal his joy on this occasion; and when he affected a concern for her being detained in a place she had so often declared an aversion for, he did it so aukwardly, that had she not been too much taken up with endeavouring to disguise her own sentiments on this account, she could not but have seen into his.

AS neither of them seemed now to take any delight in balls, plays, operas, masquerades, cards, or any of the town diversions, they passed all their evenings together, and, for the most part, alone, as I before observed; – their conversation was chiefly on serious topics, and such as might have been improving to the hearers, had any been permitted; and when they fell on matters which required a more gay and sprightly turn, their good humour never went beyond an innocent chearfulness, nor in the least transgressed the bounds of the strictest morality and modesty.

HOW long this platonic intercourse would have continued, is uncertain; but the second term was near elapsed, the suit determined in favour of *Charlotte*, and her stay in town necessary but a very days before either of them entertained any other ideas, than such as I have mentioned. *Natura* then began to regret the diminution of the happiness he now enjoyed, and indeed of the total loss of it; for though he knew it would not be wondered at, that his complaisance should induce him to attend *Charlotte* in her journey to his sister's, yet he was at a loss for a pretence to remain there for any long time. – *Charlotte*, on the other hand, considered on the separation which, in all appearance, must shortly be between them, with a great deal of anxiety, and was even sorry the completion of her business had left her no excuse for staying in town, since she could not expect it either suited with his inclinations, or situation of affairs, to live always in the country.

THESE cogitations rendered both very uneasy in their minds, yet neither of them took any steps to remedy a misfortune equally terrible to each; and the event had doubtless proved as they imagined, had not the latent fires which glowed in both their breasts, been kindled into a flame by foreign means, and not the least owing to themselves.

ONE of those gentlemen who had been council for *Charlotte*, and had behaved with extraordinary zeal in her behalf, had been instigated thereto, more by the charms of her person, than the fees he received from her; – in fine, he was in love with her; but his passion was not of that delicate nature, which fills the mind with a thousand timid apprehensions, and chuses rather to endure the pains of a long smothered flame, than run the hazard of offending the adored object, by disclosing it.

HE had enquired into her family and fortune, and finding there was nothing of disparity between them, he declared his passion to her, and declared it in terms which seemed not to savour of any great fears of being rejected. – He was in his prime of life, had an agreeable person, and a good estate, the consciousness of which, together with his being accustomed to plead with success at the bar, made him not much doubt, but his eloquence and assurance would have the same effect on his mistress, as it frequently had on the judges: but the good opinion he had of himself, greatly deceived him in this point; he met with a rebuff from *Charlotte*, which might have deterred some men from prosecuting a courtship she seemed determined never to encourage: but though he was a little alarmed at it, he could not bring himself to think she was enough in earnest to make him desist: in every visit he paid her, he interlarded his discourse on business with professions of love, which at length so much teized her, that she told him plainly, she would sooner suffer her cause to be lost, than suffer herself to be continually persecuted with sollicitations, which she had ever avoided since her widowhood, and ever should do so.

NATURA came in one day just as the counsellor was going out of her apartment; he observed a great confusion in his face, and some emotions in her's, which shewed her mind a little ruffled from that happy composure he was accustomed to find it in. On his testifying the notice he took of this change in her countenance, *It is a strange thing*, said she, *that people will believe nothing in their own disfavour! – I have told this man twenty times, that if I were disposed to think of a second marriage, which I do not believe I ever shall, the present sentiments I am possessed of, would never be reversed by any offer he could make me; yet will he still persist in his impertinent declarations.*

THERE needed no more to convince *Natura* he had a rival; nor, as he knew *Charlotte* had nothing of coquetry in her humour, to make him also know she was not pleased with having attracted the affections of this new admirer: this gave him an inexpressible satisfaction; for tho', as yet, he had never once thought of making any addresses to her on the score of love, death was not half so terrible to him, as the idea of her encouraging them from any other man.

Then, madam, cried he, looking on her in a manner she had never seen him do before, *the councellor has declared a passion for you, and you have rejected him? – is it possible? – Possible!* interrupted she, *can you believe it possible I should not do so, knowing, as you do, the fixed aversion I have to entering into any second engagement! –but were it less so*, continued she, after a pause, *his sollicitations would be never the more agreeable to me.*

NATURA asked pardon for testifying any surprize, which he assured her was totally owing, either to this proof of the effect of her charms, *which*, said he, *are capable of far greater conquests; or to your refusal of the councellor's offers, after the declarations you have made against a second marriage, but was excited in me meerly by the novelty of the thing, having heard nothing of it before.*

This had not been among the number of the few things I conceal from you, answered she, *if I had thought the repetition worthy of taking up any part of that time which I always pass with you on subjects more agreeable*; – *besides*, continued she, *it was always my opinion, that those women, who talk of the addresses made to them, are secretly pleased with them in their hearts, and like the love, tho' they may even despise the lover. For my part, I can feel no manner of satisfaction in relating to others, what I had rather be totally ignorant of myself.*

Natura had here a very good opportunity of complimenting her on the excellency of her understanding, which set her above the vanities of the generality of her sex; and indeed he expressed himself with so much warmth on this occasion, that it even shocked her modesty, and she was obliged to desire him to change the conversation, and speak no more of a behaviour, which was not to be imputed to her good sense, but to her disposition.

Never had *Natura* found it more difficult to obey her than now; – he could have expatiated for ever on the many and peculiar perfections both of her mind and person; but he perceived, that to indulge the darling theme, would be displeasing to her, and therefore forced himself to put a stop to the utterance of those dictates, with which his heart was now charged, even to an overflowing.

Such was the effect of this incident on both: *Natura*, who till now had thought he loved only the *soul* of his mistress, found how dear her lovely *person* was also to him, by the knowledge that another was endeavouring to get possession of it; and *Charlotte*, by the secret satisfaction she felt on those indications *Natura*, in spite of his efforts to the contrary, had given of a more than ordinary admiration of her, discovered, for the first time, that he was indeed the only man whose love would not be displeasing to her.

After *Natura* came home, and had leisure to meditate on this affair, he began with thinking how terrible it would be to him, to see *Charlotte* in the arms of a husband; and when he reflected, that such a thing might be possible, even though he doubted not the sincerity of her present aversion, the idea was scarce to be borne: – from this he naturally fell on figuring to himself how great a blessing that man would enjoy, who should always have the sweet society of so amiable a companion; – and this made him cry out, *Why then, what hinders me from endeavouring to become that happy man? – If I resolved against any future marriage, it was when I knew not the adorable* Charlotte, *nor believed there was so excellent a woman in the world.* – In this rapturous imagination did he continue for a moment, but then the improbability of succeeding in any such attempt, struck him with an adequate despair. *Though the uncommon merit of the woman I adore*, said he, *compels me to change the resolution I had taken, there is not the same reason to prevail on her to recede from her's. – Past the bloom of life, and already twice a husband, can I flatter myself with the fond hope she will not reject the proposals I should make with the same scorn she did those of the councellor?*

CHARLOTTE, on the other hand, was engrossed by reflections vastly different from those she was accustomed to entertain: – never woman was more free from vanity, or thought less of the power of her charms, yet she could not hinder herself from thinking there was somewhat in the behaviour of *Natura*, in his last visit, that denoted a regard beyond an ordinary friendship for her. – This apprehension, at first, a little startled her, or at least she imagined it did so, and she said to herself, *If he should really harbour any inclinations for me of that sort, how unhappy should I be in being obliged to break off my acquaintance with a person so every way agreeable to me; and to continue it, would be to countenance a passion I have determined never to give the least attention to. – Yet wherefore did I determine*? pursued she, with a sigh, *but because I found the generality of men were wandering, vague, inconstant creatures; – were guided only by fancy; – never consulted their judgment, whether the object they pretended to admire, had any real merit or not, and often too treated those worst who had the best claim to their esteem; – besides, one seldom finds a man whose person and qualifications are every way suited to one's liking: –* Natura *is certainly such as I should wish a husband to be, if I were inclined to marry again; – I have not taken a vow of celibacy, and have nobody to controul my actions: – but then*, said she again, *what foolish imaginations comes into my head; perhaps he has not the least thought of me in the way I am dreaming of; – no, no, he has suffered too much by the imprudence of one woman, to put it in the power of another to treat him in the same manner; – he trembles at marriage; – I have heard him declare it, and I am deviating into a vanity I never before was guilty of.*

SHE was debating in this fashion within herself, when *Natura* came to pay his morning visit: she blushed at his approach, conscious of the meditations she had been in on his account. – He, full of the sentiments I have described, saluted her with an air more grave and timid than he had been accustomed, and which all who are judges of the tender passion, know to be the surest symptom of it. – They sat down, and on his beginning to renew some discourse concerning the councellor's pretensions, she desired him to forbear so disagreeable a topic, telling him at the same time, he could say nothing else she would not listen to with satisfaction. – *How, madam*, cried he, *are you sure of that? – Alas, you little know what passes in my heart, or you would not permit me this toleration*. This might have been sufficient to make some women convinced of the truth; but *Charlotte*, either fearful of being deceived by her own vanity, or willing he should be more explicit, answered, *I have too high an opinion of your good sense, and too flattering an idea of your friendship to me, to imagine your heart will ever suggest any thing which would be offensive to me from your tongue.*

Suppose, madam, said he, *it should not be in my power to restrain my wishes in those bounds prescribed by you, to all who have the happiness of conversing with you; and that I were encroaching enough not to be content with the marks of friendship you are pleased to honour me: – in fine*, continued he, *suppose I were guilty of the very same presumption, you have so severely censured in the councellor!*

That is impossible, replied she, *since you are a foe professed to marriage, as well as myself*; – she was about to add something more, but was prevented by emotions, which she attempted, but in vain, to conceal; and *Natura* saw enough to keep him from despairing he had forfeited her *esteem* by aiming at her *love*.

HAVING thus made a beginning, it was easy for him to prosecute a suit, which he soon discovered he had a friend in her bosom to plead in favour of: – in a word, he left her not, till he had obtained her permission to entertain her on the same theme, and to use his endeavours to prevail on her to exchange the friendship she confessed for him into a warmer passion.

IT would be altogether needless to make any repetition of the particulars of this courtship; the reader will easily believe, that both parties being animated with the same sentiments I have described, it could not be very tedious; – love had already done his work in their hearts, and required little the labour of the tongue. *Charlotte* had entirely compleated every thing appertaining to her law-suit, yet she seemed not in a hurry to quit the town; a business of a more tender nature now detained her; – she had resolved, or rather she could not help resolving, to give herself to *Natura*, and the shame of doing what she had so often, and so strenuously declared against, rendered the thoughts of returning into the country in a different state, from that with which she had left it, insupportable to her.

AFTER having agreed to the sollicitations of her importunate lover, she expressed her sentiments to him on this head; on which it was concluded, that their nuptials should be solemnized as privately as possible in *London*, and that they should set out immediately after for his country seat, where *Charlotte*, being utterly a stranger, would not be subjected to any of those little railleries, she must have expected, in a place where every one knew of the aversion she had testified for a second marriage.

NO cross accident intervening, what they designed was, in a short time, carried into execution; – never were any pair united by more indelible bonds; those of friendship sublimed into the most pure and virtuous tenderness, and a parity of principles, humours, and inclinations.

THUS does passion triumph over the most seemingly fixed and determined resolution; and though it must be confessed, that in this instance, both had reason, from the real merits of the beloved object, to justify their choice, yet nature would certainly have had the same force, and worked the same effect, if excited only by meer fancy, and imaginary perfections.

A PLATONIC and spiritual love, therefore, between persons of different sexes, can never continue for any length of time. Whatever ideas the *mind* may conceive, they will at last conform to the craving of the *senses*; and *the soul*, though never so elevated, find itself incapable of enjoying a perfect satisfaction, without the participation of the *body*. –As inclination then is not always guided by a right judgment, nor circumstances always concur to render the indulging an amorous propensity either convenient, or lawful, how careful ought every one to be, not to be deceived by a romantic imagination, so far as to engage in an affection which, sooner or later, will bring them to the same point that *Natura* and *Charlotte* experienced.

CHAP. VI.

How the most powerful emotions of the mind *subside, and grow weaker in proportion, as the strength of the* body *decays, is here exemplified; and that such passions as remain after a certain age, are not properly the incentives of nature, but of example, long habitude, or ill humour.*

THE bride and bridegroom were received by all the friends, tenants, and dependants of *Natura*, with the greatest demonstrations of joy; and the behaviour of the amiable *Charlotte* was such as made every one cease to wonder that he had ventured again on marriage, after the disquiets he had experienced in that state.

THE kindred on neither side had nothing to condemn in the choice which each had made of the other; and though perhaps a motive of self-interest might make those nearest in blood, and consequently to the estates they should leave at their decease, wish such an union had not happened, yet none took the liberty to complain, or testify, by any part of their behaviour, the least dissatisfaction at it. – The sister and brother-in-law of *Nature*, it must be allowed, had the most cause, as they had a large family of children, who had a claim equally to the effects of both, in case they had died without issue; yet did not even they express any discontent, though *Charlotte*, within the first year of her marriage, brought two sons into the world, and a third in the next ensuing one, all which seemed likely to live, and enjoy their parents patrimony.

WHAT now was wanting to compleat the happiness of this worthy pair, equally loving and beloved by each other, respected by all who knew them, in need of no favours from any one, and blessed with the power of conferring them on as many as they found wanted, or merited their assistance. – *Charlotte* lost no part of her beauty, nor vivacity, by becoming a mother, nor did *Natura* find any decrease in the strength, or vigour, either of his mind or body, till he was past fifty-fix years of age. – The same happy constitution had doubtless continued a much longer time in him, as nature had not been worn out by any excesses, or intemperance, if by unthinkingly drinking some cold water, when he was extremely hot, he had not thrown himself into a surfeit, which surfeit afterward terminated in an ague and fever, which remained on him a long time, and so greatly impaired all his faculties, as well as person, that he was scarce to be known, either by behaviour, or looks, for the man who, before that accident, had been infinitely regarded and esteemed for the politeness of the *one*, and the agreeableness of the *other*.

HIS limbs grew feeble, his body thin, and his face pale and wan, his temper sour and sullen, seldom caring to speak, and when he did it was with peevishness and ill-nature; – every thing was to him an object of disquiet; nothing of delight; and he seemed, in all respects, like one who was weary of the world, and knew he was to leave it in a short time.

IT is so natural to feel repugnance at the thoughts of being what they call *no more*; that is, no more as to the knowledge and affections of this world; that even those persons who labour under the severest afflictions, wish rather to continue in them, than be eased by death: – they are pleased at any flattering hopes given of a prolongation of their present misery, and are struck with horror at the least mention of their life and pains being drawing to a period. – More irksome, doubtless, it must still be to those, who having every thing they could wish for here, find they must soon be torn from all the blessings they enjoy. – This is indeed a weakness; but it is a weakness of nature, and which neither religion nor philosophy are sufficient to arm us against; and the very endeavours we make to banish, or at least to conceal our disquiets on this score, occasion a certain peevishness in the sweetest temper, and make us behave with a kind of churlishness, even to those most dear to us.

FEW, indeed, care to confess this truth, tho' there are scarce any, who do not shew it in their behaviour, even at the very time they are forcing themselves to an affectation of indifference for life, and a resignation to the will of Heaven.

THE great skill of his physicians, however, and the yet greater care his tender consort took to see their prescriptions obeyed with, the utmost exactitude, at length recovered *Natura* from the brink of the grave. – He was out of danger from the disease which had so long afflicted him; but though it had entirely left him, the attack had been too severe for a person at the age to which he was now arrived, to regain altogether the former man. – He had, in his sickness, contracted habits, which he was unable to throw off in health, and he could no more behave, than look, as he had done before.

THE mind would certainly be unalterable, and retain the same vigour it ever had in youth, even to extreme old age, could the constitution preserve itself entire. – It is that perishable part of us, which every little accident impairs, and wears away, preparing, as it were, by degrees, for a total dissolution, which hinders the nobler moiety of the human species from actuating in a proper manner: – those organs, which are the vehicles, through which its meanings shoot forth into action, being either shrivelled, abraded by long use, or clogged up with humours, shew the soul but in an imperfect manner, often disguise it wholly, and it is for want of a due consideration only, that we are so apt to condemn the *mind*, for what, in reality, is nothing but the incumbrances laid on it by the infirmities of the *body*.

IT is true, that as we grow older, the passions naturally subside; yet that they do so, is not owing to themselves, as I think may be easily proved by this argument.

EVERY one will acknowledge, because he knows it by experience, that while he is possessed of *passions*, his *reason* alone has the power of keeping them within the bounds of moderation; if then we have less of the *passions* in old age, or rather, if they seem wholly extinguished in us, we ought to have a greater share of *reason* than before; whereas, on the contrary, *reason* itself becomes languid in the length of years, as well as *the passions*, it is supposed to have subdued: it is therefore meerly the imbecility of the organical faculties, and from no other cause, that we see the aged and infirm dead, in appearance, to those sensations, by which their youth was so strongly influenced.

AVARICE is, indeed, frequently distinguishable in old men; but this I do not look upon as a *passion*, but a *propensity*, arising from ill-nature and self-love. – Gain, and the sordid pleasure of counting over money, and reckoning up rents and revenues, is the only lust of age; and since we cannot be so handsome, so vigorous, cannot indulge our appetites, like those who are younger, we take all manner of ways to be richer, and pride ourselves in the length of our bags, and the number of our tenants.

I KNOW it may be objected, that this vice is not confined to age, that youth is frequently very avaritious, and grasps at money with a very unbecoming eagerness: – this, I grant, is true; but, if we look into the conduct of such men in other respects, I believe we shall generally find their avarice proceeds from then prodigality; – they are lavish in the purchase of pleasures, and must therefore be parsimonious in acts of generosity and justice: – they are guilty of meanness in some things, only for the sake of making a great figure in others; and are not ashamed to be accounted niggards, where they ought to be liberal, in order to acquire the reputation of open-handedness, where it would better become them to be sparing.

NATURA, however, had never discovered any tendency to this vice, either in youth or age; yet did that peevishness, which the infirmities of his body had occasioned, make him behave sometimes, as if he were tainted with it.

CHARLOTTE observed this alteration in her husband's temper with an infinite concern; yet bore it with an equal patience; – making it her whole study to divert and sooth his ill humour: – he was not so lost to love and gratitude, and even reason too, as not to acknowledge the tender proofs he continually received of her unshaken affections, and would sometimes confess the errors he was guilty of, in point of behaviour towards her, and intreat her pardon; but then the least trifle would render him again forgetful of all he had said, and make him relapse into his former frowardness.

IT is certain, notwithstanding, that his love for her was the same as ever, though he could not shew it in the same manner; and to what can this be imputed, but to the effect which the ailments of his external frame had on his internal faculties.

THOUGH, as well as those about him, he found a decay within himself, which made him think he had not long to live; yet could he not be prevailed upon, for a great while, to settle his affairs after his decease, by making any will; and whenever it was mentioned to him, discovered a dissatisfaction, which at last made every one desist from urging any thing on that score.

IT was in vain that they had remonstrated to him, that the estate being to descend entire to his eldest son, the two youngest would be left without any provision, and consequently must be dependants on their brother, by his dying intestate: – in vain they pleaded, that taking so necessary a precaution for preserving the future peace of his family, would no way hasten his death, but, on the contrary, render the fatal hour, whenever it should arrive, less dreadful, he had only either answered not at all, or replied in such a fashion, as could give them no room to hope for his compliance.

IN this unhappy disposition did he continue between two and three years; but as his latter days came on, he grew much more calm and resigned, *reason* began to recover its former dominion over him; and, when every one had left off all importunities on the account of his making a *will*, he, of himself, mentioned the necessity of it, and ordered a lawyer to be sent for to that end.

HAVING settled all his affairs, relating to this world, in the most prudent manner, he began to prepare for another, with a zeal which shewed, that whatever notions people may have in health, concerning futurity, they become more convinced, in proportion as they grow nearer their dissolution.

HE finished his course in the sixty-third, or what is called the grand climacteric year of life; – had the blessing to retain the use of all his senses to the last; and as death had long before assailed, though not totally vanquished him, he was too much decayed by continual wastings, to feel any of those pangs, which persons who die in their full vigour must unavoidably go through, when the vital springs burst at once.

HE took leave of his dear wife and children with great serenity and composure of mind; and afterwards turned himself from them, and passed into eternity, as if falling into a gentle slumber.

THUS have I attempted to trace nature in all her mazy windings, and shew life's progress thro' the passions, from the cradle to the grave. – The various adventures which happened to *Natura*, I thought, afforded a more ample field, than those of any one man I ever heard, or read of; and flatter myself, that the reader will find many instances, that may contribute to rectify his own conduct, by pointing out those things which ought to be avoided, or at least most carefully guarded against, and those which are worthy to be improved and imitated.

FINIS.

EDITORIAL NOTES

The Rash Resolve; or the Untimely Discovery

1. *Woman is soft, and of a tender heart ... nor hits so sure: Ovid's Art of Love. In Three Books. Translated by Mr. Dryden, Mr. Congreve etc.* (1712), book 3, ll. 43–6, translated by W. Congreve (1670–1729).
2. *Lady* RUMNEY: Lady Elizabeth Romney, *neé* Shovell (1692–1750). She was the eldest daughter of Admiral Sir Cloudsley Shovell, and married Sir Robert Marsham, the first Baron Romney, in 1716. Lady Romney is listed as a subscriber to *Plays written by Mr. Cibber, In Two Volumes* (1721), and *The Adventures of Milinthus ... done from the French* (1728).
3. *Spain* yields in Fiction: Savage might be thinking here of the Spanish prose romances of the sixteenth century, or of Cervantes' *Don Quixote* (1605–15) which parodies these. However, there was also a tradition of Spanish short fiction influenced by his *Novelas Ejemplares* (1613). There were popular seventeenth- and eighteenth-century translations, notably Sir Roger L'Estrange's *The Spanish Decameron*, a translation of five of the *Novelas Ejemplares*, and five short stories or novellas from *La Garduña de Sevilla* (*c.* 1634), by Alonso de Castillo Solórzano (1584–1648). *The Spanish Decameron* went through four editions between 1680 and 1720.
4. *Richard Savage*: Richard Savage (1697/8–1743), an aspiring poet and playwright, who claimed to be the illegitimate offspring of Richard Savage, fourth Earl Rivers, and Anne Gerard, Countess of Macclesfield. In the 1720s he was a member of the literary circle that included Aaron Hill, James Thomson, John Dyer, Martha Fowke Sansom and Eliza Haywood. Another poem by Savage praising Haywood prefaced *Love In Excess, Part the Second* (1719–20). Haywood's *Memoirs of a Certain Island* (1724) supported Savage's version of his birth and parentage. It used to be assumed that Savage was Haywood's lover and that he fathered one of her two children, but no concrete evidence exists. (See K. King, 'Eliza Haywood, Savage Love, and Biographical Uncertainty', pp. 722–39.) Whatever relationship existed between them seems to have been over by 1725, when Savage attacked Haywood in his poem *Authors of the Town*. Haywood responded in *The Tea-Table ... Part the Second* (1726), and Savage characterized Haywood as a 'strolling actress' in *An Author to be Lett* (1728).
5. *the name of* Manly: The description of Emmanuella possibly draws on Aaron Hill's praise of Haywood in his poem 'The Vision': 'There lives a Charmer whom, divinely fir'd, / Ev'n her whole Sex's Virtues have inspir'd / Where all that's manly, joins with all that's sweet, / And in whose Breast engross'd Perfections meet'.
6. Porto-Rico: Puerto Rico (the 'rich port') was a Spanish colony from 1508 to 1812.

7. *the* Spanish West-Indies: the Caribbean archipelago as colonized by Spain from the fifteenth century. Spain recognized English possessions, including Jamaica, under the terms of the Treaty of Madrid (1670), and the French presence on Hispaniola (later Haiti) in the Treaty of Ryswick (1697).
8. *his most Catholic Majesty*: a conflation of the titles conferred by the Pope on the French king (his most Christian Majesty) and the king of Spain (his Catholic Majesty).
9. Madrid ... *entertainments suitable to her Genius*: It is possible that Haywood visited Spain. A poem by Aaron Hill, entitled 'To Eliza, on her design'd Voyage to Spain', was included in *Miscellaneous Poems and Translations ... Published by Richard Savage* (1726).
10. *Don* Pedro ... *to ingratiate to the Affections of this young Heiress*: The setting, characters and plot of *The Rash Resolve* owe much to the so-called 'Spanish intrigue' plays of the late-seventeenth and early-eighteenth centuries made popular by Aphra Behn and Susannah Centlivre, and performed and reprinted well into the eighteenth century. Behn's *The Rover* (1677) has another Don Pedro who would choose a husband for the heroine. Behn's Florinda, like Emanuella, resists his choice. Common tropes are the imprisoned girl, enforced marriage, the threat of a nunnery and abduction.
11. *Goal*: gaol, or jail.
12. *Standish*: an inkstand.
13. *to bait*: to take, or make a stop for, refreshment on a journey.
14. *Don* Jabin: 'Jabin' means 'discerning' in Hebrew, as well as being the name of kings in the Old Testament.
15. Escurial: The Royal Monastery of San Lorenzo de El Escorial, built by Philip II between 1563 and 1584. The building is a royal palace as well as a monastery, a basilica, a library and a mausoleum. Demonstrating the power of the Spanish monarchy and the Roman Catholic religion, it came to symbolize the Counter-Reformation.
16. *the* Inquisition: in Spain, the tribunal established by the monarchy in 1480 to maintain Catholic orthodoxy. It was not definitively abolished until 1834.
17. *for eight or nine hundred Crowns ... for their Lives*: The practice of placing young women for whom an adequate dowry could not be provided in convents was not uncommon. See S. Evangelisti, *Nuns: a History of Convent Life, 1450–1700* (Oxford: Oxford University Press, 2007), p. 4: '[C]onvents were vital to the patrimonial needs and marriage strategies of the élites and middling sorts'.
18. Emilius: the name of a Roman Catholic martyr, tortured to make him abjure the Christian religion. He was said by St Cyprian to have been overcome by the first trial, but strengthened by God to make him victorious in the second. See *The Roman Martyrology. An English Translation* (London: Burns, Oates and Washbourne, 1937), pp. 129–30.
19. *the Freedom of the Diversions used in that Season*: Carnival was celebrated in Roman Catholic countries immediately before the penitential period of Lent that lasted from Ash Wednesday to Maundy Thursday. It was marked by a relaxation of normal social order and often characterized by the use of masks to conceal personal identity.
20. *Jessamin and Fillaree*: jasmine, an evergreen with fragrant flowers, and filaree (or fillaree), a winter annual of the geranium family.
21. *the most binding Vows of everlasting Constancy had pass'd between them*: Before the Marriage Act of 1753, promises exchanged between a man and a woman in private – known as *per verba et praesenti* – could constitute one stage of a marriage process, and were regarded as a binding contract under canon law. Either party could then insist on the performance of the contract, that is, the celebration of the marriage in church, but solemnization was necessary for full legal rights and responsibilities to arise. Sexual intercourse

after private vows was a grey area: couples were guilty of contempt of canon law, but not fornication. The ambiguities created by canon law were resolved by the Hardwicke's Act, so called after Philip Yorke, first Earl of Hardwicke (1690–1764), and Lord Chancellor from 1737 to 1756. A public ceremony became legally necessary for the marriage to have any validity. See Probert, *Marriage Law and Practice in the Long Eighteenth Century*, p. 35. Haywood could interpret the issue differently in different novels, as it suited her heroine's, or hero's, desires. In *The Rash Resolve* and *Life's Progress*, vows or a contract allow for sex, but in *Betsy Thoughtless* (1751), Haywood has Betsy tell her husband-to-be that promises grant him 'no right to liberties of that nature' (vol. 4, ch. 51).

22. *no more but so?*: Ophelia's response to Laertes in *Hamlet* I, iii, l. 10. Laertes tells her to regard Hamlet's apparent love for her as mere amorous play:

    Laer. For Hamlet, and the trifling of his favour,
    Hold it a fashion and a toy in blood,
    A violet in the youth of primy nature,
    Forward, not permanent, sweet, not lasting,
    The perfume and suppliance of a minute,
    No more.
    Oph. No more but so?

23. *a Nunnery of* Pourclaires: an eccentric spelling of 'Poor Clares', the popular name of the Order of St Clare, founded at Assisi in 1212 to follow the Franciscan ideal of poverty.
24. *Hercules*'s Shirt: a poisoned shirt innocently given to Hercules by his wife Deianeira. Hercules called on the centaur Nessus to carry Deianeira across a river. Nessus attempted to violate her, and was killed by Hercules. As he died, he told Deianeira to mix his blood with the semen on the ground, telling her it would become a love potion. Later, when she believed her husband was in love with Iole, she sent him the shirt, but it burned Hercules's flesh, and he threw himself on a funeral pyre.
25. *bigotted to*: prejudiced in favour of.
26. *Eclaircissment*: to come to an éclaircissement is to come to an understanding or to explain behaviour that seems equivocal.
27. Alcala: the city of Alcalá de Henares, 35 km north-east of Madrid.
28. Guadalaxara: Guadalajara, a city 60 km north-east of Madrid.
29. Tortol: the present-day municipality of Tortola de Henares.
30. ALCALA ... *being famous for Learning*: Alcalà had an important university founded in the sixteenth century by Cardinal Ximénez de Cisneros.
31. *Leagues*: a league was conventionally a distance of around three miles.
32. *Cousin Germain*: first cousin.
33. *the Empire*: presumably the Holy Roman Empire.
34. Andaluzia: Andalusia or Andalucia, a region on the southern coast of Spain.
35. *a criminal Conversation*: legally, adultery, but also used as a euphemism for any illicit sexual act between a man and a woman.
36. Toledo: the city of Toledo, one-time capital of Spain, 70 km south of Madrid.

Life's Progress through the Passions: or, The Adventures of Natura

1. *if the pattern laid down ... small in comparison with those presented to us*: A version of the neoclassical doctrine which ruled that the hero of a tragedy should not be completely good or bad. Based on the *Poetics*, xiii, where Aristotle states that such a character should

be 'someone just like ourselves ... not conspicuous for virtue and justice, and whose fall into misery is not due to vice and depravity', the principle was upheld by René Le Bossu (*Traité du Poeme Epique* (1675), book 4, ch. 6), John Dryden (Preface to *Troilus and Cressida*, 1679), Joseph Addison (*Spectator* 548, 1712), Shaftesbury (*Characteristics* (1710), Miscellany V) and many others. It can be found restated in Henry Fielding's *Tom Jones* (1748–9) in book 10, ch. 1, the first three volumes of which appeared in September 1748.

2. *the poet's words*: 'the poet' is probably Haywood herself.
3. *an enemy to all* romances: 'Romance', understood as an unduly long and implausible kind of fiction, had been falling into disfavour since the beginning of the eighteenth century. One of the most significant attacks on romance in the 1740s was Henry Fielding's chapter prefacing book 3 of *Joseph Andrews* (1742). See Introduction, p. xvii.
4. eclat: éclat, meaning a striking effect.
5. *his mother's cravings ... badge of distinction*: The belief that the cravings of a pregnant woman could have an effect on the appearance of her child, in the form of birthmarks or even deformities, was disputed in the eighteenth century. Daniel Turner, in *De Morbis Cutaneis* (1714) called on Hippocrates, Galen, St Augustine and others to support the case, while James Blondel attacked it as a 'vulgar error' in *The Strength of the Imagination in Pregnant Women Examin'd* (1727).
6. *the passions ... sole authors of all human actions*: a view expressed by Joseph Addison in *Spectator* 408 (June 18, 1712): 'Passions, which are to the Mind as the Winds to a Ship', and given poetic form in Pope's *Essay on Man* (1733–4), Epistle 2, l. 108: 'Reason the Card, but Passion is the Gale'.
7. Fear ... sorrow ... avarice ... anger: A similar account of the passions may be found in Haywood's *Female Spectator* (1742–4), vol. 1, book 3 and vol. 2, book 9. Haywood owes something to Thomas Hobbes' account of human nature as moved by appetites and aversions in *Leviathan* (1651), book 1, ch. 6, and Locke's *An Essay Concerning Human Understanding* (1690), book 2, ch. 10, 'Of Modes of Pleasure and Pain'. Locke does not mention avarice.
8. *such opposites, that the one is a sufficient check upon the other*: The notion of 'countervailing passions' cancelling each other out, or of passion balanced by self-interest, often for the public good, is common in accounts of man's moral nature in the period. Pope: 'Passions, like elements, though born to fight, / Yet mix'd and soften'd, in His work unite', (*Essay on Man*, (1733–4), Epistle 2, ll. 111–12); '[T]he passions either take place alternately; or if they encounter, the one annihilates the other', (D. Hume, *A Treatise of Human Nature* (1739), book 2, section 2); '[A]s ... all Passions center in Self-Love, so [Passion] may be subdued by any Superiour Passion, to sooth that same Self-Love' (B. Mandeville, 'An Enquiry into the Origin of Moral Virtue', Remark C, 1723). An important critical work on this subject is Hirschman, *The Passions and the Interests: Political Argumemts for Capitalism*; for a more recent discussion see V. Kahn, N. Saccamano and D. Coli (eds), *Politics and the Passions 1500–1850* (Princeton: Princeton University Press, 2006).
9. Men are but children ... full as vain: J. Dryden, *All for Love* (1678), Act IV, Part 1, ll. 43–6.
10. *to send the child ... to corrupt the morals of youth*: A view articulated most influentially for the early eighteenth century by John Locke in *Some Thoughts Concerning Education* (1693). Locke argued that a domestic, or private, education was more likely to produce a virtuous gentleman, as his 'Innocence and Modesty' would be better preserved at home. He conceded that 'the emulation of School-fellows often puts Life and Industry into young Lads', but believed that public schools generally encouraged 'malapertness, trick-

ing and violence'. The debate is rehearsed in *Pamela ... in her Exalted Condition* (1741–2), as well as *Joseph Andrews* (1742) and *Tom Jones* (1748–9). In Tobias Smollett's *Peregrine Pickle* (1751) the hero is roused from indolence by a public education, but also exhibits the kind of 'tricking and violence' Locke deplored.

11. *had not* Natura's *own curiosity led him to examine into the sources*: 'Curiosity in Children ... is but an Appetite after Knowledge; and therefore ought to be encouraged in them, not only as a good sign, but as the great Instrument Nature has provided, to remove that Ignorance, they were born with, and which without this busie *Inquisitiveness*, will make them dull and useless Creatures'. (Locke, *Some Thoughts Concerning Education*, section 118).
12. Precept *must be constantly and artfully instilled ... confirms it*: 'one Thing I think a Fault in the ordinary Method of Education; and that is, the Charging of Children's Memories, upon all Occasions, with Rules and Precepts'. (Locke, *Some Thoughts Concerning Education*, section 64 ff.) Fielding made a similar point in *Joseph Andrews* (1742) book 1, ch. 1.
13. pride *is intitled the original sin*: The idea that pride (*superbia*) is the original sin, or the root of all sins, or the 'queen' of sins, is a tradition in the Christian Church principally associated with the *Magna Moralia* of Pope Gregory I, or Gregory the Great (d. 604). There is scriptural authority for the tradition, but also authority to give the priority to avarice.
14. *fleers*: jibes or mockery.
15. *dishabillee*: dishabille, a state of undress, or an undress garment.
16. NATURA *now considering her as his wife ... to do before*: see *RR* p. 34, n. 21.
17. *money-scrivener*: a money lender.
18. *the disgrace of the punishment inflicted ... him the most poignant anguish*: '*Esteem* and *Disgrace* are, of all others, the most powerful incentives to the Mind, when once it is brought to relish them'. (Locke, *Some Thoughts Concerning Education*, section 55).
19. *bagnio*: here meaning a boarding-house, but can also signify a brothel or a bath-house.
20. *so overcome with the unhoped-for gentleness of his behaviour*: Locke counselled against the punitive treatment of children: '[K]eep them to the practice of what you would have grow into a Habit in them, by kind words, and gentle Admonitions, rather as minding them of what they forget, than by harsh Rebukes and Chiding, as if they were wilfully guilty'. (Locke, *Some Thoughts Concerning Education*, section 64).
21. a full confession of all your misbehavior ... and that I can expect from you: 'If therefore when a Child is questioned any thing, his first Answer be an *Excuse*, warn him soberly to tell the truth; and then if he persists to shuffle it off with a *Falshood*, he must be chastised. But if he directly confess, you must commend his Ingenuity, and pardon the Fault, be it what it will'. (Locke, *Some Thoughts Concerning Education*, section 125).
22. *his governor*: a gentleman usually undertook the Grand Tour between the ages of sixteen and twenty-one, accompanied by a male chaperone, or governor.
23. *ten leagues*: see *RR* p. 203, n. 31.
24. *almoner*: at this time, a distributor or giver of alms.
25. *being intended for a monastic life ... as a pensioner*: a pensioner could lodge in a convent or monastery for the payment of a sum of money.
26. *the* Turnabout: a revolving hatch that allows cloistered nuns to pass items to visitors and vice versa.
27. *He would doubtless have been so, had his retreat ... than* France: It is likely that Haywood visited France. In the *Female Spectator* she has one of her correspondents write: 'I had the pleasure of being in that elegant Country for three Years, and but for the unhappy Eruption between the two Nations [England and France] had not so soon left it' (vol. 2, book

12, p. 416). Later, in *The Husband* (1756), the writer refers to 'a trip I was once taking to France' (p. 59). Haywood's references to France are almost always positive.

28. *coming to an eclaircisement*: see *RR* p. 49, n. 26.
29. *intitled* the garden of the world: a clichéd description of Italy even in the seventeenth century. It occurs in *The Taming of the Shrew*, performed in 1593 or 1594 and published in the First Folio of 1623: 'the pleasant garden of great Italy' (I.i.4); in W. Harris, *A Description of the King's Royal Palace and Gardens at Loo* (1699), p.4, and other accounts of the Grand Tour.
30. *by the way of* Burgundy, *and passing through* Dijon, *proceeded to* Lyons: Natura is following a conventional route taken by tourists, that is from Calais to Paris, then via Dijon and Lyons. A choice then had to be made about the route to Italy, either going by boat or across the Alps: a coastal route by land was not practicable. The usual crossing was made through the Mont Cenis Pass, and then on to Susa and Turin. See J. Black, *The British Abroad. The Grand Tour in the Eighteenth Century* (Phoenix Mill: Sutton Publishing, 1992), p. 20.
31. *the* Protestant *cantons of* Switzerland: during the Reformation, the cities of Bern, Basel, Geneva, Lausanne, Schaffhausen and Zurich were more receptive to reform than the conservative rural cantons. Conflict between the cantons was resolved by the Peace of Aarau (1712), which allowed parity of religious rights within the Old Swiss Confederacy.
32. Avignon: As Natura takes the land route to Italy, his trip to Avignon represents an unusual detour. There is a possible Jacobite link. Lady Mary Wortley Montagu, having left the town, and writing to her husband from Italy in August 1746, explained that 'Avignon has long been disagreeable to me on many Accounts, and now more than ever from the concourse of Scotch and Irish Rebells that choose it for their Refuge', (*Selected Letters*, ed. I. Grundy (London: Penguin, 1997), p. 319). Avignon was the seat of the papacy from 1309–78.
33. *to moralize on the amazing and different subjects he beheld*: Most travellers gave prosaic accounts, occasionally adding political reflections, but John Dennis, in a letter dated 1688, rhapsodized thus: 'the *Alps* are works which [Nature] seems to have design'd, and executed too, in fury ... I am delighted, 'tis true, with the Prospect of Hills and Vallies, of flowry Meads and murmuring Streams; yet it is a Delight that is consistent with Reason, a Delight that creates and improves Meditation ... But transporting Pleasure follow'd the Sight of the *Alps*; and what unusual Transports, think you, were those, that were mingled with Horrors, and sometimes almost with Despair?' (*An Useful and Entertaining Collection of Letters upon Various Subjects*, 1745). In his *Remarks on Several Parts of Italy* (1705), Joseph Addison comments only on the 'agreeable horror' of the experience, but in *The Tatler* 161 (1710) he makes the Alps the location for a dream-vision of the Goddess of Liberty, and in the *Spectator* 412 (1712), he writes of the delight given by 'huge Heaps of Mountains, high Rocks and Precipices', which is one of the pleasures of the imagination.
34. *that vast preference given them over the moderns*: It was usual for visitors to Rome to reflect on lost greatness, as Joseph Addison did in *Remarks on Several Parts of Italy* (1705), a much reprinted work. He contrasted the desolation and poverty of, especially, papal territories, with the empire that had flourished under ancient Rome. Addison attributed the decline, ultimately, to 'the very Genius of the *Roman* Catholic religion', and his sentiments were echoed by many other English travellers. Such thinking informed Edward Gibbon's *Decline and Fall of the Roman Empire* (1776–89).
35. *the exquisite music performed at the churches*: Italian church music in the eighteenth century was influenced by opera. Composers such as Alessandro Scarlatti brought elaborate solo vocal music to the church, and there were accompaniments by string and wind instru-

ments. After the Reformation, the dominant tradition in the Church of England was the unaccompanied singing of metrical psalms (psalms translated into lines with metre).

36. *the* Romans *are allowed to be the best bred people upon earth*: Not a common sentiment, nor even a common topic in travellers' accounts. Many early eighteenth-century visitors viewed Rome as an illustration of their youthful classical reading, or as a 'cabinet of curiosities'. See R. Sweet, 'The Changing View of Rome in the Long Eighteenth Century', *JECS* 33:2 (2010), pp. 145–64.
37. Tirolose: the Tyrol, a region of present-day western Austria and northern Italy.
38. Florence ... Venice ... Vienna ... Germany: again, Natura would visit destinations typical of the Grand Tour in the eighteenth century. (See Black, *The British Abroad*, p. 46ff.)
39. Leghorn: Livorno, on the west coast of Italy.
40. *as* France *was in alliance with* England ... *her service*: France and England were allies from 1716 to 1731, placing the action of the novel between those years. However, to say that there was no shame in serving in the French army glosses over more conventional English hostility towards France, an hostility associated with the Whigs after their opposition to the Treaty of Utrecht (1713). Such feelings became more pronounced in the 1740s. There was a 'belief that the national interest had been rediscovered in the shape of opposition to France, and that this interest was more urgent because of the prospect of France and its allies taking advantage of the death of Charles VI without male heirs in 1740 to overthrow the balance of Europe'. (J. Black, *Debating Foreign Policy in Eighteenth-Century Britain* (Farnham, Surrey: Ashgate, 2011), p. 130.) Louis XV had declared his intention to restore the Stuart king, and France was poised to invade Britain in 1744. Competition for trade and empire became more pronounced after 1745. (See B. Harris, *Politics and the Nation. Britain in the Mid-Eighteenth Century* (Oxford: Oxford University Press, 2002), p. 102.) Soldiering in the army of a Catholic power was a route more usually taken by Roman Catholics who were Jacobite in sympathy. (See S. Conway, *Britain, Ireland, and Continental Europe in the Eighteenth Century. Similarities, Connections, Identities* (Oxford: Oxford University Press, 2011), p. 274.) By 1748, France and England were on opposing sides in the War of the Austrian Succession. See also below, n. 47.
41. Fauxbourg: faubourg, a suburb, or a quarter of the city.
42. *goal*: see *RR* p. 13, n. 11.
43. *an exempt*: normally, an officer commanding in the absence of his superiors, and therefore exempt from ordinary duties.
44. *in chancery*: in litigation.
45. *the compter*: obsolete term for a prison.
46. *spoke too favourably of the chevalier* St. George: The Chevalier St George was the king in exile, James Edward Stuart. The title is significant: it would only be used by Jacobite sympathizers. Haywood was arrested over her authorship of an allegedly Jacobite pamphlet, *A Letter from H— G—* in 1749. She reflected obliquely on the need for circumspection in the matter of Jacobite sympathies in *The Wife* (1756). In an episode depicting an argument between a Jacobite husband and a Hanoverian wife, she omits the husband's reply to the wife's defence of Hanover, as 'it is more than barely possible that some one or other, in this scrutinising age, might take it into his head to imagine I was glad of an opportunity of venting my own sentiments through the mouth of a third person'.
47. *he could not possibly enjoy a commission there ... the* Romish *church*: After the Edict of Fontainebleau (1685), the French army under Louis XIV and Louis XV was Roman Catholic, although foreign regiments could retain their own chaplains. Most Huguenot officers were converted by compulsion.

48. *the* Stadthouse: the Stadhuis, built between 1648 and 1655 in Dam Square, Amsterdam. More than 13,000 piles were driven into marshy ground for the foundations, and the classical design by Jacob van Campen (1595–1657) reflected Amsterdam's confidence after the achievement of Dutch independence from Spain. A marble floor inlaid with maps of the world, dominated by Atlas supporting a starry globe, symbolized colonial and commercial power. It is now a royal palace.
49. *the magnificence with which King William ... had ornamented his palace at* Loo: Descriptions of Loo more usually focussed on the fine gardens, or the hunting available nearby. The anonymous author of *The Present State of Germany* (1738) described the palace as 'a noble Structure of modern Architecture'. 'Admire' is an ambiguous term in this context, since it can mean to wonder at, without necessarily approving.
50. *a prince, whose brows were one day to be incircled with the crown of* England: Given that the action of the novel takes place between 1716 and 1731, the Elector of Hanover and heir to the British throne would be the prince Georg August, later George II, who became monarch in 1727 and died in 1760.
51. *pride, which came pretty near ferocity*: Haywood's focus on the manners of Viennese people is most likely to be a reflection of her animosity towards the Hapsburg queen, Maria Theresa, whose contested entitlement to the throne was the cause of the War of the Austrian Succession (1740–8). In the *Female Spectator* Haywood portrayed her as ruthless, driven by pride and ambition, 'wading thro' whole Seas of Blood to reach the Goal' (*Female Spectator*, vol. 2, book 9, p.332). Haywood was in the minority: many contemporaries applauded Maria Theresa's use of military force, and Hanoverian troops supported her cause. (See K. R. King, 'Patriot or Opportunist? Eliza Haywood and the Politics of *The Female Spectator*', in *Fair Philosopher*, pp. 112–15.) Hostilities ended with the Peace of Aix-la-Chapelle, 11 October 1748, seven months after *Life's Progress* was published.
52. *no small difficulty to maintain his sobriety among them*: The stereotype of Germans as dull, boorish and frequently drunk stretches back to the sixteenth century, if not earlier. As Daniel Defoe put the sentiment in *A True-Born Englishman* (1701), ll. 106–8: 'Drunkenness, the Darling Favourite of Hell, / Chose Germany to rule, and rules so well, / No Subjects more obsequiously obey'.
53. *the repeated obligations ... profess the doctrines of* Calvin *and* Luther: In the *Female Spectator*, vol. 2, book 9, Haywood makes it clear that obligations are owed 'to *Great Britain* for that Expence of Blood and Treasure lavish'd in her [the Queen of Hungary's] Cause'.
54. *things of meer form and ceremony*: Haywood's indifference to matters of form is in keeping with the prevailing Latitudinarianism of the time, which stressed moral duties rather than points of doctrine. However, matters of 'mere' form and ceremony were usually seen as dividing Dissenters and Anglicans, not Anglicans and Catholics.
55. *sceptism*: that is, scepticism.
56. *health and sickness make a wide difference in our way of thinking*: Spedding infers that Haywood suffered a period of ill health between 1737, the year of her final performance at the Haymarket theatre, and 1740. In her preface to *The Virtuous Villager* (1742), she writes that the translation was begun long before 1740, but had to be laid aside on account of a 'severe Indisposition' (Spedding, *A Bibliography*, p. 355). Further illness would delay the publication of the second volume of *Epistles for the Ladies* from 1749 to 1750. (See King, *A Political Biography*, p. 162.)
57. Spa: Spa, in the Ardennes, 'the most popular continental watering place for British tourists' (Black, *The British Abroad*, p. 56).
58. *falchion*: a broad, short sword, bent rather like a sickle.

59. *Spaw*: another form of spa, or spa-well.
60. Westminster *school*: an ancient and prestigious school, whose origins can be traced back to 1179.
61. *levee*: a bedside or early reception of visitors, especially by a person of distinction.
62. *her person was his property by marriage*: Eighteenth century wives had no separate legal identity after marriage. Under common law, the husband and wife were one person, and that one person was the husband.
63. *the authority the laws had given him*: see above, n. 62.
64. *regale*: A regale is a feast or a choice dish.
65. *a regiment that was going to* Gibraltar: Gibraltar was captured by Anglo-Dutch forces in 1704, and was ceded to Britain under the terms of the Treaty of Utrecht in 1713. There were continuing skirmishes with Spain, and it was besieged by Spanish forces from February to June 1727.
66. *criminal conversation*: see *RR* p. 67, n. 35.
67. *a bill of divorce was granted on very easy terms*: Before 1858, a divorce could be obtained by Act of Parliament, in a lengthy and expensive procedure. A legal pre-condition for divorce in the case of adultery was a suit brought by the plaintiff (usually the husband) against his spouse's lover. The plaintiff could then be awarded damages and costs. (See R. Phillips, *Putting Asunder. A History of Divorce in Western Society* (Cambridge: Cambridge University Press, 1988), pp. 227–8.) There was no legal obligation for the husband to support his ex-wife, particularly an adulterous ex-wife. Although common and canon law still did not recognize the wife as a legal person separate from the husband, 'many wives guilty of adultery succeeded in negotiating ... separate maintenance contracts' (S. Staves, *Married Women's Separate Property in England, 1660–1833* (Cambridge, MA: Harvard University Press, 1990), pp. 168–9.)
68. *variated*: here meaning variable or varying.
69. *Term was approaching*: Then, as now, the legal year was divided into four terms: Hilary, Easter, Trinity and Michaelmas. Hilary and Michaelmas are the winter terms.

SILENT CORRECTIONS

The Rash Resolve: or, the Untimely Discovery

p. 13, l. 23	arthy] earthy
p. 24, l. 28	his Barbarity had deprived him of,] his Barbarity had deprived him of expired,
p. 60, l. 31	ever to banished thence] ever to be banished thence

Life's Progress through the Passions: or, The Adventures of Natura

p. 144, ll. 21–2	at hand, might have employed] at hand, and might have employed
p. 186, l. 36	none but those by nature] none but those who by nature

For Product Safety Concerns and Information please contact our EU representative GPSR@taylorandfrancis.com
Taylor & Francis Verlag GmbH, Kaufingerstraße 24, 80331 München, Germany

www.ingramcontent.com/pod-product-compliance
Lightning Source LLC
Chambersburg PA
CBHW071521110726
47908CB00003B/916
* 9 7 8 1 1 3 8 2 3 5 4 7 2 *